ONLY
IF YOU'RE LUCKY

ALSO BY STACY WILLINGHAM

All the Dangerous Things

A Flicker in the Dark

ONLY
IF YOU'RE LUCKY

A NOVEL

STACY WILLINGHAM

MINOTAUR
BOOKS
NEW YORK

First published in the United States by Minotaur Books, an imprint of St. Martin's Publishing Group

ONLY IF YOU'RE LUCKY. Copyright © 2023 by Stacy Willingham. All rights reserved. Printed in the United States of America. For information, address St. Martin's Publishing Group, 120 Broadway, New York, NY 10271.

www.minotaurbooks.com

Designed by Omar Chapa

Library of Congress Cataloging-in-Publication Data

Names: Willingham, Stacy, author.
Title: Only if you're lucky : a novel / Stacy Willingham.
Other titles: Only if you are lucky
Description: First edition. | New York : Minotaur Books, 2024.
Identifiers: LCCN 2023036541 | ISBN 9781250887931 (hardcover) | ISBN 9781250341365 (international edition) | ISBN 9781250887948 (ebook)
Subjects: LCGFT: Thrillers (Fiction). | Novels.
Classification: LCC PS3623.I57726 O55 2024 | DDC 813/.6—dc23/eng/20230822
LC record available at https://lccn.loc.gov/2023036541

Our books may be purchased in bulk for promotional, educational, or business use. Please contact your local bookseller or the Macmillan Corporate and Premium Sales Department at 1-800-221-7945, extension 5442, or by email at MacmillanSpecialMarkets@macmillan.com.

First Edition: 2024

10 9 8 7 6 5 4 3 2 1

For my mom, my hero

If I ever read Satan's signature upon a face, it is on that of your new friend.

—ROBERT LOUIS STEVENSON

ONLY
IF YOU'RE LUCKY

PROLOGUE

One day we were strangers and the next we were friends. That's usually how it works with girls.

How effortlessly we glide from cold shoulders in public to applying each other's lipstick in sweaty bar bathrooms, fingertips touching in a swarm of warm bodies. From spreading hot-breathed rumors behind cupped hands to tossing compliments across the room like darts, aiming for a bull's-eye, but really just hoping for something to stick. I remember thinking she chose me, specifically, for some reason I'd never understand. Like she spotted me from across the hall, eyes on the carpet and shoulders hunched high as I tried to hide my underwear at the bottom of the laundry basket—flowers and stars and little pink pinstripes, embarrassingly high school—and decided: I was it, it was me. Her best friend.

And from that moment on, I was.

"Spin it," Lucy says, and I feel myself blink. My eyelids are heavy, the room twirling gently like our old dorm washing machines, slow and clunky and always broken. There's a permanent cloud of smoke in the house—cigarette, candle, incense, weed—

caked into the blankets, the couch cushions. Like if you slapped them, they'd cough.

I can still picture all my mom's country clubbers tucking my hair behind my ear, fingers lingering against my cheek like I was their own personal porcelain doll. Thinking me delicate, breakable, as I loaded boxes into the trunk while they gushed about their own time at school with distant smiles and tears in their eyes.

How sure they were that I would finally find *my people, my girls.*

"Just you wait," they had said, strings of pearls wound tight around their necks like designer nooses, my own mother watching curiously from the lawn. *"College is different. They'll be your friends for life."*

That's what I had been hoping for. Different. But *friends for life* is a myth, a fable. A feel-good fairy tale we tell ourselves to avoid having to think too hard about facing the world alone. I had believed it once. I had held it tight against my chest like some kind of feral animal I'd claimed as my own before it scratched my neck and wriggled itself free, leaving me battered and bloodied and alone.

"Margot."

I look up to find Lucy staring straight at me, her pupils wide and round like cigarette butts. I swear there's smoke coming from her eyes, curling into nothing.

"Spin."

I blink again like I just woke up from a dream and found myself here: thighs stuck to the hardwood, back digging into the corner of the coffee table. Everything feels dreamlike, hazy, faded like the milky bottom of the stale water glass sitting neglected on my nightstand. We're in a circle—Lucy, Sloane, and I—our legs pretzeled on the floor with the knife Lucy yanked from the kitchen block between us. Nicole is on the couch, detached as usual, and I reach for the knife, finally flicking it with my fingers. Watching as the shiny tip rotates in a circle like we're a strange kind of clock: three, six, nine, twelve.

We all hold our breath as it slows to a stop, the point aimed directly at Lucy.

I see Sloane perk up out of the corner of my eye, her back lengthening like a meerkat suddenly aware of some distant danger. Even Nicole darts a look in our direction, skinny frame slumped over a pillow. Hugging it hard with toothpick arms.

"Truth or dare," I say, my voice raspy and raw. My lips are pulsing, tingling, and I take another swig from the Svedka bottle between us because I need something to coat my throat.

Lucy smiles, like the question is rhetorical. Like I shouldn't have even bothered to ask. Then she leans over and grabs the knife, her fingers curling around the handle, one by one, as naturally as grabbing the base of a curling iron, a bottle of beer. The same way her hand grips my wrist when she finds me in a crowded room, pulling me away and into the night.

They were right, those women. College friends are different. We would do anything for each other.

Anything.

CHAPTER 1

We're seated next to each other, shoulders touching, side by side like a prison lineup.

I can feel Nicole's hip bone jutting into my side; Sloane can't stop picking at her cuticles, sprinkling dead skin across the floor like salt. We're in our pajamas, cheeks still smeared with last night's mascara, and Nicole looks about five years younger with her baby-faced skin and braided pigtails, barely a teenager. Sloane's dark hair is knotted up in a scrunchie, a single curl jutting out like a corkscrew, and I don't even know what I'm wearing. Some T-shirt I probably picked up off someone else's floor and claimed as my own, armpit stains and everything.

"Girls."

I look up at the detective in front of us, hands on his hips. I don't like the way he says that—*Girls*—like we're children being scolded. Some words should be ours to own, at-times-vicious yet tender terms of endearment we toss around like glitter that suddenly taste sour in the mouths of men.

Girls is one of them.

"When was the last time you saw your roommate, Lucy Sharpe?"

I glance to my left, my right. Nicole is staring at the table; Sloane's staring at her nails. We're all thinking about that night, I'm sure. Just last week but also a lifetime ago. We're all thinking about sitting on the floor, the knife spinning in circles between us, metal tip catching the lamplight and casting shapes across the wall. Lucy's wild eyes as she reached out and grabbed it and that Cheshire cat grin curling up into her cheeks, baring her fangs. The way she raised the blade higher and the glimpse I had caught of myself in the metal.

I remember thinking that I looked different in that moment. Distorted. Rabid and wild and alive.

"Someone's gonna have to say something eventually."

I look at the detective again, forehead like an old tire, cracked and slick. His face looks red and swollen like someone is squeezing him from the bottom, waiting for him to pop. I take in his hands next, finger skin bulging around his wedding ring like a sausage link. They're still on his hips with his legs spread wide like he's trying to copy some old Western gunslinger or a stance he saw on an episode of *Cops*.

"It's been three days, I think."

He looks at me, the first to speak up. "You think?"

I nod. "Yeah. I think."

Sloane and Nicole keep staring at the floor, their silence loud enough to fill the room, curling and twisting and seeping into the corners like the lingering smoke I can still smell in my hair.

"Nobody is getting into trouble, girls, but she hasn't been accounted for since Friday. She didn't show up to work all weekend. Have you talked to anyone in her classes?"

"Lucy doesn't go to class," Sloane says, and Nicole grunts, stifling a laugh.

"So you aren't at all concerned?" he asks, shifting his weight from one leg to the other. "Your roommate is missing and you aren't worried about where she might be?"

"Detective"—Sloane stops, making a point to stare at the nameplate pinned to his chest—"Frank, if you knew Lucy at all, you'd know this isn't unusual."

"Meaning?" he asks.

"*Meaning*," she sighs, "she probably decided to go out of town with some guy for the weekend, I don't know. If you find her, tell her the rent's due and we're not covering for her again."

I shoot Sloane a look, hypnotized at the chill in her tone: menthol cool and sharp as an ice pick, almost like he's boring her.

Detective Frank shifts again, switching gears, and I think I see him flush a bit more, heat rising into those chipmunk cheeks like he's embarrassed or flustered or a little bit of both.

"So, three days ago," he says to me next. "Where were you?"

"We stayed in that night, just hung out in the living room."

"All of you?"

We nod.

"What were you doing?"

"Girl things." I smile.

"How was Lucy acting?" he asks, not taking the bait. "Any different?"

"No," I lie, the first of many. I remember the depth of her pupils, oversized like two black holes, swallowing everything. The way she kept sucking on that Tootsie Pop, an orb of red, until it looked like her teeth were bleeding. "Just Lucy."

We're all quiet and I'm starting to feel squirmy in my seat. My eyes dart to the clock—it's almost eleven—and I think about open-ing my mouth, making up another lie about running late to class, when Detective Frank takes a step forward and rests his hands against the table, leveling his eyes with ours.

I hear the wood creak, straining under his weight. Almost like he's hurting it.

"Did Lucy tell you girls we brought her in for questioning?"

Nicole perks up, finally. "Questioning for what?" she asks, even though, of course, we know. We know so much more than this man thinks we do and I see his lips twitch at this little victory—at thinking he's finally said something important enough to make us care—as he drums his fingers against the table, preparing his quick draw.

"For the murder of Levi Butler."

CHAPTER 2

BEFORE

She was everything and I was nothing. That's always what I thought, anyway.

We spent our entire freshman year just a few doors down from each other. We were in the all-girls dorm, the unlucky few who got placed in the only same-sex building on campus: Hines Hall. It sat at the top of the single hill downtown, trapping us inside like a bunch of Rapunzels, untouchable, though it only made us more desirable. Like things to be won. I still think about move-in day: pulling my pile of boxes on a metal trolley, a neon 9 taped to the back and the hot flash of embarrassment every time a wheel squeaked too loud. Watching the boys loll past with their hands punched into their pockets, craning their necks, already scheming on how to get inside.

Everybody whined about it at first, skin slick with sweat and throwing scowls in every direction as we lugged comforters and futons up that long, winding stairwell, blaming each other for our own anatomy.

I remember that first night so vividly: the twenty-four girls of hall 9B being called into the common room. We stood there in oversized T-shirts and gym shorts so short we might as well be bottomless, arms like seat belts wound tight around our waists. Our RA was a junior named Janice, who recited the rules in a cursory clip: no drinking, no boys. Silence after midnight. And we just stood there quietly, nodding, mentally chewing over the fact that we had finally escaped to college just to be met with the same old restrictions, with a glorified babysitter to boot. Then she walked out and left the rest of us to *get to know one another,* everyone simply staring in a timid unease until Lucy seemed to appear out of nowhere, stepping forward from the corner and unzipping her bag.

We watched in silence as she pulled out a case of beer before plopping it onto the carpet, bottles jangling.

"Now that *that's* over," she had said, as if Janice had been nothing more than her own opening act. "Everyone, grab one."

I can still hear the uncomfortable murmur rippling across the room; the nervous laughs and darting eyes. Then, as if showing us how, Lucy leaned forward and grabbed the first bottle, twisting off the cap and taking a sip.

"To us," she had said, tipping the lip in our direction. "Nine floors of whores."

After that, I always knew she was there—it was impossible to miss her, and that was probably the point. I'd catch a glimpse of her raven-black curls as she walked past my open door or pushed her way into the bathroom, neon-green shower caddy hooked into the crook of her arm. She used to bring canned wine coolers into the communal showers, sickly sweet smells like strawberry mango and peach fizz rising with the steam and fogging up the mirror; the *crunch* of the empties before her hand popped out of the curtain and dropped them onto the tile like crumpled candy wrappers. She was the only one who never covered up before stepping back out. While the rest of us swathed ourselves in towel wraps or monogrammed bathrobes, self-consciously gripping the gap before ripping back the curtain and flip-flopping past the stalls in our shower shoes, she would just step out naked, brazen and beautiful, like she owned the place.

And in a lot of ways, she did.

"I don't know what they see in her."

I glance up at my roommate now, trying to blink away the memory like a speck of dirt stuck in my eye. Lucy's presence is like the first blast of air from an AC unit: noisy, chilling. The kind of thing that demands attention and makes your skin prickle. Her eyes are so blue they're almost white, glacial water iced over until it turned cold and hard, and when she caught me staring at her once through a hand-swiped section of the fogged-up mirror, it made me physically shiver, the feeling of her gaze traveling down my spine like an ice cube dropped down the back of my shirt.

"Hmm?" I ask at last.

"Don't act like you weren't staring."

Maggie and I are lying on the grass outside Hines, psychology textbooks splayed out in front of us and a torn-open bag of Cheetos wedged in the middle. She flips from her stomach to her back, propping herself up on two kickstand elbows.

"Everyone's staring."

She's right: everyone is staring. I can see their eyes darting in Lucy's direction from behind their sunglasses, their notebooks. Stealing a glance as she pushes her bikini top an inch to the right, head flopped back as she stares into the sun. She acts like she doesn't even notice; like she's on her own private beach somewhere, not sunning herself in the middle of campus. A busy intersection of horny teenagers who watch her rub lotion on her skin and immediately start to salivate like Pavlov's dogs.

"She's crazy."

I peel my eyes from Lucy and look back at Maggie, jealousy radiating from her skin like a bad smell. "Why do you say that?"

"Because she *is*," she says. "I heard she blinded her boyfriend in high school."

"What? No way."

"I'm serious. They were arguing about something, fighting at a party, and she reached out and scratched him across the face," she says, clawing at the air. "Like a fucking cat."

"I don't believe that," I say, eyeing her closely. Maggie isn't usually like this: gossipy, mean. She's one of the nicest people I know, actually. Irritatingly so. But at the same time, Lucy seems to bring out this side of people. It's like her existence alone is somehow threatening to the rest of us—we know we can't compete, so instead, we recoil, snarling at her from the corner to make ourselves feel safe.

"Swear to God, it's true," Maggie says, holding her hands up, defensive. "Her nail was kind of jagged or something and it ended up puncturing his cornea."

"Where did you hear that?"

"Rachel down the hall had a friend visit a few months ago. She said her boyfriend knows a guy who saw it happen."

I cock my eyebrow.

"I'm just relaying what I heard."

I turn back toward Lucy, noticing the way her fingers itch absentmindedly against her chest; the way her long, skinny nails leave little white streaks in the angry red of her sunburn. It isn't the first rumor I've heard about her, each one more outlandish than the last. Some other girl on our hall swears she's a foreign exchange student, undercover royalty shipped over from somewhere rich and exotic, although I've detected zero trace of an accent any time I've heard her speak. Another is convinced she's sleeping with her professors—all of them, females included—the only logical explanation for how she seems to get by without studying.

"Anyway," Maggie says, rolling back over and grabbing a Cheeto before popping it in her mouth. "I think I found us an apartment for next year. Two bed, two bath. It's on the second floor, thank God. No more elevators."

I hear myself mumble some distant *mhmm*s, but I'm not listening. Not really. Two other girls have joined Lucy now—a blonde with braids and a dark-skinned girl with calves like baseballs that bulge beneath the skin. They live on 9B, too. Nicole Clausen and Sloane Peters. They're almost always with Lucy, the three of them swigging from water bottles everybody knows aren't filled with water before stumbling back hours later, eyes glassy and lipstick smeared. The first time I saw them, there was something about the way they walked that stuck with me: side by side, Lucy in the middle, arms hooked together like a chain-link fence. Like they couldn't break apart even if they wanted to.

"Did you hear me?"

I whip back around at the sound of her voice to find Maggie looking at me, eyebrows raised.

"Sorry, what?"

"I said it's close to the library so we won't have to take the bus."

"Oh, yeah. That's great." I smile, then turn back toward the girls. "Thanks for doing that."

I watch as Sloane lays a towel on the grass and Nicole starts to slather sunscreen on her arms, though Lucy hasn't even looked at them. Her eyes are still hidden behind her sunglasses as she stares up at the sky and the truth is, I do know what everyone sees in her. I've seen it myself all year. It's the way her eyes seem to pierce you so deep, leaving behind microscopic little puncture wounds like a snake or spider bite. Something you can still feel on your skin long after she's left. It's the easy confidence she exudes, as natural as breathing, and the way she took control of that first night so effortlessly, just a handful of words making twenty-four strangers not only break the rules but simultaneously shatter some widely held belief about ourselves.

Some latent voice telling us to be embarrassed about our situation—*nine floors of whores*—when we should have been emboldened.

"All right, I'm done," Maggie says suddenly, slapping her textbook shut with too much force. I crane my neck as she stands up, noticing the thin lines of sweat that have soaked their way through her tank top. Everyone is cramming for finals, meaning it's only May, but it's already hotter in Rutledge than it'll ever be in most of the country by August. We're used to it, though, students lugging backpacks through hundred-degree heat before stripping off their clothes and heading to the beach, drowning their stress in salt water and sweat.

"Do you want to grab dinner or something?" she adds, offering me one last chance at conversation I should probably take. Instead, I give her an apologetic smile, already feeling my neck threatening to turn back in Lucy's direction like a quivering magnet.

"I'm going to stay a little longer," I say. "Sorry."

I watch as Maggie shrugs and walks off, a little string of pollen dangling from her thigh, but by the time my gaze makes it back to the girls, I'm not staring at the side of Lucy's face anymore, her head tilted back with her face angled to the sun—instead, I'm staring straight into the sharp blue of her eyes as she looks into my own, sunglasses perched on the tip of her nose.

I feel a sudden jolt in my body, like the shock of wet fingers grazing the outside of an outlet. Then, before I can even realize what's happening, she waves.

CHAPTER 3

My room is empty by the time I make it back to the dorm. I was hoping to catch Maggie, maybe. Join her for dinner like she had asked. She's probably sitting in the dining hall by now, pretending to study or read something riveting on her phone to mask the embarrassment of eating alone. For a second, I consider walking down there, scooting in beside her. I can even picture her looking up at me, relief flooding her features as she realizes she won't have to pretend anymore. The silent apology we would exchange before launching into some pointless small talk about our summer plans.

Instead, I grab a carton of Easy Mac and rip off the lid, dumping a splash of water inside before popping it in the microwave.

It's not that I don't *like* Maggie. I like her fine. She's nice enough; the perfect roommate even, kind and considerate. Always letting me bum one of her Diet Cokes out of the mini fridge and never letting her dirty clothes pile up. We hang out together almost every night, sitting silently on the futon with some mid-tier movie drowning out the shrieks from the other girls down the hall; the laughs and the screams we pretend not to notice, instead munching on popcorn and convincing ourselves we chose this instead. During those first few weeks of freshman year, I remember watching the other girls scramble around, mad and frantic like headless chickens, everyone desperate to make their friends and find their place. Maggie and I never really found ours, so instead we just made our own and lived there quietly, settling into a friendship that was born out of nearness and necessity and sustained by a lack of effort on both of our parts to find anything better.

And the worst part is: she knows it, too.

I still remember meeting her, a blind-match pairing the college cobbled together a month before move-in. It could have been awful; I had no idea what to expect. I spent the entire drive wondering what kind of person would need to rely on a campus questionnaire to find a single friend—a person like me, I supposed—but when I showed up, her overeagerness was the only flaw I could find. I remember her being antsy, fidgeting with her fingernails as she greeted me with an obviously rehearsed introduction the second I stepped inside. Her side of the room had already been decorated and I noticed that she had purchased two of everything: matching floral throw pillows for my bed and hers; two picture frames for each of our desks. I could tell she had dreams of us becoming instant best friends, filling those frames with photographs of us . . . but the second I saw her there, all eager and excited like the runt of the litter just dying to be picked, I didn't see visions of us sharing clothes or pulling all-nighters or giggling uncontrollably after sneaking a bottle of wine into the dorm and passing it back and forth, lip gloss on the rim sticky and smeared.

Instead, all I saw was Eliza.

Eliza, my best friend since kindergarten who asked me to sleep over the first day we met. Eliza, who dipped her finger in sunscreen and drew broken hearts on our hips so when we lay out in the sun and our skin turned tan, we could push our stomachs together and make them whole. Eliza, who pierced my ears in her closet and taught me how to dive; who blasted oldies in her parents' convertible with the top dropped down the day she got her license, pushing eighty on abandoned back roads and letting her hair tangle in the wind.

Eliza, my would-be roommate who died three weeks into the summer after our senior year.

So, yeah, that's the problem: Maggie reminds me of everything I should have had. Eliza and me living together the way we had talked about for all those years, curled up in a blanket on her parents' dock, night after night, imagining us together in some other life. Decorating our dorm together just the way we wanted it, filling the walls with an entire decade of memories we already had and leaving room for the ones that would follow. I had applied to Rutledge *because* of her: my parents wanted me at Duke, somewhere prestigious and important, but Eliza convinced me that this was the place for us.

Not for me, for *us*.

So we wrote our admissions essays together and checked the mail for months, calling each other screaming the night we both got accepted. I broke the news to my parents, weathering their disappointment and distress over me choosing a small liberal arts school that was *so far away,* even though South Carolina was only one state over from our house in the Outer Banks. I could come home for the weekend if I really wanted to—but they knew, of course, that I wouldn't. Then we submitted our roommate applications and put down our deposits and talked all night about finally being free of the cocoon of high school that always felt so smothering and small.

It all felt so perfect, so according to plan . . . until that night.

That night that changed everything and I found myself coming here, alone. Without her.

A body slams against my open door, startling me out of the memory as quick as a slap. I spin around, expecting to see Maggie— still angry from earlier, frowning at me from the hallway—but that's not who it is.

Instead, I see her.

"Hey."

Lucy is leaning against my doorframe, arms crossed tight and her denim shorts unbuttoned to reveal the cherry red of her bathing suit bottoms.

"Hey," I echo, though it comes out more like a question. I can feel my heart beating hard in my chest and I wonder if she's going to ask me about earlier, finding me staring at her on the lawn like some voyeur sneaking a peek through a peephole. I had snapped my neck back down when I saw her waving at me like that, shame burning my cheeks like a sunburn, before collecting my textbooks and taking off fast.

I feel an apology start to bubble up my throat like bile, some half-hearted attempt to explain it all away.

"Are you staying for the summer?"

I close my mouth, suddenly speechless, and realize she's looking at me like we're old friends—like this isn't unusual, her showing up here. Like this isn't the first time we've ever actually talked.

"Um, no," I say, jumping slightly as the microwave beeps. "I'm leaving after my last final."

"I have an open room," she offers. "Great house right off campus."

I look at her, confused, my fingers picking at a hangnail to give them something to do. The truth is, I don't want to go home for the summer—really, I don't want to go home at all. I can feel Eliza's absence here, in this very room, but at home, it's even worse. At home, I can feel it everywhere: the ghost of her trailing me around, hovering over my shoulder. A persistent, painful reminder of everything that could have been.

"It's not just for the summer, actually," Lucy nudges, shifting her weight from one leg to the other. "We can stay through next year. Have you signed a lease yet?"

"No," I say again, noticing a small silver necklace resting in the dip of her clavicle. It looks like a constellation of some sort; a little cluster of diamonds as stars. Eliza used to wear something like it, I think. A birthday present from her parents that she never took off, though I don't know if they're actually similar or if I'm still just seeing her everywhere I look. "Not yet."

Technically, it's the truth. I never signed a lease. Maggie did.

"Wait," she says suddenly, a little curl to her lip. "You weren't going to live with Mary again, were you?"

"Maggie," I correct, embarrassed for us both. "I . . . haven't decided yet."

I think of my roommate and what she said to me earlier: the apartment she got for us by the library and the fact that I couldn't have cared less. Suddenly, it feels so depressing, another year spent together because neither of us ever found anyone else. I pull my gaze from the necklace and look at Lucy again, standing in my doorway with those bright blue eyes. They're mesmerizing, truly, like looking into a kaleidoscope and watching the world contort into something else entirely. I register a little twitch in her lip, like she's finding something funny she can't bring herself to say. I think of the way she, Sloane, and Nicole always walk like one— the way Eliza and I did, too—and suddenly, I crave that. I crave it more than I've ever craved anything: the kind of friendship that I once knew so well, not comfortable and contained but something messy and maniacal and real.

"Well," Lucy says, that twitch of a smile morphing into a full-blown grin. "Looks like I just decided for you."

CHAPTER 4

By the end of the week, I'm standing on the sidewalk with three suitcases full of stuff, a single bead of sweat trickling down my spine and an old gray house looming before me. The past few days have gone by in a blur: finishing finals, packing up the dorm. It's like I've been operating on autopilot, my mind blank and body simply going through the motions as if all of this is normal.

As if I'm not about to move into a house with three girls I know nothing about.

"Why me?" I had asked.

Lucy had invited herself into my room by then, trailing her fingers along my desk, her eyes drinking in all the knickknacks tacked to my corkboard. I've always been something of a hoarder—no, that's the wrong word. A *collector,* maybe. The kind of person who saves ticket stubs and old receipts, applying sentimental value to inanimate objects. Like they have feelings. The idea of tossing even a single happy memory into the trash is enough to make my eyes prickle—and that's not even the worst of it. There's also the whittled-down pencil stubs and practically empty nail polish bottles; the crusty tubes of expired mascara and the used notebooks that pile up in my desk drawers for no reason other than the fact that I just can't seem to throw them away. Mom says I have attachment issues; Dad says I'm a slob. I think I'm just afraid of getting rid of something prematurely; of dipping my hand into my purse and looking for some familiar comfort only to remember that I had disposed of it.

That it's gone forever. That I'm left with nothing.

"Why not?" Lucy had responded, picking up my perfume and spraying a spritz on her wrist. I watched as she brought her nose to her skin and sniffed, wincing, before setting it back down.

"You don't even know me," I continued. "Why do you want to live with someone you don't know?"

She looked up at me then, saucer-round eyes drilling into mine. "Why do you?"

I blink now, my own eyes stinging in the brightness of the summer sun, and start to wonder if this was a mistake. I think about breaking the news to Maggie, admitting that I had made other plans in the hour between her telling me about the apartment and coming back from the dining hall, my mind still trying to process what had just happened. My vague explanation of a house off-campus and the hurt in her eyes as her lower lip quivered. The twist in my chest as she turned away, pretended to look for something in her backpack, too humiliated to even act mad. The truth is, she had every right to be mad. I left her, abandoned her, flicked her to the side like a cigarette the second some swanky new vice came prancing along.

Not only that, but Maggie saved me this year. Without her, I don't know what I would have done.

It's true that I didn't feel any real attachment to her, I didn't love her in the way I loved Eliza, but that's only because I didn't feel any attachment to anything. I spent the entire year floating, totally unmoored, completely removed from not only my body but from reality, too. In hindsight, I was definitely depressed: spending day after day in that concrete box, Eliza's smiling face tacked to my corkboard mocking me as I got ready in the mornings, studied in the evenings. Lay in bed and stared at the ceiling, replaying the events of that night over and over and over again. My parents never noticed; my teachers didn't, either. I was required to go to counseling after the college learned of Eliza's passing but my grades never suffered so they simply egged me on, signed my slips, told me to keep doing what I was doing.

That whatever it was, it was working just fine.

Somehow, though, Maggie could always tell when that film started to descend over my eyes. The one that turned them glassy and gray, somewhere far away, my mind wandering to all those deep, dark places it sometimes escaped to when the memories of Eliza became too much. Maggie could see when my attention would start to dart around the room, wildly searching for something to distract me—a handful of painkillers, swallowed dry, a few too many to knock me out; the sharp bite of a thumbtack pushed into my finger until the skin popped—and she would gently nudge me back, suggesting we watch another movie or grab an ice cream, anything to snap me out of it.

All that to say, Maggie deserved more than the awkwardness of this past week together. The tension between us was physically painful: sidestepping one another in our little box of shared space, murmuring apologies and avoiding each other's eyes. Saying goodbye with an uncomfortable arm hug and a promise to hang out after summer was over—a promise we both knew was dead the second it left our lips. Maggie is a good person, a great person, a person I don't deserve.

But now, with an entire year lost since I lost Eliza, I don't just need to be saved anymore. I need to be resuscitated.

I pick up my bags and start walking up the steps, the splintered wood in desperate need of a power wash. There's yellow pollen caked to everything: the porch railing and rocking chairs and giant cooler situated between them, smudges of it everywhere like crusty mustard stuck to the cap. I drop my bags and open the cooler, peeking inside at the collection of beers bobbing in a foot of warm water, the ice long since melted. There's a mosquito floating on its back, spindly legs thrashing in the air, and I close the lid again, wondering how long it's been in there. I take in the portable speaker on the windowsill next, the collection of lighters piled up on a small table, black ash dotting the wood. The giant pair of flip-flops with dirty toe stains like someone just kicked them off before standing up and walking inside.

Already, the house feels lived-in, even though the lease just started a week ago.

I raise my hand, ready to knock, but before my fist can connect with the door, it swings open on its own, a burly boy standing directly on the other side of it. I stare at him for a second, wide-eyed, trying to keep my attention from traveling down his bare chest, the thin line of hair sprouting beneath his belly button and pointing like an arrow to the waistband of his shorts.

"Who are you?" he asks, a mop of brown hair tousled like he just rolled out of bed.

"I'm Margot," I say. "I'm . . . supposed to live here."

Suddenly, a sense of horror descends upon me and I cannot believe it didn't dawn on me before.

I peer past the front door and into the house, a place so disheveled it looks like a cave occupied by animals. I think about the shoes outside, the *men's* shoes, and take in the shirtless guy in the living room staring at me with a smirk on his lips. It's the same way Lucy had looked that day in the dorm, almost like she was laughing at some joke I didn't understand.

This is a prank. All of it, a prank.

She must have seen me staring at her that day on the lawn and thought it would be funny: inviting me here to live with her, with *them,* knowing I was desperate enough to say yes. I wonder if she's watching me right now through the window of some neighboring house, pointing. Laughing.

I wonder if it's too late to call Maggie and apologize. Beg for mercy, take it all back.

I feel the tears well up and start to mumble excuses, ready to pick up my bags and run away, until the door opens wider and I see Lucy standing on the other side of it.

"Sorry," she says, pushing the boy out of the way. Her hair is pulled up into a bun and she's wearing a Pink Floyd T-shirt and black biker shorts, her toned legs bronzed and beautiful. "This is Nicole's boyfriend. Trevor, Margot. Margot, Trevor."

She gestures between us and the boy smiles at me again, nodding that thick shock of hair before sticking his hand down his waistband and scratching his crotch. Lucy rolls her eyes at me like we're sharing some kind of mutual disgust and I smile, feeling the relief fill me up fast.

"Everyone's still asleep," she says, gesturing for me to come inside. I grab what I can of my bags and watch as she motions to the empty beer bottles littering the floor. There's a giant bong on the coffee table, cloudy water specked with debris, next to a glass ashtray shaped like a peace sign. I notice a bowl of assorted candy in the center; a handful of coasters I doubt anyone uses. "I'll show you to your room."

The house is one of those old homes Rutledge is known for: two stories with a giant front porch, big white columns, and defunct fireplaces in almost every room. The floors look like original hardwood, and they would be nice, if someone had cared enough to take care of them. Campus is small—a cluster of old buildings situated between bars and restaurants, coffee shops and independent boutiques—and although most students live in apartments downtown, out here, mere minutes from city center, there's space to roam. Room to breathe. Already, I can feel the rural air infiltrating my lungs; the weight of the last year slowly easing off my chest. We're about a mile from downtown, only a few blocks to a campus bus stop. Greek row looms large on the street perpendicular to ours and I can't help but think about how this section of town has been overrun by students who can only afford to live in big houses like these because their rich parents pay for them to.

My own parents weren't thrilled about me ditching out on a summer back home, but at the same time, when I explained the situation—a group of friends, *real* friends, the kind my mother's friends were so sure I would find—they begrudgingly agreed to send me a security deposit and the first three months' worth of rent.

"Nicole and Sloane sleep upstairs," Lucy says now, weaving me through the living room. It's furnished with two mismatched couches, a coffee table, and a floor lamp; on the opposite side of the room there's a TV on the floor and an old record player propped open on a side table, a collection of vinyl covers decorating the main wall in a grid. "You and I are down here."

When we get to the back of the house, Lucy gestures to two closed doors: one, apparently hers, and the other, mine. She swings open the one on the right and I peer inside, my eyes scanning it all.

"It came furnished, so it's actually good you don't have much to bring."

There's a little twin bed in there, a bedside table, and another fireplace, though it doesn't appear as if it actually works. I thought about bringing my own furniture from home at first, but now, after seeing the way this place looks, I'm overwhelmingly glad I didn't—I can just imagine her smirk watching me lug my wrought iron headboard and lace duvet into this place, the kind of stuff that fits right in in my parents' beachside mansion but would feel horribly childish in a house like this.

"It's perfect," I say, dropping my bags in the center of the room. And I'm not just saying that: really, it is. The house radiates an effortless cool the way Lucy does, too: a kind of grunge aesthetic that could not be more different than Maggie's matching throw pillows. Exactly what I want. "Thank you."

"Don't thank me just yet," Lucy says, hands on her hips. "You just got here."

CHAPTER 5

It doesn't take long to unpack my things: I have one suitcase full of clothes that are still on their hangers, easy enough to put away, and another full of school supplies, books, electronics, and cords, most of which I'm unsure of their function. I grab a few handfuls of hardbacks first, their spines cracked and gnarled like overworked hands, and push them to the side before emptying the rest.

The truth is, a truth I rarely acknowledge: I've barely opened a book in a year. I used to get so lost in these imaginary worlds, slipping into another skin every time I parted their covers. The musty scent of the pages curling beneath my nostrils like an elixir that ripped me from one reality and implanted me into the next. That's the beauty of fiction, of words: when your life becomes too boring, too bland, too hard or depressing or chaotic or calm, they allow you to simply float away and inhabit another, try it on for size. With so many options so ripe for the picking, it would be a shame to only taste just one.

I still read for school, of course—as an English major, that's impossible to avoid—but ever since I lost Eliza, every time I've tried to flip open the pages of an old favorite, immerse myself in something mindless, the words won't melt in my mind the way they used to, warm and smooth like freshly whipped butter. Instead, every sentence feels clunky, hard, taunting me like they're written in some foreign tongue, completely illegible.

I guess that's the thing about grief, loss: it changes everything, not just you. Colors are duller, foods are blander. The words don't sing like they used to.

I push the empty suitcase across the room and reach for the last one, the one I've been avoiding. The one full of sentimental stuff, all that collectible trash I can't bring myself to throw away. I don't exactly know when I started doing this: saving things like concert bracelets and grainy photobooth strips. Sea glass and lanyards and an empty box of Milk Duds from the first time Eliza and I went to the movies by ourselves. I've done it since childhood, I know, but it's become something of a compulsion now. An irresistible urge to tuck away the things most people would toss, made even stronger since the night she died. Maybe it's because these are the only things I have left of her, the objects that keep her partially alive in my mind like some kind of shrine: one of her scrunchies with thin strands of hair still knotted into the fabric, an old tube of lipstick she didn't live long enough to finish. If I were to get rid of them now, it would feel like getting rid of her, too. Throwing her memory in the trash along with an embroidery floss bracelet, a broken ornament we made together in kindergarten. A cookie from her tenth birthday party I never took out of the packaging, so rock-hard stale I couldn't bite into it now even if I wanted to.

I do my best to organize the clutter before setting it aside and pulling out my pictures. I stare at the one of Eliza and me first, resting on top in a delicate gold frame. It's of the two of us in our bathing suits, a grinning selfie we snapped while lying out on her parents' dock. I can't even remember when we took it—freshman year, maybe, still early in high school—and behind it, there's a second one of us in our graduation caps, taken just before walking into the auditorium on commencement day. We look so effortless in that first one, all limbs and teeth glowing bright against our summertime tans. We spent so many afternoons out there: Eliza's blond hair turning even blonder, a cascade of freckles popping out across her nose. Salt water and sunburns turning our skin crispy and tight. That was our element: just the two of us, together, unrestrained.

But in the second picture, there's a rigidity to our smiles that makes me sad.

I remember when that one was taken, of course. Just three weeks before the night she died. The last picture we'd ever have together and we don't even look happy.

I wonder now what Eliza would think about all this: Lucy, the house. Me agreeing to move in with three strangers I know nothing about. She'd probably love it, honestly. It's the kind of thing she would do. She was always the one pushing me to get out of my comfort zone, try new things. She'd be disgusted at the way I spent my freshman year, too cocooned in the safety net of my dorm room to venture out and experience anything new. She was never shy about that. I remember an argument we had once, junior year, me whining about wanting to stay in instead of show up at some party with a bunch of public-school people we barely even knew.

"You're wasting your life," she had said, me glowering in my sweatpants as she shimmied on some cutoff shorts. She was wearing makeup, too, which was weird to look at. She never wore makeup. *"You're only young once."*

It hurt to realize she had started to think of our Friday nights together as a waste, but I knew what she meant. We had been doing the same thing for practically a decade: bike rides to 7-Eleven to spend our allowance on sweet things and Slurpees before high-tailing it back home. Staying up late, giddy and gossiping, then sleeping in in the mornings before doing it all over again. Of course, things evolved as we grew older, swapping gummy worms for wine we grabbed out of her parents' refrigerator, occasionally the good stuff Eliza found hidden in her dad's office, but the thing that stayed the same was the way I lived for those weekends, cling-ing to them even harder once I sensed her desire to start doing something different.

I remember wondering if that kind of power imbalance was normal in a friendship—if every pair consisted of one half who seemed to love the other just a little bit more—but I didn't want to question it. I was content with the way things were.

I never felt like I needed anybody else—but slowly, inevitably, Eliza did.

"I'm sorry," I say to her now, my fingertips touching her static face. I wish I could take back every stupid argument, every mean-ingless fight. Her death had shocked the Outer Banks, sending a ripple of uncomfortable contemplation across everyone who ever knew her. It was a stark reminder that none of us are immortal—especially the ones, like Eliza, who lived like they were. And it had scared me for a while, realizing that any second could be the end of it: something as simple as a trip into traffic, a cramp while you're swimming. That a life as bright as hers could be extinguished with-out even the courtesy of a heads-up. But at the same time, the abruptness of it all made me realize that she was right.

You're only young once, and only if you're lucky.

"Margot." I jump at the sudden banging on my door. "Girls are up. Get out here."

I take one last glance at the picture, guilt washing over me. It's pretty obvious, now, what I'm doing here. I'm trying to replace her. Eliza is my phantom limb: an amputation that still hurts me, haunts me, despite the fact that she doesn't even exist. She is the dull, constant throb that wakes me in the night and doubles me over; sometimes, in those early morning hours, I forget she's even gone. I'll click open my eyes and reach out to the side, half expecting to feel her warm body beside me like during those summertime sleepovers. My fingers dragging their way across my comforter, searching for the familiar feel of her—but then, every time, I find it cold and empty, the pain increasing until it's so unbearable I think I might faint.

I know now that if I'm ever going to move on, if I'm ever going to be whole, I need something to take her place. Someone else who can slip into her skin; who can give me everything she once did—or, rather, someone who can show me who I am without her. Because the truth is, I've only ever been Eliza's best friend, ever since that first day in kindergarten when we clicked so easily. And even though we were opposites—me, brainy and bookish, and her, wild and alive—I was the yin to her yang, the quiet sidekick who talked reason into her ear when she got the sudden urge to do something stupid. I used to think that her standing next to me was the contrast I needed to stand out on my own, but I know now that was never the case. Instead, she was simply something I could cling to; a safety blanket that felt familiar and warm.

While nobody else ever remembered my face, knew my name, when I walked into a room with her, I saw it click: the recognition, the respect. *Eliza's friend.*

"Coming!" I yell, standing up before propping the photo onto the mantel.

That's why, when Eliza died, it felt like my identity did, too. Her death erased us both completely and I wonder if that's the reason why I feel so drawn to Lucy. Why my eyes always gravitated to her when she walked down the hall or lay out on campus. Why I agreed to any of this. There are certain similarities between them and I wonder now if I had sensed them all along, my subconscious pulling me toward the closest thing I could find to my friend. After all, being loved by Eliza was like a sudden hit of adrenaline—a gateway drug, something addicting and freeing that left you craving your next hit the second she stepped away. And if Eliza was adrenaline, that makes Lucy something even more. Something more addicting, more dangerous.

Something I probably shouldn't be dabbling in—but at the same time, something impossible to refuse.

CHAPTER 6

AFTER

I plop down on my bed with an exaggerated huff. Detective Frank is gone, finally, and I want to take advantage of the precious time to think.

I glance around my room, taking in all the subtle changes that have taken place over the nine months since I've made this space my home: the pictures cluttering up the mantel are with Lucy, Sloane, and Nicole now, our lips pursed in puckery pouts and our cheeks smashed together with too much force. Most of them were taken in the early days: those sweet weeks of summer when we were just getting to know each other. Those first few months when everything was fine. You can tell by how different we all look, Nicole especially, her cheeks still baby-round and not the concave craters they would slowly shrink into. Then there's the string of Christmas lights hung up around the walls that I never bothered to take down; the cigarette burns visible on the floor, little black dots peppered across the hardwood from when Lucy was too lazy to grab an ashtray. All of the evidence of the life I've built in this house. The person I've become.

That person is almost unrecognizable to the person I was when I first stepped foot in here—though, I suppose, that was the point.

I wonder how much time we have until the search for Lucy really ramps up. I know, right now, they're grasping at straws: an adult gone for three days is hardly enough to call her a missing person, especially considering what they'll soon come to learn. And Sloane wasn't lying when she said it before: Lucy does this kind of thing. Everyone who knows her knows it.

But still, Levi is dead. Levi is dead, Lucy is gone, and someone has to pay.

I roll over now and reach for my bedside table, yanking the drawer open. Inside, I sift through all the typical clutter: a TV remote, a couple empty lighters I haven't bothered to throw away. Wrinkled receipts and dried-out pens, until finally, my fingers wrap around something cold and smooth shoved into the back and I pull it out, tap it awake.

It's Lucy's phone, a smattering of stars sprinkled across the lock screen.

I know I can't hang on to this forever. I know they'll eventually track it and it'll lead them back here, to this house. To the three of us—Sloane, Nicole, and me—her roommates and confidants. Her best friends. But it's better than Lucy having it, we all knew that. There were certain things that made sense for her to keep: her ID, her wallet. A handful of credit cards, although of course she'd have to use those to be tracked down. Her phone, on the other hand, was something we couldn't risk. At least this way, by the time they find it, it'll be stashed underneath her bed or something, completely obscured by dirty clothes and rogue shoes. The battery will be dead, which will explain how we never heard the ringing of various people trying to reach her.

Which will explain why, after always getting voice mail we stopped trying ourselves.

But by the time that happens, they will have already found their answers . . . only they won't be the answers I know they're expecting. Lucy's unpredictable like that. No, the answers they'll find will only lead to more questions, and slowly, carefully, we'll slink back into the shadows and let all those other things crawl quietly into the light. We'll remove ourselves from the story completely, letting it morph into something different, better. Staged.

What Detective Frank doesn't yet know is that nothing with Lucy is ever as it seems.

I stare at the stars on her phone now, my eyes gravitating toward all the constellations she once taught me: Orion, the hunter, and Taurus, the bull—but it's Gemini where they linger. I couldn't see it at first, Lucy and me lying on the roof, her hand in mine as she lifted my arm into the air and traced it for me.

"Just there," she had said, her smoky breath warm against the early fall chill. *"See the two people? They're holding hands. Like us."*

Then, once I saw it, it never went away. Every single night I would look up and find it, my eyes gravitating to it naturally like one of those inkblot pictures: something that, once seen, could never be unseen. Lying on my back, a once-smoldering fire dying in the night and mounds of warm bodies passed out around it. I remember training my eyes on the sky, thinking of Lucy. Knowing that she was out there, somewhere—that *they* were out there, Lucy and Levi. Spending his final few hours together without him even knowing it.

I remember lying there, staring at those stars, and feeling the familiar pinch of envy in my chest.

I remember thinking that, wherever she was, she was looking at them, too.

CHAPTER 7

BEFORE

The living room has been picked up, sort of, beer bottles collected and tossed into the trash. There's a candle burning on the coffee table, something citrusy and herbal like eucalyptus and lemon, the equivalent of spraying Febreze on dirty laundry. As if the scent alone could somehow render the place clean.

I walk out of my room and clear my throat, three pairs of eyes turning toward me.

"Girls," Lucy announces, a grin on her lips. "This is Margot. Roommate number four."

I raise my hand, a sheepish wave, and walk toward them on the couch, trying to make a quick calculation in my mind: Do I plop down, too, just pretend that I'm one of them? Or stand at a distance and wait to be invited?

"Where'd you find her?" Sloane asks, eyeing me like I'm some stray dog Lucy dragged in from the street. Like I might have fleas.

"She lived on our hall."

"*Our* hall?"

"Yes," Lucy says, a hint of annoyance peeking through. "The last door on the left."

"Why have we never met her before?"

"You're meeting her now."

I stay standing, taking in Sloane's skeptical gaze. Nicole is chewing on her lip, like she's trying to work out some math problem in her mind. I'm not surprised they don't know my name. I barely left my room at all last year—but still, the fact that my face isn't even vaguely familiar sends a deep sting through my chest.

"Sit," Lucy says, and I glance around, deciding to take a seat on the couch adjacent to them. A little distance suddenly seems safe. "Tell us about yourself."

I blink, my eyes flitting between the three of them as they stare at me expectantly, and I feel a sudden sense of vertigo, a sharp pang of panic, like I'm standing on a hot stage and suddenly forgot my lines.

"I'm Margot," I say at last, even though they know that already. "I'm an English major from the Outer Banks—"

"No," Lucy says, interrupting me. "All of that is bullshit. That's not you. Tell us about *you*."

I can feel my heartbeat rise into my throat, my cheeks growing warm as my mind goes blank. The sad truth of it is, there's not much else to say.

"Why'd you pick Rutledge?" Nicole asks, wide doll eyes and a gentle tone. Already, I can tell she's the nicest.

I turn toward her, offering a smile. She's giving me an opening, I know. A hand to grab because she can clearly see me flailing—but at the same time, I'm not going to talk about Eliza. Not yet.

"I had to get out of North Carolina," I say at last, a watered-down version of the truth. "I just needed to go somewhere new."

I think of home again and the way my parents had suggested I defer my acceptance after we lost Eliza, giving me some time to sort through it all. A year to deal with my grief. I had considered it for a while before realizing what their true intentions were: an attempt at making me change my mind and choose Duke instead. It's like they knew, without her, that I'd default back to them, doing whatever they asked me to do. The future we had planned together gone forever, buried with her, like the friendship bracelet we made together back when we were eight.

I remember looking down at my own, all those colorful threads woven together on my wrist, and suddenly feeling so angry about them capitalizing on her death like that. Using it for their own purposes: to control me, use me, their straight-A daughter just another thing for them to brag about at the country club cocktail parties.

In a way, I think I came here to spite them. I think I wanted them to know that, even dead, I would still choose her first.

"Why?" Lucy asks now, leaning forward. "What happened that made you want to leave so bad?"

I look up at her and swallow, something swirling in those crystalline eyes. A challenge or a dare I'm suddenly sure I'll fail.

"Jesus, Lucy, would you stop with the third degree?"

I look over at Sloane, her toned arms crossed tight in front of her chest. Her scowl is still there, but suddenly, it no longer feels directed at me.

"I'm getting to know her," Lucy says, a feigned innocence dripping from her lips.

"You're interrogating her," Sloane snaps back. "Lay off."

The room grows silent again, the four of us sitting in a beat of uncomfortable quiet. The arguing, the hostility: for a second, it concerns me, thinking that the three of them might not be as tight as I thought—but then, I realize it's the opposite. Eliza and I used to bicker like this, too, throwing the kind of sharp jabs at each other only best friends could survive. Words can stick, wedging themselves fast into the tenderest parts of you—but when you have years of memories to thicken the skin, they aren't quite as fatal. Instead, they bounce off, land with a whimper. Most of the time, anyway.

"Come on, I'll show you the rest of the house," Sloane says, standing up from the couch. "Then you can meet the boys."

"The boys?" I ask.

"The boys next door," Lucy says, pulling her legs beneath her. "They own the house—well, technically, the fraternity does. Kappa Nu. They use it for extra rooms when they need it, rent it out when they don't."

"That's why it looks like this—" Sloane grunts.

"—and why it's so cheap," Nicole cuts in. "Our rent is, like, unheard of."

"Trevor's the president," Lucy says. "Nicole gets defensive."

"I'm not defensive," she spits, definitely defensive. "I'm just saying we're lucky to live here. Most people pay four times the amount to be on this side of town."

Sloane and Lucy shoot each other a look, like they've had this conversation so many times before, and slowly, their blank stares break into smiles. Nicole looks annoyed for a second, being on the outside of this inside joke, but when Lucy and Sloane start to laugh, her shoulders slouch and she joins in, too.

"You're whipped," Lucy says, throwing a pillow in her direction.

"Trust me, I'm not." Nicole laughs, tossing it back. "This is your fault, anyway. I told you I wanted to be single and you wouldn't listen."

"If you don't want him, I'll take him," Lucy mocks, provocative but playful. "I'm not going to apologize for introducing you to the most beautiful boy on campus."

The three of them are grinning now, devious little smiles that make me feel even more like an outsider as I watch this unspoken thing blooming between them, beautiful and mysterious and entirely theirs. It's like we're back on that lawn again, all four of us in the exact same roles: me, watching curiously from a distance. Them, oblivious to their surroundings and the strange effect they have on everyone else.

I continue to sit, not wanting to intrude, until Lucy throws the pillow at me next and I catch it quickly against my chest, my heart slamming hard against the fabric.

"Margot saw him this morning," she says. "She knows what I mean."

It feels like an unspoken invitation, an outstretched arm pulling me into whatever this thing is between them, and I hold the pillow tight between my fingers and watch as she winks, that little curl in her lip making my cheeks flush hot.

Making me think, for just a second, that I would take her hand and follow her anywhere.

CHAPTER 8

Sloane and I have covered it all, starting with the upstairs. She took me into her room first, then Nicole's, both of which were adorned with the type of modest, mass-produced décor that comes with a college budget, though even the smallest peek into their respective spaces revealed so much. The focal point of Sloane's room was a giant white desk covered with textbooks and papers and a sleeping laptop; a large calendar on the wall with old exam dates obsessively circled before getting crossed out in red. Her bedside table held a scrawny lamp and a colorful glass bowl with a nug of weed waiting patiently inside. A stack of thick paperbacks, a cup of water. A pack of matches with some bar logo I vaguely recognized.

Nicole's room, on the other hand, showed no evidence of study. Hers was cluttered with clothes and makeup and mismatched shoes; it wasn't dirty, but *messy*, like she had a habit of simply flinging off her outfit and letting it live wherever it landed. I noticed some of Trevor's things peeking out from behind her own: a pair of blue boxers, a white crew sock. A Kappa Nu sweatshirt draped over the back of her chair. The air was unusually stuffy up there—heat rises, naturally—and I found myself suddenly grateful for a room on the lower level. Mine, in comparison, was unusually cold, the floor frigid to the touch, and I wondered why. Maybe there was a vent by my bed I hadn't noticed earlier.

I saw Sloane and Nicole's shared bathroom next, tiny and clean and smelling of lavender, but mine and Lucy's, I learned once we ventured back downstairs, had a malfunctioning toilet tank that caused water to run at all hours of the night.

"If it gets really annoying, just jiggle the handle," Sloane had said, wiggling it with her fingers as if to show me how. "We've asked the boys to fix it, but, you know."

She rolled her eyes and I nodded, inherently understanding the headaches that must come with frat boys as landlords.

Lucy's bedroom door remained mysteriously closed and we skipped past it wordlessly, moving next into the kitchen, then the backyard, a surprisingly large plot of land obscured from view from the street. I survey the patchy grass now, the row of azaleas pushed tight against the side of the house. The single magnolia tree with its milky white flowers and the gravel driveway big enough for half a dozen cars, squinting my eyes in the sudden brightness of the sun reflecting off the bleached-white pebbles.

"This is the shed," Sloane says, walking me over to a little wooden shack at the edge of the property. "It connects our backyard to Kappa Nu's. It's the quickest way to get over there."

She opens the double doors and a blast of musty air hits me, a combination of smells fighting for attention. I recognize the metallic tang of rust; the cold damp of fresh dirt. But there's something else, too. Something different: earthy and sweet-smelling like barrels of hay or freshly mown grass. It isn't until I peer over the edge of the door that I see what's inside: tight rows of leaves dangling from ropes on the ceiling, each of them swaying gently like hundreds of hangmen in the breeze.

"They're drying tobacco," she explains, reading my mind. "Don't ask."

I'm momentarily speechless as I stare at the maze of leaves in front of me. They're absolutely massive, the size of my head, bunched in clusters of three and five. I can barely see past them, the inside of the shed much deeper than it appears, though Sloane forges on, pushing the leaves out of her way like a stage curtain as she moves farther away. I move in quickly behind her, a swirling scent of moss and wood and sweet vanilla making my eyes water. Most of the leaves are yellowing, but some of them are brown, and before I can think twice, I reach up and touch one, its sticky consistency making me think of a spoiling corpse: juicy and putrefied.

"Here's the frat house," Sloane says as we make our way out the back doors and into the Kappa Nu backyard. I'm strangely relieved to be out of that place, though I try not to show it. There's just something about it that makes me uneasy: the ropes and the leaves hanging from the ceiling, obscuring my view, like someone could come up behind me and I'd never even know it. The long, curved blades I had glimpsed dangling from hooks on the wall, dried animal blood caked to their edges. The way the scent of gore and tobacco seemed to mix in my mind, creating something sweet and unsettling like looking down at a rare steak on your plate, stomach roiling as you lick your lips and watch the blood pool.

We stand there for a second, right outside the open shed doors, an uncomfortable quiet relaxing over us as we stare at the side of the house. I realize now that it isn't the shed that's strange, or even the things in it. I've seen my share of shotguns and hunting knives, fishhooks and fillet blades. We're in South Carolina, after all. Rutledge is a tiny little town in the middle of nothing but forest and fields: thirty minutes to the water in one direction, thirty minutes to the woods in the other. What seems strange to me is the unrestricted access we have to someone else's property. How easy it was for us to simply let ourselves into their space . . . and by that logic, how easy it would be for them to let themselves into ours. I don't want to say anything, though, knowing that a full year spent living in Hines probably just made me too sheltered. I never got to experience the co-ed dorms. The shared living between *us* and *them*.

"Are you sure you want to do this?" Sloane asks suddenly, the bluntness of her question taking me by surprise. I turn to face her, realizing too late she's already looking at me.

"Do what?" I ask, wondering how long she's been doing that: staring. Taking in my expression as I tried to work through my thoughts, a jumbled coil in my brain I still can't untangle. "Meet the boys?"

"This," she says, gesturing vaguely around us. "Live here. All of it. You seem . . . I don't know. Too nice."

I have a sudden flash of Maggie in my mind: *too nice*. What she really means is too boring, too bland, masking the bite of her words with a pinch of politeness in hopes that I won't taste that comment for what it truly was.

"How do you know Lucy?" she asks again.

"Remember, I lived on your hall—"

"No," she interrupts, shaking her head. "How do you *know* her? How did you meet?"

"Well, I don't know her," I say, suddenly embarrassed. "Not really. We didn't actually *meet*—"

"Look, don't take this the wrong way, but you seem like her flavor."

"Her *flavor*? What does that mean?"

"You're very vanilla."

"Thanks," I say, not bothering to hide the sarcasm.

"That's not a dig," she says.

"Kind of sounded like it was."

"I just mean that's what Lucy looks for," she says, resting her arms on her hips. "You can turn vanilla into anything, right? It's a blank slate. It's malleable."

"Okay—?"

"She's a fucking liar," Sloane interrupts, a viciousness in her voice I never expected from her. "Like, pathological. Did you know that?"

"I . . . don't really know anything about her."

"Yeah," she says, looking away, as if that somehow proved her point. "Just take everything she says with a grain of salt. Trust me."

"Look, don't *you* take this the wrong way, but if that's how you feel, then why are you friends with her?"

I don't know what drove me to say it, but suddenly, standing here listening to Sloane bash her best friend sitting just inside, a strange protectiveness has settled over me, like Lucy somehow needs me to defend her honor in her absence. I don't know her, not really, but she gifted me an opportunity—an opportunity of belonging, of *friends*—and so far, she hasn't given me any reason to doubt her intentions.

So far, she's been nothing but nice.

Sloane looks back at me, her eyebrows bunched like she's never actually asked herself that question before. Maybe she's jealous, I think, the same way Maggie was jealous in the courtyard outside Hines. Maybe she's threatened by Lucy—or, I realize with a sudden sense of surprise, maybe she's threatened by *me*. By another person stepping in, taking her place. I can understand that: the envy that blooms in your chest when you see your best friend with somebody else. The fear of being replaced.

Sloane is quiet for a while longer, considering, before turning back toward the shed like she's afraid Lucy might be hiding in it.

"She's fun," she says at last. "She gets you into places."

"Lots of people are fun," I counter.

"When you're friends with Lucy, she makes you feel special," Sloane says, exhaling, like the statement finally unburdened her from a truth she's been carrying around for far too long. "Like she chose you for a reason."

That, too, I intimately understand. I've been feeling that way ever since she stepped into my dorm room, the piercing blue of her eyes pulling me into some kind of trance. It's almost as if I've been hypnotized ever since, entranced by the spell of her, moving through the motions of whatever she tells me to do without a second thought.

"I don't know." She sighs again, like she's doubting herself now. "Maybe I'm being harsh."

"Maybe a little bit."

"Or maybe I'm afraid of what would happen if I stopped."

She looks at me now, an intensity in her eyes that makes my skin crawl. This veiled warning of hers cloaked as concern is making me feel light-headed, dizzy, like standing on a ledge and looking down, feeling my body start to sway. I know I should probably take a step back and reassess what I'm doing here, but I also know that if I think too hard about it, I'll come to my senses and scamper back to safety. To a place where I can feel my own two feet planted firmly on the ground.

I think of what Sloane just called me: vanilla, *malleable*. A blank slate. That's what I was with Eliza, too, if I'm being honest with myself; not my own person but a mirror she could stare into and see a reflection of herself gazing back. Sloane is trying to tell me that, if I'm not careful, Lucy will do the same. She'll turn me into something I'm not. She'll twist me and mold me until I'm unrecognizable, transforming in her hands like soft, wet clay. She'll shape me into whatever *she* wants me to be. Something useful to best fit her needs, a deliberate instrument of her own design.

But here's the thing Sloane doesn't know: I want to be changed.

That's all I've ever wanted, really: for someone to scoop me up and tell me what I'm supposed to be. My entire life, I've contorted so easily in the hands of others—my parents, Eliza—shape-shifting at any given second to be the thing that everyone else wants. So maybe that's who I am: a chameleon that can take on the appearance of its surroundings. A master of camouflage to stay invisible and safe. I need someone to mold me like putty; give me function and form.

I want Lucy to bend me, break me. Rip me to pieces and reassemble me into something different, better. New.

CHAPTER 9

A scream echoes across the backyard, startling Sloane and me out of our standoff.

"What was that?" I ask, eyes darting, though Sloane doesn't look concerned. Instead, she looks annoyed.

"Come on," she says, taking off toward the Kappa Nu house, cutting her way through a sea of weeds and apparently forgetting about our conversation entirely. "Let's meet the boys."

We walk the length of the yard and approach the house from the back. The door is cracked open and we step through it, entering a massive living room, though I hesitate to call it that because I can't imagine people actually living here. I've wondered about the inside of this place so many times—and not just *this* place, in particular, but all these places. The houses students flock to in packs, themed parties and coordinating outfits. Greek letters hanging haphazard against the siding and music beating against the walls like the house itself is a living, breathing thing. I don't know what I was imagining before—something grandiose, maybe; something to at least justify the exorbitant membership fees—but instead, the space is giant, square, and almost entirely unfurnished with the exception of one ripped-up leather couch, a few lopsided composite pictures, and a folding table in the center of it all. There are about a dozen boys huddled around it, red Solo cups knocked over and dripping foam onto the carpet, and I can feel the crunch of it beneath my shoes, a crust of fossilized fluids built up over the years. Even the air feels sticky, a concoction of sweat and smoke gripping my skin like cling wrap.

"SLOANE!"

A shorter boy in the middle with sleepy eyes and an exaggerated grin throws his arms up in way of greeting. He's brunette and overly muscular, not bad looking but clearly overcompensating, and I look over to Sloane next, trying to study the way she acts around them: passive and uninterested. Like she couldn't care less.

"Boys, this is Margot," she says, ignoring him completely. "She's taking the room next to Lucy's."

I stand still as their collective gaze turns in my direction and I can feel it slipping all over me: my face, my neck. My chest, where their eyes linger too long, then down the length of the skintight camisole I changed into while unpacking. I can practically see the cogs turning behind their bloodred eyes, trying to imagine how everything looks underneath.

"Hi," I say, feeling my cheeks turn hot. The scream, I realize now, was coming from them—or, at least, one of them. A few of the boys are holding Ping-Pong balls between their fingers; that, and the dripping beer, tells me they were in the middle of some type of game.

"Looks like you've made yourself at home."

I catch sight of Trevor in the back; he's eyeing my spaghetti straps, smiling, and I can feel myself burn even hotter, my mind flashing back to the image of him shirtless in the living room without my permission.

"You're a sophomore?" he asks, and I nod quietly. "I've never seen you around. You ever come to the house?"

"I'm sure she had better places to be," Sloane says on my behalf.

Trevor grins and I feel suddenly indebted to her for making me sound more interesting than I actually am.

"You two wanna play?" he asks, holding up the Ping-Pong ball and twisting it in the air. Sloane looks at me, eyebrows raised, and this feels like another test. An on-the-spot assessment to see what kind of person I am: the kind to crack open a morning beer in a house full of strangers or the kind to politely decline and retreat back to my bedroom.

"You seem . . . I don't know. Too nice."

"Sure," I say, forcing myself to head toward the table. Trying to exert the same indifference as Sloane, the same cool demeanor, but instead, I feel like I'm walking on stilts: awkward and rigid. My entire body put on display.

The game resumes with Sloane and me on one side of the table and Trevor and the other one, who is apparently named Lucas, on the other. I try to focus, try to block everything else out, but the sudden sting of irony is too sharp not to notice: this is the exact type of situation Eliza and I used to wrestle with. She was so much more outgoing than I was. Whenever we found ourselves approached by other people, invited to some house party or bonfire on the beach, she would say yes, always, flinging herself into any situation with the kind of calm confidence I could never grasp. The concept of not knowing anyone never dissuaded her; instead, she embraced it, reveling in the idea of sauntering into a circle of strangers, their eyes on her making her walk even taller. Talk even louder. I, on the other hand, had a hard time understanding what was supposed to be fun about the things she so desperately wanted to do: standing around, self-conscious, drinking warm beer somebody's brother had been hiding in the bed of their truck. The pimple-pocked boys with their greasy hair and gangly arms, sour breath on our necks as they leaned in close. I hated having to act like I knew what I was doing in those situations. That I was somehow born with the knowledge of how to shotgun a beer, pack a bowl, tamp a pack of cigarettes like everyone else seemed to be. I still remember the first time I ever tried one: lighting the wrong end, burning my thumb on the flame and proceeding to suck the tobacco particles straight onto my tongue. The embarrassment as I sputtered and gagged, tried to smile through the smoke in my lungs and the tears in my eyes.

The blister that later formed on my thumb, round and clear, a little bubble I proceeded to pop with my fingernail. The sting of it like a punishment I didn't want to forget.

"So, tell us about your friend."

Lucas arcs his arm with inflated finesse and I watch as the ball slaps straight into the center cup. He grins, all his attention directed at Sloane.

"Why don't you ask her?" she says, picking up the cup and downing it in a single gulp. "She's right here."

"Touché," he says, looking at me next.

"I'm from the Outer Banks," I say, not knowing how else to fill the sudden silence. I twist the ball in my hands, trying to remember the rules from the handful of times I played at a house party with Eliza. I'm suddenly grateful for those nights now, saving me from having to ask, and I do my best to mirror Lucas's stance, extending my arm long and high—but when I release it, it soars straight over their heads and onto the floor.

"We have a pledge coming in from the Outer Banks," Trevor says, jogging across the room to grab the ball. "He's here this weekend, actually. Went on a beer run with some brothers. He's a legacy, so, you know. Special treatment and all that. At least for now."

He looks at Lucas and smirks and I listen to him chatter on about recruitment, relieved to have the conversation steered so quickly away from me. Greek life isn't everything at Rutledge, but there's a decent amount of it given the size. It's still early in the summer, meaning most incoming freshmen won't start rush until fall, but apparently Kappa Nu has lined up a few summer events to get early commitments. The strategy, essentially, is to take them out and give them the time of their lives: bottomless booze, all-night parties, older girls. Show them the college nirvana that could be theirs if only they pledged their life and loyalty to Kappa Nu—and then, once school starts, the hazing begins.

"Speaking of which, there's a party tonight," Trevor continues, tossing the ball again. It lands in my cup this time and I pick up the beer and down it quickly, the warm, flat liquid like malty urine. I peel a strand of hair from my tongue and I can sense Sloane staring at me, her eyes on the side of my face. "Y'all coming?"

"We'll be there," I say, not waiting for Sloane to speak first.

The game stretches on for another thirty minutes: the toss of the ball, the slap of the beer. Foam spraying across the table, my forearm, my shirt. Trevor and Lucas are all too willing to talk about themselves, which means Sloane and I are mostly just drinking, her chiming in with the occasional laugh or disparaging quip. Standing next to her is an immersive study in effortless cool—and judging by the way Lucas looks at her, whatever she's doing, it works.

We're getting ready to start a new game when the front door bangs open and another group of guys gush in. They're all talking over one another, laughing, each one carrying a cardboard case of beer in one hand and a handle of liquor in the other.

"Come over here and meet the girls!" Trevor yells, waving them closer. "If you commit to Kappa Nu, they'll be your new neighbors."

The way he says it makes me flinch, like we're two slabs of meat being dangled in front of a pack of animals. Sloane makes an effort to catch my eye, rolling hers.

"This is the shit we deal with for cheap rent," she whispers, and I let out a laugh.

I look down at the table and decide to busy myself with racking the cups; I want to act disinterested, bored, the way Sloane does, too, even though I can see the group of them moving closer in my peripheral vision. The nearness of them makes my neck grow hot. I grab a few cups and accidentally tip another one over in the process, the remnants of backwash beer trickling down my hand. The room is spinning gently, I realize, the last hour going by in a daze. I don't know how much I've had to drink—a few beers, at least—and I concentrate again on the table, trying to keep my legs from tilting.

"This is Sloane," I hear Trevor say, my eyes still glued to the table. I register a few mutters, Sloane dispensing all the right lines, until finally, I feel their collective attention turn toward me. "And this is the new girl from OBX. Where's Levi?"

The shock of the name makes my head snap up; surely, I've imagined it. It can't be. *He* can't be the incoming freshman from my hometown; the one visiting for the weekend that Trevor wanted me to meet. I blink a few times, trying to reorient myself as I look at the boys, their smug expressions and too-short shorts, when my attention lands on a familiar face in the back.

"Levi," I echo, my voice tight. It's him, of course it is, and the reality of him, *here,* standing in this very room crashes over me like an unexpected wave, practically knocking me back. I can feel the past suddenly pulling me under, taking me down, a rip current in water that I'm powerless to fight. Because if there's a single person who brings back memories of Eliza, a body from before that could have stopped what happened, saved her from it all, it's Levi.

Levi Butler.

CHAPTER 10

We were in the water the first time we saw him, his slow approach down the dock thieving our attention.

"Who's that?" I had asked, my legs kicking beneath the calm of the current like a hidden panic, concealed from the surface.

Eliza's dock was long and lean, over one hundred yards of salt-stained wood spooling into the ocean like a red cedar carpet. It was the summer going into our senior year and we had spent every day out there, flip-flopping down to the floating dock in the mornings, marinating ourselves in tanning oil until our skin started to crisp. That day, we had been out there for hours already, our towels wet and rumpled and smelling of musty coconut, before deciding to dive in to cool off—but suddenly, we could just barely make out the outline of a person walking our way.

"I think it's my neighbor," she said, her lips just above the waterline. The house next to Eliza's had been vacant for years; like lots of homes in the Outer Banks, it spent most of its life as a vacation rental until the owners simply decided to stop renting it. They must have been pretty wealthy to let it sit like that, unoccupied, but when they did finally decide to let go of it, it was barely a week before the "For Sale" sign was replaced with "Sold." By then, though, Eliza and I had gotten used to the dock being solely ours. We didn't want to share it with anyone—despite the fact that it straddled the property line and, technically, was just as much *theirs* as it was *ours*.

Or, rather, *hers*. The Jeffersons'. My home away from home.

I always thought of Eliza's family as flawless, and I guess that's why I spent so much time there. It was like I hoped proximity alone could get some of whatever they had to rub off on me like a barbed hitchhiker sticking to my clothes, traveling back with me before planting itself in our home. Their love like an invasive species that could take over us all. I felt bad sometimes, resenting my parents like that, wishing they were different, but the reality was that while my parents tried to be perfect, Eliza's seemed like they actually were. My mother was a stay-at-home socialite, bleached blond and impossibly chatty, the textbook complement to my dad, who spent most evenings stoically silent, fingers clutching a whiskey highball and eyes perusing the room in a way that made you wonder what was wrong. We lived in a house on the same street as Eliza's, but other than that, they couldn't be more different. My dad was in finance, the kind of industry you enter into with the explicit purpose of getting rich, whereas Eliza's used to play guitar in a band, a trust-fund child who spent his youth roaming around before eventually deciding to settle down on the coast. He was passionate and peculiar and completely unfazed by the things they had, almost as if he didn't even notice them. Didn't even care. Their waterfront oasis was kept cluttered up and lived-in whereas ours was always perfectly pristine, cold like a museum and just as impersonal.

And they always ate dinner together, just the three of them, except when I was invited and they set the table for four.

I'll never forget those little moments I got to witness: Mr. Jefferson scooping up Eliza's mom on the dock, olive skin and dark hair glistening like tar melting in the sun. Those massive hands all over her bare bikini legs before he cannonballed the two of them into the water together, Mrs. Jefferson emerging with a slicked-back ponytail and mascara tears dripping down pale, freckled cheeks. Head thrown back, maniacally laughing.

My mother would have been livid, I remember thinking as we watched them splash each other like smitten teenagers. My dad wasn't even allowed to kiss my mom when she was wearing lipstick, not that he ever really tried.

I turned to look at Eliza, the memories evaporating and replaced by this unknown person walking into our space. New neighbors could change everything. They could alter the very air itself, making it lighter or heavier with their presence alone. The figure was getting closer now, both of us treading water as his lanky outline grew larger in the distance, and we could tell it was a boy. A teenage boy. A tall, tan boy with moppy brown hair and board shorts and a bare, hairless chest. He wasn't looking at us—not yet, at least, still a few too many yards away to catch sight of our bodies in the water below—and it gave us mere seconds of interrupted time to scrutinize him before he could scrutinize us.

"Come on," Eliza said at last, taking a deep breath before slipping beneath the surface like a water moccasin, silent and slick. I watched her silhouette disappear below the floating dock and I plugged my nose and followed her under, reemerging in the gap between the top of the water and the underside of the wood. It was one of our secret spaces, a private little corner of the world that we had discovered as kids and claimed as our own. I could still remember the day we found it, years ago, doing somersaults in the water and our fingers digging into the pluffy bottom. I had been afraid of it at first, getting that claustrophobic feeling like being trapped inside a submerging car, the pocket of air above me growing smaller as we sank. But Eliza had explained that as the tide rose and fell, the dock did, too. The air would never run out.

She had convinced me it was safe, that *we* were safe. That we always would be.

"Do you think he saw us?" I whispered. There was something so intimate about that space: that little bubble of shared air and the wet wood smell and the way the algae-flecked water seemed to tint our skin, too, turning our faces a glowing emerald green. We were covered from all sides, the floating buoys that held up the dock encompassing us completely. Unless you were standing directly above us and happened to look down, you'd never even know we were there.

"I don't know," she said at last, water dripping off the tip of her nose. "I don't think so."

We listened in silence as his squeaking footsteps ambled closer until, eventually, the sound of wood turned to metal and we knew he was retreating down the ramp that led to the floating dock itself. The platform bobbed above us as his bare feet made contact and we both held our breath, watching. Waiting. The presence of him on top of us suffocating and strong. We felt him move to the edge of the dock next and that's when I caught a glimpse of him from between the gaps: one hand pushed into his bathing suit pocket and the other holding a cigarette, the bare skin of his back a burnt-almond brown. He could clearly see our stuff up there—our damp towels and flip-flops and matching burlap beach bags; our phones folded into our jean shorts, an attempt to keep them cool and dry—but still, he didn't seem to sense us. He didn't look down.

Instead, he just stood there, staring straight into nothing. Claiming that spot like he would soon claim everything. Welcoming himself right into my life.

CHAPTER 11

"Margot?"

I watch as Levi's once-familiar eyes dissect me from the top down, like my presence here must be some kind of mistake. He looks as surprised as I feel and I can't help but dissect him right back, noticing how much he's changed in the year since I've seen him. Those lanky legs that once carried him down the dock are muscular and toned now; his arms are wider, thicker, juicy blue veins bulging out of biceps that didn't used to exist. His right hand is gripping a can of Natural Light so hard I can hear the aluminum crack and a newly ripened Adam's apple juts out of this throat, bobbing when he swallows, pulling a spray of patchy stubble tight across his neck.

"So, you two are already acquainted," Trevor says, nudging Levi with his shoulder. The insinuation makes me nauseous and I swallow it down, wincing at the taste.

"Why are you here?" I ask, even though it's obvious. He's here because he's *going* here. He wouldn't be at a fraternity, spending the weekend getting coaxed and courted, if he wasn't planning on returning come fall.

"Why are you?" he counters.

"I live here."

"So do I."

"Is that a *commitment*?" Trevor whoops, but we both ignore him. I suppose we should have known this was inevitable, running into each other like this, but maybe I thought he would come to his senses and change his mind. Stay in the Outer Banks or go somewhere else entirely, far away from both me and the memory of her.

I look around, unable to escape her. Eliza is everywhere now, her absence between us so pronounced it's impossible to see anything else. It's like Levi brought the ghost of her into this very room with him: sitting on the couch with the bong in her lap, fingers around the mouthpiece and her eyes cast down. Blond hair hanging, obscuring her face, naturally comfortable the way I'm naturally not. She turns her head slowly and she's staring at me now, a violent kink in her neck like a sharp right angle and a glare beneath those spider-leg lashes, the whites of her eyes a deep, bloodred.

She smiles at me, a curl to her lips as they hover above the glass, and I know she's waiting to see how I'll react, what I'll say, like this is one big test she orchestrated herself. Plopping two rivals in a ring and watching as we fight to the death—for her.

"Listen, Margot—"

If it had all been different, I wonder if we still would have found ourselves here, together, like this. All three of us: Eliza, Levi, and me. I wonder if *she* would have befriended Lucy first, tucked me under her wing and let me tag along the way she always did.

I wonder if she would have been the fourth roommate, leaving me behind the way I left Maggie.

No. I shake my head. *No, she wouldn't.*

I realize too late that everyone is looking at me now, a sea of craned necks, watching. Waiting for my rebuttal to whatever Levi just said. I had tuned it out, a hissing static ringing in my ears, and the room is tilting harder now, though I can't tell if it's from the beer or Levi or everything all at once, so I force myself to smile and turn toward Sloane.

"I should probably finish unpacking," I say, facing Trevor next. "Thanks for the beer."

"Margot, wait—" Levi says, but I turn around and walk out the door before he can finish. I vaguely wonder if he'll run outside, too, chase me down and force me to talk—but, deep down, I know he won't. Levi never really cared about me. I was nothing more than a gnat to him that hovered around Eliza: a pesky annoyance, something to be tolerated. A price to be paid in exchange for proximity to her. He never let me spoil his fun and I know this time will be no different. He'll continue to do what he wants to do, take what he wants to take, batting me away or just ignoring me completely. Meanwhile, this was supposed to be my fresh start, a place to redefine myself, but now, with Levi here, I don't see how that can happen. His presence alone is a reminder of the person I used to be, the person I lost when I lost Eliza—not only that, but I lost her *because* of him.

She wouldn't have been where she was that night if he hadn't brought her there. She wouldn't have said what she said, did what she did, if he didn't drive her to it.

If Levi Butler never came into our lives that day, invading our space as the two of us huddled beneath the dock, legs cramped and fingers pruned, Eliza would still be here, safe, with me.

Eliza would still be alive.

CHAPTER 12

I slam into my bedroom after making my way across the Kappa Nu backyard, through the shed and into the house, stalking past Nicole on the couch without uttering a single word. I'm hanging my head and massaging my temples—trying to think, to organize my thoughts—when I realize there's someone already in here, a body hovering next to my bed.

"Jesus." I jump, my hand shooting to my chest once I register her there. "You scared the shit out of me."

"Hi," Lucy says, smiling like that day in the dorm. Like there's nothing unusual about her being here, in my bedroom, without my permission.

"What are you doing?" I ask, though I regret it the second I say it. This is her house, after all. My room for just a few hours and my boxes barely unpacked.

"I left something in here," she says, even though her hands are empty. "Who's this?"

She points to the picture of Eliza and me on the mantel, the only decoration I've managed to put up, and I walk over to it, our tanned bodies tangled together on the dock mere feet from the spot Levi Butler once stood. Even now, after all this time, I can still feel the claustrophobic weight of him as we held our breath below; I can still register the hammering of my heart, the nervous energy generated from his presence alone.

"That's my best friend," I say at last. "Eliza."

"If she's your best friend, how come she's never visited?"

I look at Lucy, eyebrows bunched, wondering what she could possibly mean by that. I haven't even lived here a day. How could she have already visited?

"I would have noticed her in the dorm," she clarifies. "She's pretty."

I tilt my head, realizing now that maybe Lucy had been watching me all year the same way I had been watching her—secretly, from a distance, eyes darting in the other direction after hovering in the same spot for a beat too long. I just never noticed. I open my mouth, ready to respond, when the door creaks behind me and I whip around, registering Sloane in the entryway.

"What the hell was that?" she asks, brown eyes boring into mine as she steps deeper into my room. "Who was that guy, an ex or something?"

"What guy?" Lucy asks, an eagerness in her tone. I see Nicole appear behind Sloane now, too, the dependent pet who can't stand to be left alone for too long. The stares from all three of them attacking me at every angle.

They want answers, all of them, a thirsty need for information that won't be quenched until I spill.

"It's a long story," I say instead, already knowing that won't cut it.

"We've got time," Lucy says, throwing herself onto my bed. Sloane and Nicole follow her lead, taking their own places on the mattress, and I stand in the center of the room for a second, eyeing them there. Numbly watching as Nicole flashes a smile and pats an empty spot on the comforter like she's trying to seduce me.

I chew on the side of my cheek, thinking. Trying to decide how much to reveal. These girls are still strangers to me, still enigmas I can't quite crack—but isn't this how friendships are born? From shared traumas and bedroom bonding? Eliza and I used to do this, too, curled up on her dock in the dark, whispering secrets that drew us closer in the night. It was always the topics that felt taboo that ended up pulling us in the tightest: Eliza, age ten, revealing that she had bought her first bra but was too embarrassed to wear it. Too afraid of the straps poking through the fabric of her T-shirt; of the boys zeroing in and snapping them against her skin. Me, age twelve, showing her my ravaged ankles from trying to shave with my mom's old razor I had dug out of the trash; the nicks and the cuts and the dried, crusty blood. Her fingers grazing over all those prickly patches I couldn't quite reach. The two of us talking about boys and tampons and growth spurts and braces, all those tumultuous things that present themselves during the fragile years—years so fragile they were always in danger of shattering completely if not for that one friend who helped you hold it all together.

How many times had we come home from school with our uniforms on, shirts untucked and bras flung off, retreating into her bedroom to talk about our problems, each one seemingly larger than the last? Every conversation tying us tighter until, at last, we were two threads knotted into one: indivisible, inseparable. Eternally intertwined.

I grab the picture from the mantel now and hold it in my hands. I know I can't keep Eliza from them forever. I know I'll have to explain it all eventually: her, us. What happened back then and how I came to be here, alone. Levi Butler and why his appearance next door was enough to make me break down completely, buckling like rotten lumber beneath the overwhelming weight of him. A stilt house just waiting to collapse. The truth is, Levi was the very first splinter between us. Like salt-stained wood, it started small: a hairline fracture, skinny as a paper cut, but still, I could feel it. Even then, I could feel it. Beneath that dock, I had been hiding—but Eliza, she had been watching. Watching Levi, her lips dipped beneath the water and a dark curiosity washing over her like an ominous cloud blotting out the light. I watched her while she watched him and somehow, I knew that splinter would just continue to grow, expanding slowly from a crack to a crevice to something else entirely.

I knew it was only a matter of time until he would split us apart: forcefully, violently. I just didn't know how violent it would be.

"Margot," Lucy says, and I pull my gaze upward at the three of them sitting frog-legged on my bed. They're looking at me so strangely and that's when I register the wetness on my cheeks, two twin tears that have managed to snake their way down my face.

I lift my hand and wipe them away, smiling weakly.

"You can tell us," she continues, Sloane and Nicole on either side of her, nodding like bobbleheads. "We're your friends."

CHAPTER 13

AFTER

"It's gonna work."

I look up from my bed, Lucy's phone still clutched in my hand. Sloane is in the doorway; behind her, Nicole hovers, like neither of them quite want to come in.

"Margot," she prods when I don't answer. *"It's gonna work."*

I sigh, letting the phone fall asleep and sliding it back in my bedside table before gesturing for them both to come closer. They push the door all the way open, scampering across the floor in their bare feet, and I fling the covers back, inviting them in.

"They won't find her," she adds, scooting in beside me. "It's Lucy."

"I know," I say, knowing Sloane is right. Lucy, who is known to take off on her own without warning. Whose only predictability is being impossible to predict. Lucy, whose own mother is still blissfully unaware that she's even gone. I wonder if she's even thought about her recently, Lucy's mom—if there's been some kind of primal tickle in the back of her subconscious, alerting her that something is wrong—or if this kind of sustained silence is so normal for them that maternal instinct has long since left.

I wonder if she even cares.

If I was the one to disappear, my parents would already have "MISSING" posters stapled to every light pole across the state. I know I complain about them, I know they have flaws, but I can't deny that they are the ideal family for a missing girl. They have money and resources and endless time; the kinds of faces that would look nice at a press conference, their televised grief still achingly attractive. There would be manned tip lines and a million-dollar reward set up within the first twenty-four hours.

Probably a hashtag, already trending.

I can't help but remember now how we all sat here together, in these very same spots, on that very first day: Lucy, Sloane, Nicole, and me, squeezed together on this tiny little twin. Maybe it was the cheap beer still sitting stale in my stomach or the knowledge that Levi Butler was just next door or the fact that Lucy had been looking at me, blue eyes wide and attention rapt, in a way I had never seen her look at anyone before—but whatever the reason, something changed in that moment.

My guard dropped and I started talking. I started telling them everything.

"You're getting scared," Sloane says now, her hand on my leg. "You shouldn't be. This was her idea to begin with."

"I know," I say again.

"She's the one who got us into this."

"I know."

"The Butlers are filing a lawsuit against Kappa Nu," Nicole adds. "Wrongful death."

I nod, my eyes drilling into my bedspread. I had heard that, too, the breaking news alert chirping across my phone. Even though Levi's death was initially deemed an accident, it happened at a fraternity function. Alcohol was involved . . . a lot of it. None of us were of age, yet all of us had been wasted, guzzling cheap booze before passing out around a giant open flame as the temperature plummeted around us, frozen fingers and plumes of breath visible in the night. He had marks and bruises on his skin, possible evidence of being hazed. His blood alcohol content was three times the legal limit.

It's a miracle, his parents would argue, that there weren't more fatalities.

I can see the impending articles now; all the blame being pointed at Rutledge and Greek life and the way we students were able to run wild, drinking ourselves into a stupor with barely any oversight. Surely, it would go national: endless headshots of Levi flashing across the television, poised and professional and not at all the party animal I had always known him to be. He would be painted an athlete, a scholar, despite the fact that he ran track for one year in high school before dropping out, his smoking habit decimating his lungs. Despite the fact that he was a solid C student who was probably only admitted because his dad was a donor. Nevertheless. The entire country would still mourn his promise, his potential, all of it washed away with the water of an outgoing tide. Kappa Nu would be seen as a mere casualty; an innocent bystander caught in the cross fire.

But were they innocent? Were they, really?

I can't bring myself to feel bad about the consequences that have already come for the rest of the brothers: the suspensions and the fines. The collective black spots that will follow them around campus, the rest of their lives, forever marring them as the reason one of their own had died. Because they brought this upon themselves, too, the way they looked at us like part of their property.

The way they treated us like things they owned; mere decorations that came with the house itself.

The way they used us, dangled us like carrots. Hung us up like a neon sign flashing in the night: GIRLS, GIRLS, GIRLS.

They deserve it all.

"Yeah," I say, nodding, remembering. The brightness of the stars that night and the way they shone like diamonds in the sky. The totality of the darkness around us, a deep, dank, velvety black. The way Levi stood up and immediately stumbled, pitching forward in his bare feet before lurching off into the distance.

The way Lucy had stood up, too, glancing in my direction before following him into the cattails, quick and quiet. Disappearing into the night.

"Yeah," I repeat, my confidence growing. "It's gonna work."

CHAPTER 14

BEFORE

"Levi Butler was my best friend's next-door neighbor," I say at last, picking at a loose cuticle until it bleeds. The three of them are sitting beside me, chins in their hands. "And he's the reason she's dead."

The bluntness of the statement catches me by surprise, the way it spewed out of my mouth like a sneeze. Powerful and without permission. I look up at them, registering their shocked expressions. Their bunched-up foreheads and wide, white eyes.

"Like, he *killed* her?" Nicole asks.

I open my mouth, then immediately close it, the answer too difficult to form into words.

"It's complicated," I say at last. "It was ruled an accident, officially, but there was more to it than that."

"What happened?" she asks, and eventually, I sigh, my body back in that lukewarm water. The tangle of seaweed caught in my toes and the flitter of minnows grazing my thigh. Later that night, during dinner, Eliza's parents told us that the Butlers were from somewhere in state. That their son, Levi, was a year younger than us and rightfully bitter at having been yanked out of high school the summer going into his junior year.

"He doesn't know anyone in the Outer Banks," Eliza's mom had said, stabbing at a chunk of salmon with her fork. I still remember the sound of the metal scraping against the inside of her teeth, harsh and grating, spraying goose bumps across my arms. "So you girls be nice."

"Why did they move?" I had asked, my sun-stung eyes darting in the direction of the Butlers' house. Even though there were two thick walls and a full yard between us, I could still feel him there, as if he were sitting at that very table, nestled between Eliza and me. Already cutting me out.

"Said they needed a lifestyle change." Mr. Jefferson shrugged. "Didn't elaborate more than that."

Eliza was unusually distant that night, lost somewhere deep in the fissures of her own wild mind. I watched as she sat there quietly, gnawing on a fingernail as Mr. Jefferson stood up and cleared the plates before lowering the needle down on an old record player; grabbing Mrs. Jefferson's hand and swinging her around the kitchen the way he always did after dinner. I remember closing my eyes, listening to the music leaking out through their wide-open windows; the acoustics and laughter drifting across the water like some kind of birdsong that felt exotic and rare.

I remember thinking she'd get over it, that it was just another one of her brooding moods, but in the weeks that followed, it only got worse.

"What happened," I echo back, Nicole's question haunting me like a whisper in the night. I can't even count the number of times I listened to those words tumbling out of the mouths of my parents that summer as they watched the news in the dark, shaking their heads and a film of tears sitting stagnant in their eyes. How many times I imagined the Jeffersons screaming them into the phone, at each other. Overheard my curious classmates as they tried to pry information out of anyone they could find. Running on repeat in my mind like a broken record, night after night, as I tried to understand it, come to terms with it all—and not just the singular moment, the accident itself, but everything that came before it.

"I don't really know what happened," I say at last. "That's the hardest part."

The three of them shift on my bed, uncomfortable, perhaps knowing on some subconscious level not to interrupt.

"I think she was just curious at first," I say, remembering how I would catch her eyes skipping over to the house next door: to Levi, sweaty and shirtless, pushing around a manual lawn mower or doing push-ups on the patio while we sunned ourselves out back. She seemed only vaguely interested in the beginning, a window-shopper's curious detachment. Strolling around the backyard the way she always did in nothing but her bathing suit, eyes on her phone as she walked the dock like a runway, pretending he didn't exist. And he kept his distance, mostly. Sneaking the occasional glance when he thought we weren't looking. Eliza sneaking it back. But then she caved after those first few weeks and searched for him on Instagram, scrolling through an endless array of Levis before throwing her phone onto her bed in defeat. His anonymity just made him more interesting to her, her mind filling in the blanks with details that were far more exciting than what likely existed. It didn't help that we went to an all-girls school, either. That we spent every day of our lives enveloped in a heavy cloud of body mist and estrogen, dreaming about boys instead of seeing what they were actually like in real life.

If our parents sent us there with the intention of keeping us focused, of *eliminating the distraction,* it had the opposite effect.

Instead, we were clueless and curious, a lethal combination, drawn to their bright colors like moths to a flame.

"She was always trying to branch out, meet new people," I continue. "Then all of a sudden, this new guy shows up from somewhere different and starts taking an interest."

"So, they dated," Sloane says, and I shake my head.

"It was never serious."

I look at Lucy and register the indifference in her expression; while Sloane and Nicole are totally rapt, shaken at the idea of a murderer next door, Lucy is looking at me in an almost clinical sense, cold and detached. Like she doesn't quite believe what I'm saying. Like she's trying to form a hypothesis of her own.

"The thing you need to understand about Eliza is that everyone loved her," I say at last, looking down at the picture again. "But just because you loved her, it didn't mean she loved you back."

"What was so *lovable* about her?" Lucy asks. I can't help but startle at the way she says it, venom dripping, almost like she's jealous.

"Everything," I say, and that's the truth. Despite our differences, our occasional spats, I wouldn't have changed a thing about her. "She was kind and funny and fearless . . . almost to a fault, you know? Nobody was a stranger."

Lucy simply nods and I realize, despite how alike they sometimes seem, the two of them probably wouldn't be friends. There would be too much envy between them, too much competition. That's the whole reason girls like them choose friends like us: too-nice Nicole and studious Sloane and malleable Margot.

The kind of friends who are more than happy to take the back seat. The kind of friends who won't get in the way.

"So, was he obsessed with her or something?" Nicole asks, scooting forward, fully absorbed like she's soaking in a movie and not my real life, some slow-motion car chase seconds before the crash. "Like an 'If I can't have her, nobody can' type of thing?"

I nod, remembering. It had started small between them: a mutual fascination, an innocent crush. A bud of a thing still curled up and cautious, but slowly, inevitably, it began to bloom. By the middle of that summer, I would come over and catch the two of them talking on the dock, one of Levi's cigarettes dangling between her fingers. Eliza never used to smoke during the day like that, only at the occasional party when she was too drunk, but with Levi, her bad habits became more abundant. They mutated and metastasized; took on a life of their own. So I would approach them gently, respectfully, sitting cross-legged next to Eliza and trying to keep my distance, smiling weakly as their conversation hushed into a smothered silence—but at the same time, my very presence signaling that I wasn't the intruder in that situation.

I wasn't the outsider. *He* was.

Because that was the thing with Eliza, the thing Levi never realized: she was like that with everyone. She was just passing the time with him, a shiny new plaything to keep her occupied during those long, lazy days of summer. She liked the feeling of his eyes on her skin; the thought of him just next door, lying in bed, his mind on her. She was just starting to realize the power her own body could have on other people, just learning how to wield it like a weapon: moving her legs and chewing her lip and twirling her hair. A single batted eye bringing a boy to his knees.

"A couple months before she died, she told me she felt like she was being watched," I say at last.

I'll never forget it when she finally told me. We were halfway into our senior year and whatever this thing was between them had stretched on from the summer and into the school year, a curling tentacle holding her tight. I thought it would naturally fizzle out once classes started up again, but the distance only seemed to make it stronger. Nobody else looked at her the way he did. At school, she went back to being just another carbon copy of everybody else—long hair, starched skirt, knee socks, and scuffed-up clogs that made us all sweaty and shapeless—but back home with Levi, prancing around in her tank tops and short shorts, she was different, special. Perfect.

I remember studying on her bed that night, stomachs flopped down on the mattress and Eliza's long legs scissoring in the air. We were still in our uniforms, shirts untucked and skirts riding high, and she kept glancing over her shoulder, toward the window, tucking her hair behind her ear like she was playing some kind of role in a movie. Like she knew she was on display.

"What are you doing?" I asked at last, tired of acting too stupid to notice. "Why are you being so weird?"

She just smiled at me, condescendingly coy, like I was on the outside of some inside joke.

"Is someone out there?" I asked, twisting around so I could look, too. I realized then how exposed we were: the brightness of her bedroom juxtaposed with the darkness outside; how the two of us, framed by the window, would be perfectly visible to someone outside, yet they would be perfectly invisible to us.

"I think he watches me," she said at last, her chin tucked into her chest and her voice an inch above a whisper. "I think he's out there right now."

"*What?*" I gasped, standing up quickly. I started to walk over to the window but before I could reach it and peer outside, she grabbed my arm and yanked me back down.

"Don't *look*," she hissed. "Are you crazy?"

"Are *you?* Eliza, that's so creepy. Do you not see how that's creepy?"

"It's not creepy," she said. "It's cute."

"I'm sorry, but what exactly about being stalked is cute?"

"Don't be so dramatic," she said, rolling her eyes. Shifting her weight from one arm to the other, letting the neck of her button-up yawn open wide.

"What is with you lately?" I asked her then, not bothering to hide the disdain in my voice. The judgment, the scorn, the frustration that I had been keeping bottled up at that point for far too long. "Why are you being like this?"

"Like what?" she asked.

"Like *this*," I said, throwing my arms up, gesturing to it all. "He's just a boy, Eliza. Since when do you change yourself like this for a boy?"

"I'm not changing myself—" she started, but I interrupted her before she could finish.

"Yes, you are. You've been different. Distant."

"You wouldn't understand," she muttered, and I let out a scoff. "Try me."

She looked up at me then, front teeth digging into her lower lip. I raised my eyebrows, egging her on, and watched as her eyes darted back to the window.

"There's nothing wrong with letting him look."

I stared at her then, disbelief washing over me, the thin line between danger and desire evaporating completely and melding the two together into something else entirely. It was so classically Eliza: driving without a seat belt, diving into the marsh when the tide was too low. Sometimes I thought she genuinely enjoyed the prospect of getting hurt, the threat of impending danger dangling over her heightening the sensation of being alive.

"Pretty soon he's gonna want to do more than just look," I said at last, my arms crossed tight. "What are you going to do then?"

Eliza just shrugged, ignoring me, lifting her pen to her lips and chewing on the cap in the same mindless way she used to saunter down the dock, adjusting the triangle of her bikini top before flipping onto her stomach and untying the straps. She was doing it on purpose, I realized, all of it cunning and calculated and entirely for him: cracking the window but never opening it completely. Flashing a glimpse of her bare back before clicking out the light and closing the curtains, letting him wonder what was happening in the dark.

I shot another look out the window, squinting my eyes against the inky beyond, and in that moment, I swear I could see him: a silhouette in the distance, standing on the dock.

The outline of Levi watching us both.

CHAPTER 15

I wake up to the sound of rolling thunder, a shuddering through the house I feel deep in my bones.

We're three weeks into summer and the noise reminds me of that very first day, the bloated clouds encroaching on campus turning the sky a marbled gray. The way I had glanced out the window as the four of us sat on my bed, the spray of rain suddenly fogging up the glass. I remember thinking Levi had summoned it, somehow, his presence alone turning a perfect morning into something dreary and dark—but the truth, I knew, is that summer storms are normal around here, those reliable rumbles showing up as soon as the sun peaks in the sky. Those flashes of lightning; the torrential rain.

Quick, violent things that disrupt everything before disappearing again once they've found their release.

We ended up skipping the party at Kappa Nu, opting instead for a girls' night in. And I was grateful for it, relishing the opportunity to both avoid Levi and settle into my strange new life. Nicole and Sloane latched on to my stories about him immediately, swigging straight from a bottle of bourbon they brought into my bedroom when I described the way we once found a cigarette butt smoldering in the grass outside Eliza's window, proof of him moving even closer in the night.

"What a perv," Sloane said, her hand wringing the bottleneck, mindlessly twisting. I watched as Nicole shivered, long fingers pulling my duvet tight around her shoulders. I didn't tell them about how Eliza had picked it up, though; that curl of a smile as she rolled it slow between her fingers. The way she lifted it higher until her lips grazed the spot where his had been. I didn't want them to blame her, somehow, but I also couldn't help but feel a little thrill about the way we had all started to settle in so seamlessly together—though the irony wasn't lost on me. The fact that Levi Butler was the thing bonding us all together when he was also the one who tore Eliza and me apart.

"Yeah, just stay away from him," I said, turning toward Lucy next. I expected to find her nodding along, eyebrows bunched in the same cloak of concern, but she seemed more fascinated than frightened, drawn to the danger just like Eliza.

The more I talked, the more I watched, the more I realized how alike they really are.

It was the little things, at first. Things that made me do a double take every time Lucy walked into a room, my mind believing, for a single second, that it was Eliza instead. It doesn't matter that they look so drastically different: Lucy is dark, dangerous, a blur of black curls and bronzed skin compared to Eliza's fair hair and freckles. Lucy has blue eyes, Eliza had green, but beneath the surface, they're so much the same: the way Lucy walks with an acute awareness, swaying the important parts of her in a way that causes heads to turn, throats to clear. The decibel of her voice, loud enough to command attention before dipping into something more intimate in the moments that matter. Making you feel like the only one in the room. But then those things got even sharper, clearer, and I couldn't tell if they were really there or if I was just imagining them, overlaying Lucy over Eliza like a sheet of tracing paper, my subconscious trying to copy her completely. Every last curve. The little tics that no one else seemed to notice: Lucy tugging twice on a hunk of hair before pushing it behind her ear. Rolling the diamonds of her necklace between her fingers when she was deep in thought or gnawing on a pencil, dreamy and deliberate, leaving little bite marks behind in the wood.

I roll over in the dark now and grab my phone, limbs slippery and duvet damp. The last few weeks have stretched by without incident since that confrontation at Kappa Nu, Levi going back to the Outer Banks and leaving me in a strange state of quiet unease: I'm happy he's gone, but at the same time, I know he'll be back. I try to tell myself that maybe he'll change his mind, go to another school or at least pledge another house. I tell myself that I can handle it, that this time will be different.

I tell myself, but I never believe it.

I tap my phone now and watch as it glows in the dark, eyes squinting as I search for the date. I'm hoping to find it flipped over to tomorrow. Hoping to learn that I've slept straight through it, spent the worst hours of my life entirely unconscious. Hoping to feel the relief of a new day flood into my chest, release the unrelenting pressure from my lungs—but of course, it's still today. Eliza's death day.

One year since the night it happened. A full rotation since she's been gone.

They don't know when she died, exactly, though the coroner estimated it was sometime just before midnight, about two hours from now. I roll back over, eyes trained on the ceiling, a single bead of sweat snaking down my spine and the gentle sound of rain on the window numbing me into oblivion. The storm gave me a plausible excuse to stay in bed—to refuse to turn on the lights, peel myself from the covers—though everyone seems to instinctively understand what today is, why I've locked myself in here without explanation. I've heard the muffled sound of footsteps as the others approached from down the hall and stopped in front of my door. I've felt them hovering, waiting, before giving up and leaving again. I've ignored their gentle knocks, their throat clearings, allowing myself this single day to slip back into the person I was last year. This cracked-open shell of a thing I never wanted them to see. If I were a stronger person, I would have gone home for this. I would have spent the day with the Jeffersons, cozy in their living room as we swapped stories about her, laughing and crying and licking our wounds. I would have visited my parents, maybe even the spot where it happened, laying flowers on the ground in memory of her.

Instead, all I can do is lie here, counting the hours until it's over. Until today turns into tomorrow and I can finally breathe.

I hear another rumble, but this time, it's not coming from the sky. It's coming from my stomach, gaping and hollow beneath the covers, and I remember with a sense of curious detachment that I haven't eaten all day. I sit up and attempt to turn on the light, only when I twist the switch nothing happens, so I fling the covers from my legs before walking across my room and stepping into the hallway, following the familiar hum of voices upstairs.

"There she is," Lucy says when I step into Sloane's bedroom. The three of them are sitting on the floor in the dark surrounded by candles, Lucy flicking a lighter so close it looks like the flame is coming straight out of her fingers. "I was about to do a wellness check. Make sure you were still breathing."

"Sorry," I say, wincing a bit at her choice of words, though she doesn't seem to notice. I walk over to join them, eyeing a skillet on the floor before glancing up. There's a steady drip of rainwater erupting from a damp spot in the ceiling, each drop landing on the cast iron with a rhythmic *plink*. "Is the power out?"

"Has been all day," Sloane says, a sheen of sweat across her upper lip.

"Next door, too?" I ask, sitting down, wondering why they aren't over there. They're always over there, all four of us are, especially on gloomy days like today.

"No, but Nicole and Trevor are fighting."

"When are they not fighting?" Lucy adds, and I can see Nicole's jaw clench in the dark.

"I told you you could go without me," she cuts in, but Sloane just leans over and nudges her shoulder, smiling, before turning back toward me.

"We didn't want to go anywhere without you," she says. "Are you hungry?"

"Starving," I say, a little bubble of warmth blooming in my chest.

"We could go to Penny Lanes," Lucy suggests, her eyes still trained on the flame.

I had learned about Lucy's job earlier in the summer and something about it caught me off guard. Admittedly, Nicole and I don't have to work. Our parents provide our rent and tuition, and while Sloane spends most afternoons doing admin for the registrar, Lucy devotes four nights a week to a hybrid bar and bowling alley downtown. It seemed so strange the first time she told me; I couldn't picture her gliding around in retro roller skates with plastic cups of beer balanced on a tray, her skin slick with French fry grease as she cleaned up other people's messes. Sneaking into the walk-in freezer, maybe, dragging her finger around the rim of a Jell-O shot before popping it into her mouth. From the outside, it always looked like the world was just given to Lucy—like she was owed it all for simply existing—so the mere suggestion that she had to actually work for something like everybody else was a contradiction so jarring it left me unmoored.

"It's ten o'clock on a Sunday," I say at last, looking around for confirmation before remembering all the clocks have stopped. Nobody answers, the room silent other than another crack of lightning followed by a low, slow rumble. "Isn't it closed?"

Sloane smirks and I watch as the three of them exchange glances, something unsaid traveling between them, before Lucy leans over and purses her lips, a stream of breath extinguishing the last of the light between us.

CHAPTER 16

We sprint the four blocks to Penny Lanes, our feet damp and dirty by the time our sandals slap against the puddles in the parking lot. It's only drizzling now, but my skin is still clammy beneath my raincoat, my hair wiry from moisture. The outside air musky and vegetal, smelling of wet grass and churned-up dirt, and I inhale it slowly, a welcome change from the stuffiness of my bedroom.

We approach the building and I start to walk toward the front door, but instead, Lucy grabs my hand and leads us into an alleyway and I watch as she hoists herself on top of a dumpster, shoes squeaking against the wet metal.

"What are you doing?" I ask, although it's obvious from the second I see the window just above, too tiny to fit most adult bodies but perfectly adequate for someone as small as her.

"Getting inside," she says, so matter-of-fact, standing on her toes as she pushes it open. I watch as she pulls herself over the ledge and slithers into the building on her stomach, disappearing in the dark like a burrowing snake.

"They don't lock that?" I ask, addressing no one in particular, my neck swiveling as I check our surroundings.

"They do," Sloane says, turning to look at me, eyes wide and blank. The insinuation is clear, what she's saying. They lock it, but Lucy unlocks it.

Sloane and Nicole lead me back around to the front and we wait for what feels like an unusually long time, though I don't want to keep asking questions, appearing concerned when nobody else seems to be. Finally, I hear the sound of the door unlocking and watch as Lucy pushes it open from the inside, lifting her arms above her head like a magician reappearing after her final trick.

"How often do you do this?" I ask as I step inside, simultaneously anxious and impressed. I watch as she flips on the lights, bracing myself for an alarm to blare.

"Special occasions," she says, walking past me before squeezing my arm.

Everyone disperses slowly and I watch as they fall into what feels like a familiar rhythm: Sloane walks over to an old jukebox in the corner, sliding in her spare change and flipping through song selections before music starts to trickle out of the speakers above. Nicole plops down on one of the leather benches, bright red and ripping at the seams, while I take in the gumball machines and other dispensers pushed up against the wall, the kind that trade quarters for cheap jewelry trapped inside plastic capsules. There are racks of multicolored shoes stiff from foot sweat and sanitizer; arcade machines and basketball hoops and long wooden lanes leading to pins arranged in perfect arrows.

"Relax," Lucy says, a grin in her voice. I whip around to find her behind the bar, various bottles plucked from their homes and lined up in front of her. "The security sucks in this place. Trust me, I've seen it."

I watch as she pours a clear liquor into four plastic cups, top-ping them off with soda from the gun before scooping them all up in her hands. She walks over to me then, arms extended so I can take the one closest to me, and my mind flashes back to Hines in this moment. To how she took charge in the common room and everyone else simply slid into place behind her, grabbing those bottles from the floor and pressing them to our lips.

How she had walked into my room without warning, trailed her fingers along all my things. Flashed me this exact same smile until I found my head nodding, my lips agreeing, seemingly all on their own.

"I guess this makes it official," Lucy says, raising her cup. Sloane and Nicole are suddenly here now, too, sidling up beside us before grabbing their drinks and forming a circle. "You're one of us now."

I smile, clinking my drink before taking a sip, and in this moment, despite the warmth blooming in my chest, I can't help but wonder again why she chose me. Why *I'm* the one Lucy is pulling into her circle like this, why I deserve to be brought into her space. I've been her roommate for three weeks now, and still, I haven't seen any glimmer into her thought process, any indication of why. I've been waiting patiently for it to arrive, some *aha* moment that explains it all away, but so far, it hasn't. Nothing has. I haven't brought it up again since that day in the dorm, either, the moment I had looked at her and asked: *"Why me?"*

The indifference in her eyes, the bored curiosity, when she responded with a flat: *"Why not?"*

Now, for the very first time, I wonder if it really is that simple. If she really chose me because, well, why not? Here are three girls who lucked into a four-bedroom house too perfect to turn down. They had a spare room, nobody to fill it, and a lonely girl down the hall who seemed desperate enough to say yes. Maybe Lucy saw me on the lawn that day, staring in their direction with a longing in my eyes, and simply saw an opportunity, an answer to a problem.

Decided to do what she always does: take what she wanted and never look back.

The next four hours go by in a fluorescent haze: guzzling sweet margaritas and Amaretto sours so fast they make my throat feel wrecked and raw. Lucy coming up behind me with a refill every time my cup goes dry. Dancing to the music from the jukebox and devouring ice cream from the freezer; sliding down those long, slick lanes like some scene out of *Risky Business* and using the pins as microphones, screaming out every word. At some point, we collapse into a pile on the floor, limbs sweaty and tangled and warm to the touch, the ceiling spinning slowly above us.

Sloane checking her phone, muttering *"Shit, we gotta go,"* before pulling me up and into the night.

I vaguely remember Lucy putting back the liquor, flipping out the lights. The three of us leaving through the front door and waiting in the alley for her to shimmy back out the window, listening to her laugh as she landed hard on the dumpster. The four of us stumbling home with our arms threaded together like a daisy chain, wild and delicate, Lucy's words pulsing through my mind like a meditation, a prayer.

"You're one of us now."

It isn't until I wake up the next morning when I realize what happened, how the moment of Eliza's passing came and went and I didn't even feel it. How I had lost myself in Lucy completely, her attention the remedy I needed to make the pain go away. Instead, when the clock clicked to midnight and just kept going, time marching mercilessly on without her, I wasn't suffocating the way I had expected to be, thinking about Eliza lying flat on the ground, her final breath ejected out of her with too much force.

Instead, I had been dancing, singing, wholly lost in the moment.

I had slept soundly for the first time in a year.

CHAPTER 17

I glance up at my door, a prickling on my neck alerting me to the presence of Lucy. She does this sometimes: appears without warning. Watches from the hallway all silent and still, waiting for me to notice.

"Hey," I say, looking back down at my feet. I'm sitting on the floor of my bedroom, legs arched, painting my toenails a neon blue.

"Where is everyone?" she asks.

"I think they're next door."

It's the last week of summer, somehow, and we've been drinking it up madly, wildly, like roots in dry soil. Going out every night and sleeping until noon; sweating out our hangovers before starting the process all over again. We've passed the days at the beach, mostly, the four of us piling into Lucy's old Mazda in the mornings; windows perpetually down, a warm breeze tangling our hair because her air conditioner is always broken. It's a short drive to the coast—thirty minutes, tops; twenty when you're speeding—and we've spent the empty hours burning patterns into our backs, eating watermelon bloated with vodka. Taking cold showers, napping in our towels, then going over to Kappa Nu in the evenings to smoke a bowl and play some beer pong, our cheeks and eyes poppy red.

The truth is, I've absorbed more in these three months than I did my entire freshman year: how to shotgun a beer and roll a joint and blow perfectly circular smoke rings by arcing my tongue in just the right way. I'm still a little quiet around the boys, sometimes on edge, but Lucy has been opening me up slowly like a finicky houseplant still learning to be loved. She's been hatching me out of my shell—gently, gradually—but in a way I know would have made Eliza proud . . . and I've been starting to understand why Eliza wanted this, too, the thrill of it unlike anything I've ever experienced. It wasn't the parties or the games or the drinks she craved, I know that now, but the little things that appear in the moments in between: the way it feels to have someone recognize your face, know your name. Call you over to the other side of the room like they genuinely want you there. It's the roar of laughter when a joke lands just right or the feeling of someone's eyes on your skin that makes you feel so achingly alive.

Finally, I'm starting to get it—I'm starting to get *her*—and every single night, I collect those moments like I collect everything. Sentimental souvenirs I can't stand to toss away.

"I have to work tonight," Lucy says, leaning against the mantel. I look up again and notice she's wearing her regular uniform: short shorts and crew socks and a red T-shirt with a bowling ball in the center, the logo for Penny Lanes emblazoned across the front. "You want to get the girls and come by after close?"

I smile, nod, eager to soak up these final few days together. I don't know how things will change once everyone else comes back to campus but somehow, already, I know that they will. I can feel it, the shift in the air. The buzzing energy of other bodies nearby.

I've noticed the moving trucks appearing around town, the first trickle of freshmen scoping out the dorms, and it's strange, seeing them here. The presence of other people ripping me out of this reverie we've created like a stranger showing up unannounced in a dream—because that's what these last three months have felt like. A dream, an alternate reality. The funhouse-mirror version of regular life. A college town in summer isn't actually a college town at all and our little pocket of it has felt like a ghost town to us, a bunch of bored girls roaming around with nothing to do and all the time to do it.

Deserted and dangerous and ours for the taking.

We arrive at Penny Lanes an hour after closing, leaving Lucy enough time to clean up, close down, and ensure that everyone is gone. Sloane knocks three times on the front door as we wait, the summer air like a steam room, our skin like an oil slick. Another hot, humid night that siphons the energy out of us the second we step outside.

"I hope they have tater tots," Nicole says, her left leg bouncing. "They're so good here."

Sloane looks at her, eyebrow cocked. "You know they just buy all their shit from Costco, right? It's all frozen."

Nicole shrugs. "Everything tastes better when it's free."

"It's not free." Sloane laughs. "We're stealing it."

"Still free to me."

The door pushes open with a cool gush of air and I immediately know that something is different. Lucy is smiling at us from the other side of the building, beckoning us in, but the last time we showed up here, the inside of the alley was stone-cold and quiet, almost as if it was waiting for us to breathe it back to life.

This time, though, there are other people inside. Familiar voices. Boys.

"What's all this?" I ask, stepping through the door. "Did we come too early?"

"Nope," she says. "Just in time."

I look around, recognizing Trevor and Lucas and a couple other brothers from next door. I've gotten to know them all intimately this summer, the small pocket of them who stayed behind, too. Trevor is boorish and loud—the polar opposite of Nicole, who's always too nice to set him straight. It's hard to know what they see in each other, to be honest, besides their uncannily good looks: poreless skin, milk-white teeth, both of them almost too perfect to be real. I have a feeling there's something between Sloane and Lucas, too—something she doesn't want to admit—and they're an odd match themselves, but one that makes sense when I catch little glimpses when they think nobody is looking. Sloane is always so serious, so stoically bored, and Lucas makes her laugh in a way no one can.

I glance at the two of them now, Sloane and Nicole, though they don't look as surprised as I feel.

"I didn't realize they came here, too," I mutter, staring at the boys, my cheeks burning hot the second I say it. I don't want to admit it, the attachment I've grown in such a short amount of time—and not just to the roommates, the girls, but to this place, too. Ever since my first night here, I've come to think of Penny Lanes as something sacred, the four of us swinging in circles, holding each other's sweaty hands. A secret spot, like that pocket of air beneath the dock, where we can go to hide, to get away.

A thing we share and keep from everyone else.

Lucy turns to look at me, a flash of what feels like pity appearing across her face. Then she grabs my hand and gives it a quick squeeze before walking over to a group of them and leaving me alone.

I decide to walk over to the bar and mix myself a drink before turning around and surveying the room. It's giant, square, and completely windowless, the way bowling alleys usually are. The cavernous atmosphere makes it the ideal place to do something like this—nobody on the outside could possibly know that there are people on the inside—and as a result, it's easy to feel a little punch-drunk in here. The concrete walls make everything feel impersonal, teetering on clinical, time stretching on the same way it did when my dad let me tag along to the casino once: with no natural light to indicate the passage of time, your mind feels perpetually suspended, like you're reliving the same scene over and over again.

I look to my left and see a couple guys flinging themselves down the lanes, laughing hysterically as they slam into the bumpers. Nicole is sitting on Trevor's lap on top of the ball return and Sloane has wandered over to the jukebox again, flipping through various options before deciding on Fleetwood Mac.

"Hey, Margot."

I twist around, my eyes bulging at the sight of him. Levi is here, self-consciously gripping a plastic cup so hard it's beginning to bend beneath the pressure. I've been bracing myself for his return, of course, my eyes continually darting over to the Kappa Nu parking lot, scanning the cars for his rusted white Jeep with the Outer Banks bumper sticker peeling at the edges. I've been on high alert every time we venture next door, ears tingling with the emergence of every new voice. Chest squeezing with each peripheral glance I got of a tall, tan boy with tousled brown hair . . . but I hadn't been expecting him *here*, of all places.

I look around again, my gaze darting madly around the room,

trying to understand what he's doing. Why he's hanging out with Trevor and Lucas and all the guys a grade above him instead of people his own age, when I remember what Trevor had said that very first night.

"He's a legacy, so, you know. Special treatment and all that."

"Hey," I respond, trying to somehow swallow my heartbeat. I can feel it rising, slowly making its way up my throat. Levi's father was in the fraternity, which means he's always going to get the invite to these things, at least in the early days when they're still trying to schmooze him. Still trying to convince him that he's different, special. Somehow immune to the hazing that's inevitably headed his way.

"Look, let's just get this out of the way, okay? I know you don't want me here," he says, almost urgently, like he had been bracing himself all summer to say it. "You made that clear from the beginning. The very beginning."

I bite my lip, remembering that first day under the dock. The way Eliza and I had watched him walk toward us before we dipped beneath the water, reemerging in that secret space. How interesting: that female instinct to duck, to hide, like prey catching sight of glowing eyes in the night. Something inherent in our very genes, our very DNA. I wonder now if he knew we were down there all along, planting his feet and refusing to move.

If he liked the feeling of being on top of us, smothering us. If it made him feel big.

"But I'm here," he continues. "And I'm not going anywhere, so you're going to have to get used to it."

I remember the way I used to walk up to them, after, once they became friends. Smiling politely as I plopped down, too. The way an awkward hush would settle over the three of us, whatever they were saying before screeching to a halt.

"We don't have to be enemies," he continues, and I think about the way he would smile back, biting his cheek, hating me for existing. For being there, too. "We both loved her—"

"Stop," I say, holding out my hand. Remembering his silhouette in the yard, watching her in the dark. I can't listen to him say that word. "Just stop talking."

"I swear I didn't mean—"

"*Stop,*" I repeat.

A sharp whistle erupts from behind us and I spin around, grateful for the interruption, my eyes landing on Lucy. She's making her way down one of the lanes like a model on a catwalk, a single pin in one hand slapping against the opposite palm. Her legs are long and lean in those little short shorts, crisscrossing each other in flashy finesse, and I think of Eliza again, sauntering her way down the dock.

They are so similar, those two, reveling in the watching. The wanting. The risk.

"Everyone, gather round!" Lucy yells. "It's game time!"

I watch as she makes her way to the front of the lane and plops down at the base of it, pretzeling her legs on the floor. Then she places the pin in front of her and flicks it, sending it spinning in a circle.

I look back at Levi, registering the way his eyes swell at the sight of her. Then he cocks his head, intrigued, before turning back toward me.

"Do you know her?" he asks at last, a curiosity in his voice he can't contain.

"That's Lucy," I respond. "She's my roommate."

He opens his mouth, then closes it again, apparently deciding against whatever he was about to say, and I wonder if he sees it, too. The similarities between them. The magnetism of Lucy and the way she pulls people in against their own will. The power she has over everyone else, a dominant force like gravity itself.

I wonder if he feels it: that elusive aura, tugging at us both just like Eliza.

CHAPTER 18

"The game is Spin the Pin," Lucy says, satisfied with starting now that we're all in a circle. It's amazing how quickly she can command the attention of a room; the way a cleared throat or snapped finger sends us all scampering, so eager to please. "It's a mash-up between Spin the Bottle and Truth or Dare."

I feel a catch in my throat, thinking of Levi. I can't bring myself to look at him, but I know he's thinking it, too. There is no way I could kiss him. If I spin that pin and it lands on him, Eliza would be the only thing on our minds. It would feel like a gross betrayal—on both our parts—and suddenly, I'm so angry at Lucy for not thinking of that.

"Rest assured, there will be no making out," she says, as if reading my mind. "Not yet, at least. The night is young."

Lucas whistles and shoots a wink at Sloane, who rolls her eyes before taking a long sip of her drink.

"We go around the circle and spin the pin," Lucy continues, flinging it again and watching it wobble. "Once it stops, whoever it's pointing at will choose between truth or dare."

"And if we don't want to do whatever stupid thing we're dared to do?" Sloane asks, looking back at Lucas, though I have a feeling she's only asking so I don't have to.

"Then you're lame," Lucy says. "And you drink. I'll go first."

We all watch as she reaches into the center with one long arm, the bowling pin between us rocking back and forth as it twirls. I look around the circle, mentally tallying the players. There's me, of course, and Levi sitting on the other side of it, as far away as humanly possible. There's Nicole and Trevor; Sloane and Lucas. Lucy, obviously, and three other guys who I've met before but whose names, up until this point, I've never bothered to remember. Will, maybe. James sounds right. Something that starts with a G.

"Nicole!" Lucy shrieks as the pin slows to a stop. "My first victim! Truth or dare?"

Nicole groans, taking a dramatic sip of her drink.

"Truth," she says at last.

"Where's the raunchiest place you and Trevor have fucked?"

Trevor barks out a laugh while Nicole flushes red, hiding her face behind her cup. I see Sloane smirk, like she already knows the answer, while the rest of the guys take self-conscious sips, trying to hide the fact that they're already picturing it.

"Probably right there," Trevor says, laughing, pointing to the red bench behind us before Nicole can chime in. Lucas belts out an *"Oh shit!"* jaw dropped low, while Nicole's eyes bulge impossibly wide, her hand reaching out to slap her boyfriend's shoulder.

"Trevor, what the *fuck*?" she whispers, her face burning brighter. He just shrugs, smiling into his drink and looking satisfied.

The game keeps going, each of us taking our turn with the pin, and with every passing round, I can see our eyelids growing heavier, our cheeks flushing warmer. The familiar mutation from sober to buzzed to something else entirely making our skin droop like overworked clay. Someone brought a collection of bottles over to the circle so we didn't have to keep getting up to refill our drinks, and every time the pin lands on me, I hold my breath and pick dare. My legs feel tingly when I stand, that rush of cold blood as it floods back in, and so far, I've taken three shots of Rumple Minze, given James a lazy lap dance, and eaten a slice of room-temperature pizza some customer left beneath a table, a single bite mark already nibbled out of the crust.

"That's disgusting," Lucas muttered as I forced myself to chew, the coagulated cheese sticking to the roof of my mouth.

I have no idea how long we've been playing—minutes, maybe. Hours. Days. It could be light outside for all I know, but in here, underneath these fluorescent bulbs, it feels like we're in a vacuum. Like we're the only people in the world.

I vaguely register Sloane to my left, though she's more of a smudge than anything; a blur of color as she shifts her weight, flails her arms, whatever story she's telling growing more animated by the minute. Lucas is rambling on about his latest truth, turning what should have been a simple answer into something heady and profound. The more we drink, the more we talk—our inhibitions are lowered, emotions raised—and the room is spinning slightly, Stevie Nicks still seeping through the speakers around us, her raspy voice pulling me into a trance as she drones on about things lost and had.

I close my eyes, drop my head, my mind once again wandering over to Eliza. She would have fit in so perfectly here. This is all she ever wanted, really: all those nights when she had tried to pull me away from the safety of our bedrooms, begging me to get out. Meet people. *Do* something. I never wanted to go. I was perfectly content with the way things were—just the two of us, the way it had always been—and suddenly, I feel like a hypocrite for even being here. For living this life she wanted more than anything.

"Levi."

I snap my head up, his name slicing through the music and bringing me back to life. It came from Lucy, her cerulean eyes trained on him like a predator in the night. Maybe it's the disarming nature of her gaze, or the fact that my cup is alarmingly empty, or even the contrast of her voice to that of Lucas's—hers crisp and clean, compared to his disjointed rambling—but I suddenly realize I haven't seen her take a drink all night.

Her cup is right there, sitting by her side, but she's barely even touched it.

"Yeah?" Levi looks up at her, his own eyes inflamed from the fluorescent light or the alcohol or a little bit of both. He seems surprised to find her addressing him directly like this, though he's been eyeing her all night, drawn to her the way everyone is. A feral tension radiating between them that's come to feel normal for Lucy. I can tell he's been wanting to talk to her, catch her eye, and I watch as he looks back down, realizing the pin is pointed at him. "Oh." He lets out a laugh, self-consciously dragging one hand down his face. "Ah, truth, I guess."

Lucy smiles, her lips curling up into that feline grin like that was the answer she was hoping he would pick. Then she leans forward, dramatic, hands on the floor in front of her like she's about to let him in on her deepest secret.

"Levi Butler," she whispers, her body tilting closer, a seduction in her voice that makes my skin pulse. The air around us is suddenly so charged, we've practically stopped breathing. "If you knew you could get away with murder, would you do it?"

CHAPTER 19

AFTER

Sloane is right: it was Lucy's idea.

Right there, sitting in that circle, the seed was planted in all our minds. We didn't even know it was there in the beginning. It was still a hidden thing, tucked away and biding its time, though over the next few months, its roots would dig deep into our brains, settling in. Spindly little things that would grow thick and strong, tendrils curling. Suffocating us. Holding us tight.

We knew what we were doing, though. We knew the risks. We can't blame it all on Lucy, because while she was the one who started it, we were the ones who finished it.

My phone buzzes loud against my bedside table, the violent jolt of it startling me back to life, back to the present. Away from my memories of those early days, utopian and distant, and back to the stark reality of now: Levi dead, Lucy missing.

Sloane, Nicole, and me at the beating center of it all.

I glance over to my phone, finally, and roll my eyes when I see who's calling, pulling myself from my comforter and answering after the fifth ring.

"Hey, Mom," I say, wishing almost immediately that I let it go to voice mail instead.

"Margot, honey, oh my God," she says, not bothering with a *hello* herself. "Are you okay?"

"I'm fine," I say, rubbing my eyes. Lucy has been gone for a full week and none of us have been getting much sleep. It's even worse now that it's officially hit the news, the police asking for the public's help to find her.

They still have no idea where she is. They're starting to get desperate.

"Where is Lucy?"

"I don't know," I say. "She does this sometimes."

"What do you mean she *does this sometimes*?"

"She just does her own thing. It's not the first time she's gone somewhere without telling anyone. You remember Christmas."

My mom is quiet, thinking. They had met once, my mom and Lucy; a whirlwind of a week that was, other than that night at Penny Lanes, the unofficial start of all this.

"I knew I had a bad feeling about her, even then—"

"No, you didn't. You said you loved her."

"Did she have something to do with that Butler boy?" she interrupts, the real reason she's calling. "Margot, honey, this is serious."

"*No*," I say. "God, Mom, are you kidding? You're really asking me if Lucy killed someone?"

"It's just strange," she says. "Another freak accident, especially after what happened to Eliza . . ."

"This has nothing to do with Eliza," I snap. "Why are you even bringing her up?"

"Because that boy was the last person to be seen with her alive!" she practically screams into the phone. "Your best friend, Margot!

And now he's dead, and your *new* best friend is missing after being interrogated about it! It doesn't make sense!"

"You're being hysterical," I say, only because I don't want to admit she's right.

"If he hurt her, I would understand," my mother says after a heavy silence. I hear her exhale, finally, and I can so perfectly picture the way her free hand is probably worrying its way around her pearl necklace, yanking it from her skin like a too-tight turtleneck. "I would understand if she had to, you know, *protect* herself."

"It wasn't like that, Mom."

"You know as well as anyone what that boy might be capable of."

"I said it wasn't like that."

"I'm just worried about you."

"You're worried about how it looks," I correct.

"Well, yes, of course I am," she snaps. "People are going to start avoiding you like the plague if everyone you hang out with keeps winding up missing or dead."

I close my eyes, let her talk. There's no point in arguing.

"I can't believe they're letting you stay in that house after everything that's happened," she mutters, and my eyes click open again, relieved at the shift in topic.

"Actually, they're not," I say at last, leaning against my bed-frame. "They're giving us a week to move out."

"That's good," she says, her tone softening. "I never liked the idea of you living there, anyway. All those boys just next door."

"It's not as bad as it seems."

"Where are you going?" she asks.

"The college found us an apartment a few blocks away," I say, glancing around my room, trying not to think about the fact that I still need to pack. I've known this was coming for a while, but still, I've been avoiding it. We all have.

"What are they going to do with the house?" she asks, and I pinch the bridge of my nose, bottling a scream.

"I think it'll just be vacant for a while," I say. "Kappa Nu's suspended until the investigation wraps, and they own it, so we can't just live here without landlords."

"Maybe now is the time to reassess Rutledge," my mom says, a noticeable pep in her voice like the thought just occurred to her, even though I know she's been thinking it since the day we put down the deposit. "Distance yourself from all this nonsense. Plenty of students transfer after a year or two, and you do still have the grades for Duke, don't you?"

"I'm not transferring," I interrupt. "And I have to go, Mom. I'm really busy right now. Midterms start in two weeks."

"I don't know how they expect you to get through exams in the midst of all of this," she says, sighing. "It's not right. One student missing and another one dead."

"Yeah," I say, chewing over that second sentence: *One student missing and another one dead.* "Guess they just want to keep us feeling normal."

"Well, there is nothing normal about this," she says, her voice dipped into a whisper, muttering to herself like she forgot I'm even here. "Nothing normal at all."

CHAPTER 20

BEFORE

The room is silent except for the electric piano drifting around us, the floor tilting and spinning like a merry-go-round. It almost feels like we're swept up in it, unable to escape, moving around and around with the music as it mounts louder in our ears.

I think I might be sick.

"Well?" Lucy asks, and I feel myself blink. I look over at Levi, at his stunned expression, then back at Lucy. Her eyes haven't left his for even a second.

"Fuck," Lucas mutters. "Way to kill the buzz, Luce."

"I'm being serious," she says, leaning back, the tension in the room lifting slightly like that simple shift in posture somehow altered the very air. I look around and notice how everyone else seems to mimic what she does exactly: the placement of her hands, the tip of her head, all of us subconsciously miming her movements. "If you could kill someone and know for a fact you wouldn't get caught, would you do it?"

Levi lifts his hand to the back of his neck, massaging it gently.

His cheeks are flushed and he won't look at me, he can't look at me, because he knows what I'm thinking. What we're both thinking.

"I don't know," he says at last. "I'm a lover, not a fighter."

And there's that word again—*love*—or at least a derivative of it. I don't know if Levi actually loved Eliza, and to be honest, I don't care. I loved her, too, but that didn't stop me from hurting her; from making her feel guilty about the things she wanted. The life she craved. In fact, I think I hurt her *because* I loved her—that's what people do, after all. Destroy the very thing they desire the most.

"Bullshit," Lucy spits. "That's bullshit."

"Would you?" Levi shoots back, suddenly angry, and I can't help but flinch at his abrupt change in tone, the way Lucy so easily burrowed beneath his skin.

"Of course I would," she says, satisfied with his reaction. "We all would."

We turn to look at her, tired eyes trying to focus, and I wait for her to smile, let out a laugh. Instead, she simply crosses her legs before picking up the pin and twisting it in her hands.

"The only thing that makes bad things bad are the consequences, right? Think about it. The fact that we're all here right now means we're all a little morally loose."

She grins as she says it and everyone is quiet, looking around, suddenly feeling so exposed. I can't help but flush as I take in the empty bottles we pulled from the bar; the liquor we drank that isn't ours. The way we're all sitting here in this place we don't belong, acting like we do. She's right, I realize. If there's one thing Lucy's taught me since the moment we met, it's that once you bend one rule without consequence, it feels a lot easier to break the others.

"If we could indulge in life's dirty deeds without the repercussions, we'd be animals," she continues. "We are animals. All of us."

"I disagree," James chimes in, and I turn to look at him, though I'm barely listening. Not really, not anymore. I'm still thinking about Lucy, entranced by her confidence. Mesmerized by the way she asserts herself with no apology before inevitably bringing everyone around to her side. "That's not the way it works."

"It's not?" she asks.

"No, it's not," he says. "Morally, most people would draw the line before killing someone."

"Moral is subjective."

"Moral is straightforward," he argues. "It's *right* versus *wrong*—"

"Nothing in life is straightforward."

"Okay," Nicole juts in, an uncomfortable twinge in her voice. Her eyes keep darting over to Levi, his long, tanned legs knocking into hers. "We get it. You've made your point."

"No." Lucy shakes her head. "I haven't. And my point isn't about morality, anyway. My point is that if you claim you're above killing someone, it's only because you haven't found a reason to do it yet."

She looks at me and winks, a shot of adrenaline spiking through my chest.

"We break rules when we decide the cost of getting caught doesn't outweigh the reward of doing it, right?" she asks. "You can say the same for everything. Once you find the right person, the right *reason* . . . the scales start to tip."

We're all quiet, considering it in our drunken stupor. The idea of it like some distant dream.

"I'd kill my stepmom," Trevor says at last, his expression blank. He nods once before bringing his cup to his lips, like the matter is settled.

"Professor Lund," Sloane adds, nudging Nicole to let her know she's kidding. "He gave me a B in pre-cal for no reason at all."

"We all have it in us," Lucy continues, ignoring her, crossing her arms tight against her chest. "Joke all you want, but under the right circumstances, we'd all do it. I know we would."

"What about you?" I ask without even realizing I said it out loud. I'm still looking at Lucy, at the glimmer in her eye that I swear wasn't there just a few seconds ago. Only she could make something like murder sound so straightforward. Only Lucy could make you feel like you might actually consider it—or that there's something seriously wrong with you if you don't. "Who would you kill?"

I watch as her head turns in my direction, pointy teeth digging into her lip and those pinprick pupils trained on me. Then she cocks her head, eyebrows furrowed like she doesn't understand the question. Like she's disappointed in me, somehow.

Like I shouldn't have even had to ask.

"I would kill someone who deserves it."

CHAPTER 21

I'm up early, six A.M., the gin and tonics I drank the night before making my tongue feel raw. I don't know if I ever fell asleep, really, but instead just lay rigid beneath my comforter in some kind of comatose state, staring at the ceiling. My head pounding gently to the rhythm of my heart.

I pull the covers up to my chin, a chill traveling down the length of my spine. It isn't just the temperature that's making me shiver, although it is freezing in here. I had noticed it on that very first day, the way the upstairs was so stifling hot compared to my room, constantly cool. I had chalked it up to shitty insulation at the time, cracks in the windows, although technically, that should be making it *hotter* in here, not the other way around. But right now, it's thoughts of Lucy that are making my body react like it had that day in the dorms, her glacial gaze on my back turning my spine cold and hard. An icicle materializing from the chill of her eyes alone.

I can't stop thinking about the way she looked last night, elbows pressed together as she leaned into Levi. The concentration on her face and that little twitch of a smile as she bit her lip, watched him squirm.

"If you knew you could get away with murder, would you do it?"

I climb out of bed and creep toward my door, pushing it open in the dark. It's just starting to get light outside, the hazy start of a new day, but the silent stillness of the house tells me everyone is still sleeping. I'm not surprised. I can't even remember what time we stumbled home last night—only a few hours ago, surely—but still, I slink into the hallway, past Lucy's room, and tiptoe up the steps until I reach the second floor.

"Sloane?" I whisper, knocking gently on her door. "Are you up?"

She doesn't respond, but still, I enter, her blackout curtains choking any trace of light from outside. I climb onto her bed and shake her gently. "Sloane," I say. "Wake up."

"What?" she groans. "What time is it?"

"Shh," I say, dipping my voice low in case Lucy is around. I know it's illogical—I know her door was closed when I walked past, I know she's sleeping—but still. She has that habit of creeping up behind you, popping up unannounced. You never really know when she might be around. "I need to talk for a second."

"And I need to sleep," she says.

"What was up with last night?" I ask, ignoring her. "That was weird, right?"

"What about last night?"

"Lucy," I say. "That question."

"Oh, I don't know," she says, eyes still closed. "Lucy likes to play games."

"Well, yeah. I gathered that."

"I don't mean that game," she clarifies. "I mean *games*. Head games."

"You think she was trying to get into Levi's head? Because of what I told you?"

"Like I said, I don't know."

I'm quiet, chewing it over, remembering the way she dipped her chin low like she was sharing a secret, a confession, and the way she had chosen Levi, specifically, as the person to share it with. We had been playing the game for hours at that point. She could have asked anybody . . . but instead, she asked him.

"I don't like that," I say at last, thinking out loud as I cross my legs. "I don't like her dangling it in front of him like that—"

"Then you shouldn't have told her," Sloane interrupts. "That's what Lucy does. She dangles."

She's right. I know she's right. I risked this when I decided to tell them about Eliza and Levi and the history they shared. The accident that killed her and the fact that Levi was there with her. The unanswered questions, all those loose ends. Everyone looked at him differently after that, rumors mounting when he was identified as the last person to be seen with her alive. Silent speculation trailing him around like an invisible odor, turning up noses.

I suppose I just hoped they would keep it to themselves.

"What is she going to do?" I ask at last. "She isn't going to *confront* him about it, is she?"

"Are you really asking me what Lucy is going to do?" Sloane asks, finally flipping over to face me. "You should know by now that's a stupid question. Nobody ever knows what Lucy is going to do."

"It's a bad idea," I say. "It could make him feel cornered or something. People are dangerous when they feel cornered."

Sloane is quiet, her head pushed into the pillow and her tired eyes open just barely. Finally, she sighs, rolling onto her back so she's staring at the ceiling.

"I don't think she'd do that," she says at last. "But she is gonna fuck with him."

"What do you mean?"

"She's gonna play with him. Scare him. Paw at him like a little mouse."

I remember the way Lucy had looked that night on my bed, her expression impenetrable as I told her about Levi and the things he did. I could tell, even then, that there was something churning around in her mind. Something gaining substance, growing solid. I just didn't know what.

"Why do you care, anyway?" Sloane asks, pulling me from the memory. "Why should he get to come here and live a perfect life after what happened to your friend?"

"He shouldn't," I say, sinking lower into the comforter, the feeble resolve getting harder in my chest.

"Right," she says. "So let him squirm."

We settle back into the silence, Sloane's chest rising and falling until I'm certain she's asleep again. I think about getting up, heading back into my own room and trying to do the same, when my mind wanders back to Lucy's cup last night, sitting untouched by her side.

"Did you notice she wasn't drinking?" I ask at last.

"Margot, I have a raging hangover," Sloane says, eyes still closed. "I didn't notice if Lucy was drinking."

"She wasn't," I say, thinking about how we all got so drunk so fast while she seemed to stay sober, voice straight and words unwavering. "I mean, I'm pretty sure she wasn't."

Sloane sighs, finally pushing herself up and resting her head on the headboard. I watch as she gestures to a half-empty glass of water on her side table, a smudge of old lipstick kissing the rim, and I hand it to her, watching as she takes a small sip.

"Lucy likes to know everything about everybody," she says at last, licking her lips. Then she exhales, long and hard, and closes her eyes like she just ingested some kind of drug. "She wants to know it all."

"She's inquisitive," I say, but Sloane shakes her head.

"She's cunning. If she wasn't drinking, it's because she had some kind of agenda last night. She wanted to keep her wits about her. You still don't know anything about her, do you?"

I think for a second, knowing she's right. Sloane had asked me this very same question on that very first day, the two of us pushed against the side of the shed, and now, months later, my answer is the still same. I consider Lucy a friend at this point, no longer a stranger on the hall or an object sunning herself on the lawn. Not just an enviable face I looked at with wonder and awe but something more personal now . . . and still, when it comes to who she is at her tender, pulsing, meaty core, I know next to nothing. Lucy never offers up anything of substance, shunning *truth* for *dare* and always guiding the conversation to avoid any questions that threaten to get too personal. She never opens up, instead focusing her attention on prying anything and everything out of the people around her. It's what makes her so mysterious, so interesting. The reason those rumors swirled around her like a cloud of gnats our freshman year; why people made up stories, her very existence an urban myth, a far-fetched legend. Something whispered about behind cupped hands, passed down from person to person, each iteration more fictious than the last.

They were just trying to understand her. Trying to make sense of this curious girl living among us who nobody knew anything about.

"What do *you* know?" I ask, leaning forward slowly.

Sloane looks at me for a beat longer than necessary, like she's trying to make some calculation in her mind. Finally, her eyes dart to the door, her mouth starts to open, but the moment is interrupted by a wooden groan in the hallway, long and grating, and we both look to the side, the sudden noise sending an inexplicable pang of panic through my chest. This house makes sounds, it's old like that, and even though I know it's probably just the air conditioner kicking in, Nicole getting up to pee in the dark, I have the sudden sensation of someone standing just outside, ear flush against the door.

"It's a waste of time trying to figure Lucy out," Sloane says at last, rolling back over to face the wall. "Just trust me on that."

CHAPTER 22

It takes time to settle back into classes. Like trudging through marsh mud, relaxed and lazy, my mind fights me on it every step of the way. Maybe it knows, on some subconscious level, that the farther I move away from the summer, the deeper I sink into Lucy and this house and all the thoughts of Levi just next door, the harder it'll be to pull myself out. Crawl back to safety before it's too late.

For the first few days, I sit in class and zone out completely, the slow drone of my professors turning into static as I reminisce on the last few months, trying to convince myself that they were, in fact, real. Back in the presence of other people, it feels like a fantasy, like something imagined. An old movie that runs on repeat in my mind, my favorite scenes popping back into my awareness without warning: Nicole and me side by side in the sand, both of us in stitches over something stupid that happened the night before. Sloane and me watching movies in bed, burning popcorn in a saucepan and drinking wine straight out of the bottle. Lucy bursting into my room at random, each time sending a nervous quiver down my spine like that very first day when I swung around in my dorm, her presence sharp and sweet like a shot of morphine. Penny Lanes and those syrupy cocktails and the four of us belting out old songs with new meaning until the whites of our eyes were bleeding red.

Maybe the madness of these last three months has finally caught up to me, the beer and liquor and cheap, shitty weed causing my brain to slow way down, processing things that used to be easy in a kind of sluggish slow motion. I'm definitely sleep-deprived, consistently hungover, but in truth, I think I just miss the way those days bled together like watercolor, twelve entire weeks stitched into a single memory like a mosaic, a quilt. One long fever dream that couldn't possibly end. But when it did end, I blinked my eyes and found myself loopy and disoriented like waking up wrecked after a cough syrup stupor: bumbling and bleary-eyed, unable to discern the real from the imagined. Fact from fiction. Reality from dream.

I'm curled up on the couch now with a pile of books on the cushion beside me, the smallest of them nestled in my lap. I'm enrolled in a Great Books class this semester and the reading list is exorbitant, a fast slap back to reality: Homer and Dostoevsky and Twain and Tolstoy, all of us warned on the very first day that we'll need to get through a book a week in order to be prepared for the final, no matter if the selected text is ninety pages or nine hundred. I never could have gotten through them all last year, the way my mind constantly wandered without warning, but now, somehow, I find that I'm able to relax into the words again, the sentences stringing together in my mind without effort as I slip into another body, another world.

More undeniable evidence that this summer has changed me in more ways than one.

I look up just as Lucy bursts out of her bedroom, her open door revealing a peek inside. I can see clothes cast away on an unmade bed, a single dreamcatcher spinning sluggish beneath the air vent. She keeps stick-on stars on the ceiling, the same kind I had when I was a kid, and the quick glimpse reminds me of my very first day here, taking stock of every single space, trying to piece together what the clues might say. Sloane's and Nicole's were fairly easy to decipher, the pictures their rooms painted straightforward and clear, but I still can't get a grasp on Lucy's, even after so much time spent inside. I still can't discern what, exactly, it says about her. What it reveals.

I probably never will.

"What are you reading?" she asks now, walking over to the couch. She stands above me, peering over the pages, and I hold the book up, showing her the cover: *The Strange Case of Dr. Jekyll and Mr. Hyde*. "What's it about?"

"You've never heard of Dr. Jekyll and Mr. Hyde?" I ask, with an incredulous stare. Everybody knows Dr. Jekyll and Mr. Hyde. Even though this is the first time I've ever actually read the story, the characters themselves are so deeply saturated into society, it's hard to imagine having never even heard of it: the eternal battle of good versus evil, the ability for one body to possess two entirely different natures. The constant clashing between them and the question of which will rise up, victorious.

Lucy just shrugs, shakes her head, and I look back down at the book again, eyeing the passage I just highlighted.

"It's about . . . human nature, I guess."

"Huh," she says.

"You'd probably like it."

I think back to that night at Penny Lanes again, the scene flaring up like an itch begging to be scratched. Lucy's voice, soft as silk, as she presented us all with that question: *"If you knew you could get away with murder, would you do it?"* I can still see her devilish grin, the way she was examining us all, pushing and pulling, daring us to indulge in the dirty little parts of ourselves we're constantly trying to repress. I've shrugged it off since then, discounted the entire conversation as just another one of Lucy's stunts meant to shock and awe—but at the same time, I can't deny that, in the moment, we had all been thinking it, considering it. Pondering the perfect balance between risk and reward, scales quivering, each of us wondering what it would take to finally make them tip. The mental tally of everyone in our lives who had wronged us flipping through our minds as quick as a deck of cards.

"Can I read it when you're done?" she asks, and I look at her, studying the way her face is cocked so curiously. Her eyes dart back and forth between me and the book as if she wants it, desperately, so I flip it closed, toss it across the couch.

"Take it," I say at last, curling my legs up beneath me. "It's yours."

CHAPTER 23

Fall arrives in the way of all the seasons: slowly, at first, a sense of giddy anticipation spreading through campus with each unusually crisp morning or crunch of dead leaves beneath our feet. We could all feel it happening, the creeping change in the air. Our spiked fruit and summertime tans being slowly replaced with warm whiskey cider and bonfires behind the shed.

We still go next door, of course, but with eight A.M. lectures and late nights at the library bookending our days, the frequency has dwindled to a steady trickle at best, no longer every night, but strategically scattered depending on our workload. And not only is the frequency different, but the feeling is, too: now, there are always other people there, no longer just the small, exclusive pocket of us it was in the weeks before. There are girlfriends back from summers abroad, sorority girls eyeing us with not-so-subtle curiosity. I can't help but feel territorial every time I step into the place and find someone else sitting in my usual spot on the couch, some other girl chatting up Trevor when Nicole isn't around. I try to let it slide, shooting over a shy smile when I catch them staring, but the gush of other students on campus has been an unexpected shot of reality, a splash of cold water just when I was starting to get comfortable.

A humbling reminder, really, that the place was never truly ours to begin with.

"Costume parties are stupid," Sloane says to me now as she sits cross-legged on my bed, watching me fling various clothes around my room. We've been watching the pledges decorate the house all week: stuffed bodies swaying from the magnolia tree out back, faux cobwebs strangling the branches. A skeleton doing a keg stand and strobe lights pulsing to the rhythm of a playlist that's been running on repeat for so long, I've started hearing the songs in my sleep. "Draw whiskers on your cheeks and call it a day."

"I'm tempted," I say, taking in her flannel button-up and baggy jeans. She has a green beanie sitting snug over her hair, a budget-friendly lumberjack she pulls off well, and I'm jealous I didn't think of it first. "How seriously do they take this thing?"

"Like a heart attack, unfortunately."

I flip through a few more hangers, chewing on the inside of my cheek. Out of all the roommates, Sloane is the one I've seen the least of since school started back up again. If she isn't in class, she's at work at the registrar's, and she's the smartest of us all by a landslide, vanishing every Monday morning and rarely making another appearance outside of fishing around in the kitchen until it's time to go out on Friday night. I've caught glimpses of Nicole studying at the kitchen table, Lucy reading in front of the TV, but they're both more than willing to party on the weeknights in a way that Sloane typically isn't. Nicole tends to power through her hangovers, shamelessly reporting to class in sunglasses and sweatpants, whereas Lucy just skips them entirely, spending entire days in her room with the lights off and door closed.

"Dressing up shouldn't be a prerequisite to get drunk," I say, pulling out a cheetah-print sweater—but before I can hold it up to my chest, I feel that familiar presence behind me, already knowing it's Lucy in the door.

I twist around, registering her costume: a black tank top, leather pants, and combat boots complete with felt ears and thin little lines scratched across her face. The outfit makes her mane of curls look even darker, her eyes glow even brighter, and there's something chilling about the contrast: cold and hard like the silent slink of a panther as it weaves its way through the dark.

"Well," I say. "There goes that idea."

"Be a prisoner," Lucy says, walking toward my closet and plucking a black-and-white-striped dress from the back. "I have some handcuffs you can attach to your wrist."

"A *prisoner*," I echo, tossing the sweater onto the floor and slipping the dress off the hanger instead. "And why do you have handcuffs?"

"Do you really want to know?" she asks, and I fake a gag. "I'll go get them."

I twist back around and face the mirror once she leaves, pulling my T-shirt over my head and tossing it on the floor with the discarded sweater. Then I slip on the dress, running my fingers through my hair to tamp down the flyaways.

"Where's Nicole?" Sloane asks suddenly, her eyes darting around like she just now realized our foursome isn't complete. "I haven't seen her all day."

"She's already over there," Lucy says, walking back into my bedroom with a pair of handcuffs hanging from her finger. "She's doing Tinkerbell again."

"She did that last year," Sloane says, and Lucy shrugs.

"She likes the way the dress makes her boobs look."

I smile, grabbing the handcuffs and slipping one of the silver bracelets around my wrist, hesitating before I close them.

"Do you have the key?" I ask.

"Of course I have the key. And I have this, too."

She walks over to Sloane first, dropping something in her hand before making her way back over to me. I can already tell she's up to something. She always gets the same expression: smug, mischievous, an illusionist seconds before her biggest trick. She likes the bated breath, the anxious anticipation, the thought of us all wondering what she could possibly pull out of her hat next.

I watch as she stops in front of my mirror, her body pushed close to mine and an impish smile pulling at her lip. Then she grabs my hand and uncurls my fingers, placing a little white pill in the center of my palm.

I look down at it, a prickle of sweat erupting across my skin. I've experienced a lot of firsts in this place, but hard drugs aren't one of them. I'm not naïve enough to think they aren't around: I can see the dusty remnants beneath the boys' noses, bodies buzzing like a live wire and their pupils stretched to three times their natural size. I can tell by the way their money always has a subtle curl to it; all the crumpled-up plastic bags stuffed to the bottom of the trash can and the flimsy mirror stashed beneath the coffee table. The way they lock themselves in the bathroom in packs before coming back out, alert and alive. I just know they aren't comfortable enough with me to offer it yet and honestly, I've been glad, dreading the inevitable moment one of them beckons me into an empty bedroom. Imagining myself nervous and fumbling like that first cigarette, not knowing what to do.

I look over at Sloane, as if asking permission, and watch as she inspects it, the little tablet pressed between her thumb and forefinger. There's a certain energy vibrating through the room right now, a dangerous anticipation for a night we've been watching unfold through the window for weeks. It feels like the start of something, a new season and semester, but also, somehow, the end of it, too. The four of us so desperately wanting to go back to those dog days of summer, reclaim what was rightfully ours. Live in that little bubble of fantasy we had somehow deluded ourselves into thinking would last.

I watch as Sloane tips her head back and pops the pill into her mouth, swallowing it dry. She grimaces a bit, her jaw clenched tight like she just sucked on a lemon, and before I can think twice, I close my eyes and do the same. It goes down slow, painful, a jagged scrape against my throat that makes my tongue curl. Then I stand silent for a minute, as if waiting for some sudden transformation to take place, and when I open my eyes, I find Lucy staring straight at me like that day on the lawn: a diabolical gaze, a gentle nod of approval.

It only dawns on me later: I never even thought to ask what it was.

CHAPTER 24

The house is packed so tight it feels like the walls are bulging, the seams are ripping, the compound weight of us too heavy for its fragile frame to hold. I've grown so used to it being just us and the boys, the boys and us, a small, select group as opposed to what feels like half the college standing shoulder to shoulder, the crush of warm bodies and the rhythmic thumping of bass so loud it's making my teeth rattle.

"So what's your major?" a guy in a pirate hat yells, a single black patch cinched tight over one eye. "I've never seen you around."

I blink in quick succession—three, four times—and take a sip of my drink to coat my throat.

"English!" I yell back, but very quickly, judging by the way his exposed eye refocuses as if seeing me for the very first time, I realize my mistake.

"I was talking to your friend."

"Yeah, sorry," I say, turning to look at Lucy. She's standing by my side, eyes skimming the crowd, looking bored as ever.

"Luce," I say, nudging her, in case she didn't hear. "Captain Hook wants to know your major."

She turns to look at him, downing the rest of whatever bottom-shelf liquor is sloshing around in her cup before grabbing my fore-arm and pulling me away.

"I'm sure he does."

We spend the next hour gliding around the house, making small talk with the people we know. Mostly ignoring the ones we don't. Whatever that pill was, it's making me feel alert, alive, the tips of my fingers tingling like they're hovering over an outlet and channeling the charge. At some point, I realize I'm sweating pro-fusely, the house so stuffed it feels like an oven, and I turn toward Lucy, grabbing her hand.

"I'm going outside!" I yell, probably too loud. "I'll meet you out there."

I'm pushing my way out of the house when my shoulder slams into another body, hard, so I swing around, start to apologize. Mumbly little words trickling out of my mouth. It takes a second to realize who's standing in front of me—but when I do, it feels like a plug has been ripped out from beneath me, all the blood draining from my face.

"Margot," she says, and although I can see her jaw tense, she offers a smile. Of course she does. "It's so good to see you."

I look at my old roommate, a strange mix of emotions coursing through my chest. She's wearing black leggings and an orange T-shirt, awkwardly oversized, a jack-o'-lantern drawn onto the stom-ach in a strange kind of grimace. She looks so out of place here, so uncomfortable, and as I think back on the life we lived together, the kind of friends we used to be, I realize with a sense of startling clarity that I don't regret what I did to her. I don't regret it at all.

I wonder what kind of person that makes me.

"Maggie," I say, realizing now that it's been months since I've thought about her. In the beginning, my mind used to flash back to her constantly. Every time I started settling in, feeling content as I curled up next to Lucy or Sloane or Nicole on the couch, our limbs tangled together as we watched a movie in the dark, I would see her, always, the outline of Maggie burned into my brain: the two of us on the futon, so comfortably uncomfortable. Her perpetual small talk, always polite. I would see that look on her face when I first broke the news; the hurt in her eyes as she packed her things quietly, bottom lip quivering through another forced smile. And I used to dread this moment, the inevitable moment when I'd have to face her in the flesh instead of in my own mind. The place where I rehearsed the apology I knew I'd never say to her over and over and over again.

"How are you doing?" she asks, taking a step closer. I watch her eyes focus in on mine, a look of concern flashing across her face. "Are you okay?"

"I'm good," I say, trying to smile, act normal, ignore the incessant hammering of my own heart in my neck. "Yeah, I'm good. How are you?"

"I'm great," she responds, polite but clipped.

"How's the apartment?"

"It's fine," she says. "I found someone to take your—I mean, the room. The extra room."

"That's good."

"We met at the dining hall," she offers, even though I didn't ask.

"I'm sorry," I blurt out, unable to take it any longer: the tiptoeing, the tension, even though I'm not sure if it's really there or if it's just me, projecting and paranoid. I rub my palms against my dress, trying to fight the deep, debilitating urge to keep blinking. "I'm really sorry, Maggie. About, you know—"

"Oh, don't worry about it," she says. "Really, I understand. It's just good to see you out. Happy."

"It's not that I wasn't happy living with you—" I start, but she waves me off, shaking her head.

"It's fine," she says. "You don't have to explain it. You wanted a different life."

We stand in silence for a second, the crowd around us humming like a beaten hive: too many bodies, too small of a space. The very air around us chaotic and charged. I can't help but think about the contrast of this setting from the way she probably remembers me—frozen on the futon, eyes glazed over, nothing but Eliza's face thumping through my mind like a heartbeat pulsing in an open wound—and I wonder what she's really thinking right now, seeing me like this.

If she really understands it, if she's really this kind, or if it's all an act manufactured to avoid any more tension, any more hurt.

"Well, listen, I should get going—" I start, but before I can finish, I feel a hand on my shoulder, five long fingers curling their way around my neck.

"Oh my gosh, Mary!"

It's her eyes that get me: the subtle bulge, that flash of pain, not unlike a character in a movie the second they realize they've been shot. I watch as Maggie looks back and forth between Lucy and me, disbelief and understanding settling over her at the exact same time.

"Is this—" she starts, looking at me, motioning to her.

"Roommates," Lucy interrupts, nodding. "We live over there, just next door."

Maggie swallows, nods, and I'm horrified to find the faintest prickle of tears magnifying her eyes. I'm sure she's thinking it; I am, too. That day on the lawn. Maggie telling me about the apartment she found and Lucy sunning herself in her bathing suit as we gossiped, imagined, pretended we could possibly know her at all.

The disdain in her voice, the skepticism in mine, as I listened to that unusually sharp hiss between her teeth.

"I heard she blinded her boyfriend in high school."

Somehow, after getting to know her, it feels more believable now.

I watch as Maggie sputters out a *good to see you,* and then a *goodbye,* making her way back inside. It's not lost on me that these two roommates of mine could not be more different—if Lucy is darkness, then Maggie is light; pure, clean, angelic light—and that's probably what's hurting her the most right now: the realization that I met Maggie, got to know her, and actively chose the opposite. But the truth is, this has nothing to do with her and everything to do with me. Maggie's only flaw is that she reminds me too much of *me*: too mild, too meek. Like Sloane said that day in the yard: *"You seem . . . I don't know. Too nice."* I had tried that before. I had tried to be the watchful one, the protective one, the one that was always cautious and careful. Like Maggie coddling me in the dorm, always alert for some subtle sign that I was putting myself in danger, I had been that person for Eliza, too. I had been her voice of reason, trying my hardest to keep her safe. I had pushed back against her perilous urges and none of it ever worked.

She just pushed back harder, pushed me away.

So maybe that's the reason I had to get away from her, this kind, quiet girl who not only reminds me of me, but of all my failures. Of everything I *didn't* do.

Maybe that's why I'm finding myself oscillating toward the opposite, toward Lucy, a swinging pendulum making my way slowly to the other side.

CHAPTER 25

I wait until Maggie is out of sight before Lucy and I join Sloane and Lucas sitting around a makeshift bonfire out back.

"How are you feeling?" Lucy asks, a smirk on her lips. I'm still a little rattled about the encounter, a little on edge, but the chemical concoction coursing its way through my bloodstream is making it impossible to feel too bad.

"Good," I say at last. "I feel good."

And that's the truth, at the heart of it, despite the guilt still tickling for my attention. I do feel good. And it isn't just the pill, either. Or the alcohol. Or the fact that I finally got in my apology to Maggie, albeit I can't quite tell if it was actually accepted or if she was just being nice as always. It isn't even the way every single person in this circle suddenly feels like family to me, the little shed between us a portal to another world. It's because I've just now realized, whether consciously or not, that I haven't been looking for Levi this entire time. We've spent the last two months tiptoeing around each other, attempting to coexist like two plants repotted into too small a container. Our respective roots trying to branch out, bury deep, but instead getting tangled together in the process.

It's almost felt like a competition between us—like one of us needs to wither in order for the other to thrive—but right now, sitting here, I'm not so sure it has to be that way.

"This is some party," I say, turning to Lucas. He's reclining in a lawn chair so ratty and worn he's practically sitting on the ground, a cowboy hat tipped low over his eyes.

"This is nothing," he responds, staring into the flames. "Just wait until January."

"What's in January?"

"Initiation," Sloane says on his behalf. "The first party where the pledges aren't pledges anymore."

I nod, reminiscing on the last few months. The freshmen are required to spend every free second at the house during their first semester. I'm always seeing them coming over in the mornings and in the evenings after class, cleaning the house and running errands. Sacrificing Friday nights to be the upperclassmen's designated drivers, chauffeuring them around town with no questions asked.

"There's this little island a few miles off the coast," Lucas continues. "An older brother found it years ago and it's become a tradition, throwing it out there. No neighbors, no cops. Our own little slice of paradise."

"How do you get there?" I ask. "By boat?"

I watch as Lucas tips a beer back to his lips, takes a long swallow before wiping his mouth with the back of his hand. I've learned by now that having access to a boat is the highest form of social currency at a coastal college like Rutledge, little skiffs and dinghies cluttering up students' lawns. Center consoles and speedboats for the locals who are lucky enough to use their parents'.

"Their last task is to drive everyone out there, set up camp," Lucas says, nodding. "Once we're settled, their obligations are over. It's their first real night of freedom."

I try to imagine it: hordes of students making their way to the water, bow lights bobbing as we venture out and into the night.

"Doesn't it get cold in the winter?" I ask.

"We have a fire, heaters for the tents. Liquor blankets," he adds, grinning. "It gets pretty feral."

Sloane suddenly perks up, twisting around to face the house.

"Where is Nicole?" she asks for the second time tonight, as if this conversation suddenly sparked her memory. I realize, too, that we still haven't seen her. Not since this morning.

"She's wasted," Lucas says. "She's been here for, like, eight hours."

"Should we go find her?" I ask, turning around, too. Waving my hand through the air as the wind picks up, pushing smoke from the bonfire directly toward me.

"Trevor has her. She's fine."

The circle settles back into a heavy, stoned silence, our limbs light and minds numb. The house is still thumping, still thrumming, still pulsing with the energy of hundreds of people still inside. I can practically feel the sweat dripping, the body heat radiating, and eventually Sloane and Lucas get up to grab another drink, leaving Lucy and me alone again.

I look over at her, blue eyes ablaze as she stares into the flames, feeling another rush of warmth in my chest.

"How was it complicated?"

It takes me a second to realize she's talking to me. She's still staring into the fire, completely entranced, her voice barely above a whisper. I look around, checking to see who else she could be directing the question to, but still, we're alone.

"What?" I ask at last.

"Your friend," she says. "You never said how she died. Only that it was an accident. That it was complicated."

I feel a quick twinge in my chest like a popped guitar string, my insides buzzing. Remembering that conversation on my bed, the three of them staring as I started to talk.

"She fell," I say at last, still staring at her profile. I wait for Lucy to turn and face me but she never does. "There was an argument, and she had been drinking . . . Honestly, it's one of those things that doesn't even feel real. Like I dreamed it or something."

I'm quiet as I turn back toward the fire, my eyes getting lost in the glowing logs, the licking flames. Watching them travel up the pile of wood before transforming into curling black smoke and disappearing altogether.

"Where did it happen?" she asks.

"A party," I respond. "I didn't want to go, and she went with him."

I swallow, close my eyes, remembering how it felt to be lying in bed that night, tapping through Instagram and seeing the videos of them together. Eliza and Levi. I knew she must have been drunk to be posting them like that, raw and unfiltered, one after the other in quick succession. Her eyes were glassy and unfocused, a vacant stare, and I could so perfectly picture her heavy fingers punching at her phone screen as Levi draped an arm around her shoulder, the weight of him heavy. Pulling her down.

I remember sitting up fast, my screen glowing in the dark and alarm growing in my chest. Watching the two of them giggle un-controllably, stagger around. A bottle of vodka clutched in his hand that he lifted to her lips, tipping it back.

I open my mouth, ready to speak again, when the body of a boy comes out of nowhere and slams into the seat beside me, making me jump.

"Holy shit," he says. "Lucy Sharpe?"

Maybe it's because everything feels so detailed tonight, the edges razor-sharp like a freshly whetted blade, but I can't help but register the way Lucy's eyes swell at the sight of him, her face freezing for just a second before slipping back into that indifferent façade.

"Jesus, we all thought you were dead or something," the boy continues, laughing, missing the fact that Lucy is ignoring him. Or maybe he just doesn't care. "Where have you *been*? Do you go here?"

I watch as she gives him her full attention, finally, a fair-faced blonde wearing a short blue dress slathered in blood. Even from behind, I can see his shoulders tense beneath her scrutiny, a self-conscious laugh escaping his lips.

"Yeah, I know, I didn't pick the costume," he says, grabbing the dress. "All the pledges had to wear something stupid. I'm one of the twins from *The Shining*. What year are you?"

"I'm sorry, I have no idea who you are," Lucy says at last, crossing one leg over the other. "We've never met."

"Yes, we have," the boy says, shaking his head. He doesn't seem drunk—in fact, compared to the rest of us, he seems shockingly sober.

"You said you're a pledge?" she asks, leaning forward, the light from the fire making her eyes shine. "A freshman, then?"

"Yeah, I'm Danny, remember?"

"Then why aren't you getting me a drink?"

She thrusts her cup in his direction, the liquid inside barely half gone, and I look back and forth between Lucy and the boy, her cold eyes trained on his, something heavy traveling between them. It isn't like Lucy to be so casually cruel like this. Blunt? Sure. She gets off on making people uncomfortable, commanding them around, but it's usually with an air of intimacy, like she's teasing them because she loves them. People would kill to be bossed around by Lucy, wearing her attention like a badge of honor . . . but Danny looks concerned right now, uneasy, cataloging the way she's staring at him. Like she doesn't even know him at all.

"I . . . I was just going . . ."

He gestures behind us, farther into the backyard, before closing his mouth and shaking his head, like he's suddenly thought better of whatever he was about to say.

"Yeah, sure," he says at last, standing up and taking her cup. "Coming right up."

We watch in silence as he walks away, nothing but the popping of the fire and the distant echo of music masking the utter stillness between us. I wonder if she's going to bring it up again, Eliza, nudge me to continue, but instead she turns toward me and smiles like she only just realized I'm here.

"Terrible pickup line."

"You really didn't know him?" I ask, looking back at the house where the boy disappeared, my own voice suddenly sounding strange in my ears. "It seems like he knew you."

"No idea," she says. "I bet one of the guys put him up to it. They always try to embarrass the pledges like that."

"Yeah," I say, nodding vaguely, suddenly feeling a little nauseous. Slowly, quietly, the sense of euphoria I had earlier feels like it's being replaced with something else now. Something more like unease. "Listen, should we find Nicole? I don't want to leave her—"

Before I can finish, I hear the bang of the shed door swinging open behind us; the slap of the wood hitting the siding, hard. I twist around, relieved, expecting it to be Nicole—maybe Lucas was wrong; maybe she hasn't been here after all, but instead, in her room, and now she's mad at us for leaving her behind—but almost immediately, I feel the color drain from my skin as I register the body standing before me, his familiar face streaked with dirt.

"Levi," I say, noticing the wild look in his eyes. It seems both haunted and hollow, like he's just seen something terrible—or maybe it's *my* eyes, distorting things. Twisting his face into something demonic, not unlike the way it looked immediately after they found Eliza, his pupils large and impassive as he stared into the lights, the cameras. His face on the news and his sweat-soaked skin as pale as a corpse. "What are you—?"

I stop, taking in the rest of him. He's wearing something old and tattered like some kind of Tarzan-inspired loincloth but I can't tell if it looks like that on purpose or if he's been doing something to soil it that way. His bare chest is scratched, jagged little lines like fingernail streaks dotted with blood, and his eyes dart back and forth between Lucy and me like we just caught him red-handed doing something he shouldn't.

My heartbeat picks up a little, my hands begin to shake, and I realize with a sense of sinking dread that if Levi is coming into the backyard through the shed, that means our house is the only place he could be coming from.

CHAPTER 26

"Eliza, you need to tell someone."

I can see her here, behind the fire, staring at me with an emptiness in her eyes.

Neck crooked, accusatory. The hypocrisy of it all.

I wonder what she would think if she could see the two of us together like this, like that night at Penny Lanes. If she could somehow know from beyond the grave that Levi and I are running in the same circle, grabbing beers out of the same cooler. Both of our lips touching a single joint as it passed between us.

My spit on his, his on mine, not too removed from sharing a kiss.

"He broke into your house."

Would she be happy, at last, that we were tolerating one another? That we were learning to get along? We aren't friends—we were never friends, never would be friends—but at the very least, we're being civil.

Or would she be jealous, like I was, seeing me spend so much of my time with somebody else? Would she feel betrayed, like I did, watching me slip into this other life?

"Margot, you're being insane," Eliza had said, hands on her hips, surveying her empty bedroom. "He did not break into the house."

It was nearing the end of our senior year and we had come home one night, late, to find the Jeffersons' back door swung wide open, the warm breeze snaking its way through the living room making the interior curtains flutter in the wind. We had been at the movies together—Eliza, her parents, and I, the four of us the family I always preferred—and her mother had screamed when we walked inside to find it open like that, as if someone had bolted out the back as soon as our car pulled into the driveway. Mr. Jefferson kept insisting there was a logical explanation, muttering vague rationalizations like *"Maybe we just forgot to lock it"* or *"Maybe the dog pushed it open,"* even though their golden retriever was twelve years old and could barely walk, let alone dislodge a set of French doors. He was refusing to make a scene, call the police, but there was an aura in the house that we could all feel; a foreign energy that was obvious from the second we stepped inside and found the double doors swung open, monster-sized moths flapping around the ceiling light.

"He was here," I said, even though there was no proof. Nothing was missing, as far as we could tell. Nothing was disturbed. But there was the faint smell of him on her bedsheets, a boyish odor of sweat and Old Spice, and I could picture him lying there, on top of her duvet, eyes on the ceiling as he imagined her kicking her legs for him through the window. The way her spaghetti strap would slip and her pen would dangle between her lips, his breath getting deeper, heavier, as his hand worked at his zipper. Snaking his way down, down, down.

"Wait a second," I said, my attention drifting to the bulletin board Eliza kept mounted above her desk. "Didn't you used to have a picture right there?"

I pointed to the wall, an empty rectangle of space that I was sure was covered up before. Eliza kept it cluttered with a giant calendar, posters of our favorite celebrities, snapshots of various summers spent with our backs digging into the sand. And in the very center of it was a picture of us—Eliza, her dad, and me—huddled together on the back of her parents' boat. I could still remember when it was taken, her mom pushing us together the way she always did to document some mundane memory she promised we would appreciate more when we were older. I had been wrapped in a towel, hair wet and dripping after taking a swim, but Eliza was in her bathing suit, that little string bikini she used to walk around in when Levi was looking.

It was there, I knew it was—until suddenly, it wasn't.

"Eliza . . ."

"Yeah, I see it," she said, her face suddenly a shade too pale. She crossed her arms across her torso, tight, like she was about to be sick. "There has to be an explanation. He wouldn't . . . he wouldn't do that."

I knew right then that she would never tell. She would never admit to what was going on with Levi; what she had invited into her room, her life, this leech of a boy who latched on from the beginning and refused to let go. It wasn't her fault, of course it wasn't, but in her mind, she had led him to this. She had beckoned him in, forefinger curling, daring him to get just a little bit closer. She had tested him, teased him, and now he was testing her right back. How would she explain it to her parents? How would she tell them what she was doing at night, curtains open, letting him watch from the other side of the lawn? How would she ever look them in the eye after that, the creeping shame as their foreheads bunched, their little girl no longer so little?

In that moment, holding her stomach tourniquet-tight, she must have been thinking about all those conversations between us. She must have been thinking about the way I had told her, *warned* her, tried to nudge her along so many times. She must have been remembering what I had said in that very bedroom, that very spot, the disgust in my voice as I told her soon, watching from a distance wouldn't be enough.

Soon, he would want more, crave more, feel entitled to more the way they always do.

"He would," I said, staring out the window. I was looking at Levi's house, a single light emanating from his bedroom in the otherwise dead of night. Wondering what he was doing in there with that picture, *our* picture, Eliza in her bathing suit and Mr. Jefferson and me probably ripped from the edges before being crumpled into a ball and tossed in the trash. And I know I should have walked to her then, held her. Comforted her. Told her it wasn't her fault. I should have swallowed my pride and simply let her be scared . . . but I couldn't help but feel a certain smugness in my chest about being right all along. About knowing there was something wrong with him, something sick, so instead, I crossed my arms, too, reinforcing the wall that was already building between us.

"I *told* you he would."

CHAPTER 27

"What were you doing over there?" I ask, standing up from the lawn chair. I look past Levi, through the open shed doors, the dim lights of our living room barely visible through the windows. That first morning with Sloane comes rushing back, the two of us making our way through the shed and the unease in my chest as I thought about how easy it was for us to invade their space like that.

How easy it would be for them to invade ours.

"Answer me," I say, taking a step forward, though the sudden movement makes me feel abruptly dizzy, everything going straight to my head while all the blood drops in the opposite direction.

I think of Eliza, that unmistakable feeling of someone else in her home, and all at once, I hate myself for thinking Levi and I could coexist like this.

"Nothing," he says, lifting his hand behind his head. It's the same gesture he did at Penny Lanes when he was put on the spot by Lucy, rubbing the back of his neck like that. "I was just . . . getting something. From the shed."

"What were you getting?" I ask, grabbing my chair for support, handcuffs slapping against the armrest with a metallic *clink*.

"Lighter fluid." His eyes dart around, looking at Lucy and me before landing on the flames between us. "For the fire."

The three of us are quiet—Levi and me upright in a silent stand-off while Lucy sits to the side, watching it all. His voice is cautious, careful, but I can't decide if it's because he's hiding something or because he's confused about this sudden line of questioning; about my voice, urgent and incessant.

I look over at the fire, then down at his hands, noticing they're empty. Realizing he can't have anything in his pockets, either; he's practically naked. He doesn't even have pockets.

"I couldn't find any," he adds.

"Butler!"

We all turn around at the sound of Trevor's voice interrupting us, echoing across the lawn. He's shirtless, too, even though the temperature is nearing fifty, and we watch as he walks out the back of the house and approaches us with a manic grin. Danny is behind him, Lucy's Solo cup clutched in one hand, that gory blue dress seeming even more ridiculous than before. All these people, their costumes, it's giving everything such a strange edge, like I'm standing in the center of a lifelike dream. Everyone is themselves, but also not—there's something warped about their features, something wrong, like they're all caricatures of who they should be, who they were just a few seconds ago, a strange energy emanating from them all.

I reach down and pinch my arm, feeling silly the second I do it, although I really wouldn't mind if I snapped out of whatever this is and suddenly woke up, sheets damp and skin slick, gasping for air in my pitch-black bedroom.

"You doin' okay, man?" Trevor asks, slapping his palm against Levi's shoulder. "You look a little pale."

"Yeah," Levi says, a weak smile cracking across his face. "Yeah, I'm okay."

"I've been looking for you." Trevor winks. "Where you been?"

"I was just—" He gestures to the shed again, the door still hanging open to reveal the back of our empty house. I watch as he looks at Trevor, then me, then Lucy sitting silently in the corner, a little curl to her lip as she watches him squirm. "Trying to bring this fire back to life."

"Why don't you let Danny handle that," Trevor says, squeezing his shoulder, hard. "Let's get you a drink."

Levi looks back at me one last time before nodding silently and slinking into the house, Trevor's grip still firm against his skin. There's a certain energy to him tonight, Trevor, one that sometimes creeps in when I've seen him bossing around the pledges, drunk on power and playing God. It feels coked up and dangerous, like he's looking for a fight or maybe just returned from one, adrenaline pounding around him like a pulse.

Or maybe that's just me again, my own imagination, whatever I ingested earlier making everything feel so good until it took such a violent turn in the opposite direction.

"Here," Danny says, turning to Lucy once the others are gone. He hands her the drink, arm outstretched, but she doesn't take it.

"I'm not thirsty anymore," she says instead, standing up before walking toward me and grabbing my arm. "We're going home, anyway."

We step around the fire and stumble through the grass, Lucy's fingers digging hard into my wrist as she pulls me through the shed. My head is dipping, spinning, and I'm relieved to be leaving, the sights and sounds and smells of the party suddenly too much— but at the same time, I can't stop thinking about Levi slinking around in our house just minutes before. I can't stop imagining him creeping through my bedroom the way he once crept through Eliza's, fingers flipping through my clothes. Scanning the pictures on my mantel, maybe. His greedy eyes on her still, even now.

"Wait," I say, stopping abruptly in the backyard, feet from the door. Lucy turns and looks at me, her head cocked to the side. "I don't want to go in there."

"What do you mean?" she asks, hands on her hips.

I think of him on Eliza's bed, his head on her pillow. The faint smell of him staining her sheets.

"Levi," I say at last. "He wasn't in the shed. He was in the house."

Lucy is quiet, staring at me, before twisting her head and looking at the back door.

"We were sitting around that fire for over an hour," I continue. "He wasn't in the shed for that long."

"Margot," she says, smiling. "We were out there for, like, twenty minutes."

"Still," I say, feeling my cheeks burn hot. "He wasn't in the shed for that long looking for lighter fluid."

She sighs, rolling her neck like she's trying to stretch something out.

"Maybe he was tinkering with the toilet tank or something. I told Trevor the other day they need to take care of that. The noise is pissing me off."

"Why would Levi be doing that?"

"Trevor always sends the pledges to handle that stuff," she says. "He's too lazy to do it himself, plus he can't use a tool to save his life."

"In a loincloth?" I ask. "In the middle of a party?"

"I don't know. Maybe."

"We need to start locking the doors," I say. "We always leave them open."

"Yeah, because Nicole can't keep track of her key," she says. "She lost her keycard to Hines the second day of freshman year."

"But the boys can't just come in here without asking—"

"Yes, they can," she says, cutting me off. "They own the house, Margot. They can do whatever they want."

"They own the house," I echo, realizing, for the first time, what exactly that entails. I didn't even have to sign a lease to live here. Levi isn't just my neighbor anymore. He isn't just some guy next door who looks through the windows or loiters out back.

He's more than that. He *can do* more than that.

"Look, you're messed up," Lucy says, touching my arm. "You're paranoid, having a bad trip. It's my fault, honestly. I should have only given you half."

I look down at her fingers on my forearm, feeling a twist in my chest. Thinking of the pill she placed in my palm; the bitter pinch of it as I swallowed it dry. She's right, I know she's right, but at the same time, the energy back there was unmistakably off. It felt like I was on the outside of something among all of them, Levi included, a sinister secret pulsing around them like a shared heartbeat.

"Let's go inside, get you some water," Lucy says. "Then you can sleep it off."

CHAPTER 28

The night that follows is one I'll never forget, the music from next door pulsing like blood in my ears. It goes on for hours until the sound eventually dwindles into a faint trickle of the final stragglers: a single laugh, someone tripping in the gravel. The metallic kick of an empty can skidding across the road.

It's even worse once it's quiet, though, the thought of Levi creeping through our house the same way he once crept through Eliza's forcing my brain to stay awake. It comes to me in flashes, the juxtaposition of *then* and *now* blurring together until they're indistinguishable: his calloused hands on our doorknob, twisting it gently before stepping inside. The fluttering of wind in the curtains, Eliza's living room and the marshy smell that seeped its way in like he brought something dead inside with him. Walking around her bedroom, plucking that picture from her wall and running his fingers over it before slipping it into his pocket.

Sitting on the edge of the mattress, my body sinking down with the creak of the springs.

I've slipped into sleep a couple times, but it's always a restless, stressful dip out of consciousness before I'm startled back awake after only a few minutes—and every single time, I see flashes from my past, carnivalesque and over the top. The same way the circle of us around that bonfire felt otherworldly and wrong: Eliza and me lying out on the dock, our limbs stretched so long they look like melting taffy pulling in the sun. Levi's white smile, the corners of his lips fish-hooked so high I can see his gums.

Darkness, total darkness, so disorienting that I feel myself falling far and fast until I hit the ground with a quick, wet splat.

I glance at my bedside table, little digital numbers glowing red and the pair of handcuffs coiled on the clock, serpentine in the dark. It's almost four in the morning and even though the effects of whatever I took earlier have mostly worn off, there's still that lingering discomfort that borders on fear.

My legs won't stop pulsing, thrashing, my body begging me to run.

"It's totally harmless," Lucy had said, grabbing her keys from a hook on the wall and unlocking the cuffs. Then she sat me down on the kitchen floor and fed me little sips of water, hand cupped tight under my chin. I had been shaking uncontrollably at that point, trembling jaw like a chattering-teeth toy. "Just gives everything a bit of a glow until, you know. It doesn't."

"I wish it was him," I had said, ignoring her completely. Goose bumps spraying across my skin and my voice as sharp as a blade. Lucy cocked her head and I watched as the understanding dawned on her slowly. I had been thinking of Levi, of course, visions of him and Eliza staggering around that night on my phone. Their lips slick with vodka and spit and their fingers twisted together, knuckles white in the dark. "It should have been him."

I flip to my side, eyes wide and stinging. Now that I'm coming down, I try to talk myself into believing what Lucy had said: there are so many explanations that could make sense. Maybe Levi really was in the shed, one of the other brothers sending him on some obscure errand like fetching lighter fluid that didn't exist, laughing behind his back as he fumbled around, frantic, too afraid to come back without it. It was the kind of stupid thing they did to the freshmen; the kind of thing meant to embarrass and belittle. Or maybe he really was fixing something in the house, fiddling with one of the many broken things we had to hound the boys about: the shoddy heater that wasn't a problem in the summer, but now, in October, made our toes stiff when we walked barefoot across the floor. The leak in Sloane's ceiling that still wasn't fixed or, like Lucy had said, the running toilet tank that, now that I think about it, I haven't heard all night.

I close my eyes, exhaling long and hard. It was a bad trip, that's all. A foreign chemical that managed to hotwire my brain, revving up the worst of my fears.

But then, just as my body starts to unwind, I hear the faintest sound.

I sit up quick, trying to determine where it came from. It seemed like it was both inside and outside at the exact same time: a muted *thump,* like a fist pounding or foot kicking . . . or the hard, fast slap of a door slamming shut.

I click on the lamp on my bedside table, holding my breath as I listen. I hear it once more, in my room but also out of it: a muffled shuffling, close but quiet, so I fling off the covers and get out of bed, creeping my way toward my closed bedroom door.

"Lucy?" I whisper, even though I know, from down the hall, she can't hear me. She's probably asleep, anyway. It's four in the morning. *"Luce, is that you?"*

I can feel my heart in my throat as I pray for a response—she's in the bathroom, maybe, grabbing a glass of water—but instead of her voice, I hear it again. That sound.

A thump, a groan. A single dry cough.

"Shit," I whisper, the palms of my hands prickling with damp. "Shit, shit, shit."

Even if what Lucy said is true, there is no logical explanation for why anyone should be entering our house at four in the morning. Suddenly, the thought comes to me like a punch to the chest: What if Levi was listening to Lucy and me talking when he was in the shed? She had been wondering about Eliza, after all. Pushing me along, asking me questions. I didn't say anything bad out there, I didn't say anything wrong, but still. He had looked so strange once he emerged, like he had heard us. Heard every word.

"There was an argument," I had said.

He wouldn't have liked that.

I hear it again, something resembling a dry heave, and before I can think twice, I fling open the door and step into the hallway, the sudden pitch-black of it throwing me off-balance. I take a few steps out of my bedroom, but before I get far, my bare feet brush against something on the floor, warm and wet, and I immediately jump back, squinting at whatever it is on the ground.

"What the hell?" I whisper, kneeling down. Suddenly, a familiar scent fills my nostrils: vomit, warm and sharp, something fermenting on the floor. My eyes are starting to adjust now and I can see that it's a piece of clothing, a costume, bright green fabric with torn-up edges.

I glance to the right, toward the bathroom, and see a dark figure slumped on the floor.

"Nicole?" I ask, realization dawning on me as I run toward the bathroom and turn on the light. After Levi showed up, I had forgotten all about her. Lucas said she was drunk, too drunk, but that Trevor was taking care of her . . . but now I remember Trevor, too, walking out back to boss around the pledges.

"Nicole," I say again, reaching out to shake her shoulder. She's half naked, huddled on the tile with a puddle of red bile beneath her. I turn back toward the hallway, looking at her dress. She must have gotten sick, peeling it off before stumbling to the toilet, falling asleep.

"Come on," I say, digging my arms into her armpits, hard, trying to help her stand. I don't think she was in here when I went into my bedroom earlier, but at the same time, I can't be sure. It was dark and I was disoriented, basically beelining from the kitchen straight into my bed. "Nicole, come on. Let's get in bed."

She groans, her head flopped to the side like a newborn baby, a crust of dried spit stuck to her lip.

"No," she mutters, holding up her arms before they flop back down again, gummy and boneless. That's when I see the marks on her wrist: little bruises like fingers, faint but there, and there's something familiar about the placement of them. Something about it I've seen before. "Stop."

"Come on," I say, trying to brush away the memory, focus on this. "Let's go."

"No," she says again, but she lets me lift her—really, she has no choice—the entire weight of her leaning into my side, body limp like a dragged corpse.

I look down at the toilet, chunks of bright red vomit sitting stagnant in the water, and flush it with my free hand before bringing her back into my bedroom, wiping her face and tucking her in bed. I stare at her for a second, taking in the way the back of her hair is rough and matted, the frantic twitch of her lips like she's already lost in some kind of dream. Then I curl in beside her and listen to the steady sound of her breathing, trying not to think about the fact that it couldn't have been her I heard moving around earlier. She's practically comatose.

That, and I can hear the tank running.

CHAPTER 29

AFTER

"Detective Frank is here."

I look up at Sloane, two wide eyes peeking through my doorway. Lucy has been gone for over two weeks now and they're here with a warrant, like we knew they would be.

"Okay," I say. "Be right out."

I flip my book closed and toss it onto my bed, steeling myself for these next few hours, even though we knew it was only a matter of time. We knew they would want to explore every aspect of her, peeling back her privacy and poking around. Sticking their fingers into all of it.

I walk into the living room to find everyone else already there: Sloane and Nicole on the couch, side by side, with Detective Frank standing in the center. There are a few officers with him, eyes perusing the room. The place is practically empty now, most of our belongings sealed up in boxes, but we tried to clean up as best we could, anticipating their arrival. We've been watching the news.

"I'm going to be straight with you," Frank says, eyes on me as I walk to the couch and take a seat next to Nicole. "Your roommate's last known activity was right here, in this house, two days before her employer called and reported her missing."

I think of us in this room again, smoke whirling around as Lucy picked up that knife, my reflection gleaming in the metal. The way she had gotten up and gone outside, leaving her phone behind. I know they're going to find it today. It's dead now, it's been dead for a while, stashed under her bed, beneath her clothes, just like we planned.

"So I'm going to ask one more time," he continues, shifting his weight from one leg to the other. "If you know where your friend is, you need to tell us."

"We don't know where she is," Sloane says, practically pleading, but it's all an act. I know it's an act. We've rehearsed this so many times. "We weren't concerned before but we're worried now, too, okay? We've been trying to call, but—"

"But her phone is off," he interrupts. "Or dead. We know."

"You said you questioned her about Levi," Nicole says. "Maybe she took off because she didn't know what else to do. She acts tough, but she's only human like the rest of us."

Detective Frank looks at Nicole for a beat too long, bored with her monologue.

"She was probably terrified," she adds weakly.

"You know, the more we learn about Lucy, the more questions we have," he says, ignoring her. "Does that surprise any of you?"

"No," I say when it becomes clear that Sloane and Nicole aren't going to answer. "That sounds about right."

"How exactly did you all meet?"

"She's very outgoing," Sloane says. "She's never had a problem approaching people she doesn't know, striking up a conversation."

"And charming," Nicole adds. "She can make friends with a wall."

"Did you see Lucy spending any time with Levi alone on the night he died?" Detective Frank asks, shifting gears so quick it takes me a second to catch up.

"No," I say at last, remembering the way he had stood up and immediately stumbled, legs limp and loose like a wobbly fawn. The way Lucy had looked at me, smiling, before she got up, too. "It was a big party. He was there, but we only saw glimpses of him."

"Glimpses," he repeats.

"Yes. We didn't really hang out with him."

"Who did you hang out with?"

"Each other," I say, as if that should have been obvious.

"That's not what I heard from other people who were there."

"You didn't ask about other people."

Detective Frank stares at me, put off by my tone.

"You asked about us," I add.

"What is that supposed to mean?"

"It means I don't know what other people saw," I continue. "But *we* didn't see them alone together."

"So you never saw them hugging, touching, nothing like that?"

"No, never."

"Interesting," he says. "Then why did we find her blood on his clothes?"

CHAPTER 30

BEFORE

I wake up to find my bed empty, nothing but the still-warm imprint of Nicole by my side. I glance at the clock, it's almost eleven, before flinging myself from bed and walking into the living room.

"Good morning," Lucy says, a mug of coffee in her hands, chipper as ever. They're all out here, all three of them, Sloane and Nicole looking as miserable as I feel. "You doing okay?"

"Yeah," I say, even though that's not quite true. I fell asleep eventually, the dawn-lit windows making my room just light enough for me to finally relax, but the events of last night have left me exhausted, a weariness in my mind that even six hours of sleep couldn't erase.

"Did you get sick?" Sloane asks, looking up at me. She's still in her makeup from last night, a swipe of mascara streaked across her cheek and a single gold hoop still stuck in her ear. "It smelled like puke in here this morning."

"Not sick," I say, glancing at Nicole. She's staring into her lap, skin tinged green and body swallowed by Trevor's sweatshirt, fingers pulling at the sleeves. "Just . . . scared, I guess."

"She was all paranoid about people breaking into the house," Lucy says, laughing. The sound of it grates on me, especially considering how afraid I was, but I try not to show it. "I basically had to force her inside."

"That explains why you disappeared," Sloane says, smiling. "Kind of an intense atmosphere for your first time."

"First time with what?" Nicole asks, Sloane and Lucy turning to look at her like they forgot she was there. She seems so small like that, bent into a ball in the corner of the couch, and it brings to mind the way she looked last night: curled up on the floor like a baby bird, wet and trembling, after tumbling out of a tree. I wonder if she even remembers me cleaning her up, tucking her in. Lying awake for over an hour to make sure she wouldn't get sick again and choke to death in her sleep.

"Molly," Lucy says. "I was an idiot and gave her a whole pill."

That explains the euphoria, then. The overwhelming sense of love I felt as I looked at all of them around that fire, dreamily pondering the possibility of Levi and me living together in perfect harmony. What is it about Lucy, I wonder, that causes us all to simply do as she asks? I hadn't even questioned her about what that pill was. I didn't even hesitate. I just saw the way she was looking at me, all eager and expectant, and tipped my head back. Hoped for the best.

"Speaking of disappearing, where the hell were *you*?" Sloane asks, directing the question at Nicole now. I walk to the couch and take a seat beside her, making sure to leave a little room between us.

"I don't even know," she says at last. She's holding a cup of coffee, too, but it's completely full, quivering in her hands. "I went over there early, right after class, and started drinking too fast. I think I was with Trevor the whole night."

"Not the whole night," Lucy says, putting her empty mug on the floor. "He was outside for a little."

"Maybe—" She stops, bunching her eyebrows like she's trying to remember something. I watch the side of her face as she swallows, shakes her head gently. "Maybe I fell asleep. But somehow, I got home. I woke up in Margot's room."

Lucy flings her head back and laughs again, clapping her hands together. This is our normal morning ritual—recounting stories from the night before, bleary and bashful, amused at all the little things we could hardly remember—but right now, it doesn't feel like it normally does. There's a darkness to it, a creeping dread like marbled clouds gathering before another summer storm. There were too many things about last night that went wrong and I watch as Lucy and Sloane get up, making their way into the kitchen for more coffee, but Nicole is still sitting, staring. Her eyes on the couch in a way that feels the opposite of focused—like she's no longer trying to remember something, but instead, trying to forget.

"Are you okay?" I whisper once the others are gone. She still has her wrists covered with her sweatshirt and I try to remember the look of those bruises I saw—unless they weren't actually bruises at all. It could have been a trick of the light, maybe. A cluster of shadows; a smudge of makeup. It's tempting to believe that, but still, there was something about them that felt eerily familiar. Something about the placement like five large fingers that makes my stomach twist. "Nicole?"

I reach out to touch her leg, my hand barely grazing the skin when she winces, a physical recoil that makes me yank it straight back.

"Sorry," I say, alarm creeping into my chest. "Sorry, it's just . . . are you—?"

"I'm fine," she says, placing her cup on the coffee table and pushing it away like it's something repulsive. "Sorry, I'm fine."

"Are you sure?" I nudge. "Last night—"

"Last night was a shitshow," she says, finally turning to face me. "Honestly, I'm embarrassed."

"You shouldn't be embarrassed," I say. "But when I found you this morning, I thought I saw bruises . . ."

"Oh, yeah." She laughs, rolling her eyes and pushing up her sweatshirt, the blue from before already morphing into a deep, plum purple. "I vaguely remember Trevor trying to help me walk at one point, holding my arms. I bruise so easily."

I try to picture it: Trevor grabbing her forearms, guiding her forward, not unlike the way my own fingers dug into her armpits as I yanked her up off the floor and got her in bed. For the first time, I wonder if I left bruises on her, too. I wonder if I'm capable of leaving that kind of mark, evidence of the way I had hoisted her up, clawed at her skin. The dead weight of her almost impossible to hold. I feel a small relief flood into my chest when I remember the time her thigh slammed into the coffee table last month, leaving behind a welt the size of a baseball. The time she tripped in the shed, smacked her shin, and spent three weeks slapping away Lucy's hand every time she tried to poke at the pooling blood with her finger. That maniacal laugh and devious grin.

"Thanks for being worried," she says at last, cracking a smile, though it doesn't really reach her eyes, "but I promise, I'm fine. Remind me to eat dinner the next time we go out."

CHAPTER 31

It's unnaturally cold the week leading up to Thanksgiving, the temperature dropping into the forties every time the sun dips down. Everything has felt so stilted since Halloween, so strange, and I can't help but feel like some cataclysmic change took place that I haven't picked up on. A tectonic shifting, the very ground no longer solid, but trembling. Threatening to buckle beneath us all.

The day after the party, Trevor and Nicole got into a blowout fight: screaming, crying, Nicole slamming her way out of his room and charging past the rest of us before barreling back into the house. Of course, we chased right after her, asked what was wrong, but she never told us. Never even came close. They made up hours later—they always do—but every time we're all together now, the tension is so thick, so heavy, it's almost unbearable. The weight of it all like an anvil on the chest; a crushing mass that makes it hard to breathe.

"She needs to move on," Lucy says to me now, the two of us making our way out back. The weeds have gotten out of hand this week, the grass calf-high, scratchy against my exposed ankles. "I mean, seriously. It needs to stop. I'm honestly relieved she's gone."

Lucy had convinced me to stay on campus over Thanksgiving break. *"It'll feel like summer all over again,"* she'd said, crisscross on my bed, making me yearn for those twelve perfect weeks that suddenly felt so far away. In truth, I had been dreading going home to my parents, anyway. Dreading their inevitable questions about my major and whether or not I still wanted to keep it; their nosy inquiries about my new life, new friends, sniffing around for some small detail for them to pick apart. I've told them virtually nothing about my roommates—I haven't wanted to taint them, *this,* this thing I have that finally feels so blissfully removed from my life back home—so while Sloane left this morning, Nicole two days ago, I hung back, settled in.

Starting tonight, it's just me and Lucy for one entire week.

"What do you think happened?" I ask, trying to pry information instead of share it myself. I haven't told anyone about how I found Nicole that night: dress slipped off in the hallway, hair caked with vomit and stuck to the side of her neck. She explicitly asked me not to just before Sloane and Lucy came back from the kitchen. She said she didn't want to deal with Lucy's jokes about her being a lightweight, said she just wanted to forget, so I had nodded, agreed, and kept my mouth shut. Because her story made sense. I could see it so vividly: Trevor's fingers digging into her wrists, pulling her down the fraternity halls. Trying to separate her from the rest of the party once he realized she drank too much. Maybe she got sick on his shirt and that's why he wasn't wearing one; maybe that's what their fight was all about—but lately, I've started to feel the emergence of a new feeling in my chest. The same feeling I had when I watched Eliza stomach-down on her bed, knowing that Levi was just outside, watching her in the dark. The same feeling that flared up every time she strutted down the dock, played with her bathing suit.

The same feeling that's screaming at me right now, flailing its arms. Begging me to acknowledge that something's not right.

"Oh, I know exactly what happened," Lucy responds as she slaps away a bug on her arm. "She got shitfaced on Halloween and Trevor got mad because the president's girlfriend shouldn't be acting like that."

"That seems a little harsh," I say.

"Yeah, well, that's how it is with them. He gets jealous, too. She's flirty when she drinks."

I open my mouth, then immediately close it, still not sure how much to say.

"But if she breaks up with Trevor, we lose the house," Lucy continues. "The president picks the tenants. We'll all be homeless."

"I don't think she's going to break up with Trevor," I respond, even though Lucy is right. Nicole's the whole reason we got this place.

"You sure about that?"

"No," I admit. "But it doesn't really seem like Trevor's the thing she's so upset about."

"What do you mean?" she asks as we approach the shed, double doors shut tight. "What else would it be?"

I hesitate, my mind on another memory. The same one that flared up on Halloween as I held Nicole's body in the dark, staring at those grapelike bruises clustered around her wrist. The one I had tried to push down, tried to forget.

I think of Levi leaving the shed, that haunted look on his face.

I think of Nicole half naked on the floor, fetal and broken. The way she tried to fight me off when I touched her, her pathetic little limbs pushing into mine and her voice so fragile. Those single-syllable words flopping off her tongue like they were too heavy for her mouth to hold.

"No. Stop."

Once again, there's just something about Levi, and it isn't even how he had been on our property before I found her, having free rein of our home like that night at Eliza's. It isn't even the way those bruises had been on her wrist, of all places, sending a sharp pain through my chest like a knife to the heart. It's that I've noticed, ever since Halloween, that Nicole and Levi hardly even look at each other anymore. It's not like they ever really had a friendship before—Nicole listened to me when I told her those stories about Eliza, his watching, what happened between them on the night she died—and after that, she always kept her distance, albeit pleasantly, politely, such is Nicole. But now, it isn't just her staying away. It's *him*, too. A mutual ignoring that feels deliberate on both their parts.

Like something happened between them they equally want to forget.

"I've just been thinking—" I start, but before I can finish, I open the shed and jump straight back, my hand shooting to the base of my neck. "Jesus, that's *disgusting*."

In front of us, a dead deer hangs from a rope on the ceiling, bubblegum tongue lolled out to the side and a steady stream of blood flowing into a floor grate I've never once noticed.

"They must've gone hunting," Lucy says, unperturbed, watching curiously as the carcass sways. "It's finally cold enough."

I suddenly remember the way the shed smelled the very first time I stepped inside: that metallic tang, like something decayed, that has since become as commonplace as the vanilla perfume dabbed behind Lucy's ear, Nicole's peppermint shampoo pushed into the pillows. I barely even notice it anymore, the smell of death. The odor of rust and rot that's always there, airborne, stained into the place.

"They're bleeding it," she observes, tilting her head, her eyes following that thin trickle of red. "I wonder if we can convince them to make us dinner."

"No, thank you."

"You've never had venison before?"

"No."

"You should try it. It's good."

"I don't know," I say, staring into its pupils. Seeing myself in the inky reflection before forcing myself to look away. "It feels a little different when you look into its eyes before eating it."

Lucy just shrugs, continues walking.

"Who else is here this week?" I ask as we skirt our way around the interior walls. The deer keeps turning as we move; a slow, somber circle.

"Lucas, Trevor, James, Will," she says. "They're all local so they're just going home for the day."

"That's it?"

"A couple of pledges," she adds, deliberately not looking at me. "They always make a few of them stay behind to take care of the house."

"Which ones?" I ask, suddenly more alert. We're almost to the back door now, the faint eruption of laughter leaking through the windows. The scrutiny of the deer on my back making the little hairs on my neck stand up straight.

"Levi," she says. "I'm pretty sure I saw his Jeep out front."

I stop, barely a few feet from the door now, and Lucy twists around, annoyance on her face.

"Look, I know you don't like him, but you can't hide in your room every time he comes around. You were here first."

"I know," I say, biting my lip.

"You're going to have to learn to ignore him."

"It's not that easy."

"Why not?"

"I don't know," I say. "Being around him just makes me feel guilty."

"Because of Eliza?" she asks, and for a second, I forget to breathe, hearing Eliza's name on her lips for the very first time jarring something loose in me I didn't even know was there. It feels so strange, listening to her say it so casually like that. Like bumping into someone you know in a place you don't expect them. Seeing them ripped from one world and dropped into another, notably out of place.

"Yes," I say at last. "Because of Eliza."

And that's the problem, really: Lucy and Eliza should exist on two totally different planes. They shouldn't be intersecting like this, over and over again, the two lives I've created that were meant to be parallel now painfully perpendicular.

"Why do you feel guilty?" she asks, taking a step closer. Her hand reaching out, fingers wound around mine.

I think back to that night, those videos. Levi's arm around her neck, his body hanging off her shoulders. Eliza tilting her head back in a drunken howl and the light of the moon reflecting off the water. The crash of the waves so far below.

"There are just things I wish I had done differently," I say at last.

I think of the way I had watched them, over and over and over again, restarting from the beginning every time I reached the end. It was a punishment, blinking my bleary eyes in the dark. Like popping that blister, savoring the sting, something sick I forced myself to do for reasons I still don't fully understand. I remember the disbelief, the anger. The frustration that she could be so stupid after everything we knew about him; everything we had learned.

I remember navigating to my contacts, finding her name. My

finger hovering, ready to call. Ready to pick her up, maybe. Bring her home and tuck her in bed . . . followed by the spite in my chest when I thought about how she went there without me. The wound ripping open when I just wanted it to heal.

So instead, I put my phone down, silenced it completely.

I rolled over in bed, closed my eyes, and tried, so hard, to forget about it all. To forget about her, to forget that *feeling* that was growing in my chest, instead swallowing it down so it sat in my stomach. Putrid and sour, coating my tongue.

Poisoning me from the inside out.

CHAPTER 32

"Happy Thanksgiving," Lucas says. "It's better than turkey, I promise."

I look down at the plate in front of me, a small circle of steak with a puddle of gore leaking out around it. The scoop of mashed potatoes layered beneath has already turned soggy and pink, the brassy aroma of it all tingling my tongue. I made the mistake of walking into the kitchen earlier just as James was slamming a wooden mallet onto the meat, microscopic specks of red spraying the cabinets.

"Tenderizing it," he'd said, oblivious to the little drip making its way down his cheek.

There's blood on the ceiling now, pinpricks of plasma misting the stucco. I take a sip of my water, shrugging off the thought.

"Thank you, boys," Lucy croons, lifting up a glass of wine. We set the table earlier for the first time since I've lived here, a mismatched collection of plates and silverware gathered from secondhand stores and left behind by previous tenants. Wildflowers from the backyard soaking in juice glasses and the overhead lights dulled down low. There's a handful of flickering wicks between us, skinny candelabras making the dining room look gothic and dim. "What would we do without you?"

"Starve to death," Trevor responds, pulling out the chair beside me. Thanksgiving is tomorrow, and while the locals are going home for a formal dinner with their families in the morning, they've agreed to do a Friendsgiving-style one with us tonight. Lucy had begged them, really, making them feel guilty about the two of us being here by ourselves, even though we chose it.

"That's not fair," I say. "We made the sides."

I try not to look at Levi as he takes his seat across from me, our table of seven feeling a little too intimate in the subdued light. As much as I hate to admit it, though, Lucy was right. Despite the fact that Levi is here, this past week has been wonderful, the way we've all slipped back into our summer selves. Lucas is still as much fun without Sloane as the object of his affection and I've gotten to know Will and James from the night at Penny Lanes better, too. Trevor is just as obnoxious without Nicole, but he's paid me more attention these last few days than he ever has before.

"Which one did you make?" Trevor asks, turning toward me now. I feel a flush of something in my chest under his eyes, a crawling heat that makes me uncomfortable.

"The mac and cheese," I say.

"How did you know mac and cheese was my favorite?"

Lucy clears her throat, shooting me a look from across the table that I don't like. It's suggestive, eyebrows raising, and I try to signal back a bulge-eyed innocence, communicating that I'm just as confused about his attention as she is.

"Which one of you do we have to thank for shooting our

dinner?" I ask, picking up my silverware, attempting to divert the conversation from me.

"James," Lucas says, slapping him on the shoulder. "Never seen such a clean kill in my life."

I look up, stunned at the image of James, of all people, being the one to pull the trigger. The shyest of them all, so kind and quiet.

"Beginner's luck," he says, sawing into his steak.

Lucy lets out a laugh and I glance over to find her palm cupped tight over her mouth, the corners of a smile peeking out like she's fighting to contain it.

"I'm sorry," she says, removing her hand before wiping a drip of wine from her lip. "It's just ironic."

"What is?" James asks, lowering his knife.

"You. Mister Moral Compass killing something because you can."

I think back to that night at Penny Lanes, James chiming in after Lucy asked us that question. Fighting her on it, the Jekyll to her Hyde. The only one brave enough to push back.

"It's for food," he says slowly. "It serves a purpose."

"Risk and reward," Lucy argues. "It's still a living thing. It was alive, now it's dead, and it's all because of you."

"You can't be serious," he says, his hands still holding the silverware, hovering in the air. I glance down at my plate, little threads of meat torn apart by the serrated blade, and force myself to look away. "Humans and animals are two completely different things."

"Sure," Lucy says, taking another sip from her glass before twisting the skinny stem between her fingers. "Although, *morally*, I'd consider that subjective, don't you think?"

We're all quiet, the soft glint of the candles the only movement between us. Lucy smiles again, the glass lip hovering just beneath her mouth, warm breath fogging up the reflection.

"Not so straightforward, is it?"

We gather in the living room after dinner is over, candles reduced to nubs of wax and bottles of wine lying empty on the floor. Lucy keeps trying to talk us into playing Spin the Pin with one of them, but they're half-hearted attempts, more in jest than anything. For the first time in a long time, she actually seems drunk like the rest of us, maybe too drunk, her body slumped over the couch and her bare legs draped across Levi's lap.

"Truth or dare," she says, twirling around a puddle of wine in her glass. There's a crescent of lipstick stuck to the rim and I wonder if she snuck into her room to apply it after dinner. She wasn't wearing any earlier. I'm almost positive she wasn't.

"Lucy, enough," Lucas says, flipping through a pile of old records in the corner. "We're not doing that shit right now."

"Levi's a pledge, so he has to," she taunts, leaning up so her flushed chest is facing him, practically sitting in his lap.

I watch as Levi glances at Trevor like a child looking for an escape, but Trevor only shrugs, his eyes red and worn.

"She's not wrong."

The entire room is silent again, bated breath as we stare at Lucy, wondering what she has in mind. A single sentence from her has the power to change an entire night's dynamic, alter the very air between us, and I try not to overanalyze how she's clearly singled Levi out again, almost all of her attention directed at him like that night at Penny Lanes.

I wonder what she's doing, what this new game is, the way she plopped down right beside him on the couch, her legs kicked up on his lap and her fingernails trailing their way down his arm. If she really doesn't find anything wrong with the way she's acting or if there's something more to it. Something I can't yet see.

"Fine, truth," Levi says, downing his drink. Lucy reaches for the open bottle on the floor but he holds his hand over his glass and shakes his head. I hear a faint scratch from the corner of the room, Lucas setting a record on the turntable and lowering the needle down.

"What are you afraid of more than anything?" she asks, resting her head in her hand. "Anything in the whole world?"

A long, dense silence packs the room—the kind that makes it feel like there's cotton in my ears, drowning the sound—before the hazy hum of Janis Joplin trickles into all of us.

"Heights," Levi says at last, looking into his drink like he's studying something hidden in the bottom. "I'm afraid of heights."

I stare at him, trying to decide if this is some kind of sick joke, and without warning, his words summon her again: Eliza, materializing out of nowhere. Sitting beside Levi with her hand on his thigh, her eyes on mine.

A single trickle of blood, skinny and serpentine, snaking its way out of her mouth.

"And small spaces," he adds, making me blink. "I'm kind of claustrophobic."

Trevor clears his throat, like he's trying to mask a laugh, and I look over at him smiling into his cup. I can see it in Lucas, too, and James and Will and even Lucy: some unsaid thing bouncing around the room, pinging off all of them.

"Heights and small spaces," she echoes as she finishes her drink. "Good to know."

CHAPTER 33

Lying in bed, staring at the ceiling, it feels like I've traveled back in time to two years ago. To that night in my bedroom, my phone alight in the dark, watching my best friend play with fire while I stayed wrapped in the cool safety of my duvet, wound around me like a fiberglass blanket. Looking at Eliza and Levi on that screen felt like looking through someone else's window and seeing something I shouldn't, something dangerous: a child in the kitchen reaching for the knife block. Little fingers fiddling with the safety of a loaded gun.

Watching, waiting, wondering what would happen.

Knowing, deep down, how it would end.

We had always been so different, Eliza and me, but that's the reason we worked so well. Without her incessant nudging, her never-ending efforts to get me to go out, do something spontaneous, I never would have left the house—but without me around to constantly reel her back in, remind her of her own mortality, she never would have come back.

And then, that night, she didn't.

Now, sitting in the living room and staring at Lucy, it's like

I'm looking at a carbon copy of all those nights together, fuzzy and fading and just different enough to let me know that this is real. This really is happening: Lucy's legs stretched across Levi like a seat belt, pinning him back, long and lean and smooth under his touch. The way she laughs when he talks, twirling a curl around her finger the same way Eliza used to tinker with that pen in her bedroom, suck on her diamond necklace. Kicking her legs, biting her lip. Anything to get him to look.

I suppose I shouldn't be surprised, Eliza and Lucy being as similar as they are. Even when I talked about Eliza that first night on my bed, Lucy had a wariness to her, an obvious envy emanating from her eyes like she felt the need to compete with someone already in the grave. Eliza loved the danger and Lucy does, too, so maybe the idea of dangling herself in front of someone who might lash out and bite, someone who already *has,* makes him all the more appealing. A danger so palpable she can taste it every time he gets close, like metallic on your tongue just before lightning strikes.

I keep turning it over in my mind, trying to understand it, when I hear a noise from outside. The same muffled movement I heard on Halloween: a slapping door, a gentle scraping. Someone clearing their throat.

I sit up, listening quietly before climbing out of bed and turning on my light. Just like last time, it sounds too close to be coming from the yard—but it's not coming from inside the house, either. I open my door and tiptoe into the hallway, glancing into the bathroom, just in case.

It's empty, like I knew it would be: no Nicole on the tile, loose limbs at harsh right angles. The heave of bile trying to claw its way out.

"Lucy?" I whisper, walking to her room next. The door is shut, the way it usually is, and I think about knocking, but instead, I just place my hand on the knob and twist. "Luce, do you hear that?"

Her room is partially illuminated by the glow of the moon through the curtains, those neon stars alight on the ceiling, and almost immediately, I see that it's empty.

"Lucy?" I ask again, opening the door wider, even though she's clearly not here. Her comforter is flung back, an imprint of where her body once was on the mattress. A single pillow housing the shape of her head. I resist the urge to step in farther, instead closing the door again and making my way into the living room, perching myself on the edge of the couch.

I think back to earlier in the night, when the boys were leaving. I had stood up, collected our glasses, a silent cue that the evening was over. Lucy acted like she was heading to bed, too, hands on her hips, yawning in the hallway. Watching until they all filed out the back door, into the shed, and disappeared into the dark.

Unless, of course, she was waiting for me to shut myself in before she left, too.

But if Lucy went next door, who would she have gone with? In the months we've lived together, I've never once seen her spend the night anywhere other than here. It can't be Trevor, surely. Judging by the way she looked at me at dinner, eyes on mine as he worked his charm, she would never go home with our roommate's boyfriend . . . although I do remember her laughing about it the day I moved in, teasing Nicole as she tossed the pillow in her direction.

"If you don't want him, I'll take him. I'm not going to apologize for introducing you to the most beautiful boy on campus."

Maybe, once I left, Trevor had stayed, lingering in the yard before walking back inside, convincing Lucy to head home with him, too. She was drunk tonight, more so than usual, but it still doesn't feel like the kind of thing Lucy would do. It's definitely not Lucas—she always acts so annoyed at his immaturity, his silly sense of humor—and she couldn't care less about Will or James. She hardly even talks to them.

Which only leaves Levi.

"She wouldn't," I whisper, but already, I know that she would. She's just like Eliza: drawn to the risk of him like adrenaline, like pheromones, some chemical reaction that leaves her helplessly high. The fact that he's been dubbed dangerous, off-limits, is only making him more desirable to her, the same way Eliza would flaunt herself in front of her window. The way she was still out with him that night, even after we found the proof of what he did, who he was: the missing picture, her open door. The stomach-churning smell of him everywhere we looked.

I think about going back to my room, getting in bed, trying to forget about it all the same way I tried to forget about those videos on my phone, when I hear a noise again—but this time, it's different. Unmistakable.

This time, it's coming from above. A heavy *thump* like someone walking on the roof.

CHAPTER 34

I run outside and crane my neck, the sky above granite black. There isn't a cloud in sight and the stars look like little pinpricks in fabric, so sharp and clear they take my breath away.

"Hey!" I yell, the sound of my voice making me strangely self-conscious in the otherwise silence of the night. It feels like talking out loud in an empty room, searching for proof you really exist. "Who's up there?"

I hear more shuffling and turn to the right, squinting my eyes, trying to make out shadows in the dark. I still can't see anything so I walk around to the side of the house, angling for a better view, when a figure emerges out of nowhere, like whoever it is was lying flat on their back and suddenly decided to sit up straight.

"Hey," she responds.

"Lucy?"

The voice is unmistakable. It's Lucy up there—maybe alone, maybe not—and I get the distinct feeling I've interrupted something.

"What are you doing?" I ask, walking closer. "How did you get up there?"

"The lattice," she says, leaning back on her hands. I can see the red glow of a cigarette between her fingers, the shadow of her feet bobbing to some undetectable beat. "If you stand on the railing, you can get your foot on the bottom one and climb up."

I glance at the lattice, the jasmine growing around it dormant this time of year, though the leaves are still lush and green, thick vines working their way up the wood like juicy veins on an out-stretched arm.

I grab the nearest stake and shake it, testing its strength.

"Why are you up there?" I ask. "Is there . . . someone with you?"

"No," she says, finally giving me her full attention. I can some-how sense her sitting up straighter, eyes intent on the shadow of me below. "Who else would be up here?"

"I don't know."

I bite my lip, too embarrassed to admit what I was thinking. It was stupid, my own insecurities rearing their ugly head. Not only that: it was impractical, too. Levi wouldn't be up on the roof, not after what he admitted to earlier. He's afraid of heights, apparently. Even though that didn't seem to stop him the last time.

"Just come up," she says after a beat of silence. "It's nice."

I look at the lattice, then back at the roof, my heartbeat thump-ing hard in my chest. This would normally be the kind of thing I'd scoff at—Eliza on the roof, beckoning me up while I rolled my eyes and shook my head, nagged her to come down before she broke her neck—but instead, I hoist myself up and grab the stake to the side, scooting my way over until I find my footing. I can sense Lucy watching me from above, silently observing, and even though the cheap wine coursing through my bloodstream is making every-thing feel a little airy and light, I'm still acutely aware of how high up she is. How flimsy this thing feels beneath my weight, like one wrong step will make me tip back and fall.

"Here," she says, leaning over with an outstretched hand. I'm almost to the roof now, practically parallel to Nicole's second-story window.

"Thanks," I say, grabbing her arm. Feeling her fingers wrap around my wrist as she helps me up. Then, once I feel secure, I push off from the lattice and land on my knees, crawling around to the other side of Lucy, farther away from the edge.

"So," I say once I sit down next to her, palms stinging at my sides. I cross my legs, mirroring her stance, trying to come across as relaxed even though I can still feel my heart beating hard in my chest. "You always come up here in the middle of the night?"

"Sometimes," she says, taking a drag. She offers it to me and I shake my head.

"What do you do?"

"Just sit," she says. "Stare. Think."

We're quiet for a while, no noises between us outside of the suck of Lucy's cigarette: the crackling tobacco, the long exhale. The curl and crisp of the paper and the gentle flick of her fingers, red-hot ash scattering at her feet.

"Why are you awake?" she asks at last, not bothering to look at me. She's staring out at something I can't see, her gaze settled on one of those invisible spots in the distance.

"I don't know," I say, not wanting to reveal the real reason: all those thoughts of her and Eliza, Eliza and her, the two of them dancing around in my mind like the stars of some terrible ballet. "I couldn't fall asleep."

"How come?"

I look at her, the side of her face revealing nothing.

"I heard noises," I say at last. "It was you, I guess, although it didn't sound like it was coming from above before." I look back ahead, the realization just now dawning on me. "It sounded like it was coming from below."

That's why those noises were so odd, so hard to pin down: they weren't coming from inside or outside, but somewhere else entirely. Both and neither at the exact same time.

"Did you hear it on Halloween, too?" she asks. "The noises?"

"Yeah, actually. I did."

I think back to those strange sounds that had lured me out of bed: the rustling, the cough. That fast slap of a door opening and closing again. I had forgotten all about them once I stumbled across Nicole on the tile, all my attention focused on her, and I watch as Lucy sucks down the last of her cigarette and flicks it off the roof, the tip of it sailing like a firefly in the night. She lies flat on her back as she blows the smoke out, a single fat cloud funneling into the air.

"Levi wasn't in the house that night," she says at last. "Not technically, at least."

"What do you mean?" I turn my head to look at her, trying to understand, though she just continues to stare at the sky.

"He was in the cave."

"The cave?" I ask, my eyes flicking across her face. They're starting to get adjusted now, just enough to see the inky outline of her features in the dark: the gentle slope of her nose, the jut of her chin. "What's the cave?"

"The basement."

"This house has a *basement*?" I ask. "I didn't think houses around here could have basements. The water table—"

"Yeah, too high, I know," she says. "Less of a basement and more of a crawl space, then. You can't even stand up in there."

"What was he doing in our crawl space?"

"It's stupid," she says, finally rolling her head to look at me, the wet whites of her eyes glistening in the dark. "It's a part of their pledgeship. All the freshmen have to spend a certain number of hours down there before they're initiated."

"You're not serious," I say, but as I think back to Halloween, it actually makes sense. I picture the blond boy first, the one in the dress, coming out to the fire before gesturing to our house like he was on his way there—then shaking his head, pursing his lips. Realizing, perhaps, who he was talking to. What he shouldn't say. Levi next and how he looked so haunted, so scared, stuttering to find an explanation to defend his presence.

His eyes landing on the fire, finally, and then to Trevor. That sick look on his face like he had turned feral.

"You doin' okay, man? You look a little pale."

"What do they do?" I ask.

"Just lie there," she says. "It's too narrow to do anything else. I've seen it before. It's literally a hole, like being buried alive."

My mind wanders back to Levi again, that tortured expression, and I wonder how long he had been down there before he came barreling back out, running through the shed, eyes wide and full of terror. An hour, maybe two, body rigid in the dark as he listened to the sound of his own heart in his ears. His own rushing blood. The feeling of little legs crawling across his skin as he opened his eyes only to see the vast expanse of nothing staring back.

"Extra cruel to do it to a guy who claims to be claustrophobic," she adds.

That's why Trevor had been laughing tonight. Hearing Levi admit that, his fear of small spaces, and knowing what he was forcing him to do.

"They think it's some big secret but Trevor told me when he

was drunk," Lucy continues, and I think back to that night at Penny Lanes, her finger tracing its way around the rim of her cup. Her listening, the rest of us talking, spilling our secrets like she slit us right open.

I suddenly wonder how much she knows about people. I wonder what all she's heard.

"The next morning, he made me promise not to tell anyone," she continues. "If Rutledge found out, they'd definitely get disbanded."

"Why would anyone agree to do that?" I ask. "It's . . ."

"Degrading?" she interrupts. "Disgusting? It's because they're desperate."

"Desperate," I repeat.

"Desperate to *belong*."

She says it like a slur, like something to be ashamed of, but for the first time since I've known him, I can see the smallest piece of myself in Levi: so eager to be a part of something, to be accepted, that you make yourself do things that you would otherwise never do. Sucking on the wrong end of a cigarette, tobacco grit burning hot on your tongue; eating old pizza off the floor or letting a drug dissolve into your bloodstream just because someone placed it in your palm and held your hand tight. It's no different than what I did to get here, really: agreeing to live with three strangers I knew nothing about. Blindly going along with whatever they said, whatever they did, like if I faked it hard enough, I'd be one of them.

"Trevor says it *bonds them*." She laughs. "Like trauma bonding."

"That's fucked up," I say.

"Yeah. It's just a matter of time before something happens."

I turn to her again, eyes narrowing, waiting for her to continue.

"There's a little door on the side of the house you open to get into it, behind the azaleas, but if it closes all the way and latches from the outside, you're stuck in there. This house is not up to code," she adds. "It's too old."

I hear those noises again in my mind, so distinct in the dark: a sliding door, a body scraping against something as it shimmied itself inside. A cleared throat, a dry cough. Settling in before the awful, endless waiting.

"They leave it cracked open when they're in there, but . . . you know. Accidents happen. One little push and you're trapped."

I'm quiet, my heart beating hard in my throat. Thinking of Levi on Halloween; his bare chest, scratched and bleeding, like jagged fingernails cutting across the skin.

"Did you mean it?" Lucy asks me suddenly, twisting her neck so she's facing me again. "What you said on Halloween? In the kitchen?"

It takes a second for me to realize what she's referring to, but then it returns to me slowly, like recalling a dream. It's been living quietly between us for the last four weeks, really, my admission curled up like a hibernating animal. Neither of us wanting to poke it awake, acknowledge its presence. Talk about those words I had muttered as my body trembled cold in the kitchen; Lucy feeding me water, baby sips in the dark. It had barely been conscious, the thought ejecting itself from my mind like an exorcism: demonic and violent, completely out-of-body. I just had to get it out, the terrible belief that had been living inside me for far too long.

"I wish it was him. It should have been him."

"Of course I meant it," I say at last. And I expect to feel ashamed afterward, maybe even embarrassed. I expect to feel disgust or surprise but instead I feel lighter the second I say it, like the thought itself had been tied around my ankle. A ball and chain weighing me down. "Eliza didn't deserve to die like that. Levi did."

CHAPTER 35

AFTER

I can feel the collective intake of breath, all three of us sucking it in. This is a detail we hadn't accounted for, a fuzzy memory we had forgotten all about.

Lucy's blood, Levi's clothes.

We can work with this, though. We can use it to our advantage if we play it right.

"How do you know it's Lucy's?" I ask at last, remembering the way it had dripped from her finger like a leaky faucet, little red spots polka-dotting the floor. Detective Frank can clearly tell he caught us off guard, a satisfied smile emerging on his lips.

"Her parents provided DNA samples for us to compare it to," he says, his eyes trained on me now. Me, and only me. "It was a match."

I rub my temples, the idea of it all so hard to grasp.

"They want to see their daughter found just as much as the rest of us," he adds.

"I'm sure they do," Sloane snaps, her voice sarcastic and sharp.

"What's important here is we know your friend was with Levi Butler the night he died and we know they were in close enough proximity for her blood to get on his clothing," Frank says, growing impatient. "Why was she bleeding, girls?"

The moment flashes through my mind again and suddenly, we're back together, all four of us, the citrus sky giving everything an unnatural glow. It had felt like another dream, another bad trip, Lucy's hand bleeding in such a steady, rhythmic drip that the sound of her blood hitting the floor reminded me of the second hand of a ticking clock, strangely soothing in the silence.

I see her lift her finger to her lips, eyes on mine as she sucked it dry.

"Did he hurt her?"

"No," Sloane says, and I blink out of the memory. "It wasn't like that."

"Did he hurt any of you?"

We're all quiet, hands wringing nervously in our laps.

"We know this boy's background," Frank says, eyes darting back over to me again. "You can tell us."

"It wasn't like that," she repeats.

"The marks on his body . . . they weren't natural. This wasn't just some accident—"

"You heard her," I interrupt, realizing too late that my fingers are digging into my palms so hard the thin skin is starting to sting. I release my grip and wipe the sweat from my hands, placing them on my lap to hide the little crescents left behind by my nails. "It wasn't like that. And we don't know where she is."

The room falls into a heavy silence and Detective Frank just stands there, waiting for us to fill it, even though he knows, by now, that we'll only refuse. Finally, he exhales, looking at the officers still standing behind him and jerking his head toward her bedroom door before turning his attention back at us.

"Well, all right," he says, chubby fingers back in his belt loops. "If that's the way it's gonna be, I'm going to need you girls to wait outside while we search."

CHAPTER 36

BEFORE

We've been in a state of comfortable quiet since Lucy told me about the cave, Levi, that secret thing they do when the four of us are fast asleep.

It feels strange now, thinking about it: all those nights I had been lying in bed, closing my eyes, not even knowing there was another body beneath me. Their hidden presence like a fifth roommate I never knew we had. But now that I'm in on it, now that I know, it's hard to imagine I didn't somehow feel the company of another person down there. That I didn't pick up on the reason I always felt so cold, that underground pocket of concrete and dirt drafting into my bedroom, emitting through the floor.

That I didn't feel their nervous energy, hear their shallow breaths. Pick up the panicked beating of their pulse beneath the floorboards, shrill and haunting. My very own telltale heart.

"That guy from the fire," Lucy says to me now, breaking the silence. "His name is Danny DeMarcus. I do know him. He went to my high school."

I roll over to my side, curled up in a ball like we're lying in bed and not on rigid asphalt, shingles rough beneath the weight of us.

"Danny DeMarcus," I repeat, remembering him from Halloween. The blond boy in the blue dress who had plopped down next to us, striking up that conversation Lucy desperately didn't want to have. He had been so insistent, so sure he was right, and Lucy had just brushed him off the way she always does, asserting ignorance. But still. I had seen something different in her expression that night. I knew she was lying.

"I guess I just prefer for people around here not to know about my past," she says, rolling over to face me, too. "I wanted a fresh start. I figured you'd understand."

"Yeah," I say, nodding, hand under my head like a pillow. "I understand."

"There are things from back then I didn't want to bring with me."

I'm quiet, not knowing how to respond, Lucy's eyes on mine like she's waiting for me to say something next.

"It was such a shitty school," she continues when the silence stretches on for a beat too long. "There were nine people in my graduating class. *Nine.* I would go years without meeting a new person."

I think of Eliza and me, just like this, two years ago: the hard wood beneath us, the stars up above. Listening to the cicadas on the dock, reliable like a metronome, steady as a sound machine, their lullaby soothing me into a trancelike state. Nodding vaguely as she talked about all the places she wanted to go, people she wanted to meet, our little town and private school suffocating her like a boa constrictor: the harder she fought, the tighter they squeezed. It was hard not to take it personally.

"I honestly didn't think any of them would go to college, let alone come *here*," Lucy says. "This random little place."

It only dawned on me later, after I arrived at Rutledge, that maybe Eliza actually liked being the biggest fish in a small, simple sea, despite her grand plans. The things that she said. She had picked this school, after all. She could have gone anywhere and I would have followed—but instead, she chose here, another small town where she could outshine us all.

"I just thought I'd never see them again," Lucy continues, and I blink away the memories, focusing back on her. "So when Danny came up to me like that, catching me off guard . . . I don't know. I just lied."

"You never see them around town?" I ask. "When you go home?"

She's quiet, staring at me as she chews on the side of her cheek. For a second, I think she didn't hear me until she rolls back over and faces the sky.

"I don't go home."

I don't understand it, at first, what she's trying to say. She didn't go home for summer, that's true, but I didn't, either. She didn't go home for Thanksgiving, convincing me to stay here with her, keep her company—but slowly, it dawns on me. The quiet confession she's trying to make.

She doesn't go home, ever. She doesn't have a home.

This is her home.

I suppose it shouldn't come as a shock. Lucy has always given off an air of independence, of being on her own. Her parents never seem to pay for anything the way ours do and a sudden sense of naïveté settles over me as I think about Lucy stalking off to Penny Lanes each night, permanent pimples around her hairline from the fryer grease and wet blisters on her heels from Rollerblades that are always half a size too small. Meanwhile, I've been blindly reliant on a direct deposit that appears by some dependable magic on the first of every month: rent, tuition, the very food that feeds me still being doled out by Mom and Dad. I've never seen Nicole want for anything, either—she flashes around her credit card so carelessly it can't possibly be linked to her own account—and Sloane has that job with the registrar, sure, but it feels more like a résumé cushion, the kind of thing she uses not only for the money but as an extra opportunity to do her homework in an air-conditioned office with free coffee and snacks.

Not the kind of job, like Lucy's, that keeps her on her feet all day. The kind of job that relies on tips for cash.

"I don't get along with my mom," she adds after a beat of silence. "Never have."

"I'm sorry—" I say, the raw truth of it all stunning me into silence. It's not the reality of Lucy being untethered that shocks me, a tumbleweed roaming through life by herself. That part actually makes sense in a strange sort of way. It's the admission, the vulnerability of it.

I've learned not to expect this kind of openness from her.

"Don't be," she says. "I'm better off without her."

"Do you ever talk?"

"No." She shakes her head. "I left right after school, figured I'd just come here and get a job and a cheap apartment. I haven't reached out since and she hasn't, either. She doesn't even know where I am."

"And your dad?"

I ask it hesitantly, tender as a tiptoe, the cloak of night making me feel bolder, braver, pushing me to venture into territory I would otherwise run from. But Lucy's showing herself to me right now.

She's telling me things, intimate things, the kinds of things she's always extracting from other people and never revealing herself.

I think of Sloane's voice that morning in her bedroom, dipped down low so nobody else could hear: *"You still don't know anything about her, do you?"* Lucy's usually so bottled up, so tight-lipped, that bearing witness to this version of her that spills her secrets so freely is leaving me gutted, ripped apart like the corpse of that deer once the boys plunged a knife into its ribs and worked their way down. On the one hand, I don't want her to regret this in the morning. I don't want her to wake up, blink her bleary eyes, and think about the things I had pulled out of her in the dark, my nudging questions like a pair of fingers tugging at a piece of yarn. I know these are all things she would never tell me if we were sober. If we hadn't just spent the entire week together, completely alone. If we weren't sitting on top of a roof right now, the nightfall so dark and disorienting, it almost feels like talking to yourself.

But on the other hand, I don't want her to stop.

"He didn't know how bad things were," she says at last.

"Why didn't you just go live with him?"

I wait for her answer, but she's suddenly so quiet, I feel the overwhelming urge to repent. I pushed too hard, pried too much, causing her to shut back down instead of open up further—but just as I'm opening my mouth to apologize again, attempt to reel her back in, she starts to speak.

"I don't need him," she says at last, and I can feel her lean over, her hand holding something silver around her throat. "But he gave me this."

I lean in, too, my nose practically touching her neck, trying to see through the darkness. She's holding a necklace. The same necklace I noticed that day in the dorm, the one I've seen her wear every day since: a silver chain with a cluster of tiny diamonds arranged around her clavicle like a constellation of stars.

"He said it reminded him of me because I was named after that song. Lucy in the sky with diamonds."

"You were named after LSD?" I joke, an attempt to ease the tension. Lucy snorts, punching my shoulder, but I can tell she's smiling.

"That's one interpretation," she says. "But I think it's because of the stars. I've always liked them."

"Yeah, they're nice," I say, somewhat dazed. Thinking of all those stickers on her ceiling. I don't even know what time it is anymore, how long we've been up here. "Eliza and I used to sit outside, too. Try to find the constellations. She had this big telescope we broke out sometimes when it was clear enough to see."

"Do you know any?"

"The Big Dipper," I say. "The Little Dipper."

"Those are easy. Look, there's Orion," she says, pointing into the sky with her finger. Tracing the arms, the legs, the sword, and the belt. "And Taurus. Gemini, the twins."

"Where are the twins? I don't see them."

"Just there."

She grabs my hand from the roof, hers unusually warm in the otherwise chill of the night, and thrusts it into the air above us. Then she uses my own to draw the outline of two figures, arms connected, and I watch as the pattern emerges before my eyes.

"See the two people?" she asks, and suddenly, I do. I can see them so crisp, so clear, it's hard to imagine there was ever a time I didn't. "They're holding hands. Like us."

CHAPTER 37

"What did you guys do when we were gone?"

I'm sitting on Sloane's bed, watching as she folds clean clothes on the floor, though I don't know why she's bothering to unpack. She got back in town this morning and there are only two weeks of classes left until winter break. Pretty soon, she'll just be packing again.

We'll all be packing, preparing ourselves for an entire month apart.

"Just hung out," I say, watching as she pulls a pair of jeans from her duffel. "It was nice."

"*Nice,*" she repeats. "Sounds cryptic."

I think back to that night, Lucy and me, the two of us eventually climbing down the lattice in silence. The way we had crept quietly into the hallway, said our good nights. The silent click of our bedroom doors behind us before we crawled into our respective beds and pulled the covers close.

I think about how I had lain there, reminiscing about our conversation, wondering if she was doing the same. The way I had longed to be alone with her, but at the same time, feared it more than anything.

Maybe it's because Lucy has a way of talking that makes me uncomfortable, her voice burrowing into my skin like an insect, digging in deep and living there quietly. Maybe it's the way she makes people admit things so readily, those eerie eyes that feel borderline hypnotic powerful enough to make your lips part without your permission; to force your arms to stretch out and hand her anything she wants.

Or maybe it's because I've been starting to listen to her, really starting to believe the things she says. Over the summer, the way she spoke of murder at Penny Lanes with such indifference had sent a sharp chill down my spine. It had scared me, that murky moral logic—but in the months since, talking about life and the way I wished things were, the harshness of it all has started to dull like she's been kneading the idea in my mind slowly, gently, until the jagged edges are no longer there.

"It was pretty low-key," I say at last. "We didn't leave the house much."

I wonder now if anyone else knows what I do. If Lucy has told the others about the crawl space, her parents. Held their hands in the dark as she drew pictures in the sky.

"Have you seen Nicole?" Sloane asks, jolting me from my daydream. She says it bored, almost like an afterthought, but I can tell by the way she avoids my eyes that she's curious about my answer.

"Not yet," I say. "I heard her come in earlier, but then she left again."

"She's lost, like, ten pounds."

"In a *week*?"

"Margot, I can see her spine."

I chew on my lip. Nicole has always been skinny, a trait she attributes to genetics and a fast metabolism, but now that I think about it, ever since I found her that night cheek-down on the tile, she's been picking at her food more than eating it.

I think of her holding that mug of coffee in her hands, eyes empty as she pushed it away.

"Do you know what happened?" Sloane asks, looking at me now. "On Halloween?"

"No," I say slowly, hesitantly, remembering the way Nicole had asked me not to tell. "I mean, not really."

"Margot," she says again, eyes trained on mine. "She's my best friend. Please."

I'm quiet, thinking about those bruises on her wrist. The way Nicole's been so different lately, so reserved. The way the dynamic between us all has been so indisputably off. I want to keep my promise to her, but at the same time, this isn't Lucy asking—Lucy, who would never let her live it down. Who would bring it up again and again, using her embarrassment as the butt of some joke. This is *Sloane*.

"I found her," I say before I can change my mind. "Late. After everyone was already asleep."

"What do you mean you *found* her?"

"She was on the floor in my bathroom. She got sick . . . it was pretty bad."

Sloane sighs, stretching her neck, eyes on the ceiling.

"I mean, we knew she was wasted," she says at last. "Lucas told us, right?"

"Yeah, but the next morning, she seemed a little weird."

"What did she say?"

"She didn't say anything," I recount, remembering the way she had flinched, crossed her arms, muttered that apology like she had just snapped out of a daydream. "It's just the way she was acting."

Sloane looks down at the floor again, busying herself with a T-shirt. I watch her fold and refold it—three, four times—trying to work it out in her mind, fit the pieces together.

"Levi was on our property that night," I blurt out, against my better judgment. Not only do I have no idea if Sloane knows about the cave, but I don't have any proof of Levi being anywhere other than inside it all night. If what Lucy told me is true—if he wasn't in the house on Halloween, but instead, below it—then that means he couldn't have done anything to Nicole, anyway . . . unless, of course, he wasn't in the cave at all, a possibility I've been massaging around in my mind ever since I remembered that admission he made on Thanksgiving.

Maybe he had walked through the shed, toward the little door behind the azaleas, but instead of going under the house like he was supposed to, he went in. Maybe it started simple: he didn't want to do it. He was claustrophobic, dreading another night in that cramped little space. He thought nobody was home, that we were all next door, so he decided to go inside and wait it out there. Just lie to the brothers when he came back out.

But he wasn't alone. Nicole was there, the worst possible person.

Nicole, Trevor's girlfriend.

I wonder what he would have thought: seeing her in the house, her big eyes bulging as he walked inside. Nicole was afraid of him already. She had listened to my stories, shuddering as I described the way he broke into Eliza's bedroom. Maybe she thought it was happening all over again and started yelling, calling out for Trevor, and Levi knew that a single slip of the tongue about him coming into our house uninvited, waiting out his hazing on a comfortable couch instead of where he was supposed to be, would lead to him not only getting in trouble, but being kicked out for good. So maybe he had run to her, tried to stop her from screaming as her nails scratched at his chest.

Maybe he had grabbed her wrists, twisting just a little too hard.

"What are you insinuating?" Sloane asks. "Are you saying—?"

"I don't know," I interrupt. "I don't know what I'm saying. Just . . . he was here. That's all."

Sloane looks back down at her laundry, unfolding that same T-shirt. Folding it again. Whatever happened to Nicole that night, Levi is somehow involved. I'm sure of it. I think of those fingerprint bruises and the way they completely ignored each other after, a tension between them that didn't exist before. The fight between Trevor and Nicole the next morning and the way nothing has been the same since. Maybe she tried to tell Trevor and he got jealous, blamed her instead of Levi, the idea of the two of them alone in the house together too much for his brittle ego to take. Or maybe he didn't believe her. Levi is a legacy, after all. Trevor couldn't just kick him out without some kind of solid evidence.

I can practically hear him now, that belittling voice. Commanding and masculine; always right. *You were drunk, Nicole. You don't know what you saw.*

"We need to start locking the doors," I say. "Lucy told me Nicole keeps losing her key, but we can't just leave them open for anyone to come in."

Sloane looks at me, opening her mouth like she's about to tell me off.

"I'm not blaming Nicole," I add, holding up my hands. "That didn't come out right. I'm just saying we need to protect ourselves."

She closes her mouth again and glances down at her lap, fingers working at the seam of a skirt for so long the thread has pulled, unraveling the fabric.

"Yeah, you're right," she says at last, nodding slowly. "We need to protect ourselves."

CHAPTER 38

Finals go by in a sleep-deprived blur: waking up early, slogging to campus, those bleary morning hours desolate and dark despite the string lights wrapped tight around the fronds of the palmetto trees. Entire days spent hunched over textbooks in an always-abandoned corner of the library, underslept and overcaffeinated, my body buried between archaic desktop computers like the only mourner left in a forgotten graveyard.

Saying goodbye is strange once the semester is over and it's finally time for us to all part ways. Maybe it's because we've spent every single day of the last seven months together, suddenly inseparable the way Eliza and I once were: hips attached, finishing each other's sentences. Oftentimes falling asleep in the same bed. So many nights, I wake up with a jolt to the glow of some old movie playing in the background, the sticky sensation of cotton mouth on my tongue. Turning to the side to see the three of them curled around each other like plaited roots, eyelids twitching in the dark and the twinkle of Christmas lights hung haphazard around my bedroom as I'm left wondering what I did to find myself here.

How I've gotten so lucky with this second chance I know I don't deserve.

Or maybe it's because I know, once we all leave, that Lucy will stay. That while the rest of us will be making our way home, four whole weeks getting fattened up with home-cooked meals and spoiled with piles of intricately wrapped presents, Lucy will still be here, alone. Without us. She'll be making her own meals or probably picking up takeout, plastic fork nudging at the leftovers from Penny Lanes. The house will be eerily quiet around her—even Kappa Nu will be empty, every last one of the boys gone, too— and it's such a depressing thought, so un-Lucy-like, picturing her all forsaken and small.

"Are you going to be okay?" I ask now, my hand on the door as I hesitate outside my running car. Exhaust is billowing out as Lucy stands on the porch in sweatpants and bare feet, arms crossed tight against her chest. "Being here by yourself?"

"Margot," she says after a beat of silence, the tip of her nose chapped and pink. "Are you serious?"

"You can come home with me. We'd be happy to have you."

Ever since that night on the roof, her voice raspy and raw as she told me her secret, I've felt the offer threatening to rip right through me so many times before simply swallowing it back down and forcing myself to forget. I know she'll refuse, maybe even get angry at me for feeling an ounce of pity for her, but now that I'm standing here, the last one to leave, it feels wrong to just drive away without saying something.

"I'm touched," she replies, hand over heart, monotone and mocking.

"Really. My parents are . . . I mean, they're parents. They get annoying sometimes. They'll probably interrogate you the second you step inside—"

"You're doing a really great job selling me on this."

"—but at least you won't be by yourself on Christmas," I finish. "Come on, Luce. You don't deserve that. Nobody does."

She hesitates, and for a single second, I imagine her stomping down the steps and wrapping me in a hug, her nose nuzzled tight into my neck and her breath warm on my ear. I picture her sliding into the passenger seat, fiddling with the radio. Bare feet on the dash as she pokes around the cupholders, curious fingers collecting loose change.

Instead, she crosses her arms tighter and leans against the doorframe.

"I want to be by myself," she says at last. "Really, it's fine."

I see the silhouette of my mom in the yard the second I pull onto my street. She's waving frantically, standing on her tiptoes with one long arm flailing in the air while my father hovers behind her with his hands in his pockets, looking uncomfortable.

I haven't seen either of them since last March, nine long months ago, over freshman year spring break. Maggie went on a family vacation to Disney World and everyone else on my hall had apparently planned some trip to the Keys that I only learned about the day before they departed. I would have happily chosen to stay in my room by myself, spending the week catching up on schoolwork or simply watching TV, but Hines was closed during break. All the dorms were. For one fleeting moment, I thought about staying behind anyway, getting locked inside after the RAs left. Roaming the abandoned building like some kind of purgatoried ghost. But I hadn't moved quick enough when Janice came around, poking her head into every room to make sure they were empty.

When she saw me sitting on the futon, eyes wide and faking

innocence, I heard her swear under her breath before walking into our room and hovering while I packed.

"Oh, sweetie," my mother says to me now as I step out of the driver's seat, pulling me in for a hug. She smells the same: a permanent scent of sunscreen seeped into her arms mixed with the perfume my father gifts her each year for Christmas. She's always dropping hints that she wants something different, but every single year, she unwraps it and acts surprised. "Thank God you're here."

"Hey, Mom."

"How were finals?"

"Fine," I say, detaching myself. "I feel good about them."

"You're still wanting to major in English, then?"

I stay quiet, already knowing what she'll say next.

"I'm really not sure about that, Margot. It's not practical, and the longer you wait, the harder it'll be to change it—"

"I like English," I say. "I'm not changing it."

"But what are you going to *do* with that, though?"

"Honey," my dad interrupts. "Let's let her get unpacked first."

"Right, right," my mother says, holding up her hands. "And your friends?" she asks. "They're good?"

"They're good."

I force myself to smile, walking around to the trunk and hoisting a duffel bag out of the back.

"Well, I would hope so, considering they've completely stolen you from us."

"They haven't *stolen* me," I say, pulling the bag over my arm. "I've just been busy."

"You'll tell us all about them," she continues, a command more than a question, before turning around and making her way back toward the house. My father nods at me, his version of a hug, before twisting around and trailing her silently. "Everything there is to know."

Dinner goes by in the way it always does: the clinking of silverware against my mother's best china, the three of us rattling off the kind of sterile small talk you'd expect to overhear at a networking event. It's so vastly different than the family dinners I used to have at Eliza's, I can't help but compare them: the ever-present music filling their house compared to the long, heavy stretches of silence in ours. Their belly laughs and genuine conversation next to our stale, recycled lines. I know there's nothing inherently *wrong* with my parents. They've always loved me, provided for me, given me whatever I've needed and more—it's just that they don't really seem to like each other that much. Their marriage feels like a transaction, purely business, and I am the output of twenty years' worth of work. Maybe that's why my mother hounds me so much about my life, my choices. Why my father always seems to be silently assessing me like I'm a line item in one of his spreadsheets.

I am an investment to them, their only child. If I fail, they fail, and everybody knows it.

My mother leaves my dad to the dishes once we're finished and the two of us walk to my bedroom together, like she's positive I must have forgotten the way. I open the door to find they've left it virtually untouched, the entire space like a time capsule preserving the person I used to be.

"You know, you can donate this stuff," I say as I flip on the lights, scanning it all. The stuffed animals I used to sleep with are still propped on my bed like they've been waiting for me this entire time, disappointment stamped across their fuzzy faces at how long I've stayed away. The clothes I didn't take to college are still hanging in my closet, by now outdated and most likely too small, and there's even a picture of Eliza and me tacked to the wall: that one in our graduation caps, stiff smiles in the auditorium, the edges curling in on themselves like a ribbon of shaved wood. "I don't need it anymore."

"I would never," she says, crossing her arms in the doorframe.

"You could make better use out of this room, too," I say, taking in the faint lines of the vacuum on the carpet, the chemical smell of Windex on the windows. Imagining my mom coming in here, week after week, cleaning it for nobody. "Turn it into an office or something."

"Why are you so eager to move on from us, Margot?"

I turn to face her, the comment taking me by surprise. I never really thought my mom registered the way I'm always shrugging her off, pushing her back, letting her adulation slip away like salt water on sunscreened skin. I never considered myself worthy of such praise—I know I am, and always have been, painfully average—so I always assumed she was doing it for her own benefit: inflating all my attributes, reciting them in the mirror like an affirmation, a prayer. Like if she said it often enough, I might actually become the daughter she always wanted me to be.

"I'm not," I say, cheeks burning.

"You are. You never come home. We missed you on Thanksgiving."

"I'm busy at school—"

"You're avoiding us."

My mother gestures vaguely around the room and I know what she's saying, the silent insinuation: that I'm not only avoiding them, but *this*. Her. Eliza and the memories of the two of us here, in this very room: faded pencil lines etched onto the trim, marking our growth spurts. The pictures we ripped out of magazines and taped to the wall. There are reminders of her everywhere, and I drop my bags on the floor and sit on the bed.

If only she knew the reminders were even stronger at school: between Lucy and Levi, Eliza is everywhere now. There's nowhere safe.

"You should go see them," my mom says, walking over to sit next to me. "I bet they'd love it."

"Yeah," I say, although the thought of visiting the Jeffersons is almost too much to bear.

"They're bulldozing it, you know. Where it happened."

I look at my mother, eyebrows lifting. Just like I've been avoiding home, I've been avoiding the thought of that place, too. Like a pothole in the road, a puddle in my path, my mind skirting around it if only to make myself more comfortable. I saw it on the news in the days immediately after, of course, that old, abandoned building with caution tape stretched tight across the ash-black entryways. Little red flags stuck in the grass, plastic flapping in the breeze.

"When?" I ask.

"Three weeks."

"That's good."

"It is good," she says. "They should have done it a long time ago. It's completely unsafe, not to mention an eyesore."

I nod, my mind on those videos again. On Eliza stumbling her way up the steps, one by one, the empty beach roaring beneath her and the glow of the moon high up above. That's why they had been there: the moon. What a strange, stupid stroke of bad luck. If it wasn't full that night, the party wouldn't have happened. If it wasn't so clear and cloudless, she wouldn't have gone.

If she hadn't been there with Levi, of all people, howling at it like a lonely wolf trying to find her pack, she wouldn't have gotten so sloppy, so drunk.

She wouldn't have fallen. She wouldn't have died.

CHAPTER 39

It takes a few hours for me to finally fall asleep, my childhood bed feeling more foreign than my room back at Rutledge. Nestled between bursts of deep dreams that always startle me back awake—scared and sweaty, eyes darting madly around the room like my own body can't remember where I am—I come to realize that my mother is right. She's right about all of it.

The reason I haven't been back is that I'm avoiding them, her. *Here.* The last conversation that took place in this very room.

I knew it the second Eliza started seeing him again. It was like an intuition, barely there, my eyes picking up on the subtle way she would smile when her phone chimed at night or how she'd started getting dressed up again any time we ventured out onto the dock. She had kept her distance for a while, the break-in spooking her just enough, but it didn't last long, the pull of his attention stronger than anything I could say to convince her to stay away. And I'll admit it: I liked the fact that I had been right. All along, I had been right about Levi. I had been right to be wary of him and it was always so tempting to remind her of that, the ever-present urge to pick at the crust of a scab before it could fully heal. I don't know why I did it. I was boasting, I guess, reminding her in my own little way that I was useful, necessary.

I had seen something she hadn't—but Eliza, she hated it. She resented me for picking up on what she didn't.

"How can you just forget about him breaking into your house?" I asked one night, hands on my hips, the anger surging out of me as she tapped away at her phone. Even though graduation was approaching, only a handful of days left before we were set to walk across the stage, I had to ask her about it. I had to know. I knew it would only be temporary—only one more summer spent with Levi lingering and then we would both, finally, be free—but I couldn't handle the thought of her keeping something from me, something secret. Something as big as this. "Eliza, that is such a violation. We should have called the *cops*."

I realized, too late, that I was mirroring the way my mother sometimes stood when she was berating me about a mediocre test score, her judgment like a physical thing between us, sucking the very air out of the room. Even my tone was the same, harsh and grating, so I dropped my hands to my sides, suddenly unsure where to put them.

She looked up at me, a beat of silence before she dropped her phone onto my bed.

"He said he didn't do it."

"What do you mean—" I started, then stopped, my eyes growing wide as understanding dawned. "You *asked* him about it?"

"Yes," she said. "I asked if he came into the house while we were gone."

"And what did he say?"

"He said he would never do that. That there had to be some other explanation."

"Well, yeah, of course he's gonna deny it—"

"I could have misplaced the picture, Margot. Maybe my mom took it to use in the yearbook or something. We never even told my parents it was missing."

"That's stupid," I said. "You didn't misplace it."

"Levi also suggested that maybe *you* took it."

I stared at her, a wave of disbelief washing over me, trying to process what she just said.

"What?" I asked, although I heard her fine. I just wanted her to repeat it. I wanted to give her a second to reconsider what she just said; the opportunity to apologize, take it back. "He said that?"

"He suggested it."

"And what did you say?"

"I said it made sense."

I blinked—two, three times—a substantial silence settling over us. It had been almost an entire year of Levi trying to weasel his way between us, break us apart like a splinter in dried wood, but that was the very first time he had been so deliberate about it. Like instead of just sitting back and waiting for the crack to travel, growing slowly, naturally, until the fissure was complete, he decided to take a sledgehammer to it. Smashing us to smithereens.

"You've done it before," she said, averting her eyes, like she was suddenly embarrassed for me.

"What do you mean?"

"You collect things. I've seen you take stuff out of my room before . . . ticket stubs, receipts—"

"That's *different*," I said, my cheeks burning at the knowledge that she had seen. At all the little mementos that were stashed away in that very room, at that very moment. "I would never *steal* something of yours."

"You wouldn't?" she asked, infuriatingly calm.

"No, I wouldn't. Besides, why would I steal a picture and blame it on Levi?"

"Because you hate him, Margot. You've always hated him."

"I don't hate him—"

"Yes, you *do!*" she yelled, finally getting angry. "Just admit it. Why *wouldn't* you try to turn me against him?"

"I just have a bad feeling about him, okay?" I yelled back, throwing my arms in the air. "I'm trying to protect you!"

"I don't need you to protect me. You're not my mother."

"Yeah, but I'm your friend," I said, trying to calm down. I walked toward the bed and took a seat on the edge, resting my hand between us. "There's just something about him that bothers me, Eliza. Something that doesn't feel right."

"You're being dramatic," she said.

"I'm not being dramatic."

"Okay, then you're being *jealous,*" she snapped, standing up and stalking across the room. "Christ, Margot, what is it with you? Am I not allowed to have other friends now? A boyfriend?"

"Yes, of course you can have other friends," I said. "It's just . . . he's too . . ."

"Too what?" she asked, hands stuck to her hips. "Too cute? Nice? Interested?"

"Clingy!" I yelled again, too frustrated to keep my voice down. "He's obsessed with you, Eliza. It's not healthy. It's *weird.*"

"Well, I guess that makes two of you."

I froze, her words hitting me like a slap to the face. I stared at her as the silence mounted and I could tell she regretted it instantly. I could tell, the second she said it, that she wanted to reel it back in, swallow it back down, but no matter how she apologized, no matter how she backtracked, it was out in the open now. The way she really felt.

"I didn't mean that—" she started, but I held my hand up, shook my head.

"Clearly you did."

"I didn't," she said. "I'm sorry, I really didn't. It's just . . . I have a lot going on right now, okay? And I really like him, and you've been trying so hard to break us apart—"

"Get out," I said, standing up myself and pointing to the door. I had to look to the side then, lip quivering, trying not to show the mounting tears crawling up my throat. The cry threatening to spring free with a single glance in her direction. "I tried to warn you."

"Margot—"

"I tried to keep you safe," I said, finally turning to face her, surprised to find that she was crying, too. "I'm not breaking you apart, Eliza. *He's* breaking *us* apart. He's manipulating you."

"Just sit back down," she said, gesturing to the bed. "We can talk about it."

"I already tried that," I interrupted, my voice cold as I grabbed her wrist and ushered her out of my bedroom. It wasn't the first time we had tried to hurt each other like that, our words more painful than any physical act of violence; our tongues sharper than any freshly whetted blade. We knew each other's weaknesses better than we knew our own—we had touched every single soft spot, pushed on them like purple bruises just because we could—but until that moment, I never stopped to wonder what would happen if we went for the kill. Never even considered the possibility of one fatal blow that had the power to end it all.

"I tried to talk but you wouldn't listen," I continued. "You're choosing him over me."

"That's not true," she said, whimpering in the hall.

"Congratulations, you fell for it."

"Margot, stop—"

"He's gonna hurt you, Eliza. It's only a matter of time."

"Please don't say that."

"And whenever it happens," I said, staring at her in the hallway, those bright pink eyes and tear-streaked cheeks begging me not to say it, "don't call me."

CHAPTER 40

I wake up on Christmas morning to a text from Mr. Jefferson.

> Merry Christmas, sweetie. Saw your car drive by last week.

I lie in bed, staring at the message, my own cursor taunting me to come up with something to say. Before I can make up my mind, it pings again.

> Would love to see you today.

I sigh, my head sinking deep into my pillow, thinking about the last time I'd seen Eliza's parents. It was the summer she died, the night of her funeral. Even then, I had been avoiding them, the guilt I felt over Eliza's death rearing up like a storm surge every time I drove by their house.

I'll never forget their faces that day, the makeup smudged heavily beneath Mrs. Jefferson's eyes as Mr. Jefferson pushed her around the room by the small of her back. Shaking hands, glumly nodding. Accepting condolences on her behalf.

"I just wish you had been there," he said to me that night, a haggardness in his face I had never seen in him before. We were sitting on the back porch together, tie loosened around his neck, and I could smell the bourbon on his breath, warm and stale. I knew, whatever came next, he'd probably regret in the morning. "You kept her safe."

I stayed silent, wondering if Eliza ever told him about our argument; the things we said to each other that were so hard to take back. I doubted it. She had died with her parents still thinking I was a good person, and I watched as he continued to sip, picturing myself in bed that night, staring at my phone.

"Whenever it happens, don't call me."

"You talked sense into her," he continued. "She listened to you."

"Not always," I said, looking down at my lap. "Sometimes I think she did things specifically because I told her not to."

"Welcome to my life." He smiled into the distance, then turned toward me. "Was anything bothering her?" he asked at last. "Any reason you can think of why she might've—?"

He trailed off, like the rest of the sentence was too painful to say.

"Mr. Jefferson, you don't think—?" I stopped, tried to wrap my mind around what he was insinuating. Finally, I spit it out. "She didn't *jump*."

"No," he said after too long a pause. "No, of course not. But she never mentioned anything to you? Nothing seemed . . . wrong?"

I stayed quiet, our final conversation running through my mind.

The tears in her eyes and that quiver in her voice. The betrayal leaking out of us both for reasons related, but also entirely apart.

"No," I said at last. "I can't think of anything."

"And you never saw anyone giving her a hard time? Someone who might have gotten under her skin?"

"Mr. Jefferson, it was just an accident. She fell—"

"Humor me, Margot."

I couldn't keep looking into his eyes anymore, inflamed and unblinking, so I turned to stare into the backyard, the long dock stretching out into a darkness so dark, I couldn't even see the end of it.

"Nobody disliked Eliza," I said at last. "She was friends with everybody."

He sighed, squeezing the lids of his eyes with his fingers, probably realizing how desperate he was starting to sound. How deranged. I looked at him and felt a pang of pity flare up in my chest because I knew what he was doing, what he had been doing ever since he got the call that night. Ever since he was startled awake at two in the morning, looked down at his phone, and saw Eliza's number on the screen but heard someone else's voice on the other end. That heavy silence, a long exhale. The sound of sirens in the distance and the words no parent is ever equipped to hear.

He was grasping at straws, blindly searching for anything and anyone to blame other than Eliza's own recklessness. Her own stupidity.

I knew, because I was doing it, too.

"There were bruises," he said at last, and I jerked my head toward him, a hitch in my throat that made it hard to breathe. I watched as he opened his eyes, stared into his glass. Inspecting something invisible at the bottom.

"What do you mean?" I asked slowly.

"On her wrist," he said. "Like fingers. The coroner said they were . . . fresh."

I glanced over to Levi's house, the little pinprick of light coming from his bedroom. He had been at the funeral, too, keeping his distance. Sitting silently in the corner before standing up and walking away as soon as it was over. He had been interviewed by the police that night, then later on the news. Skin pale and eyes haunted after leaning over the edge, seeing the way her body looked after falling fifty feet in the dark. We later learned that her bones had broken immediately upon impact. Her neck snapped in half like a raw noodle.

The small mercy, I supposed, was that she was dead as soon as she even realized what was happening.

"Of course, she was all banged up," Mr. Jefferson continued, his eyes glistening with fresh tears. "She was covered in them. Bruises. But I don't know . . . I guess I was just wondering—"

"She was with Levi," I interrupted, still staring at his window. "They went to the party together."

"I know," he said. "I know that. They were dating?"

"I don't know what they were, but he was always around."

"How did you feel about that?"

"Honestly?" I said, turning to face him. "I hated it."

"Why?"

"He's just a bad influence, a bad guy."

"How so?"

"He just *is*," I said. "Things got so different once he showed up. Eliza told me—"

I stopped, my chest flushing as Mr. Jefferson snapped his head in my direction. Even though she was dead, I still felt a strange sense of allegiance toward her. A deep-seated obligation to keep my best friend's secrets.

"Eliza told you what?" he pushed.

"She told me Levi used to watch her at night. Through her window," I said at last, the admission making me uncomfortable. "That he used to follow her around."

"She told you that?"

I nodded, shame creeping into my cheeks.

"Why wouldn't she—?"

"She didn't want you to be upset," I continued, talking fast. "She thought it was cute, I guess. That he was that interested."

I watched as he sighed, took another long sip of his drink, more resigned than anything. We both stayed quiet, listening to the sounds of the cicadas in the distance. The occasional thrash in the water, the gentle waves.

"You know, you try to instill a sense of right and wrong in your kids—"

"This isn't your fault," I started, but he held his hand up.

"But as a parent, you usually get it wrong more often than you get it right." He was quiet, twirling the melting ice in his glass. "It's hard to be mad at her."

I stared at the side of his face, new lines etched deep into his skin like he had aged years instead of days. He was right: it was hard to be mad at her, but I couldn't tell him that. I couldn't tell him about the awful things we had said to each other, all the terrible things we had done.

I couldn't tell him that I blamed myself, too, in so many different ways. So instead, I just sat there silently, staring into the distance. My eyes trained on the Butler house until Levi's light finally switched off.

CHAPTER 41

The morning crawls by in a sluggish daze: sugary casseroles and Christmas carols running on repeat as I unwrap my gifts. I feign delight over a new set of plaid pajamas, a sterling silver charm bracelet I'll probably never wear. My mother unwraps her annual perfume—my father, a stack of books he always picks out himself—then I throw on a pair of jeans and a sweatshirt before making the walk down to Eliza's.

It's a quick journey, just a handful of houses between us, and as I round the bend to the Jeffersons' driveway, I can't help but notice how empty it looks. Not just the yard, all the old flowers long-since dead, but the house itself, too. None of the regular decorations are cluttering up the porch; there are no candles flickering in the windows or wreaths hanging from hooks on the door. Mrs. Jefferson always used to set up an inflatable Nativity scene on the lawn, something my own mother chastised as *tacky* whenever we drove around the neighborhood to look at the lights, though I know I can't blame them for not feeling festive this year.

Finally, I reach the front and push my finger into the bell, waiting impatiently as I hear the sound of footsteps approaching on the other side.

"Margot."

The door swings open and I try my best to conceal the surprise, though I'm sure it's apparent all across my face. Eliza's father is barely recognizable beneath the tuft of a newly grown beard, wiry hair peppered with gray. His skin is still a deep, dark tan, but there are more wrinkles now, too. Fine creases where it used to be smooth and bags that didn't exist before hanging heavy beneath his eyes.

"Hi, Mr. Jefferson."

"Thank you for coming," he says, opening the door wider, ushering me in. "Merry Christmas."

"Merry Christmas to you."

I step in closer and let him wrap me in a hug, the sour smell of body odor tickling my nostrils. Then I pull away, glancing around the living room. Noticing how different the interior looks, too, like all the blood has been sucked from the place.

"Where's Mrs. Jefferson?"

"Running errands," he says, leading me into the kitchen. I smell brewing coffee, burnt bacon, and watch as he turns toward the cabinet, opening it up to grab a couple mugs.

"On Christmas?"

He's quiet, his arms suspended in the air until his shoulders slouch just slightly.

"Today isn't easy for her," he says at last, still not facing me. "She needed some space."

I walk up behind him and grab the mugs from his hands, gesturing for him to take a seat. He smiles, grateful, and I pour enough coffee for the both of us before sliding into the chair beside him. It vaguely reminds me of that night after the funeral, the two of us sitting on the porch in silence. His whiskey dwindling while I stared into the distance, telling him things that were meant to be secret.

"How's school?" he asks at last, ringing his hands around the mug.

"Fine. I liked my classes last semester."

"Still majoring in English?"

I nod, taking a sip of my coffee, even though it's scalding.

"Good for you," he says. "You've always been good at that."

"My mom isn't too happy about it."

"Well, she's not the one getting a degree, is she?"

I smile, remembering with a surge of warmth why I liked being here so much. Eliza and me sitting at this very table, doing our homework while Mr. Jefferson picked up a poem I wrote. Reading it quietly with a nod of approval.

"You have a real gift," he had said. My own dad, on the other hand, had muttered something about iambic pentameter being useless in the real world.

"She told me they're bulldozing the old school," I say now.

I eye him carefully, trying to gauge his reaction. I wasn't planning on bringing that up, but at the same time, maybe it'll be good for him. I get the distinct feeling that Mr. Jefferson doesn't talk about it much. That if I didn't bring it up myself, we'd never actually acknowledge the reason why I'm here, alone, sitting in Eliza's spot on Christmas morning.

"Yeah," he says at last, rubbing one hand against the back of his neck. "It's been wrapped in caution tape ever since—well, you know. But it doesn't stop kids from sneaking in."

"Still?"

"Oh, yeah. They think they're invincible at that age. Just like she did."

"At least it won't happen again," I offer, and he shrugs.

"I guess the town finally decided it was time. There's talk of some kind of memorial going up in its place. A public park and a tree. Some kind of plaque."

"That's great."

He smiles at me, but it doesn't make it to his eyes.

"Have you made any friends at Rutledge?"

I hesitate, picking at my cuticle. I know Eliza's parents want me to be happy, but at the same time, I don't want them to think of her as replaceable. I don't want them to remember all those scenes of the two of us together—reading on her bed, painting our nails on the bathroom floor, lying horizontal on the dock, day after day, giggling about nothing—and suddenly find her ripped out of all of them, another face and body superimposed on top. I almost wonder if it would have been a comfort to them seeing how lost I was last year; knowing that I could hardly bring myself to leave my room, eat a proper meal. Peel myself from bed without first thinking of her.

"A few," I say at last. "Nobody as good as Eliza."

Mr. Jefferson smiles as he grabs my hand and squeezes it, hard.

"Do you mind if I go upstairs?" I ask, returning his gaze. There's something about being here, back in this house, that makes me suddenly desperate to stick my fingers into all of it, reacquaint myself with every single corner. Every last smell. Especially after the uneasiness of my own home, my own bed, I long to feel the familiar comfort of her room. My safe haven for so many years.

"It's just . . . I haven't been in her room since the last time," I say. "I want to see what you've done with it."

"It's exactly the same," Mr. Jefferson says, leaning back. "I've barely been inside since. But go ahead, take all the time you need."

I thank him and excuse myself, making my way into the living room, then the foyer, noticing the lack of tree in the corner and the nonexistent stockings that should be hanging above the fireplace. A trail of goose bumps erupts down my arms when I see those double doors swung open again, yawning wide like the night of the break-in. A cool marsh breeze leaking into the house and the almost imperceptible flutter of wind in the curtains.

I approach the stairs and ascend them slowly, imagining Levi's calloused hands gripping this same railing. Wondering if Mr. Jefferson knows he's at Rutledge now, too. Walking the halls his daughter should have walked; living the life she dreamed of first. I move farther down the hall, my eyes skimming over the collage of family portraits, Eliza's school pictures, the Jeffersons' wedding photo. They look so young there, high school sweethearts married just after they turned eighteen. Sometimes I wonder if that's why Eliza felt such a strong pull to Levi. I wonder if she looked at her parents—in love from the start, together for so long—and wanted the same thing for herself, no matter who it was with.

I shrug the thought away, turning into her bedroom next and flipping on the light.

Mr. Jefferson was right: it's exactly the same. A shrine to Eliza just like my own parents had preserved my room for me, all her old things situated in all the same places as if they've been waiting for her to walk back in. I roam around the edges, taking in all the same posters. The empty glass on her side table and the permanent water ring stained into the wood. The kiss of her lipstick still stuck to the rim. I look over at the giant corkboard next, cluttered up with pictures, the bare spot still right in the middle.

The window by her bed, curtains pulled open the way they always were.

I can hear her voice now, dipped into a whisper, the same way she always materializes when the memories of her become too much. I can see the swing of her legs in my peripheral vision; the flick of her eyes darting outside.

That flash of excitement as she chewed on her pencil, tugged twice on her hair.

"I think he watches me. I think he's out there right now."

I walk toward her dresser next, opening the drawers before I can think twice, resisting the urge to pull something out and inhale it deeply. Wrap it around my shoulders and call it mine. Instead, I let my fingers trail across the clothes still folded neatly inside, skirting the edges, feeling the fabric, until they brush against something different, rougher.

Paper, I realize. A torn-open envelope shoved deep in the back.

I glance over my shoulder, toward her open door, then back to the dresser, grabbing the envelope and pulling it out from between two sweaters. It's thick, bulky, and I stick my fingers inside, eyes widening as I pull out a stack of cash.

"What is this?" I whisper, my thumb flipping through the bills. There's several thousand dollars in here, easily, every bill a hundred.

I shove the money back inside and close the flap, flipping the envelope around. It's addressed to a place I don't recognize—a place in Fairfield, North Carolina—with no return address at all.

I eye it carefully, trying to figure out who it might be from, who was meant to receive it. Why Eliza had it stuffed in the back of her dresser like some dirty little secret she didn't want to reveal. Maybe she found it while she was out one day and decided to keep it, claim it as her own. I wouldn't put it past her. She once found a solid-gold bracelet in the school parking lot and decided to keep that, too, instead of turn it in and attempt to find its rightful owner.

I pull my phone out of my pocket and open the camera, snapping a picture of the address before tucking the envelope back where it was. I close the dresser and walk next to her desk, an urgent curiosity sweeping over me. I don't care about the money; I just want answers. Eliza and I didn't keep things from each other—at least in the beginning we didn't—but this envelope means something, and I want to know what it is. My eyes skip over her old textbooks, still stacked high in each corner, a smattering of notes and papers leftover from senior year. I find her planner and flip it open, fanning the pages, eyes stinging as the little doodles in pen dance before me like a flipbook. I read through all the old milestones she rendered important enough to note—SAT dates, the last day of school, graduation—and blink back tears when I see she wrote future ones, too. Days that she was apparently excited enough about to write down; days she'd never get to see.

Margot's birthday. Move into Hines. First day at Rutledge!!

I slap the planner shut with too much force, my eyes watering as I walk to the bed and sit on the edge of it, fingers digging into her comforter.

"Margot, honey, you doing okay?"

I can hear Mr. Jefferson at the base of the stairs and I glance toward the hallway, wiping a rogue tear as it trails down my cheek.

"Fine!" I yell back. "Be down in a second."

I look down at her bed, the imprint of my hand, the picture of that address burning hot in my pocket. Maybe it's nothing. Maybe it's graduation money, a gift from a relative she never lived long enough to spend. Maybe it's her own personal savings stuffed in some random envelope she found; a college fund she was stocking up on, spending money for when we were finally free.

Maybe I'm trying to assign meaning to a truly meaningless thing and the very fact that I'm still sitting here, pulling at my hair in her bedroom the way I always was, sends a sharp sting of irony in my chest. A twinge of embarrassment that I'm still trying so hard to understand her, my best friend. Still attempting to read through the lines of the things she told me, separate the truth from her little white lies—but even then, it was pointless. Even then, Eliza only showed the world the face she wanted it to see: carefree and fearless, bold and brave. Everything else stayed hidden, secret, so I suppose her death should be no different.

I stand up and wipe my fingers beneath my eyes, an attempt to pull myself together, when a hint of movement catches my eye through the window. I start to walk toward it, peering through the glass.

It's coming from Levi's bedroom.

His blinds are open—the curtains, too—and I can just barely make out the back of his head as he sits on his bed, arms gesturing like he's talking to someone just out of view. I never realized how clearly Eliza could see into his room from here, though I guess it makes sense—if he watched her, that means she could have watched him, too—and I lean in closer, a little thrill traveling through my chest at the thought of spying on him like he once spied on us.

This private moment, whatever it is, something secret that I'm not meant to see.

I'm about to force myself to turn around, aware of Mr. Jefferson waiting just downstairs, when whoever Levi is talking to walks into view, pulling my attention back. It takes a few seconds for me to register what I'm seeing, her body coming into focus after a few long blinks: slender arms, that shock of black hair. Curls bouncy and wild as she saunters into the frame and sits down next to him.

Then I watch as Lucy's long fingers weave their way through his hair, holding him close, his lips on hers as she goes in for a kiss.

CHAPTER 42

I barrel back down the stairs, mind spinning and knees weak as I thank Mr. Jefferson for the coffee and babble some excuse about needing to get home.

I had stared out that window for entirely too long: frozen with shock, hands on the trim, forehead practically pushed into the glass as I willed myself to blink my eyes and find Lucy's face replaced with somebody else's. Desperate for it all to be some kind of complex mirage, a trauma-induced delusion. A misunderstanding that could be easily explained—but it wasn't. It's not.

That's Lucy next door. Lucy, with Levi, the two of them tangled together in a drawn-out kiss.

I'm rounding the corner of the driveway when the sudden sound of her laugh stops me in my tracks. I watch as Lucy emerges from his house, eyes lighting up when she catches sight of me in the street, mere feet from the door.

"Margot!" she yells, waving her hand. "There you are!"

Levi appears in the doorway now, too, hands in his pockets and his head ducked low. He's wearing a T-shirt and flannel pajama pants, caught off guard and a little disheveled, though Lucy is acting like everything is fine. Like this is entirely normal, her being here. Walking toward me in Levi's front yard, arms outstretched, the big reveal on some game show I didn't even know I was playing. It's like that very first day she showed up in my dorm, ruby-red bikini and sun-kissed cheeks as she leaned against the doorframe, messed with her hair.

The way she had sauntered in so casually, trailing her fingers across all my things as if claiming ownership over them, and me.

"What are you doing here?" I ask, my eyes darting between them. Thinking about all the times she's stepped into my room since, appeared out of nowhere, or was already in there when I walked in myself: scanning the pictures on my mantel, flipping through the books on my desk. Inserting herself into all the spaces where she shouldn't have been and acting like it was the most natural thing in the world.

Lucy stops short, hesitating in the driveway like I reached out and slapped her.

"You said—" I watch as her smile fades slightly, her excitement at seeing me being slowly replaced with something that looks like shame. It feels strange, that expression on her. I've never seen Lucy ashamed over anything. "You said I could come."

"What?" I ask, taking another step forward. Still trying to wrap my mind around seeing her, here. With him. "What do you mean?"

"For Christmas. You said if I didn't want to be alone on Christmas . . . oh God, I'm sorry. You didn't actually mean it, did you? You were being nice."

"You came for Christmas," I repeat, remembering that conversation on the porch. My offer, her decline. The sad smile on her face and the split second when I actually thought she might agree.

"I feel like an idiot."

"No, don't feel like an idiot. I just mean . . . why are you *here*?" I ask, gesturing to Levi, lowering my voice. "With him?"

"I went to your parents' house earlier but your mom said you were visiting a friend. I saw Levi's Jeep in the driveway so I'd figured I'd come by and say hi. Pass the time until you were done."

I open my mouth, ready to confront her with what I saw through the window—but then I close it again, deciding that I don't want either one of them to know I was up there watching. Even more, I want to see if Lucy will bring it up herself. If she'll try to hide it or if she'll come clean, tell me everything. Explain what she was doing in Levi's bedroom, fingers wound tight around his hair.

"I felt weird just sitting at your parents' house without you there," she says at last, a hint of embarrassment in her voice. "They didn't even know who I was."

"I'm sorry," I say, looking between Lucy and Levi, trying to force a smile. It's true that I had kept her from my parents—the details, at least. The intimate things I didn't want them to taint. It was nothing personal, just my own selfish desire to keep my two lives blissfully separate, but I can see now how that must have felt for her, showing up to her best friend's house and being met with nothing but blank stares.

I glance over to Levi's car next, a giant white Jeep with an Outer Banks bumper sticker peeling at the sides. It's also true she would have recognized it. It's noticeable anywhere, especially since she's spent the last semester walking past it every single day. And I *did* invite her here. She never said yes, but it's not unlike Lucy to show up unannounced. She does it all the time.

"I'm just surprised to see you," I add.

"I'll leave, if you want—"

"No, don't leave," I say, closing the distance between us, forcing myself to pull her in for a hug. "I want you to stay."

Her arms hang limp by her sides until I feel them wrap slowly around my neck, squeezing me back, swaddling me in all those familiar smells: her vanilla perfume and warm coffee breath. The subtle smell of smoke always lingering in her hair. It's tempting to fall back into the spell of her, to close my eyes and get swept away. Lucy never lets herself be vulnerable like this and I can just imagine her waking up this morning, the first hint of light leaking through the windows and the cold quiet of our house as she brewed a pot of coffee for one. I can see her curling up on the couch for the second week in a row, eyes glassed over as she flipped through the channels, read another book without registering the words. Pondering two more weeks of solitude and the last-second decision to jump in her car, make the drive here without asking permission or telling a soul.

Something selfish and impulsive that is, to be honest, the exact type of thing that Lucy would do.

"I'm glad you're here," I say at last, my nose nudged into her curls. Part of me means it, I really do, the idea of Lucy needing me enough to put herself out there like this sending a surge of something warm through my chest—but the other part of me can't deny what I saw through that window.

I think about these last seven months, the way Lucy has slowly singled Levi out in almost every interaction. From the moment his eyes landed on her at Penny Lanes—the moment I heard her throaty whisper as she leaned into him on the floor, asked him that question that's been ringing through my mind ever since—I had been afraid of this. Afraid of Levi swooping in and claiming another thing that was meant to be mine.

Afraid of Lucy leaving me like Eliza did for a boy who doesn't deserve her.

I open my eyes, detach myself from Lucy's grip, and notice that Levi is still standing there, observing us curiously from the porch. He seems to be turning something over in his mind, dissecting it slowly, and I watch as he runs his hand along his jaw, wipes what's left of Lucy from his lips, before he turns around and disappears into the house, closing the door behind him.

CHAPTER 43

AFTER

We've been outside for over an hour, waiting patiently as the police make their way through the house. We're sitting in the backyard with our legs pretzeled on the ground when Detective Frank finally emerges, a swarm of officers behind him carrying plastic bags of evidence to their cars.

"You're free to go in," he says at last, stopping a few feet in front of us. Sloane holds her hand above her eyes, shielding the sun as she stares in his direction, while Nicole keeps playing with a pile of gravel in her palm. The pads of her fingers are chalky as she tosses the little white rocks back onto the driveway, one by one, like skipping stones at the beach.

"What is that?" he asks suddenly, something in the distance catching his attention. I watch as his eyes dart away from us and around the yard, his nose upturned.

"The boys," I say, already knowing what he's referring to. "They keep meat in the shed."

"Meat?"

"They're making jerky."

Sloane and I watch as he walks closer, a single stubby finger pushing the door open with a creak. I can feel his grimace from here as that familiar smack of metallic hits our nostrils; watch as he takes in the long, lean strips of deer, rust-red and limp, drying from rows of metal racks. Tufts of pelt heaped in the corners and bloated flies buzzing around the room.

"Is that safe?" he asks. "For . . . consumption?"

I shrug, twisting back around.

"I don't know," I say. "They seem to know what they're doing."

Detective Frank looks back at me, at Sloane, then finally at Nicole, still busying herself with those rocks.

"You know, this whole situation seems like it has the potential to get awfully . . . volatile," he says at last. "Trouble waiting to happen."

"And what *situation* is that?" Sloane asks.

"Your living situation. Four girls living here right next to all those boys living just over there. They're your landlords?" We nod. "And how's that work, exactly?"

"They own the house, we pay them to live here," I say. "Pretty straightforward."

"You signed a lease?"

We're quiet, knowing the boys are probably breaking some kind of city rule by letting us live here. I doubt they have a rental license; we never signed anything or scanned our IDs. Like Lucy had told me that night on the roof, the house probably isn't even up to code, structurally sound, safe for daily living. We just hand over an envelope of cash every month, under the table, and they fix the things that need to be fixed when they feel like it.

"There's a power imbalance here that I don't like," he says when we don't respond. "It's probably a good thing you're moving soon."

"Did you find anything?" I ask, jerking my head toward the house, an attempt at changing the subject. They found her phone, I'm sure, among other things.

"You know I can't tell you that."

I watch as Detective Frank pokes his head into the shed again before closing the door and walking back toward us.

"We're worried about her," Sloane says. "We really think she got spooked and ran."

"And why would she do that?" he asks. "Why would she run if she has nothing to hide?"

"Because that's what Lucy does," I interject, folding my arms. "She ran away from home after high school. It doesn't mean she did anything wrong."

"Look, girls." Detective Frank takes a few more steps in our direction, squatting down. I can't tell if he's trying to come across as sympathetic, on our side, or intimidating by making himself eye level with us. Either way, seeing him wobble around on his toes like that, seeing the knees and groin of his pants pull too tight against the tension of his weight, just makes him look a little pathetic. Like an adult using the slang of kids half his age. "I know you know more than you're letting on."

Nobody speaks, a heavy silence settling over us except for the occasional click of gravel. Nicole's still tossing those stones and I wish she would stop. It's a nervous habit, I think, like Sloane picking at her cuticles. She needs to give her hands something to do.

"I've tried to be patient with you, but I'll be honest, it's starting to wear thin. So we can do this the easy way, with you cooperating here at home, or we can do it the hard way with you down at the station."

"You know what? Fine," Nicole says suddenly, finally directing her attention toward him. She drops the rest of the rocks and stands, wiping the white residue on her shirt. "Maybe Lucy did do something to Levi, okay? Maybe she did."

"Nicole—"

I watch as she juts out her hand, silencing Sloane, her gaze still on the detective crouched a few feet below her.

"I'm sick of being treated like criminals when we haven't done anything wrong."

Sloane and I are quiet, Nicole's outburst echoing around us, the tension thick and sticky like a gust of hot, humid air. Detective Frank raises his eyebrows, quiet, waiting for her to continue.

"She did say all that stuff—"

"*Nicole,*" Sloane warns.

"What stuff?" Frank asks, attention unyielding.

"About murder," she says. "Justifying it."

"She didn't mean that," I say, thinking back to that night at Penny Lanes. To all of us sitting in that circle like a séance, bobbing heads and tired eyes as we murmured to each other about deviance, about death. "We were just messing around."

"She said everyone would do it," Nicole continues. "For the right reason—"

"Okay." Sloane stands up now, too, placing her hand on Nicole's back. "If you'll excuse us, we're going back inside now. We're all exhausted."

"Withholding information from an investigation is illegal," Frank says, watching Sloane as they start to walk away. "We can charge you with obstruction."

"Can you?" Sloane asks, whipping back around. "Because we've already told you everything we know. Lucy talks a lot, okay? But half of what she says is bullshit. We all know better than to believe her."

Detective Frank is quiet, ignoring her outburst, eyes darting back and forth between Sloane and Nicole standing rigid before him.

"Whether or not you want to admit it, your friend is the key to this thing," he says at last. "She either did something, or she knows something, and there's a reason she's gone."

Sloane stares back at him, continuing to hug Nicole's fragile frame before the two of them turn back around and walk wordlessly toward the house, the screen door slapping shut behind them.

"I know what goes on in a place like that," Frank says to me next, his voice dipped low. I turn back toward him and he gestures to the shed. To the boys next door and everything they get away with. "And I know about Eliza. Levi's old fling and your friend from before."

He's trying to play good cop now—trying to extend a hand, offer me a way out—even though I know better than to take it. Even though I know if I reach out, let my fingers curl around his, he'll just grab my wrist and twist it instead.

"I would understand if something happened," he continues. "If Lucy needed to protect herself or one of you. If it was self-defense, maybe—"

"I don't know what you're talking about," I say, cutting him off.

"Are you sure?" he asks. "Because it seems like a pretty big coincidence. Your next-door neighbor, your two best friends."

I continue to stare, silent, before Detective Frank finally sighs and stands up, nodding gently and making his way out front without uttering another word. Then, once he's gone, I drop my head into my hands, pushing hard on my eyes until I see stars.

CHAPTER 44

BEFORE

Lucy and I are on our own private stretch of beach, necks sandy as we stare up at the sky. We found this spot a few days ago while we were wandering around, shoes dangling from our fingertips as we stumbled through the dunes. Trying to escape the crowds that, despite the cold weather and biting sea breeze, never really seem to dissipate around here.

There's a faint crackle of fireworks somewhere to the north of us and the crashing of waves down by our feet, though it's too dark to see how close we are to the water. I hear a sloshing to my left and turn to the side, vaguely register Lucy's outstretched arm holding the bottle of wine she snagged from my parents' pantry.

"Happy New Year, Margot."

She wiggles the bottle in my direction, the sudden sound of her voice making me realize we've been lying in silence for a long, long time: ten minutes, maybe twenty, quietly comfortable in each other's presence.

"Happy New Year, Luce."

I grab the bottle and take a pull, the sweet bite of rosé making my skin prickle. We're bundled up in sweatpants and sweatshirts, two knit blankets spread out between us, but still, it's cold out here. We should have brought hot chocolate or something. Spiked it with Bailey's.

Lucy has been in the Outer Banks for about a week now, the two of us sleeping feet-to-head in my bed, even though my parents have two perfectly acceptable guest rooms they made up for her the second they realized who she was. After we left Levi's, we had walked back into my house to find my mother doing laps around the living room until she heard our entrance and stopped abruptly, clasping her hands tight behind her back like we had caught her stealing. I tried to ignore the hot flash of embarrassment that shot up my chest at the thought of her spending the entire hour since Lucy's unexpected arrival running around in a flurry of nerves: collecting the dishes, lighting candles. Barking out orders and madly fluffing the throw pillows like Lucy might take one look at their lumpy physique and shake her head, disappointed in us all. Once we settled in, though, it turned into a slow, lazy week the way the holidays usually are and I actually found that I didn't mind it. Thanks to my mom's incessant questioning, I've learned more mundane details about Lucy's life in the last seven days than I have in the last seven months combined. She grew up with cats, apparently, even though she thinks she might be allergic. She doesn't have any extended family—no aunts, no uncles, no cousins—and even though I warned my mother not to ask too much about that, about how she grew up, she still found a way to pepper in her nosy inquiries, feigning ignorance when I shot her looks across the table.

"How about a boyfriend?" she had asked the other night, the four of us sitting close in the dining room. I could see my dad's shoulders hunch instinctively; the small cough he'd let slip, like something was caught in his throat. "A pretty girl like you has to have one."

"*Mom,*" I warned, but Lucy just laughed.

"It's fine. I had one in high school, but it didn't work out."

I heard Maggie's voice in my ear then, that hiss on the lawn as we watched Lucy lie out there. *"I heard she blinded her boyfriend in high school."* It felt like just another rumor at the time, one of the countless wild tales some student made up about her to feel relevant, but still. I felt myself leaning forward, not wanting to miss a word.

"His loss," my mom said, spearing a piece of broccoli.

"Yeah," Lucy said, averting her eyes, her voice suddenly sounding too clipped. Too strained.

"He didn't . . . he didn't *hurt* you or anything, did he?"

"Mom, seriously."

"Margot, honey, we're just having a conversation."

"It's fine," Lucy said again, cutting into a chicken thigh. "No, nothing like that. At least, not physically." She smiled.

"Truth or dare," Lucy says to me now, and I feel myself blink. I brush off the memory along with a streak of sand on my cheek before rubbing both arms with my hands to warm them.

"Truth," I say at last, another pop going off somewhere in the distance. A flash of light, a faraway cheer.

"That's new for you."

"Yeah, well, if I said dare you'd dare me to go skinny-dipping and I'm not trying to die of hypothermia."

Lucy laughs, an open-mouthed snort that's cut short by another slug from the bottle. She shakes her head, wipes her lips on her hand, and plops it down in the sand between us.

"You're not wrong about that."

I'm quiet as she thinks, fingers tickling at her chin until she flips to the side and rests her head on her arm.

"What's your New Year's resolution?"

"I don't really have one," I say, and that's the honest truth. I've never been that kind of person. There have always been things I've wanted to change about myself, things I've disliked, but until I met Lucy, I could never imagine waking up one morning and just actively choosing to be somebody else. Shedding my insecurities like a too-small skin, leaving them behind. Outgrowing my old self and simply morphing into someone new.

"You have to have one. Just pick something."

I take a minute to think about the past year, such a drastic detour from my life thus far. I can't even believe that, 365 days ago, I was still living in the dorms with Maggie, cocooned in a cradle of junk food and mediocre movies to keep myself from having to think too hard about everything I had lost. So maybe that's my resolution: to never go back to that place again. To never lose anything else so completely. And I don't just mean Eliza; I mean myself, too. I had no idea how fragile I was back then, how my very being was held together by such a perilously thin thread. Because before I was with Maggie, I was with Eliza. I hadn't lost her yet. We were still best friends, still doing everything together. We were still counting down the days until Rutledge when we could both finally be free . . . but was I happy back then? Was I, *really*? I don't actually know. I never tried to change the things I didn't like about myself, fix the things that needed to be fixed. Instead, I just latched on to Eliza, zeroing in on all the places she was full where I was hollow and hoped that if I lapped them up for long enough, they'd pool their way in and fill me up, too.

"I want to be different," I say at last, the only way I know how to put it.

"Different how?"

"I don't know," I say, rolling over now, too. "I'm sick of being weak, I guess. Of being . . . malleable."

"I don't think you're weak."

"Lucy, come on." We're both quiet, nothing but the roar of waves between us. I want her to say something, to crack some kind of joke to break the tension, but instead, she stays silent. "You saw how I was last year."

I'm grateful for the dark right now, the cover of night, so she can't see the warm flush creeping into my cheeks. We've never really talked about this before: her choosing me, the anomaly of it. How it just doesn't make sense, no matter which way you twist it.

I grab the bottle from the sand, surprisingly light in my grip, and take another drink.

"You were going through something."

"I was always like that," I say, shaking my head. "Even before Eliza. I was always too cautious. Always letting people walk all over me."

"Well, I like you the way you are, but I know you have it in you to be different. I've seen it."

We're both silent, memories from Halloween flooding right back. The way I had stood up by the fire, interrogated Levi as soon as I saw him emerge through the shed, my accusations fierce and unafraid. Later, shivering on the kitchen floor, a hatred so pure and razor-sharp it sliced straight through the silence, surprising us both.

"It should have been him."

"That wasn't me," I say now. "I was angry—"

"It is possible to be both," she interjects. "Radically both."

I twist my head, eyes straining against the night. I still can't see her, but I can feel Lucy's smile stretching through the darkness: pulling wide, cheeky and taunting. The kind that bares teeth.

"You read *Jekyll and Hyde*," I say, remembering that line, *radically both,* one of the many I'd highlighted before flipping it closed and tossing it across the couch. The concept of being mutually good and evil, dark and light, tickling my subconscious like an incessant itch growing stronger, harder to ignore. What a profound notion: that neither of those things needed to cancel out the other, but instead, could simply swirl together until you became your own unique mixture of each.

"I liked it," she says.

"I knew you would."

"It's what I've been saying all along."

I pinch at the sand between us, rubbing the grains between my fingers. If there's one thing I've learned about Lucy, one thing that's become glaringly clear, it's that to her, the entire world exists as a gradient, a sliding scale. Her moral compass isn't broken, per se, but it's definitely skewed, the magnets attracted to whichever direction she sees fit. Spinning madly around, guiding her whichever way she wants to go.

There is no good or bad for Lucy. There is no right or wrong, noble or evil, but simply the existence of people who dabble in their own combination of each.

"Your turn," I say, handing the bottle back. Trying not to think about the gradual pull of it; those scales, tipping, just like she said they would. "Truth or dare."

"In the spirit of trying new things: truth."

I curl my legs into my chest, thinking about all the things I want to ask her. All the secrets I know she keeps—but still, there's only one that comes to mind. One question I've been chewing over since the second she got here; one mystery on the tip of my tongue, the weight of it pushing my lips apart only for me to lose my nerve and swallow it back down.

"Why did you go over there?" I ask at last, picturing her in Levi's room again. Fingers twisting in his hair and her palm delicate on his thigh as she leaned in close, her lips on his. "When you went to my house and I wasn't there . . . why did you go to Levi's?"

She rolls over to face me, the shadow of her eyes gaping wide.

"I told you—" she starts, but I shake my head.

"No," I say. "You know what I mean. Why did you really?"

"I guess I was curious," she says at last.

I'm quiet, picturing those early days with Eliza. The way she sauntered down the dock, eyes darting over to Levi when she thought he wasn't looking. The way she would watch from a distance, a kind of bored awareness because there was nothing better to do. I remember her searching his name on her phone like he was some strange, exotic thing she simply wanted to study, try to understand. But then it morphed from there, an innocent interest turning into something bigger, stronger.

I can't help but wonder if that's what's happening here, too.

"He told me about the party," Lucy says, rolling back over to face the stars. "The night she died."

I freeze, my body suddenly numb from the cold and the wine; the wind whipping off the water and this conversation, everything. I had been trying to work up the nerve to ask her about the kiss next, what I saw through that window, but this feels more important now.

"What did he say?"

"He mentioned the old high school," she says. "The party that happens there every year."

I see it in my mind, the way it's always been: standing broken but tall on the edge of the beach, inside gutted from a lightning-strike fire that ripped through the rooms years ago. Structurally, it's still standing, though nobody could call it sound. There are missing walls, no roof, only three stories of ash-black empty spaces cluttered up with charred furniture nobody ever bothered to move and phallic graffiti spray-painted over old chalkboards. Empty vodka bottles collecting dust in the corners, evidence of parties past; the occasional sleeping bag left behind by someone too drunk to drive home. Even I couldn't deny that it was the perfect place for a bunch of underage kids: right on the beach, a view of the water. Abandoned and messy and ours for the taking.

"The first full moon of the summer," I say at last, nodding slowly. "It's usually pitch-black out there without any power, but when the moon is out and the sky is clear, it's suddenly light, too. You can see everything."

Even from my phone, I remember thinking it looked impossibly bright: the midnight moon reflecting off the water like a giant mirror, a pane of glass, cloaking everything in a ghostly glow. The kind of eerie luminescence that appears just before a tornado, still and haunting, dark and light, the sky itself sending a warning of certain danger to come.

"Radically both," Lucy mutters and I turn to face her, the crackle of a faraway firework like white noise in my ears.

"Yeah," I say. "I guess it is."

I look up at the sky now, the peek of the moon like something shy and wary, flitting in and out of the haze above. Picturing Eliza and Levi climbing those steps, ascending higher, stumbling perilously close to the edge. A single misplaced cloud could have called the whole thing off, made it too dark to see, but that night had been perfect, as good as they come: the moon glowing bright against the ink-black sky like a flashlight in the dark, exposing them all.

CHAPTER 45

It's our first week back at Rutledge and nothing feels the same. Nothing has felt the same since Halloween, really, that cursed night that cast a spell over everything.

I close my eyes, massage my temples, my bed cold and hard as the image of Lucy and Levi replays in my mind for the millionth time. I had hoped things would feel different once we got back, the clean slate of Christmas break wiping the bad away, but instead, from the second Lucy and I stepped through the front door together, everything just felt different, strange, like we somehow wandered into the wrong house.

Despite the week we had together, my best efforts to shrug it away, I don't know what to think about seeing the two of them together like that, my mind oscillating between the only two explanations so often I'm finding myself caught somewhere in the middle, suspended. Stuck. I honestly don't know which one I'm more afraid of: the idea of Lucy actually falling for Levi the same way Eliza did, watching him pluck another one of my friends out from under me and holding her tight in his palm before crushing her in his grip, or the concept of Lucy playing us all in another of her games.

I think about that very first night on this very bed, telling stories about Levi and who he is. The wheels turning in her eyes like she was starting to form an idea, a plan. Leaning into him at Penny Lanes and whispering that question like she already knew the answer.

Sloane and me in her bedroom, the two of us huddled beneath the sheets in the dark.

"That's what Lucy does. She dangles."

Maybe that's what this is all about: Lucy dangling her power, her knowledge, peppering Levi with questions about Eliza like pushing on a bruise with building pressure. Ripping the legs off a spider, one by one. Seeing how long she can go until he screams. What is her endgame, though? What is her goal? Like Sloane had said: Lucy is calculated, cunning. She's singling Levi out for a reason and I need to know what that reason is. It almost feels like she's testing us both, Levi and me, pulling our strings and making us dance. Worming her way into my thoughts every night like a parasite gnawing its way through my brain, making me feverish and sick.

Forcing me to think things, feel things, I never thought I would.

"Margot."

I open my eyes to see Sloane standing in my doorframe, her expression grim enough to make me sit up quick. She looks truly worried for the first time since I've known her: not bored like she usually is, mildly detached like she's simply scrutinizing the rest of us for her pleasure alone, but visibly alarmed. Maybe even afraid.

"It's gotten worse," she says.

"What has?"

"Nicole."

She scurries into my room and shuts the door behind her, dropping her voice even though, as far as I know, we're the only people in the house. Lucy's been working a shift all day and Nicole is next door, talking to Trevor. It's the first time she's willingly gone over there since I can remember, which struck me as progress until I realized the pledge party is tonight. The first Saturday of the new semester.

"Margot, this is serious," Sloane says. "She looks really bad."

"How bad?"

"Skeletal."

I chew on my lip, thinking. There was barely any time between Nicole getting home from Thanksgiving and leaving again for Christmas, so none of us said anything about her rapidly withering figure. And what would we even say? She's refusing to tell us what's wrong, why something seemed to flip in her psyche the second she woke up the morning after Halloween. All we have to work with are flashes of that night, none of which feel very concrete thanks to the chemical concoction that had been coursing through our bloodstreams: Nicole lost in that party for hours, Lucas grumbling about her getting too drunk. Me finding her on the bathroom floor, limp and confused and mottled in bruises.

Levi on our property, skulking around.

"This is all Lucy's fault," Sloane mutters, immediately snapping me out of it.

"How could it be Lucy's fault?" I ask. "I was with her the whole night."

"She's the one who set her up with Trevor," Sloane says. "She practically forced them together last year even though I told her it was a bad match."

"They're not a bad match," I say, even though it sounds hollow the second I say it.

"Margot, come on," she says, shooting me a look. "They're awful together and you know it."

I think about all the moments I've witnessed between them, Nicole and Trevor, subtle little things that always bothered me; elusive discomforts I could never quite place. It was in the way he looked at her, more lust than love, transforming into something else entirely any time he had a few drinks: animal, almost predatory, like he wanted her just for the sake of owning something. A sick pride in draining the life out of a living thing just to mount it on a wall. And then there was the time he interrupted her at Penny Lanes, telling us their secrets. The look on his face, like he was reveling in her shame. Flirting with me when she wasn't around and stalking around the yard on Halloween, shirt ripped off and that rapacious grin.

The glimmer in his eye that made me take a step back.

"Why did Lucy want them together so bad?"

"It was never Trevor," Sloane says. "It was this fucking house."

"The house?"

"Lucy wanted to live here. Trevor was going to be president."

Sloane arches her eyebrows and I finally understand: Nicole dating Trevor was a means to an end. Lucy wanted the house, and the only way to get it was to get in with Trevor. She had practically admitted it to me that first day of Thanksgiving break when the two of us were trudging through the grass together, making our way out to the shed. Her fear over them breaking up and it going to someone else instead.

"If this is all because of that fight with Trevor, then why doesn't Nicole just break up with him?" I ask. "I mean, the house is fine, the rent's cheap, but we can live somewhere else next year—"

"She isn't going to break up with him, Margot. She's too nice. Don't you get it?"

The way Sloane looks at me sends a wave of discomfort through my chest. She's right: Nicole is too nice. She always has been, ever since that very first day when she tried to pry me out of my shell, her smile cutting through the pressure like a warm wet blade. She's always the one smoothing things over, keeping the peace. That's probably what she's doing right now next door: alleviating any lingering tension before we're all marooned on an island together without our own house to run to. Without any way to escape.

"Lucy picked her for a reason," Sloane continues, leaning forward, and I can feel it now, radiating, some massive admission coming so close to barreling right out of her. The force of it something she can no longer contain. "I've been telling you that from the start."

I think back to the two of us outside the shed; the way she stopped, seemed to think hard about something before turning my way, asking that question: *Are you sure you want to do this?* The way she had called me vanilla, malleable. A blank slate. The very thing Lucy wanted like she had picked me specifically, casting me to play some kind of role for her. A preordained purpose I still don't understand.

"When you're friends with Lucy, she makes you feel special," she had said, that ache in her face like she hadn't yet decided if that was good or bad. *"Like she chose you for a reason."*

I had stopped questioning what my reason was, but I never even thought about the fact that Sloane and Nicole might have reasons, too.

"What do you know?" I ask, a chill creeping up my spine. "What do you know that you haven't told me?"

She hesitates, glancing over her shoulder again before leaning closer on my bed.

"Lucy didn't live in Hines last year," she says at last, and I notice the way she's ripping at her fingers now; pulling a loose nail so hard it bleeds.

"What do you mean? Of course she did. She was there all the time—"

"No, she didn't," she says, shaking her head. "Margot, you need to listen to me. Everything you think you know about Lucy . . . none of it is true."

CHAPTER 46

I can still see her on that very first day, stepping into the circle of us with a case of beer in hand, bottles rattling. The way she plucked one out and twisted the cap, plunging her arm into the air like a call to arms, a battle cry.

"To us," she had said, glass lip smoking. Taking a long swig and cementing herself in our minds as just that: us. One of us. Our ringleader, our North Star. The self-imposed brightest one of all. She had been everywhere, always, making her way down the hall in the dark and stepping into the showers in the morning. Rinsing off her hangover before appearing again, starting all over.

The three of them linked, forever intertwined. They did every-thing together.

"I don't understand how that's possible," I say now, trying to wrap my mind around it. "She was there. She was always there."

"She approached Nicole and me on move-in day," Sloane says. "Introduced herself in the courtyard and we clicked. By that night, she was hanging out in our room like we'd known her forever."

I picture that circle again; the RA, Janice, wrangling us into the common room, reciting the rules. The twenty-four girls of hall 9B grouped together, huddled in twos—except for Lucy. Lucy wasn't there with a roommate, hip attached to the only other person she knew like the rest of us. But she wasn't like the rest of us, was she? She never had been. She was just *there*, standing behind Sloane and Nicole. Biding her time until Janice left and she could step into the center, make herself known. Eternally comfortable with being alone.

"There were twenty-five," I say, mentally counting us all. Twelve rooms, twelve sets of roommates . . . and Lucy. But in my mind, Lucy didn't belong in a set; she belonged in a trio. It was always the three of them with her in the center.

It never struck me as odd until now.

"She told us she didn't like her roommate," Sloane recounts. "That's why she was always in our room."

"Did she sleep there?" I ask. "She was on the hall all the time."

"Sometimes on our futon. Not always."

"And you never asked to meet her roommate?"

Sloane shrugs, like the thought had occurred to her, but in the end, she'd simply dismissed it. "She said she was boring, never left her room," she says, biting her lip as soon as the words escape. I feel my cheeks flush. I can tell she feels bad. "No offense."

"It's fine," I say, waving it off. "But maybe she lived on another hall or something. A different floor?"

"That's what I thought at first, too."

"When did you start thinking otherwise?"

Sloane sighs, rolling her neck, and I can't help but dart my eyes over to my closed door again, always aware of the possibility that Lucy might be listening.

"After finals were over, when it was time to move out of Hines and into the house, Nicole and I couldn't find her," she says at last. "We were calling her phone, looking in the lobby. Even if she lived on another floor, she should have been there, too, right? Moving out with everyone else?"

"Right," I say, nodding, remembering the swarm of girls with their campus-owned carts. The metal corners crashing into our ankles; rickety old wheels and neon numbers stuck to the back.

"We finally figured she was at work or something and was going to get her stuff later, but when we pulled up to the house, she was already here unloading shit out of her car. Where did it all come from?" she asks, leaning forward. "If she didn't move it out of Hines, where was she keeping it?"

I chew on the inside of my cheek, thinking. Remembering that night on the roof; Lucy's admission that didn't feel like much at the time suddenly looking different in this strange new light.

"I left right after school, figured I'd just come here and get a job and a cheap apartment."

"Did you ever ask her about it?"

"Yeah," Sloane says. "She shrugged me off, said she moved out early because she wanted to avoid the crowds, then acted like *I* was the crazy one for questioning her about it."

I think back to my first day in this house, the very moment I met the others. Lucy calling me into the living room and the harsh hostility emanating off Sloane. The way she had been glaring at me, snapping at her.

"Where'd you find her?" she'd asked, eyeing me suspiciously.

"She lived on our hall."

I still remember the inflection in Sloane's voice when she responded, incredulous: *our* hall? I always thought she said it like that because she couldn't believe I'd lived there, too. Like it was *their* hall, not mine, that humiliating sting shooting through my chest when I thought about all the days I'd wasted tucked away in my room.

But it wasn't that; it was never that. Sloane wasn't doubting that I lived there. She was defying Lucy because she *didn't*.

"That's why you were so upset," I say now. "The day I moved in."

"She was gaslighting me," Sloane says, and our entire conversation outside the shed flares up to the forefront of my mind again. I play it back, scene by scene: Sloane, eyes darting, afraid of being watched. The venom in her voice, like somebody scorned: *"She's a fucking liar."*

"There has to be an explanation," I say at last, trying to tread lightly. I don't want Sloane to think I'm brushing her off, siding with Lucy, but at the same time, it doesn't make sense. "If she didn't live in Hines, how was she always getting in and out of the building? Wouldn't you constantly have to be buzzing her in if she didn't?"

"Nicole's keycard," she says. "You're the one who made me see it."

I think back to the two of us in Sloane's bedroom, just after Thanksgiving. Talking about Nicole and how skinny she looked. The way I had demanded we start locking the door even though she could never keep track of her key.

Sloane opening her mouth before closing it again, looking concerned. Fingers working at that seam for so long the thread started to fray.

"She lost it—" I start, but already, Sloane's shaking her head.

"She didn't lose it," she says. "Nicole still swears it was stolen. We just never figured out who took it."

The thought of it makes my skin crawl: Lucy wandering up to Sloane and Nicole in the courtyard and talking her way inside. Swiping Nicole's keycard so she could let herself into the dorm as she pleased before drifting down the hall, into the common room. Convincing us all that she belonged.

"Before I left for Christmas, I stopped by the registrar," Sloane says. "Right before they closed for the holidays. I searched Lucy's name."

"You can't just look at student records," I say, eyes widening. "You could get expelled—"

"I know," she says, holding up her hand. "But after realizing she was the one who took Nicole's key, I had to know why."

"What did you find?"

"Nothing," she says. "Every time I searched her name, nothing showed up."

"What do you mean, *nothing showed up?*" I ask, though I can see it now: Sloane sneaking to her computer, an empty office just before the holidays. Booting it up, glancing over her shoulder. Confirming she was alone. Pulling up records and typing Lucy's name; brown eyes widening when it came up blank. "Are you sure you spelled her name right? Sharpe with an *e?*"

"Yes, I spelled her fucking name right."

"Okay, sorry. I just don't understand—"

"What is so hard to understand, Margot?"

I can tell she's biting her tongue, trying not to scream, those ravaged fingers tugging at her hair as she begs me to just put it together. Figure it out. Her frustration is mounting, leaking out of her eyes, and I brace myself to hear the thing that, deep down, I've known was coming all along. All those little moments are bubbling up to the surface now. Moments with Lucy when someone asked about her major and she shrugged them off; when they mentioned never seeing her on campus and she just smirked and walked away. She never studies. Sure, she reads, but they're books I've lent her. She was like that last year, too, jealous girls speculating about all the terrible things she must be doing to get by. She's always coming and going out of the house like the rest of us, but she works, too.

She's the only one of us with somewhere to be that isn't on campus, so how do we know she isn't just grabbing her backpack and taking off to Penny Lanes instead of going to class like the rest of us?

The answer is: we don't.

"Nothing showed up because there is no Lucy Sharpe enrolled at Rutledge," Sloane says at last, and I feel the twist of something sharp in my chest: fear, cold and hard, plunging in deep like a knife to the heart. "Lucy Sharpe doesn't exist."

CHAPTER 47

AFTER

I walk inside to find Sloane and Nicole in Lucy's bedroom, tired eyes drinking it in. The place is destroyed: floor to ceiling, wall to wall, drawers thrust open and clothes disheveled. Shoes kicked out of the closet and books splayed out like a bomb went off.

"Did you check under the bed?" I ask, joining them on her unmade mattress. I can still smell her here: vanilla and cigarette. Musky and delicate. Radically both.

"Yeah," Sloane says. "Her phone's not there."

I nod, pulling my legs up under me. "How about in the desk?"

"Gone, too."

I put my hand on Nicole's knee, squeezing gently. This is the hardest for her, I know. The performance, the lies. She's a good person.

"I'm sorry—" she starts, but Sloane shakes her head, cutting her off.

"I already told you, it's not your fault."

"What did Frank say to you out there after we left?" Nicole asks me next.

"Nothing," I say. "Don't worry about it. You're doing fine."

"God, I hate this," she says, sinking farther into the bed. She lays her head on Lucy's pillow and I notice a black curl there, long and coiled, resting delicately on top. A little piece of her still stuck to the sham.

I bet, if we looked hard enough, we'd find pieces of her everywhere.

"It'll be over soon," Sloane says. "Give it a couple days. They'll find the stuff on her phone."

"How long until you think it all comes out?"

They both look at me and I just shrug, attention drifting around the room. I feel a bit dazed, seeing it like this, sort of like taking in the ruins of a place you once loved. Her room the epicenter of the earthquake that shook our lives apart.

"I have no idea," I say at last. "The press is still reporting she's a student. Rutledge has got to say something eventually."

"They're probably scrambling," Sloane says, laughing a little. "Can you imagine the dean admitting that a random person spent an entire year shacking up in their dorm and nobody knew about it? She kept a shower caddy in the bathroom, for Christ's sake."

"The parents will have pitchforks," I say. "And my mother will be leading the pack."

Nicole smiles, finally, and I feel something lighten in my chest when I look at her. She glances at Sloane, then at me, and the three of us burst out laughing, a violent fit that leaves us in stitches. We must be tired, delirious, the stress and surreality of these last few weeks doing something strange to our brains.

It is sort of ridiculous, though, when you really think about it. The things Lucy was able to get away with. The people she fooled.

The people she's still fooling.

"The cops have got to know by now," Sloane says, wiping a tear from her eye.

"Yeah, well, we didn't lie."

And that's the truth: we didn't lie. Not outright, only by omission, crafting our responses slowly, deliberately, every time Detective Frank hit us with a question that could come back to bite. That very first morning, sitting in the dining room, the three of us swallowed by our oversized T-shirts as our plan lurched into motion: slow, at first, but gaining momentum. Soon it would take off and leave us all behind.

"Nobody's getting into trouble, girls, but she hasn't been accounted for since Friday."

We held fast, doe-eyed and innocent, and it was easy, really, because that's all we are to him: underestimated always. Just children, just girls.

"Have you talked to anyone in her classes?"

I can still hear her so clearly, stone-faced Sloane, chiming in with the perfect response while Nicole and I bit our tongues, tasted blood, a blend of terror and triumph pumping through our veins as we tried so hard not to laugh.

"Lucy doesn't go to class."

"Frank's gonna be so pissed," Nicole says now, threading her hands behind her head. "It makes him look like an idiot."

Sloane's the one to laugh this time, plopping down beside her and nuzzling close. "That's because he is."

I slide my way between them now and the three of us lie quietly in bed together, the way we have so many times before: staring up at the plastic stars on the ceiling, meticulously arranged.

Thinking of Lucy and everything she taught us.

CHAPTER 48

BEFORE

It's unusually calm on the water, the gentle churn of the engine creating little waves that ripple out around us. Marmalade sky reflecting off the surface, casting everything in an orange glow. It would normally be such a scenic picture, something ripped straight out of a song, but the boat's slow approach to the island in the distance makes it feel like we're being transported to a prison somewhere, cut off from society with no way to escape.

"Margot."

I turn around, tallying up the bodies in the boat. Nicole is sitting on Trevor's lap, angular legs sticking out of a fleece blanket draped across her stomach. He's drinking something out of a flask, stainless steel and small in his hand, the other palm placed on Nicole's thigh as he nuzzles his nose deep into her neck. Sloane is leaning into Lucas to their left, visibly rigid as his fingers play absentmindedly with her hair, while Will and James are next to me in the back and Levi is driving, knuckles white as his hands grip the wheel.

"Margot."

"Yeah," I say slowly, twisting further, already feeling Lucy's eyes on me. Ice-cold and kaleidoscopic; curious, like she somehow knows. She's all the way in the front, perched on the bow like a figurehead pulling us forward.

Or maybe a siren, seductive and dangerous, her little lies fooling us all.

"Did you hear that?" she asks me.

"Hear what?"

"There's a full moon tonight."

I look at Lucy, registering that little twitch in her lip. Like that day on the lawn, our first talk in the dorm, laughing at something I still don't understand. I don't know why she's telling me this, what she's playing at, so I just nod, smile, and twist back around as I pull my own blanket tight around my shoulders, the sharp chill whipping off the water sending a shiver straight through me.

I think about this afternoon, just over an hour ago, the very moment when everything changed. Sloane and I pushed close on my bed; the things she told me lodged in my brain, stuck like a splinter. Harsh and throbbing as I tried to summon a single memory of Lucy on campus, in one of my classes. Black curls bobbing in a sea of other students or sharp blue eyes staring at me from the back of the library.

That whiff of vanilla hovering like the ghost of her trapped in an empty room.

It was a pointless exercise. Lucy was never there. I was starting to accept it with a certainty that was startling, so much so that it's hard to imagine how I never noticed it before—but the truth is, it's easy to blend in in a place like this. Rutledge may not be big, but it's sprawling. The classrooms are scattered across the city, historic buildings tucked into little cracks and crannies, disappearing into their surroundings so naturally it's hard to even know what belongs to the college and what doesn't. There are full sections of the school I've never noticed before, entire buildings I haven't had a reason to step inside. Not only that, but I've seen the same handful of people in my classes for almost two years now, all of us trapped inside a bubble of our own making. Completely unaware of what goes on outside it. I rarely catch glimpses of Sloane or Nicole during the day, either, both of them retreating to their respective spaces and staying there until it's time to come home again, and when I think about all this, *really* think about it, it actually seems shockingly easy to do what Lucy has done: to simply step into this place and blend in so seamlessly.

To convince us all she's one of us.

"She's still our friend," I said to Sloane, the implications of it all sitting stubborn between us, refusing to sink in. "I mean, this doesn't change anything—"

"Margot, it changes everything." She gaped. "We're living with a stranger."

"She's not a stranger," I said, somewhat mildly, humiliation blooming in my chest at how natural it was for me to keep jumping to Lucy's defense like this, no questions asked. Same as that first day outside the shed, listening to Sloane's slander, the reflex to protect her was automatic, instinctive, like a mallet to the knee.

"Well, she's not who she says she is, either."

It's still tempting, even now, to give Lucy the benefit of the doubt. Sloane hadn't been with us that night on the roof; she hadn't heard Lucy talk about her childhood, her past. The way things were and her desire to get away.

"I wanted a fresh start," she had said. *"I figured you'd understand."*

I did understand, and I was starting to convince myself that maybe it was simple: maybe Lucy moved to Rutledge on her own but didn't have the money or the grades to get in. She started working at Penny Lanes, saw the way the students lived, and wanted that for herself, too. A chance at belonging, at friends. Not so different from any of us, really, so she met Sloane and Nicole on the lawn and felt at home in their presence; she was invited into their dorm, into their lives, and didn't want to admit that she was somehow different, less than, because of her parents. The way she grew up.

Why *wouldn't* she fake it when nobody questioned her? Why wouldn't she just go along with it all, simply pretend, like the rest of us, to be something she's not?

We're so close to the island now that I can see the other boats anchoring, swarms of boys hopping off and onto the sand, carrying duffel bags and coolers over their heads to keep them from getting wet. Girls sitting on the sides with their legs dangling off, taking swigs of vodka straight from the bottle. Salt water and wind turning their hair crimped and wild. I thought about skipping the party tonight, hanging back while the others left and using the free time to sort through my thoughts, try to find some answers. Sloane couldn't get away with bailing without upsetting Lucas—that, and she didn't want to leave Nicole by herself—and neither of us wanted to tip off Lucy, either. Alert her to the fact that something was wrong. We're supposed to be sharing a tent, after all, the only two roommates who aren't coupled up—and then I had an idea.

"Luce, can you come back here?" Levi asks, bringing my attention back to the boat. "I'm getting ready to anchor."

I've never heard him use that nickname before and I watch as he pats the seat next to him while Lucy stands up, stepping over our stuff as she makes her way toward the back. Images of the two of them flash through my mind again: Lucy in his bedroom, sinking deep on his mattress. Long fingers winding through his hair as she pulled him close, her lips on his. She plops down on the bench next to him and starts poking around the cupholder, always curious and forever bored, before pulling out a rusted fishhook and using it to pick at her nails.

"Make sure you girls don't wander away when you're drunk," Lucas says, a giddy anticipation sweeping through him now that the night is so close to starting. "There are animals out there."

"What kind of animals?" Sloane asks, crossing her arms.

"Spiders," he says, his fingers crawling their way up her leg. "Alligators, snakes."

"Just stay on the beach and you'll be fine," James says, and I turn around, startled at how close he is. With everything else going on, I forgot he was even here.

"Wait until you see the stars," Lucas continues, hugging Sloane close. "It gets so dark without the ambient light—"

"Fuck!"

We all turn to look at Lucy, her sudden scream startling us all. A stream of bright red blood has erupted from her nail, running down her finger, and I watch as she throws the fishhook back into the cupholder like it somehow sprang to life and attacked her on its own.

"Here," Levi says, rummaging through various cubbies in search of something to stanch the bleeding. I watch as it leaks out in a steady gush, perfect little circles dripping onto the floor of the boat, the cushioned seat, Levi's shorts. He's distracted, simultaneously trying to look and steer as the boat hits a wave at a weird angle and slams back into the water, hard, almost sending Nicole to the ground.

"Butler!" Trevor yells. There's a subtle slur to his speech as he grabs ahold of Nicole's thigh with his free hand. She winces, straightening herself on his lap. "Watch where the fuck you're going!"

"I'm okay—" Nicole starts, but Trevor interrupts her, eager to keep fighting.

"Christ, dude, you're going to kill us all."

"It's fine," Lucy says quietly, touching Levi's arm. "I got it."

Levi peels his eyes from her and looks back ahead, through the windshield, purposefully avoiding Trevor's gaze. I can see the tendons in his neck bulging, his jaw clenched tight like he has to physically restrain himself from snapping back. The tension on the boat is so palpable, so thick, and I realize, somehow for the first time, that it isn't just between Lucy and us but the boys, too. Nicole and Trevor; Levi and me. This little group of us that was once so solid now warped and bending beneath the pressure of it all; little hairline fractures traveling slowly, threatening to burst.

"Are you okay?" I ask, my voice low as I watch Lucy hold her finger, the slow glide of blood between her hands like the wax of a melting candle dripping to the floor.

"Fine," she says. "A little blood never bothered me."

I watch as she lifts her head, eyes on mine, before pulling her finger to her lips and sucking it dry, and I get the sudden sensation of looming danger, watching her like this. Like eyeing a funnel cloud in the distance as it inches closer, collecting strength. Like we're all marching toward something big, something permanent, the slow simmer of the last eight months morphing into full-blown boil.

The boat sidles up to the shore and lurches to a stop, the anchor plunging into the water with a violent splash. The night is officially alive with the sound of drunken shrieks and wild laughs, but all I can hear is my own blood in my ears. My own beating heart like the steady thrum of drums in the distance, the executioner's call, intensity building until we hit the inevitable crescendo—and once we do, once we reach the top, there will be nothing left for us to do but fall.

CHAPTER 49

It gets dark fast, the little bubble of sun in the distance melting into the water as the boys work quickly, quietly, trying to pitch the tents and get the fire going before we're swallowed by the sky. Already, I can hear the noises of the night: the quick thrash of something feeding in the distance, the buzz of bugs as they skim across our skin.

"Whiskey?" Nicole asks, walking up behind me. I turn around, registering a bottle in her hand that's already half gone.

"Sure," I say, grabbing it from her and taking a sip. It's sweet, honey flavored, and the syrupy liquid goes down slow, like drinking sap. "Have you eaten anything today?"

I try to smile when I ask it, try to make it sound like a joke. A subtle reference to her request the morning after Halloween, reminding her to eat dinner, but she doesn't smile back when she sits down next to me.

"If not, this will go straight to your head."

"I'm fine," she says, wrapping her arms tight around her legs. They're so fragile, so thin, and I can't stop thinking about the way she looked earlier, stumbling around on the boat. No cushion on her bones to break her fall.

"Are you really?" I ask quietly. "Fine?"

She doesn't answer, both of us silent as we sit in the sand, on the edge of everyone, watching the freshmen pile driftwood and palmetto fronds into a giant pile for the fire. The rest of the boys are setting up tents in a circle around the pit; the girls by the coolers, guzzling liquor to stay warm. Suddenly, there's a shriek in the distance and we turn toward the sound, our eyes landing on Lucy in the water. It's practically freezing, but she's still up to her knees, jeans rolled up and damp at the edges. Splashing Levi as he tries to carry the rest of the supplies from the boat.

"Does that bother you?" Nicole asks, ignoring my question and nodding toward them.

"So, you've noticed," I say, shooting her a smirk.

"She's not exactly subtle, is she?"

"I guess it's just hard to understand what she sees in him," I respond, a watery truth. "After everything I've told her."

Nicole nods, her bare toes digging into the sand, and I turn to face her, knowing this is my opening. I've been so distracted lately—by Lucy, by Levi, by the two of them together and the memories they provoke; trying to understand how it all ties together, what it all means—that I know I've been neglecting Nicole, whatever she's going through. Pushing it off until later, never. Hoping it'll simply resolve on its own.

"Does it bother *you*?" I ask slowly, trying to gauge her reaction.

"Why would it?" she asks, stone-faced as she grabs the whiskey from my hand and takes a long pull, jaw clenching as she swallows.

"I just thought that after whatever happened on Halloween—"

"I said I'm fine, Margot."

"I don't *believe* you," I push, my fingers digging into the sand. "Whatever happened . . . you can tell me."

"Nothing happened on Halloween."

"Nicole," I whisper, my voice dipped low. I hadn't planned on doing this tonight, confronting her so deliberately, but there's something about us all being marooned here with nowhere to run that makes me want to keep digging. "Come on. Please."

"Levi didn't do anything," she says at last, a sudden glint of tears in her eyes. It's the closest she's ever come to a confession and I watch as she wipes them angrily, little wet streaks darkening her shirtsleeves. "I promise."

"Are you sure?" I ask, looking back at the fire. My eyes on him crouching next to it, blowing gently on a collection of sticks glowing red. Thinking about the bruises on her wrists; the ones they found on Eliza. Levi and Lucy and the thought of him helping himself to everything I love making my jaw squeeze.

"Yes, I'm sure," Nicole says, grabbing the whiskey again and draining it completely. "He didn't do a thing."

The night descends into chaos quickly, like the sinking sun took our inhibitions with it. The fire is roaring, finally, the orange glow of it sparking in our eyes; ash and embers flying into the sky before drifting into the distance, getting swept away by the breeze. Someone has music playing through a portable speaker and a group of girls are holding hands, running in circles around the fire as they sing.

I wonder what it is about the cloak of night, a sky full of stars, that makes everyone act a little strange, a little savage. "*The very error of the moon,*" Shakespeare said, a line from *Othello* that stuck with me when we read it last semester. "*It makes men mad.*"

I look up at the sky again, that single spotlight shining down, and try to push out the memories of the last time I was acutely aware of a full moon above, another party taking place in the dark. A collection of kids left on their own with too much freedom and not enough sense.

It's animal, I guess, our attraction to it. The way it empowers us to think and feel and do as we please.

I glance around, taking in the others. Lucy and Levi are standing by the flames, his arm flung around her shoulder in a way that makes me think of him and Eliza on that very last night: stumbling, laughing, fingers intertwined. Sloane and Nicole are sitting together by the tents, their eyes on Trevor as he lurches around in the sand. There's a bottle of rum clutched in his hand that hasn't left his grip since we got here, but that hasn't stopped him from barking out orders. Still bossing around the freshmen, playing God, even though their duties are over and his power is gone. After a few more seconds, I find who I'm looking for and stand up quick, brushing the sand from my jeans as I make my way toward him. I glance back at Lucy every few seconds, relieved to see her still swept up in Levi, paying no attention to my slow slink into the dark.

I approach him furtively, standing by the water with a couple other brothers, noticing he looks different than the last time I saw him: no more blood slathered across his skin, his cheeks. Long blond hair now buzzed short against his scalp.

No more costume, that stupid blue dress.

"Excuse me, Danny?" I ask, watching as he turns around at the sound of his name. He doesn't recognize me at first, but slowly, I see it: the memory of Halloween, of me, of the three of us sitting around that fire out back. Lucy pretending not to know him and the way he scurried away with his tail between his legs. "Do you have a second?"

Danny DeMarcus, Lucy's old classmate.

The only person here who might know her at all.

CHAPTER 50

We walk along the shore together, away from the fire, the sand spongy beneath our feet and the sharp shriek of whistles echoing out around us.

"Ignore them," Danny says at last, one hand in his pocket and the other nursing a can of Bud Light. The sounds from the party grow steadily more distant until we finally stop at a collection of driftwood and sit side by side, the silhouettes of the others dancing in the dark. "So, you said you wanted to talk?"

"Yeah, about Lucy," I say, trying to choose my words wisely. "Halloween."

"Right," he says, looking back at the water. I can hear it lapping in the distance, the scuttle of fiddler crabs as the tide washes out, and suddenly remember what Lucas said earlier about all the other life out here prowling around in the dark.

"She told me you went to school together," I say at last. "How she grew up. That she doesn't really like people knowing about her past."

Danny is quiet, forcing me to continue.

"I think she pretended not to know you before because I was sitting right there."

"I guess I can't blame her," he says at last, taking a drink.

"Why's that?"

He turns to look at me, eyebrows raising.

"She's your roommate. Why don't you ask her?"

"I know it has to do with her home life," I continue, using my toe to draw circles in the sand. "Not getting along with her mom."

"That's an understatement."

"Was it really that bad?"

Danny shrugs, takes another drink.

"Let's just say her mom has a reputation," he says. "I'm sure it wasn't easy to live with."

I nod, filing the information away.

"I also know she had a boyfriend who might have . . . hurt her."

Danny turns to face me, finally, and I'm suddenly grateful for the pitch-black sky shielding my expression. I'm trying to piece it together, form a narrative that might make it make sense. All the little clues Lucy has fed me, either deliberately or not: whispered truths she shared in the dark and those little admissions I extracted right out of her, pushing carefully until they came gushing out. I can't yet bring myself to say what I've started to think, the pieces slipping together like a jigsaw puzzle. The bewildering enigma of Lucy slowly starting to resemble something solid, something whole.

I can't tell Danny that ever since I saw Lucy and Levi through that bedroom window, all their little moments together have started replaying in my mind in a strange new light: the first time he saw her at Penny Lanes, that subtle look of shock as his eyes roamed all over. The way he turned to me, cocked his head: *"Do you know her?"* he'd asked, like he couldn't quite believe it. The way

Lucy would always single him out after that, almost as if they had a shared history neither one of them wanted to admit.

"I'm just worried about her," I add. "I think they might be talking again."

I glance back at the fire, and although I can't make out faces from this far, I can still see them, Lucy and Levi, huddled close in the exact same spot. I think about the way Lucy had looked when I told her those stories about Eliza and Levi, that curl to her lip like she was subtly amused. The way she kept asking about her after that, nudging me to tell her more like there was some simmering jealousy I could never understand.

"That's not possible," Danny says at last, shaking his head. "Parker's dead."

The shock of the sentence bolts me in place: the casualness of it, so matter-of-fact, not at all what I was expecting.

"Parker," I repeat, the unfamiliar name feeling strange on my tongue. The confusion on my face must be apparent because Danny keeps talking.

"Lucy's boyfriend," he explains. "They were together for years."

"What happened?" I ask, my head swimming at this sudden shift. And just like that, I'm back to square one, the flimsy theory I was starting to form already deflating slowly in my hands.

"Car accident. Right before she left."

I think about us up on that roof again; the way Lucy had looked at me and kept talking in the dark, eyes wide like there was something big she wanted to admit. Something she was working up to, maybe. Something deeper she wanted to say.

"There are things from back then I didn't want to bring with me."

"Was Lucy in the car when it happened?"

Danny sighs, rolling his neck before downing the rest of his beer and crunching the can in his grip.

"No," he says. "But people blamed her for it."

"How could people blame her if she wasn't there?"

"They were at a party the night he died and got in an argument. A bad one. People saw her slap him before taking off and he tried to chase after her. Got behind the wheel after he'd been drinking and ran into a ditch."

"That's not—" I start, my mouth hanging open when I can't find the words. Imagining Lucy's sad smile at the dinner table; the way she averted her eyes, like she was ashamed. "People can't blame her for that," I say at last. "That's not her fault."

"You know how rumors start," he says. "First, she provoked him, then she slapped him. Then the slap turned into her actually mauling the guy, scratching his eyes so it messed with his vision. Then people started speculating that she fucked with his car so the brakes wouldn't work. All kinds of stupid stuff."

I think back to freshman year, Maggie and me on that lawn. The stories about Lucy that were swirling around, ever-present, practically invisible like dandelion seeds getting swept up in the breeze. But all you really need is one to settle in your mind and plant itself there, growing slowly until it takes over everything.

All you need is one person to believe it until the others do, too.

"Sometimes people can't accept the randomness of it," Danny continues, with a gentle shrug, like this isn't the first time he's thought about death. "Sometimes, people just die."

"Yeah," I say, remembering that night with Mr. Jefferson on the porch. After the funeral, his brown-liquor breath, both of us dropping crumbs of doubt as we glanced at one another, silently hoping the other would follow. Both of us looking to ease our own guilt, for someone else to pin it on. Some stupid reason to make it make sense.

"You know, you're the second person today to ask me about

Lucy," Danny says, turning to look at me like the thought just occurred to him. "I had forgotten the girl even existed until three months ago and now she's all I talk about."

My head jerks back in his direction, another bomb I wasn't expecting.

"Who else was asking?"

"Levi," he says. "Just before we left the house."

I can feel it again: that pinch of envy, of greed, even though I don't understand it. I don't understand how I can still feel this protectiveness over her after everything she's lied about. How I can still find myself wanting to step between them like I did with Eliza, every little stolen look feeling like a personal betrayal? A knife to the back?

"Did he say why?"

"Isn't it obvious?" Danny laughs, jerking his head back to the fire. "Look at them."

I twist back around, squinting in the dark, the two bodies I assume to be theirs huddled so close they've melted into one inky black spot and I wonder, for the very first time, if I need to just swallow my pride and talk to Levi next. Ask him outright the things I've been thinking; see if there's something more that he knows.

"Anyway," Danny says, standing up from the driftwood like he's suddenly decided he's had enough. "You're a good friend for worrying about her, but there's no need. Lucy can hold her own."

"Yeah, thanks," I say, standing up, too. Trying to mask the disappointment I feel in leaving our talk with more questions than answers. "I'm sorry for bothering you."

"You're not a bother," he says. "And for what it's worth, I don't blame her for leaving. Fairfield's too small a town to shrug off rumors like that."

"Fairfield," I repeat, the familiar name pulsing through my mind like a budding headache as I try to place it. "Fairfield, North Carolina?"

"Yeah, you know it?" he asks, a surprised smile like this is the most interesting thing to come out of our conversation. "That's our hometown."

CHAPTER 51

I feel my fingers trailing their way across Eliza's clothes, folded tight and undisturbed. That worn envelope stuffed in the back and my hands sensing the bulk of it, notably out of place.

Pulling it out, opening the flap. All that money stuffed inside and an address on the back I didn't recognize. The picture of it on my phone I had forgotten all about ever since Lucy showed up, commandeering my attention.

"Where have you been?" she asks me now, plopping down in the sand beside us. Sloane, Nicole, and I are sitting cross-legged, side by side, observing everyone else's slow descent into madness. The party is still going, still raging like the fire around which we're gathered, though the crowd is beginning to dwindle now, people starting to stagger into their tents. Exploring the island, maybe. Couples sneaking off and into the trees.

"I had to pee," I say, turning to face her. Her cheeks are flushed and pink from the fire and I see that envelope again, so clear in my mind.

Fairfield, North Carolina.

I watch as she turns in the direction of the foliage behind us, a cluster of untamed shrubs and long, sharp grass. Swaying cattails and barren trunks with branches like brittle bones stripped of their skin. I wonder if she really did see Danny and me walk off in the opposite direction together. I wonder if she knows, on some subconscious level, how close her secrets are to suddenly slipping away. If she knows that I'm lying.

"I got lost," I add, grabbing the bottle of wine beside me and tipping it back, swallowing too much. For the heat, the courage. The numbness I know it'll soon provide. I can already feel the whiskey from before filling my limbs up slowly, pushing down on my eyes so they feel heavy and hard. "It's dark out there, away from everything."

I look at Sloane, nursing her beer, a tension in her jaw that calcified the second Lucy showed up. Nicole right next to her, cheekbones angular and harsh in the shadow of the flames. She looks sunken-in, hollow, like someone jabbed her with a needle and she's been deflating slowly, losing her shape, and there's something so desolate about it. About all of us, really. Sitting here, side by side, trying to pretend that everything is fine.

Trying to convince ourselves that nothing has changed when really, everything has.

"Huh."

She says it in a tone that's painfully unconvincing and the entire thing reminds me of Eliza and me in those final few days. Of graduation, bumping into each other outside the auditorium, our parents pushing us together without even registering the stiffness in our arms or the lies in our smiles. That picture still tacked to the wall in my bedroom, framed on my mantel, the saddest thing I've ever seen. In that moment, we knew something big had fractured between us, something possibly even permanent. We knew, after that argument, that we would never be whole again—but still, we tried. We tried to look happy, normal, Eliza's fingers hovering behind my back like she couldn't stand the thought of touching me. Her mom counting down, camera in hand, and the sigh of relief that escaped from her lips as soon as the flash went off and we could peel ourselves apart. We hadn't spoken a word since that fight in my bedroom. It was the longest we had ever gone without talking, an entire decade of friendship whittled down to nothing but stone-cold silence, but neither of us wanted to be the first to crack so instead we let it grow between us like a tumor, getting bigger, denser. As if ignoring it completely would make it go away on its own.

"Oh shit," Sloane mutters and I look up now, tracking her gaze, watching as Trevor trips in the sand. He goes down hard, dangerously close to the fire, limbs like rubber as his legs splay out in two opposite directions.

"I'm fine," he slurs, waving off Lucas as he tries to pull him up. He's still clutching that stupid bottle, fingers wound tight around the plastic neck, refusing to let go even to break his fall. Everyone glances over as he struggles to find his footing and I look over to Nicole next, wondering if she's going to help him. Silently hoping she won't.

"I'm grabbing another blanket," she says, standing up to make her way to the tent.

I know she's embarrassed, seeing him like this. Maybe a little resentful that Trevor's allowed to let loose and act like an idiot when she, apparently, isn't. I look back just as Trevor finally gets to his feet and lifts the handle in the air, saluting us all. The bottle is alarmingly empty, only a few fingers of liquid left sloshing at the bottom, and he tries to take another swig but his aim is off, a rush of clear liquid missing his mouth and gushing down the front of his shirt.

"Fuck!" he yells, stumbling a bit as he pulls at the fabric, the sweet smell of coconut drifting toward us in the wind. A snort of laughter erupts somewhere to my right and I twist around, looking for the source.

It came from Levi, unmistakably, a look of pure amusement on his face watching Trevor embarrass himself in front of everyone like this.

"Is something funny?" Trevor asks, taking a step toward him. His face has morphed in a matter of seconds and I recognize the same look from Halloween that made my skin crawl: dangerous, predatory. His eyes wild and unrestrained.

"Butler," he repeats when Levi doesn't answer. "I said, is something *funny?*"

"No," Levi says, shaking his head, downing the rest of his beer before reaching into a cooler and grabbing another. Everyone else seems to have stopped what they're doing now, bodies still like statues. Afraid to move, afraid to breathe.

"Give me yours," Trevor says suddenly, a challenge in his voice. We watch as he drops the bottle onto the sand and rips his shirt off before flinging it at Levi, his bare chest rippling in the shadows from the fire. The shirt lands in Levi's lap with a wet flop and he takes a deep breath as he stares down at it, still unmoving. The glow from the flames illuminating his face, eyes stretching down into two long shadows.

"Butler, I said *switch.*"

"God, he's an asshole," Sloane mutters, and I look back at her now, the way she's staring at Trevor with such disgust.

After a long stretch of silence, Levi places his beer on the ground with measured control and pulls his shirt off, throwing it over to Trevor. Even from here, I can see the trail of goose bumps erupt down his arms, his bare skin exposed to the cool night air.

Or maybe it's the humiliation, this public act of shame, his anger festering like an infection, trying to push its way to the surface. He just sits like that for a second, half naked, jaw clenched tight and eyes on the flames as Trevor pulls the clean shirt over his head and continues to glare.

Finally, Levi gives in, taking the wet wad of fabric off his lap and fanning it out before putting it on, that dribble of liquor still stained down the front.

"That's what I thought," Trevor murmurs, stalking off, and I can't help but wonder why Levi let him do that. Why he let Trevor chew him out on the boat earlier, too. Maybe he's conditioned after an entire semester of letting the other brothers walk all over him, older boys treating him like their own personal punching bag. Maybe he still feels like a pledge, only a few hours into the party that was supposed to set him free. Maybe he knew it wasn't worth the fight, that Trevor's wrath would be worse later if he turned him down.

Or maybe he's trying to keep the peace for some reason, every interaction between them like Levi is walking on glass, never knowing when he might get cut.

The party reignites slowly, cautiously, people forcing themselves back to their conversations and their drinks, though everyone's eyes are still darting furtively over to Levi as he sulks off to the side. There's something dangerous about the way he grabs his beer from the sand and downs the rest of it before crushing the can in his grip, tossing it into the water. Reaching for another and cracking it open before downing that, too.

"I'll be right back," Lucy says, standing up and walking toward him. I watch as she plops down by his side, her hand on his leg like she's trying to comfort him, and I start to look away, still uneasy watching the two of them together like that, when a flash of movement jerks my head back in their direction: Levi grabbing Lucy's arm, hard, and flinging it away with a force that feels violent. Lucy hissing something under her breath before Levi snaps back, standing up with a look of revulsion on his face.

I watch as he stumbles off, bare feet clumsy as he makes his way toward the trees. Those brittle branches like a skeletal hand reaching out, curling its fingers; the silhouette of a single bird perched on the edge like an omen. Then Lucy stands up, too, brushes the sand from her legs as she turns to look at me.

A smile forming on her lips as she follows him into the dark.

CHAPTER 52

My head is pounding as I open my eyes, the brightness of the tent borderline blinding.

I blink a few times, my surroundings materializing slowly around me before I smack my lips, try to swallow. My throat feeling like sandpaper and my spit as thick as glue. It's freezing in here, the early morning air still unthawed, and I reach my arm out to the side, instinctively looking for the familiar warmth of another person beside me only to find the second sleeping bag cold and empty and zipped up tight.

No one's there.

I sit up fast, a pang of panic flaring in my chest. Memories of Eliza, my phantom limb, all those mornings I had woken up to that blissful, bleary second when my subconscious still believed she was alive. I remember now, with a startling clarity, that Lucy should be in here with me. We were supposed to be sharing a tent last night and I close my eyes again as quick bursts of memory explode in my mind like a strobe light, sharp and blinding: the fire, the dancing, the mounds of warm bodies passed out around the giant open flame. The moon in the sky like a large, open eye and the bottles of liquor being drained faster than what should have been possible. Danny and me on the driftwood, whispering those stories: Lucy and her boyfriend, that accident. Some big argument just before he died. Trevor stumbling around, screaming out orders.

Lucy and Levi and that strange confrontation, a simmering anger as he flung her arm off.

I don't remember putting myself to bed and I fling the covers off now, looking down, realizing I'm still in my clothes from last night. Smears of dried mud caked to my pants; the cuffs of my jeans stiff with salt water. Sand and cold sweat flaking off my chest like a molting second skin.

I remember Levi leaving, Lucy following, that worm of rage writhing around in my stomach. Trying to drown it, kill it, by picking up the bottle and taking another drink.

A sense of claustrophobia comes washing over me and I suddenly, desperately, need to get off this island. It feels like those early memories with Eliza again—the two of us beneath that dock, surrounded on all sides; that bubble of damp air that got caught in my lungs and made it feel like we were sinking, drowning—and I stand up too fast in my tent, fighting the overwhelming sense of vertigo that rushes to my head before unzipping the opening and stepping outside. The island is buzzing with the kind of hungover energy that makes everything feel like it's moving in slow motion: lethargic stretches and girls sipping instant coffee out of rustic enamel mugs. Splashing their faces with palmfuls of water, mascara smearing like a bruise beneath their eyes. The boys are lolling around in sweatshirts and basketball shorts, thick heads of hair sticking up at odd angles. A few of them attempting to scramble eggs above barely there flames.

I finally catch sight of Sloane and Nicole in the water, calf-deep and moving slow, and I amble over to them, my heart hammering in my chest.

"There she is," Sloane says without turning to face me. Already, I don't like the sound of that. "And how are we feeling this morning?"

"Like shit," I say, rubbing my eyes. "I think I blacked out."

"You think?"

Sloane looks at me, eyebrows raised, and simply stares for a second before she looks back at Nicole, the tip of her hand trailing idly across the water.

"What happened?" I ask, a croak in my throat, even though I'm not so sure I want to know.

"You tell me," she says, looking back down, ripples from Nicole's fingers cracking the glassy surface. "You weren't making any sense at the end."

"What was I saying?"

"Something about how you needed to find Levi," Sloane says, and I suddenly remember the thought that flared up when I was talking to Danny. Wondering if I needed to just talk to Levi, swallow my pride and demand some answers. "I kept telling you to stop but you wouldn't listen."

"I was trying to find Levi?" I ask, twisting around, my eyes scanning the beach for any sign of him. For any sign of either of them, Lucy or Levi, although her absence in our tent has made it painfully clear that they're probably asleep, and they're probably sleeping together.

"At one point, you ran off to find him and I found you lying by the water an hour later," she says. "The tide was rising."

I look down at my jeans, the dark stain at the bottom, and her words trigger another memory from last night, blurry but there:

my fingers digging into the sand as I listened to the occasional splash in the distance, the bobbing of boats anchored offshore. The murmur of voices a few yards behind me and sounds of the party slipping away as people made their way to their tents or just fell asleep right there by the fire. My head spinning and my mind on Lucy and me up on the roof, on the beach over Christmas, curled up in those blankets as we passed the bottle between us.

The distant pop of fireworks and her voice like a whisper, a suggestion. A dare.

"If you knew you could get away with murder, would you do it?"

I remember staring at the sky, so cloudless and clear I could see every constellation like Thanksgiving night with Lucy's fingers in mine. The quick stab of jealousy once I found the sisters, the twins, their hands clasped tight while my own remained so painfully empty.

"Did I find him?" I ask, a creeping uncertainty in my voice. My cheeks burning as I remember Levi standing up and walking into the trees; Lucy's smile as she glanced in my direction before following slyly behind. It's all so familiar, this terrible feeling. Even after everything I've learned about Lucy, everything I know and don't know, there's still a possessiveness toward her I can't control. It's the same as the greed I had for Eliza, wanting her friendship all to myself. The high from her attention perfectly pure and razor-sharp, not the watered-down thing I had to stomach when somebody else wanted it, too.

"I don't know," Sloane says. "You were alone."

I sigh, closing my eyes, trying to excavate the massive pit settling deep in my stomach. I feel uneasy, sick, but I still can't put a finger on why. It's probably all the alcohol, mixing liquors, this abandoned place and the anxiety that inevitably sets in after a night of indulgence. Trying to think back on what I did, what I said.

What I might have seen. Maybe it's the full moon from last night making me feel off-kilter and strange, reminding me of that night almost two years ago. Of watching Eliza and Levi stumble around in the dark just like Lucy and Levi had been. Witnessing that argument—that violent fling of her arm, her low hiss in return—and that feeling of fear, of dread, of knowing I should step in and do something, but also just wanting to fall asleep and forget.

I try to summon more memories now, my mind grazing the feeling of something familiar but just barely out of reach. I try to picture finding them, maybe. Rounding a corner to see their bare skin glowing like ghosts in the night as I stood at a distance, watching it all.

"I wish it was him. It should have been him."

"I think I'm going to be sick," I say instead, head swimming, a slow heat starting to crawl up the back of my throat.

I turn around and walk away from the water, toward the direction of the tent before taking a turn and going inland instead. I approach the trees quickly, the foliage growing denser the farther I get from the shore, and I keep my eyes down, watch where I'm stepping. Trying not to think too hard about Lucas on the boat and his comment about all the other creatures we're sharing the place with; all the deadly things that lurk in the shadows, just waiting for an unassuming something to stumble across their path. Finally, I chance a glance up and spot a clearing a few feet in front of me, another little patch of sand in the distance with water retreating on the other side. I keep my eyes lifted, my gaze trained forward until my foot hooks around a root and I start to fall.

"Shit," I hiss, just barely catching myself.

I shake my leg free and look down, realizing, too late, that it's not a root. Instead, my foot got caught on something else entirely: a human arm stretched out in front of me, long and lean and covered in dirt. I feel something catch in my throat—shock, fear, a horrible knowing locked deep inside—and before I can stop myself, I let out a scream, shrill and haunting, before the sharp swell of vomit comes barreling out.

CHAPTER 53

It doesn't take long for the others to find me.

I can hear them before I see them, the snapping of twigs and leaves as they run in my direction, calling my name. My scream suspended in the air around me and my pile of vomit steaming warm in the cool morning air.

"Margot!"

They must think I've stumbled upon some kind of animal, visions of me clutched in the jaws of an alligator, limbs ripping as it drags me away. I recognize Lucas's voice first, just a few yards behind me, but I still can't move. I still can't speak. All I can do is stare down at the body beneath me, facedown in the mud. At the back of his head, moppy brown hair all tangled and torn. The same head I saw staring into the distance from beneath the deck-board slats almost three years ago; those long, tan arms, so muscular and toned, once holding a cigarette as he stood just above, now strewn about in all the wrong angles.

"Margot, are you okay?"

Lucas appears beside me and places his hand on my arm, slow

and delicate. Like he's afraid I might break. I can feel the moment he sees it, too: his tightening fingers, the intake of air.

The back of Levi's neck, all marbled in bruises.

"Oh shit," he says, letting go of me before pushing both of his hands through his hair. I turn to look at him just in time to register the color drain from his skin. "Oh shit, oh shit."

"What is it?"

Sloane jogs up behind us before coming to an abrupt halt, her eyes bulging impossibly wide. Nicole just behind her, her face ghost-white.

"What's going on?"

I hear Trevor's voice next, more irritated than anything, and twist around to see a handful of people trickling in behind him, too nosy to stay put on shore. I step to the side, mechanically letting him through, and watch as he follows everyone's gaze before registering the body lying limp in the mud.

"What is this?" he asks before turning to look at me, his voice picking up an octave. "What happened?"

"I don't know," I say, finally finding my own. "I just . . . found him here."

"What do you mean you just *found him here*?"

"I just found him," I repeat. "I came out here and I . . . I tripped. I thought it was a root, or a branch, or . . ."

I stop, shaking my head, shock settling over me. Making me numb.

"Butler," Trevor says, turning back toward the body before nudging Levi's side with his shoe. We all flinch as it sags back into the mud, almost like we expected him to spring up and pounce. "Butler, get up."

"Trevor—" Nicole starts, but he ignores her, pushing the torso with his foot again.

"Butler, get the fuck up," he says, louder. "He's passed out."

"He's not passed out—"

"Yes, he is," Trevor says, nudging him harder. The toe of his shoe pushing deeper and deeper as he tries to rouse Levi awake. We're all still, too afraid to move. To breathe. Just like last night, watching Trevor and Levi fight in the dark. Like if we just stand here, statue-still, we might blend into the trees and disappear.

"*Butler!*" Trevor yells, kicking his side, and before anyone can even realize what's happening, he charges toward Levi and grabs his shoulder, rolling him over so he's flat on his back.

"Trevor, what are you *doing*?" Nicole screams, lunging forward, but Sloane holds her back before she can get too far. "Don't touch him! He's *dead*."

I look down at Levi, that word—*dead*—hovering above us like a storm cloud, blotting out the light. We all knew it, deep down. We all thought it, feared it, but nobody else had been brave enough to actually say it out loud. Now, though, it's impossible to deny: Levi is dead, and he's been dead for a while. The entire front of his body is covered in thick brown mud. It's in his eyelashes, his nostrils, his mouth, his hair.

I have a sudden flash of Eliza again, the way she must have looked splayed out on the ground beneath that old burnt building. Maybe it's the position of his limbs that suddenly reminds me of her, both of their bodies lifeless and limp like marionettes simply tossed to the side.

"*Fuck!*" Trevor screams, the sound of it echoing around us, making me jump. I hear a few birds flap in the distance, too startled to stick around, and I'm suddenly so jealous of their ability to just leave.

"We need to call the police," Sloane says, quiet, before shooting a look at Trevor. "Nobody else touch anything."

"God, I'm fucked," Trevor mutters, pacing now, his hands pushed into his hair. "I'm so fucked."

"Trevor, he's dead," Nicole repeats, disbelief in her voice and fresh tears springing up fast in her eyes. "Do you not understand that? *He's dead.*"

"I'm the president," he snaps back, flinging around so he can finally face her. "This happened on my watch. This piece of shit drank too much, couldn't handle his liquor, and now *I* might go to jail for it?"

"Nobody's going to jail," Lucas whispers, trying to calm him, though his voice sounds anything but certain. "It was an accident."

"That wasn't an accident," Sloane snaps back, her voice suddenly too hard. "You saw his neck."

We're all quiet, thinking of those bruises that looked eerily like fingers. Almost as if someone had been holding him down.

"You're disgusting," Nicole mutters, her gaze still on Trevor, and we all turn to look at her now, a quiet hatred festering in her eyes. "It's impossible for you to think about anyone but yourself, isn't it?"

"Okay, come on," Sloane says, grabbing Nicole's arm and ushering her away. "Back to the beach. I'll get my phone and we can call for help."

My feet stay planted as I listen to the slow retreat of the others; their ragged breaths and stifled cries now that the initial shock has worn off and everyone has finally realized what's happened. I vaguely register Sloane calling my name, trying to nudge me along, force me to follow, but I still can't move. I still can't speak.

I still can't peel my eyes from his, from Levi's, wide open and blinding white against the thick, dark mud covering the rest of his face.

I feel a touch on my arm and jump again, expecting to see

Sloane right back beside me—but instead, it's Lucy, her expression hauntingly calm. I don't even remember seeing her show up and I look back and forth, trying to decipher how long she's been here. Where she came from. Thinking about the last full memory I have of last night: her and Levi together in the sand. Lucy's hand on his thigh and the way Levi had pushed it, standing up with that look of disgust on his face. Her voice in Penny Lanes as she talked about murder with a cool indifference; the two of us in the kitchen, my chattering teeth. Her head cocked and curious as I muttered my confession, that inky black truth.

"It feels good, doesn't it?" she says at last, her voice so low I'm not even sure if it's real or if I've somehow imagined it. Imagined it all. "To finally get what you want."

CHAPTER 54

The rest of the week is nothing more than a blur: all of us sitting in the sand, eyes wet and red, watching the coast guard appear in the distance. The police crawling the island, spinning cobwebs of yellow caution tape as a bloated man named Detective Frank pulled us to the side, one by one, scribbling notes as we gave our statements.

It was a chaotic scene, frenzied from the start. None of us were able to answer his questions, not really, the details of the night fuzzy and fading. Conflicting accounts of who was where, and when, and why. The mud had swallowed our footprints; the shifting sand made it impossible to retrace anything. The tide the night before had been higher than normal—the full moon tugging at the water like it had tugged at all of us, the gentle pull of gravity like a curling finger daring us to indulge in our own intimate extremes—and as a result, any evidence, murky as it might have been, was washed away as it fell. Destroyed by Trevor flipping over the body; the grime covering Levi's skin masking any prints, any clues. Any indication, other than those bruises, of how exactly this might have happened. Of what could have gone so horribly wrong.

By the time we made it back to land, I was shivering with shock, a trauma blanket wound around my shoulders despite the fact that I was still sweating. We were brought to the station next, every single one of us, where we were asked to repeat our statements again, and again. And again. Our hair crusted with salt; sand still stuck to the crooks of our arms, the bend of our knees. The hidden spaces tucked between our toes. Clothing damp and the smell of pluff mud permanently stuck to our nostrils so no matter where we went or how far we ran, we were still back there, back on that island. Looking down at Levi as it swallowed him whole.

By Monday, the news was everywhere: freshman Levi Butler died over the weekend at a fraternity-sponsored function. There was alcohol involved, dozens of empty handles collected from the beach and bagged as evidence. Crumpled cans bobbing with the waves and whispers of hazing, everyone remembering the way Trevor had treated him. That scary aura as he puffed his chest out. Officially, the boys swore pledgeship was over and Levi must have just drunk too much before stumbling away and passing out in the trees. That maybe he fell in the mud, his head too leaden and floppy to lift back up. Maybe he was smothered by it, thick and sticky as it lodged in his windpipe. Gagged him to death. Still, Kappa Nu was suspended indefinitely. The boys are still next door for now—most of them don't have anywhere else to go—but the parties are over and the shed doors stay closed, that pathway between us irrevocably shut. They're strangely quiet when they do venture out, eyes cast down and tails tucked tight. All of them afraid of attracting unwanted attention in a way that reeks of irony, oddly refreshing—but at the same time, we keep to ourselves now, too, because while the unfolding news is one thing, the rumors are another beast entirely. From the second we stepped off that island, they spread like wildfire set to a parched, hungry place: powerful, uncontrolled, ripping through campus with a speed that was startling.

Each one somehow both outlandish and believable and most of them, as always, revolving around Lucy.

She was with him, after all, splashing him in the water. Sitting next to him by the fire and trying to console him after Trevor humiliated him in front of everyone. Like Nicole had said as the night was just starting: *"She's not exactly subtle, is she?"* People noticed the way she touched his leg and how he recoiled, flinging her arm back onto her lap. People noticed how he walked away and she stood up and followed.

Nobody saw him after that. Nobody saw him return.

"I picked up a shift tonight."

I snap my neck up, unsure of how long I've been sitting, staring, sinking into my mattress even though it's two o'clock on a Friday afternoon. Rutledge canceled class for the week, sent out emails encouraging students to sign up for free counseling, but as a result, every second since I stumbled across Levi has been spent in this house, what once felt like my sanctuary now more like a cell.

"I have to get out of here," Lucy says when I don't answer, clearly feeling the same. "I think I'm going crazy."

I blink a few times, registering her in my doorway with the Penny Lanes logo pulled tight across her chest. Our conversations have been so surface-level lately, so stilted, a heavy silence settling over the four of us every time we find ourselves together, thick and impenetrable as we chew it over. The comfortable quiet we once had now accusatory and cruel as we wonder which rumors could be real, which could be fiction.

As we quietly develop theories of our own.

"Come by at close?" she offers, and I try to smile, even though it feels more like a snarl. "Margaritas on me?"

"Not tonight," I say, registering the subtle hurt in her eyes. "Sorry."

"Why not?"

She cocks her head, that same look of innocent interest I now know is anything but. It reminds me vaguely of a limping animal; something feigning weakness just to draw you close before whipping around and eating you alive.

"I'm just not up for it," I say at last. "With, you know, everything."

"Ah, yes," Lucy says, crossing her arms. "*Everything.*"

"Rain check?" I ask, sitting up straighter and suddenly uneasy about the way she's standing in the doorway, blocking my exit. Her eyes are drilling into mine like she's trying to extract something from me, some buried truth I don't want to give up, and I catch that little quiver in her lip like there's something else she desperately wants to ask.

"Sure," she says instead, though she's still lingering there, drumming her fingers against the wall. She nods gently, finally, and turns to leave before suddenly twirling back around like whatever's on her mind is still struggling to break free.

"You know, Margot, this is a difficult time for all of us."

She's choosing her words slowly, carefully, her mind soldering the sentence together before she reveals her thoughts to me.

"I know how you felt about Levi," she adds.

I bunch my forehead, unsure of what she's getting at. I hated Levi. She knows that more than anybody. There's a temptation, once people are gone, to sugarcoat their qualities, inflate their attributes, all the other girls I used to see next door crying to their classmates about how he was *such a nice guy*—but not me, not Lucy. I literally told her I wanted him dead and I feel a rock lodge in my throat as it dawns on me, finally:

That's her whole point.

"We should be sticking together, you know?"

She rests her head on the doorframe, reminding me of all the times she's done the same thing to my shoulder, nuzzling her nose deep into my neck. The two of us on the couch, burrowing close in my bed.

"Yeah," I say slowly. "I guess you're right."

"Okay, good," she says, the darkness that settled over her expression before evaporating completely, flashing a smile that makes my blood freeze. "Because now really isn't the time to turn away from your friends."

CHAPTER 55

I wait for the slam of the front door before I spring out of bed, run to the living room, and peer out the window, watching as Lucy makes her way down the sidewalk.

I'm no stranger to her cryptic sayings. I've known from the beginning that this is who Lucy is, what she does. Like Sloane had said that morning in bed: she likes to play games. She's drawn to the reaction, the risk, a kid with a magnifying glass angled just right. But this is the first time I've found myself directly on the other side of it. The first time I've felt the heat of her scrutiny creep across my skin, her gigantic smile amplified on the other end. The first time I've looked into her blue eyes not with comfort or curiosity but genuine fear, bulging wide as she watched me squirm.

I think about that last comment, her final line. There was a double meaning to it that I don't like, an insinuation I can't ignore. Was she trying to comfort me, a metaphorical hand squeeze as she sensed me backing away, retreating into myself the way I did on Eliza's death day? The same as a gentle knock, a cleared throat, another invitation to Penny Lanes in an attempt to pull me back out?

Or was she trying to warn me, *threaten* me, somehow remind

me that whatever happened that night on the island is something the two of us are in on together?

I watch as Lucy rounds the corner before I make my way to her bedroom, tentatively placing my hand on the knob. Of course, I've been inside her room before. I've fallen asleep on her bed, inhaled the essence of vanilla and smoke permanently pressed into her pillow. I've flipped through the hangers in her closet, tried on her clothes. Smeared her blush across my cheeks and grimaced in her mirror when the reflection staring back was still indisputably me. This house belongs to all of us now, every single corner of it sacred and shared, but with that kind of belonging comes an intrinsic understanding. An unspoken rule all roommates abide by—the good ones, at least.

I've never been inside without her permission.

That doesn't mean I've never felt the urge. Like that night on the roof when I poked my head in, I could have done it so many times: a clandestine binge, secret and shameful, like sneaking into the pantry and gorging myself sick. She keeps her door closed but she never locks it. She's at Penny Lanes for hours at a time. I've always wondered what kind of things I could learn about her by simply looking, observing, no different than flipping through Eliza's planner or digging around in her dresser.

I could have done it, but I never did.

I suppose I wanted to see if I really could be different. If I could turn into someone who wasn't probing or jealous but comfortably confident with the way things were. Someone who didn't care so much about another person that I was willing to push away my morals, my pride, just to catch a glimpse of the things they wanted to keep secret.

Now, though, going through Lucy's stuff doesn't feel nosy. It feels necessary.

I hold my breath as I twist the knob, taking a quiet step inside. Immediately, I catch the familiar whiff of her, the whirring fan in the corner churning up all those conflicting smells. Sloane and Nicole are just upstairs and I think about shooting off a text, asking Sloane to keep watch, but at the same time, so many of the things I've come to learn about Lucy are things I'd like to keep secret for now. Things I want to understand myself first.

I start with her vanity, dragging my fingers across various bottles of makeup and hair products; foundation smudged on the chipped white wood and red streaks on the mirror, little doodles in lipstick. Her purse is resting on her bed, already opened like she flung it down in a hurry, and I wonder why she didn't take it with her—but at the same time, Lucy carries more than one bag. Sometimes she has a backpack, another reason I always assumed she was a student. Sometimes a clutch, like when we go out. She could have grabbed a different one on her way out the door, so I start digging around, pulling out clumps of wrinkled receipts, a pack of Altoids. Lip balm, sunglasses, and finally, an ID. This is definitely a going-out bag, then, because the driver's license I'm holding has to be a fake. I've seen her flash it at bouncers and bartenders; grocery store clerks while grabbing bottles of wine. I've marveled at how convincing it is, the birth year listed making her twenty-three years old . . . but then I see the address, that familiar town name.

Fairfield, North Carolina.

The ID shakes in my fingers, Lucy's blue eyes staring back from that thin strip of plastic. All the other information is correct: her name, her picture. Her hometown. *It could still be a fake,* my mind tries to reason. The little part of me that still desperately wants to believe the best. She could have found someone to copy her real one and only alter her age—but already, I know I'm lying to myself.

I know, deep down, this birthday is real.

"Who *are* you?" I whisper, Lucy's expression in the picture as cryptic as always, and suddenly, I remember Danny's voice beside that fire on Halloween. His incredulous stare as the three of us sat outside, sparks glowing in our eyes.

"Do you go here?" he had asked. *"What year are you?"*

I pull my phone out of my pocket, snapping a picture of the ID before putting everything back in her purse and making my way over to her desk. I flip open her laptop next and tap at the keys—it's locked, of course it is—so I close it again before reaching for the drawers and pulling them open . . . but those are locked, too.

I stand back, eyeing the drawers, wondering how to get inside. They have to be locked for a reason. Nobody takes the time to lock their desk unless there's something valuable inside. Something they don't want anyone else to see—and suddenly, I think of Halloween again. The way I sat shivering on the floor, those handcuffs still cinched tight across my wrist. The way Lucy had walked into the living room and grabbed her keys, unlatched the cuffs, my skin red and raw from the pressure. I walk back into the living room, noticing them still hanging from their regular hook on the wall, and this, too, seems strange—Lucy left for work, why wouldn't she bring her keys?—but at the same time, she walks to Penny Lanes. It's only a few blocks away. We never lock our doors, either, a bad habit she once blamed on Nicole that I now know not to be true.

I glance out the window again before grabbing the keys and dead-bolting the door, just in case. Then I head back to her desk and flip through them, one by one, recognizing the house key we never use, her car key dangling from a leather keychain. The key to the handcuffs and finally, a smaller one that looks different, older.

I push it into the lock and it slides in easily before twisting it to the right and pulling the drawer open.

Inside, I find the usual clutter—pens, notebooks, Post-it Notes with grocery lists and random reminders scrawled in cursive—and continue to dig, fingers shaking, knowing there has to be something to find. Finally, my hands brush up against something glossy and smooth and I pull it out, flip it over, my breath catching in my throat when I register what I'm holding.

For a second, I wonder if my mind is playing tricks on me again. If I'm still seeing Eliza everywhere like I have every other day for the last nineteen months: in the living room at Kappa Nu, head bent low as she eyed us from afar. Sitting next to Levi, hand on his thigh, that skinny string of blood dripping out of her mouth. In Lucy's little tics and that diamond necklace that, now that I've actually seen it up close, doesn't really look like Eliza's at all. But it's indisputable, no matter how many times I shake my head, try to blink it away: I'm staring at a picture of Eliza and me, a picture I haven't seen in two years but that I've thought about so many times. The reason for that final fight, really. The mystery that came between us that we never actually solved.

The one that turned me against Levi, Eliza against me.

I'm staring at the picture that was stolen from her bedroom.

CHAPTER 56

AFTER

"It's on!"

Sloane calls us to the living room and turns up the volume, Dean Hightower's voice creeping into the silence of the house around us. Bouncing off the newly bare walls. We've been moving our things out slowly, methodically, hauling boxes to the new apartment between classes. The furniture that came with the house is staying, of course, and we haven't decided what to do with Lucy's room yet. Right now, it's simply sitting untouched as if we're all just waiting for her to step through the front door, throw herself down on the couch with a sigh. Hit us with some half-hearted apology for causing such a fuss before crossing her legs and tilting her head, demanding we fill her in on everything.

I make my way out of my bedroom, the sound of snapping cameras and murmuring journalists leaking from the TV, and smile at Nicole when I see her emerge on the landing.

"Can't wait to hear this," she says, plopping down next to Sloane. I take a seat next to them and pull my legs up, settling in, trying not to think too hard about how this is probably the last time we'll all be nestled together on the couch like this.

"*Good afternoon,*" he says, fiddling with his tie. The dean of Rutledge is as stereotypical as they come: white hair, tortoiseshell glasses, bulbous nose, and a slow Southern drawl. Lucy's been missing for three weeks now and while he's held press conferences since Levi's death, long-winded speeches devoid of any real detail, this is the first time he's expected to say something about *her.*

"*As I'm sure you all know, Rutledge College has been mourning the death of one of our own: freshman Levi Butler, who tragically passed away at a fraternity function on Saturday, January 12,*" he says, refusing to peel his eyes from the paper in front of him. "*The fraternity in question, formally known as Kappa Nu, has been suspended amid the official investigation and several members have been brought in for questioning.*"

"Okay, get to it," Sloane says, rolling her wrists. The dean is flanked by a few officers behind him, a show of solidarity, and I can't help but stare at Detective Frank just off to the left, twirling his wedding ring on his finger.

"*Here at Rutledge, we value honesty and transparency above all else, so we would like to inform the public of the latest development. While Mr. Butler's death is still being investigated as an accident, you may have also heard that police are searching for a missing woman who they now believe may have vital information related to the case. That woman is twenty-three-year-old Lucy Sharpe, who has not only been connected to the deceased but is believed to have been the last person to be seen with him alive.*"

"Here we go," Nicole says, rubbing her hands together. I can feel the giddiness radiating off her, off all of us, this heavy secret we've been carrying around slowly being released. Like every other time I learned a new truth about Lucy, though, the initial surprise about her age was replaced with a kind of obvious understanding once I really thought about it: that first day in Hines when she appeared with a case of beer at hand, the rest of us so fresh out of high school, so naïve. Just starting to scheme about how to find our fakes as we searched for upperclassmen with a passing resemblance, maybe. Someone we could bribe into passing one back. But Lucy always felt so much older than the rest of us, so much more mature, grabbing those bottles from Penny Lanes at random. Not at all concerned about getting caught. And while I know that twenty-three isn't all that old, when you're cocooned inside a place like Rutledge, a place where everyone is simply a carbon copy of everyone else, it's old enough to somehow feel predatory, wrong.

We're only sophomores, after all, most of us just on the cusp of nineteen. Even the seniors are barely twenty-one.

"It is important for our parents and students to know that while Ms. Sharpe deeply embedded herself into the Rutledge community, she is not, in fact, a student enrolled at the college," the dean continues, pulling me back. *"She reportedly spent a significant amount of time last year inside Hines Hall, our female-only dormitory, and while we can understand the concern about a nonstudent gaining access to a college-owned building, we can assure you that Ms. Sharpe was only allowed entry from residents she befriended, which does not, in fact, violate any school rules."*

"I knew it," Sloane says, clapping her hands before pointing at the dean, accusatory, as if he can somehow see her. "I *knew* he'd deny it."

"I mean, yeah," Nicole adds. "What else would he say? She conned her way in?"

"Furthermore, Ms. Sharpe seems to have befriended several mem-

bers of the Kappa Nu fraternity, including Mr. Butler. At the time of her disappearance, she was living with several Rutledge students in a private house off-campus, immediately adjacent to Kappa Nu, which also does not violate any school rules regarding nonstudents living in college-owned housing."

"They're not going to take any responsibility," Sloane says, an amused smile on her face. "They're going to play dumb."

"Good," I say, pulling my legs tighter beneath me. "Let them."

"Ms. Sharpe was reported missing on Tuesday, January 22, when she failed to show up for work for the third shift in a row," he continues. We watch as he pulls a handkerchief out of his pocket, dabs at the sweat dotting his forehead, and stashes it away without peeling his eyes from the podium. *"She is employed as a waitress at Penny Lanes Bar and Bowling Alley, and thanks to the cooperation of her employer, police have been able to identify her parents, who were listed as her emergency contacts and are requesting respect and privacy as they work with authorities to help locate their daughter so she can return to the station for questioning."*

I can't stop staring at the dean, hanging on to his every word, teeth gnawing on the inside of my cheek as this plan we set in motion takes off so fast.

"At this time, we'd like to reassure the public that there is not a warrant out for Ms. Sharpe's arrest as it pertains to the death of Levi Butler," he continues, finally looking up from his notes. He removes his glasses, rubs the lenses with his shirt, and replaces them again. *"However, police are collecting new evidence every day, and it is of upmost importance that any person, student or otherwise, with information regarding her whereabouts come forward as soon as possible. Thank you."*

The crowd erupts with questions as soon as he stops talking but the dean simply steps down from the podium and walks away without an offer to answer. The three of us continue to watch as a reporter appears on screen next, a picture of Lucy emerging in the left-hand corner, and I suppress a shudder when I see those eyes again: crystalline and kaleidoscopic. So lifelike I think she might blink.

"That's enough of that," Sloane says as the screen goes dark.

I turn to look at her, the remote still clutched in her grip before she tosses it onto the couch again, but when I glance back at the dead TV, Lucy's face is still there, temporarily burned into the screen like she's right here with us. Smiling at all the things we've accomplished, this stunt we've pulled because she taught us how.

Lingering, the way she always does, like she isn't quite ready to leave.

CHAPTER 57

BEFORE

This picture of my past, this snapshot in time.

I remember it being a happy memory—comfortable, at the very least, the two of us in our element like this—but I've never actually noticed before how this photo of Eliza and me so blatantly displays our differences: me, self-consciously covered by my towel, eyes looking warily away from the lens. Eliza, all brazen in her little blue bikini. Reveling in the attention of the camera the way she reveled in the attention of everything.

My heart thumps hard in my chest as I stare at it, dissect it, try to wrap my mind around why it's here, in Lucy's bedroom, tucked away like a secret. My fingers resting on the glossy paper, Eliza's face. Blond hair bleached even brighter by the sun and the freckles cascading across her nose like stars, her very own constellation.

I think about the envelope of money I found deep in her dresser; the Fairfield address scrawled across the back. I pull my phone out of my pocket now, opening my pictures, and tap on the most recent image, the one I just took: Lucy's ID. Then I flip back to the picture of the envelope from Christmas, then back to the ID.

The addresses are the same.

I drop my arm, my head feeling like it's swimming in a sea of something thick and heavy as I try to process it all. Try to think about what it all means.

Did they know each other, somehow? Lucy and Eliza?

Is this why Lucy chose me? Is Eliza the reason why I'm even here?

Maybe it was blackmail. Maybe Eliza got tangled up in something bad, something she shouldn't have. Something somehow involving Levi. This seemed to start when they met, after all, all those sullen moods and bad habits she seemed to pick up out of nowhere. All those times she flipped her phone over when I walked by, hiding her screen, or opening her mouth to tell me something before changing her mind and closing it again. Those times when the two of them fell into a whisper as I approached, their conversation cut short by my presence alone. It still feels like Lucy and Levi somehow knew each other, too, long before he got here. The way he clearly recognized her that night at Penny Lanes; the way she was always so drawn to him, so curious, every little detail filling her up like she couldn't get enough.

I faintly register a noise in the distance—a muted thumping, my own heart in my ears—but my mind still feels like it's wrapped in gauze, a padded room dulling everything. I feel too detached to react so instead, I stay floating, like I've simply left my body behind and I'm watching myself from a distance with cool indifference.

"Margot!"

The sound of my name pulls me back slowly and I wonder where it came from. Sloane upstairs, maybe. Nicole calling down from her room.

"Margot, open up!"

I twist around, toward Lucy's open door, simultaneously recognizing the voice and realizing the noise is coming from outside. And it isn't just thumping, either. It's knocking.

Lucy is knocking at the front door.

"I forgot my wallet!" she yells, banging harder. *"Why is the door locked?"*

I look down at the picture again, shaking in my grip, before pushing it back in her desk and locking the drawers, terror surging through my chest. I step back, a faint tingling crawling up my neck as I look around, frantic, trying to find something for my hands to grab. Because if Lucy is standing on the porch right now, peering through the windows and into the living room, she's going to see me walking out of her bedroom. She's going to be rightfully curious why I locked her out of the house and walked into her room the second she stepped outside.

My eyes dart around, keys still in hand, wildly searching for some excuse to be in here. Some plausible reason that she might buy—and that's when I spot it. A stack of books in the corner, piled high against the wall.

"One second!" I yell, a cold sweat erupting on my palms. I grab the familiar title on top and walk out of her bedroom, trying to act casual as I register her face through the window, her expression twisted into grim annoyance. I shoot her a smile as I walk to the front door and unlatch the bolt, letting her inside, but she storms straight past me, hands on her hips.

"Margot, what the hell?" she asks, her eyes flicking back and forth between my face and her room. Her keys are stuffed in my back pocket and I try to angle my body away from her, attempting to hide them. "What were you doing in my room?"

"Just grabbing my book," I say, holding up *Dr. Jekyll and*

Mr. Hyde. It's pure dumb luck that I spotted it sitting there, right on top, so easily within my reach. "I need it for another class this semester. I wanted to get it before I forgot."

"And the door?" she asks, gesturing back to it.

"I lock it sometimes," I say, sagging my shoulders, acting ashamed. "I told you I don't like leaving it open. I didn't think you'd be back for a while."

I stare at Lucy's expression, maddeningly neutral like a lenticular image, her very essence changing depending on which way I look at it. It's amazing how quickly she can morph in my mind from beautiful to menacing to something else entirely, the tiniest twitch of the eye or suggestive smile threatening to reveal something I've never seen in her before.

"Okay," she says at last, posture loosening, though she doesn't sound convinced. "Yeah, okay."

She walks past me and into her bedroom, my breath held as she disappears inside. Quietly, I walk over to the wall hook and replace her keys, biting my cheek. Waiting for her to notice something out of place and come storming back out, demanding the truth. Instead, she reappears calmly with the bag slung over her shoulder and I wonder, for a single second, if this was another test. If she left her purse on purpose, maybe. If she somehow knew I would do exactly this.

"I'll be taking these," she adds, elbowing me as she walks past. I watch as she grabs her keys from the hook on the wall and shakes them in front of me, dangling like a carrot. "In case you decide to lock me out again."

She walks back onto the porch and closes the door before I can respond, my head spinning as she skips down the steps. Then, once she's gone again, I walk into my bedroom and toss the book on my bed before opening my laptop and beginning to type.

CHAPTER 58

According to Google Maps, Fairfield, North Carolina, is a two-hour drive from my house in the Outer Banks. It has a population of 226 and I can't help but think about what Lucy told me that night on the roof, how she would go entire years without meeting a new person.

She wasn't lying about that, at least. Fairfield is small, claustrophobically so, her entire town easily fitting into Kappa Nu during a particularly large party.

I grab my phone and navigate to the picture of Lucy's ID again, zooming in first on her face. I look next at the book on my bed, little dots of sweat smeared from my fingers. The illustration on the cover showing the face of one person with two entirely different auras: good and evil, foreign and familiar. Some murky combination of right and wrong. I wonder, for the very first time, if the Lucy I've come to know is simply a mirage like this, an optical illusion. My own subconscious snapping its fingers and creating the very thing it thought I needed. If I merely imagined all her similarities to Eliza, those subtle little signs that they were the same, because, deep down, that's what I wanted: another shot, a second chance.

Eliza reincarnated, the sudden and startling appearance of Lucy in my life allowing me to simply forget what happened and replace her entirely.

I zoom out of the picture so I can see her address again, typing it in and watching it load. The screen zeroes in on a little red pin plotted firmly in the middle of nowhere and I switch to satellite view, a single house materializing amid what seems to be acres of untouched land. I take in the algae-green roof, the dirty white siding. The haphazard shutters and rusted red pickup parked in the grass. I can't help but feel a sting of something in my chest when I see it all, something I can't quite name, because right now, taking in this house I can only assume to be Lucy's, it's impossible not to think about the ways we grew up, so glaringly different: me in my waterfront mansion with wraparound porches, oyster tabby driveway, and luxury cars. The nearby beaches and long, winding docks that we used to run down barefoot, so untethered and free.

I switch out of Google Maps and navigate to the county website next, over to the tax department, and finally, property records. Then I type in her address again, fingers drumming against the keys while it loads. I've always wondered why tax records are made public like this—why any curious stranger should be able to simply search an address and learn everything there is to know about its owner—but right now, I'm just grateful for the opportunity to finally find some answers. After a few seconds, a single link pops up on the screen and I click it, holding my breath until the result appears—but once it does, confusion pummels me, the name glaring back looking strange and out of place.

I stare at the computer, then back at the picture, wondering, for a second, if I typed in the wrong address. If my subconscious is playing tricks on me again, making me see people from my past like they're right there in front of me, fleshy and solid and undeniably real. I was expecting to find Lucy's mom, maybe. A person to pair with the stories I've heard. Another name I could google or a phone number to call, any morsel of information I could add to my pile—but finally, I'm beginning to grasp the truth, the answers coming to me one by one like the steady drip of a faucet, filling me up with a sense of sick understanding. All the things I thought I knew are suddenly different, warped, like staring at my own reflection in the water and barely recognizing the face that stares back.

I've been wrong about Eliza, about Lucy, about Levi.

About everything.

CHAPTER 59

I read the name on the screen again, blinking my eyes, head swimming with the implications of it all. These last nine months and the little crumbs Lucy has dropped like she was trying to get me to follow them all along. Like she was daring me to put it together, figure it out. Finger curling before running back into the dark, waiting patiently for me to find her at the end.

I think about her stepping into my dorm on that very first day, diamond necklace cinched tight around her neck. How she zeroed in on Eliza's face on the mantel, jealousy radiating as she picked up the frame and asked me those questions.

The two of us on the roof, the stub of her cigarette glowing like an ember. That final drag before she flicked it from her fingers and sent it sailing into the night.

There's a reason why Lucy and Eliza are so similar. There's a reason why they share the same habits, the exact same tics. Why every time I look at Lucy, I see her. I didn't make it up. I didn't imagine it, my subconscious trying to replicate her completely. My guilt trying to scribble her back into existence, paper tearing beneath the weight of my frenzied mental strokes, so desperate to see her again. It didn't matter how wrong it all was, how deformed, this Frankenstein version of her I had cobbled together and brought back to life. I wanted it so badly I ignored all the signs and I picture Eliza again, back in her bedroom, the two of us stomach-down on her bed. Her legs kicking in the air, dainty chin cupped in her palm. The way she rolled over to the side and glanced out the window, her voice a whisper only I could hear.

"I think he watches me," she had said, twirling that diamond between her fingers before lifting it slowly, kissing it to her lips. *"I think he's out there right now."*

It was never Levi she saw, that silhouette in the distance, my body cold as I imagined him watching in the dark. He wasn't the source of the cigarette we found beneath her window; he wasn't the one who watched, night after night, a looming presence we could all feel. It was *Lucy* out there, observing quietly. Drinking in all the little things about Eliza that made her so rare: the way she moved, the way she talked, the way she made everyone around her love her so fiercely. Studying the way her fingers tugged twice at her hair, bit down on a pencil until her teeth left marks.

Played with that necklace clasped tight around her neck, a gift from her father she never took off.

Her father, Mr. Jefferson, whose name is still burned onto my laptop screen.

Mr. Jefferson, the one who owns Lucy's house in Fairfield, North Carolina.

I lean back on my headboard, letting the truth settle over me. It was Lucy who broke into the Jeffersons' that night, curtains fluttering as she wandered around the living room, up the stairs and into Eliza's room. It was Lucy who touched all her things, the source of that foreign presence we could all feel. Who saw those pictures on the wall and plucked one from the center, taking it for herself.

That picture not of me, not of Eliza, but of Mr. Jefferson tucked tight between us.

Mr. Jefferson, Lucy's father.

I think back again to that night on the roof, the way she stalled when I asked about her parents, her dad, like that bit of information was just a step too far.

"He gave me this," she had said, diamonds glinting between her fingers. Pulling me close, her breath on my neck. *"He said it reminded him of me because I was named after that song."*

The information is all here, all online, right in front of me and ripe for the picking: the deed, ownership history, property updates and tax bills. Mr. Jefferson bought the house in Fairfield back in 1999 and I do the math in my head, counting backward, just to be sure: twenty-three years ago. The same age as Lucy. Eliza's parents have been together since high school—I've seen the pictures myself; the two of them at prom, so young at their wedding—but finally, I feel the pieces slide into place and everything from the past two years suddenly makes sense.

I see it now, as clear as crystal: a young Mr. Jefferson, so charismatic and charming. So wild and free. A musician, a poet, a man with money—the temptation, I'm sure, was always there. Despite how strange it all feels, how at odds with the person I thought I knew, I let myself reach out and touch it and it feels surprisingly solid, like I've somehow known this part of him was there all along. I imagine him traveling, untethered, the way he was before settling down on the coast. I imagine him finishing a gig and meeting a woman, letting the lust take over and cloud it all. A single lapse in judgment, a fatal mistake, a weekend away from his wife that left a girl pregnant and threatened to disrupt his entire life. So he did what people with money always do: he bought her silence, her shame. A house somewhere in the country that would keep her satiated and sustained and far, far away.

I think of him the night after Eliza's funeral: the two of us on the porch together, rocking slowly in the dark. The smell of stale whiskey on his breath and his jet-black hair glinting in the night. I remember turning to him, his face heavy with emotion, with exhaustion, with all those unanswered questions he kept torturing himself with: *"Was anything bothering her? Did she have any enemies? Anyone who might want to see her get hurt?"* Something had clearly been troubling him that night, weighing on his conscience, but I assumed he was simply trying to process, to grieve. Trying to make sense out of something so senseless.

Trying, like I had been, to find someone else to blame.

Now, I can't help but wonder if he knew that Lucy had found him. If he knew she had been coming around, watching his family, seeing that their life was so different than the one she had with her mother back home. I wonder if he suspected that it was her who broke in that night and that's why he refused to call the police, made up those excuses, probably so afraid of his secret slipping out, ruining his perfect family. His perfect life. Because that's what they were, the Jeffersons: they were perfect. It was the way they ate dinner together, windows open and old music leaking out. It was the genuine laughter, the overwhelming love, Mr. Jefferson tossing Eliza's mom off the dock and bringing out his telescope when the sky was clear and the stars were out. I always thought that if I could just get close to them, it might rub off on me, too. That I could be one of them, part of their family instead of my own—but Lucy, she must have felt that longing to such an extreme, knowing what she could have had, *should* have had, but was given instead.

I think of the two of us on that beach now, New Year's Eve, the bottle between us as we stared at the sky. The distant pop of the fireworks as we whispered our secret wishes, our deepest desires, like if we muttered them out loud, they might just come true. *"I guess I was curious,"* she said, another little honesty she waved in front of me, knowing I would never see it for what it truly was. She wasn't just curious about Levi, wandering into his house on Christmas. Sitting on his bed, taking his head in her hands. Wondering what his lips might feel like on hers.

It's all so clear now, so painfully obvious.

"When you're friends with Lucy, she makes you feel special."

I think of her walking around Eliza's house, blue eyes drilling into the family photos on the hall, so proudly displayed. The ache in her chest knowing that she was something dirty, secret, banished away like a bad habit. Making her way into Eliza's bedroom, eyeing her planner. Flipping through the pages just like I had, learning all the little things she had rendered important enough to note: her best friend's birthday, her first day at Rutledge. Move-in day at Hines Hall.

"Like she chose you for a reason."

It's why she showed up in the courtyard that morning, lingering in the background until she saw me pulling my cart with that neon 9 taped to the back; why she approached Sloane and Nicole on the grass, two girls living on the same floor as me, just down the hall. Why she stepped into my dorm that day and grabbed my arm, invited me in.

Lucy didn't want to live her own life anymore. She wanted to live Eliza's.

CHAPTER 60

AFTER

It's strange: standing on the sidewalk, less than a year since the first time I found myself planted in this very spot with my bags by my side. Looking up at this house and imagining all the things that could happen: the friends I could make, the person I could become. Wondering how it would all play out. I had no idea, back then, the things I would be capable of. The way Lucy would bend me and break me; the way three strangers would slowly turn into friends, then family, the bond between us turning from liquid to solid. Curdling in the heat until it was thicker than blood.

Messier, too.

"Ready?" Sloane asks, emerging from the living room and stepping out onto the porch. I watch as she sticks a piece of paper on the front door before she closes it, locks it, and hoists the last box under her arm.

"Yeah," I say, wondering now what that girl would think if she somehow knew how it would all end. If she would be impressed or horrified.

Probably both.

I turn around to find Nicole stacking bins of clothes in her car and I catch a flash of movement out of the corner of my eye, an undercover cruiser rounding the corner and making its way toward the house.

"Frank is here."

Sloane and Nicole stop what they're doing and watch now, too, the three of us waiting as Detective Frank parks across the street, steps out of the driver's seat, and slams the door behind him, walking toward us with that familiar stride. We instinctively form a line on the sidewalk like that first day in the dining room, anticipating his questions. Rehearsing our answers.

"Girls," he says, tipping his hat.

Rutledge has finally settled back into a strange sense of normalcy, although everything still feels a little bit off, a little bit strange, like the world got knocked off its axis and we're all struggling to stand up straight, staggering around, wondering if we'll ever feel normal again. Downtown is filling up slowly, cautiously, the streets coming alive with students who are starting to trickle out of their houses. Our mandatory time of mourning complete. The sidewalks are crushed with lines again, elbows jostling to get into bars, Levi's face starting to fade from the posters that were hung up around town as a somber reminder to drink responsibly.

It's funny: I've spent my entire life being anonymous, but now I finally know what it's like to be them. To be Lucy, to be Eliza, to be the kind of girl who attracts stares. The one who elicits whispers, rumors swirling around me like a thick mist of perfume. No longer a castaway or a sidekick but a part of the pack, a piece of a whole. We're a unit now, inextricably linked. A clique that feels a little bit jarring, a little bit off, when one of us tries to venture out on our own, Lucy's aura still clinging to us like a spider's thread, sticky and strong. Something we can feel more than we can see.

And that's what I had wanted in the beginning, what I would have given anything for, but now I understand the strange feeling I got when I used to see the three of them walking down the hall together, arms attached like a chain of paper dolls.

Rip one of us away, and we'll never feel whole again.

"Moving day?" Detective Frank asks, and I blink back into the conversation, his toe kicking at a box at my feet.

"This is the last of it," Sloane says.

"And Lucy's things?"

"Still inside," I say. "We locked up so nobody would take them. We assumed her parents would be coming."

Frank looks at me, chewing on the inside of his cheek.

"The fraternity isn't using the house for anything until the lawsuit blows over," Sloane adds. "They said we can just leave it for now."

"Well then it's going to be sitting here indefinitely," he says, shifting his weight. "The lawsuit isn't blowing over and those boys aren't coming back. What's this?"

He gestures to the porch and we stay quiet, watching as he walks up the steps, peels our note from the door and holds his finger out, a blue Post-it stuck to the pad of his pointer. He skims it quickly, then looks back at us.

"Your new address?"

"It's for Lucy," Nicole says. "Just in case—"

"In case she comes back," he interrupts, understanding settling over him slowly.

"She won't have our numbers anymore," I say. "Not without her phone."

"We didn't want her to think we just left—" Sloane adds, but Officer Frank interrupts her, holding his hand up.

"Girls." He says it gently now, his eyes squinting like this is the first time he's really noticed us before. The first time he's ever seen us at all. "She's not coming back. You understand that, right?"

We're all silent, sheepish and embarrassed, staring at the piece of paper in his hand like kids getting scolded after our parents found something salacious hidden beneath our beds. Nicole looks down, rubbing the sole of her shoe against the concrete, because we know how childish this looks, leaving it behind like that. Such a desperate and deluded show of hope.

"Lucy Sharpe . . . she isn't your friend," Frank continues. "She's not who you thought she was. You understand that."

We stay firm, fierce in our commitment to her, our solemn vow, and I can see the slow shift in his face. The gentle softening as suspicion recedes and pity takes over.

We watch as he sighs, sticking the note back on the door for us and walking down the steps before planting himself on the side-walk again, shaking his head. Eyeing the three of us now, a slow scan down the line before his gaze stops on me and I see him swallow.

"The two of you can go," he says to Sloane and Nicole, refusing to avert his eyes from mine. "You and I need to have a talk."

CHAPTER 61

BEFORE

It's dark by the time Lucy comes home, the scuff of her shoes ascending the porch steps alerting me to her presence.

I've been in my room this entire time, all eight hours, my door bolted and my laptop open and dead on my comforter. My thoughts on Lucy, on Eliza, on how the two of them have more in common than I ever could have imagined. I hear the front door slam as she makes her way into the living room, her feet heavy as she stomps through the house.

"Hello?" she calls, her voice echoing through the empty living room. *"Where is everyone?"*

She can be so quiet when she wants, so catlike and contained, but now, I feel her radiating through the walls, the floor, her very being pumping hard like an organ deprived of oxygen. Something atrophying slowly, a transplant suddenly rejected by its host.

I hear a banging on my door that comes out of nowhere: a hard, closed-fist pounding that makes the bones of the house rattle in place. I eye the knob jiggling back and forth, the door jerking wildly on its hinges.

"What is with the locked doors today?" Lucy yells, slamming her palm against the wood. "Margot, get out here. We need to talk."

I stay rooted on my bed, frozen with fear, a million different scenarios running through my mind.

"All of us," she adds, and somehow, I can tell she's making her way back to the living room, waiting for me to follow.

Knowing that eventually, like always, I will.

After a few more seconds of silent debate, I stand up and walk to the door, twisting the dead bolt and opening it wide. The hallway is empty in front of me, the overhead lights all clicked off, and I creep into the living room, rounding the corner to find Lucy sitting on the couch. Her hair is frizzier than normal, her skin shiny and a little too damp, and I glance out the window, into the inky black night. Noticing, for the first time, that it's started to rain.

"What's going on?" I ask, a little tremor in my voice as I try to see through those sparkling eyes. They're impenetrable, like always, tough as diamonds and just as rare.

"That's what I'm trying to figure out," she says, glancing to the staircase just as Sloane and Nicole come creeping down. "Everyone, sit."

Sloane looks at me, eyes wide and unusually afraid, before she and Nicole walk to the second couch and sit down in tandem. I stay standing at the edge of the room and Lucy turns to me next, willing me forward. I can feel the pull of her like a rope around my waist; I can feel the tension, the physical tug, and I let her gaze guide me farther into the room, though I stop short at the coffee table, refusing to get closer.

"There are clearly some things we need to get off our chests," Lucy says at last, leading us like a meeting, and for the very first time, I see little glimmers of Mr. Jefferson in her face. I see those same faint lines around her eyes I never noticed before; the slight upturn of her mouth, his pointed chin. But it's the hair, mostly, that charcoal color. As deep and dark as a bottomless hole.

Eliza took after her mother completely, bright-skinned and honey-blond-haired. At least that's one thing Lucy got for herself.

"Come on," she says when no one speaks up.

Sloane looks at me again, her lips pursed shut, and I wonder why she's being so uncharacteristically quiet right now—until I think of that first conversation outside the shed. Me questioning her loyalty to Lucy and her shrinking back, revealing her truth.

"Maybe I'm being harsh," she had said, suddenly doubting herself. *"Or maybe I'm afraid of what would happen if I stopped."*

I glance to Nicole next, so wisp-thin it looks like she might disappear, and the tension in the room is so heavy, so solid, I can feel my insides caving like moist dirt is being heaped on my chest. The mounting pressure of being buried alive.

"I know someone wants to say something," Lucy continues, crossing her arms. "Everyone's been weird since the night on the island."

We stay quiet, bodies paralyzed with the exception of our racing hearts, our darting eyes, though it's not for a lack of things to say. The problem is I have too *many* questions, too *many* fears, all of them buzzing around in my mind like a swarm of insects, making it impossible to grab on to just one.

"Okay," she says at last, standing up fast before stalking off into the kitchen. "If this is how it's gonna be."

Sloane and I exchange a look again, silently wondering what she'll do next, before Lucy reemerges with a handle of Svedka in one hand and a knife from the knife block clutched in the other.

"What are you *doing*?" Sloane asks, instinctively scooting back, her arm launching up to shield Nicole next to her like a mother in the driver's seat just before a crash. "Put that back."

"Calm down," Lucy says, plopping onto the floor before placing the knife in front of her. "I refuse to just sit here in silence. We're going to talk, and this is how we're going to do it."

We all watch as she reaches out and flicks the knife, the metal tip turning in slow, somber circles.

"We're not playing your stupid game," Sloane says.

"There are obviously things we need to ask each other," Lucy snaps back, staring at Sloane before diverting her gaze over to Nicole, to me. "So, let's ask. Let's get it out."

She takes a swig from the bottle, smacking her lips before grabbing a sucker from the coffee table, tossing the wrapper on the floor and popping it into her mouth.

"Truth or dare," she asks, looking down at the knife. Sloane shakes her head, though I can see her resolve melting. Her desperate need for answers, all those questions she wants to ask. Her anger toward Lucy over these last few weeks steadily mounting, getting stronger. Ready to rip right out of her like a raging storm.

"Fine," Lucy says once it becomes clear Sloane isn't going to bite. She turns her attention to me next, lowers her voice. "We'll let Margot go first."

My body goes rigid as my eyes dart over to Sloane, seeking out her permission like always. She just stares at me—she doesn't nod, but she doesn't shake her head, either—so I walk over to the center of the room before taking a seat on the floor, my back digging into the coffee table and my hand slowly gripping the knife.

Sloane lowers herself down beside me slowly, a show of solidarity as she leans against Nicole's legs.

"Spin it," Lucy says, and I feel myself blink. Everything feels muffled, hazy, as the memories of the last nine months pulse around me now; the many, many times the four of us have been in this living room, sitting in a circle just like this. Telling Lucy whatever she wants; readily doing anything she asks.

"Margot," she says, and I lift my head, eyes on hers. Wondering how to word all the things I so desperately need to know. Because Lucy is a liar, yes, but I realize now that's not even the problem. The problem is she's been honest, too, and I have no idea how to tell what's real and what's not. What's the truth, sprinkled in so carefully, so casually, and what's nothing but an outright lie. She's let me in on little things, cherished things. Things that have shown me the rarest of glimmers into who she really is.

Things that still make me love her, somehow. Despite or maybe even because of it all.

"*Spin*," she repeats, and I exhale slowly, grabbing the bottle of vodka between us and taking a pull to coat my throat. Her pupils seem to be stretched to three times their natural size and she nods at me, a red stain on her teeth, before I flick the knife and watch it twirl, all of us leaning forward as it slows, breath smothered in our throats.

"Truth or dare," I whisper, watching as Lucy grabs the handle, the knife tip pointed directly at her. I feel the air exit the room as Sloane straightens up and Lucy starts to smile.

"Truth," she says, although the way she's looking at me now, eyebrows lifted, I know she means it more as a dare. She's taunting me, egging me on, challenging me to ask her the thing she knows I want to ask. This is her game, after all. It always has been.

This is what Lucy does. She dangles.

"Why did you do it?" I ask, that single question encompassing so much. The last two years pummel over me now as I picture Eliza and me in her bedroom, that silhouette outside in the dark. The missing picture and Lucy showing up at Rutledge; coming into my dorm room, singling me out. Finding out where Levi would live and casting her spell over him, too, before following him into a darkness so dark, he'd never be able to claw his way out.

I picture his body in the mud, eyes wide and afraid. The trail of death that seems to follow her around for reasons I still can't explain.

Lucy looks at me, head tilted like she's observing me from behind a piece of thick clear glass. Like I'm some foreign creature she doesn't understand until a thin smile stretches slowly across her face. The look of a person who's just realized they've won.

"Margot," she says at last. "You, of all people, should know the answer to that."

CHAPTER 62

I can still feel myself lying in bed, phone alight in the dark. Those videos of Eliza and Levi playing on repeat, branding themselves right into my brain. I couldn't help but watch them, study them: the way they swayed in unison, his arm on her shoulders. That bottle of vodka passing between them before she leaned her head back and howled at the moon.

"I don't know what you're talking about," I say now, my heart hard in my throat as Lucy stares, smiling.

"Oh, I think we both know that you do."

I had heard about the party, of course. It was an annual thing. A sacred senior tradition to descend upon that old school during the first full moon of the summer, a rite of passage before we all parted ways—but of course, I didn't go. It was three weeks into summer and Eliza and I still weren't speaking. Not since graduation, anyway, our smiles fake and fleeting as we posed for that picture. Arms rigid by our sides as we pretended to be friends. We were leaving for Rutledge in just two months and I was starting to wonder how it would work, the two of us living together when we could barely stand to be in the same room. We would have to get over it eventually, one of us would have to crack, but Eliza had yet to apologize so I hadn't either, opting instead to stay in that night and watch her life unfold through my phone.

I remember the sky growing darker, the shrieks getting louder. Eliza looking drunker as the night wore on. I wanted to hate her. I wanted to see her suffer the consequences of her actions instead of relying on me to save her the way I always did. I wanted her to stumble home drunk and get grounded by her parents, her senior summer ruined because I wasn't there to keep her quiet when we crept in late. Because the truth was, the truth I had secretly known for so long: she never appreciated it. She never appreciated *me*, the way I always propped her up, kept her safe, so instead, I turned my phone off and flipped over in bed. I pinched my eyes shut and I tried, so hard, to just forget about it all. To forget about her, about Levi, about the stinging betrayal I felt every time I thought about the way she had looked at me in my bedroom, those horrible words hissing loudly between her teeth. I tried to tell myself I didn't care, that she could go ahead and ruin her life if she wanted to—but I did. I did care.

I would always care about Eliza, even and especially when she didn't care about herself.

"What are you guys talking about?" Sloane asks, leaning forward, but I can't bring myself to respond. Instead, I'm still back there, back in my bedroom, my body hot beneath the sheets as I let out a sigh, opened my eyes. Realized I could never go to sleep as long as Eliza was still with him, that sick boy next door who watched her through the window. The one who had broken into her room, lain on her bed. Wedged his way between us in a way nobody had ever been able to before.

I remember flinging off the covers, frustration mounting as I crawled out of bed. Silently cursing her for making me take care of her the way I always did as I tiptoed through the dark and threw on my shoes, crept through the back door while my parents were asleep just down the hall. The school itself was only a short walk away and I was stewing the entire time, muttering the things I planned to say to her. That old, burnt building looking haunted and strange as the moon shone down, looming like a shadow puppet cast across the wall.

"Margot," Sloane says, but I can't peel my eyes from Lucy.

Lucy, who has asked me about that party so many times. Who has nudged me along, showered me with questions, almost as if she knew the truth and was trying to get me to say it myself. I think about that conversation back in the Outer Banks, New Year's fireworks popping in the distance and our eyes trained on the stars above. Lucy had brought it up again: that night, that final night, Eliza and Levi stumbling around that old school together. Arms like loose nooses wound around each other's necks and the vodka pouring down their gullets all tingly and warm.

"He told me about the party," she had said. *"The night she died."*

But that wasn't true; it was another one of her lies. Levi didn't tell Lucy about the full moon that night and the way they all gathered, drawn to it like a spell. Like some primordial instinct, some ancient rite, Eliza the sacrificial lamb left bleeding at the altar. Lucy knew about the party because she had been there the way she had *always* been there, the way she still is: appearing out of nowhere, all feline and quiet.

Watching in the distance, her body blending into the dark.

"I saw it happen," she says to me now, reading my mind as I remember the way I walked into that building, the party already dying by the time I arrived. Sidestepping people I vaguely recognized as they staggered onto the sidewalk, looking straight through me as if I were a ghost. I had always been invisible when I wasn't with

Eliza and that night had been no different, all those limp bodies with glassy eyes stumbling home like people possessed. "I saw it all."

I remember poking my head into every single room, each one littered with cigarette butts and empty beer cans. The sour smell of vomit mixing with the sea breeze as I made my way up the stairs. I just kept climbing—the second floor, the third—searching every corner, trying to find her. The roar of waves in the distance somehow sounding louder the higher I went.

"Margot, talk to me," Sloane says, grabbing my wrist. "What is this about?"

It's all suddenly too much—the memories, this room, the feel of Sloane's hand on my arm and the heat of their stares, all eyes on me—so I stand up fast before walking into the kitchen and out the back door, desperate for space to think. For air to breathe. But the rain is beating down hard as I stagger into the yard, loud cracks of thunder vibrating my bones.

A flash of lightning illuminating the shed, those big double doors still latched shut.

I walk toward it, the smell of blood prickling the skin on my neck as I swing the doors open and stumble inside, breathing heavily. My hair dripping wet as I drop my head in my hands, my mind fully immersed in that final night now like it's happening all over again, so unbearably real. The memory of my body ascending higher, those rickety stairs with the full moon above illuminating it all. I was so close to leaving. I was so close to just giving up, going home—until I heard that noise.

Something like a kicked can, the scrape of aluminum as it skidded across the floor.

"What was that?"

I remember my head snapping to the side, Eliza's voice just barely above a whisper. It sounded strange, slurred, so I rounded a wall and that's when I saw it: two bodies moving in unison in the corner; pale, bare skin glowing bright in the dark.

"It's fine," Levi said, his voice breathy and hoarse. "It's nothing."

"Is there someone there?"

"I said it's nothing."

I crept closer, blinking my eyes, each flip of the lids making everything a little bit clearer, a little more real. It was them, I could tell, even in the darkness: it was Eliza and Levi, completely unclothed, lying on the floor of that disgusting place. They were surrounded by empty bottles and sleeping bags, cigarette stubs and discarded trash. Levi's body moving in a rhythmic motion, his hands clenched tight around her wrists, fingers digging into her skin while Eliza lay beneath him, open eyes on the sky.

I opened my mouth and started to take a step forward—but then I stopped myself, remembering the night of the break-in. The way I could smell Levi in her bedroom, the scent of him stained deep in her sheets.

Realizing, with a jolt, that what I was watching wasn't the first time.

I still don't know which part was worse: seeing Eliza like that, the way she kept lowering her standards for him, digging herself deeper into this hole I somehow knew would trap her forever, or finally understanding the magnitude of their relationship and what it entailed. The reality of just how far apart we had drifted: all the things she had kept from me, all the things she felt she couldn't say. I remember watching with pure detachment as they finished, unable to look away. Levi rolling off with a grunt before standing up, pulling on his shorts. Eliza self-consciously gripping her chest while she looked around for her sundress, fingers skimming the floor.

"I'll be back," he had said, not bothering to help her up before heading to the stairs and walking down. "Gonna grab another beer."

It was pure reflex that finally pulled me out of the shadows, my body stepping forward as Eliza got dressed. She was standing a little too close to the edge, swaying gently as she pulled on her clothes. Her body eclipsed by the glow of the moon. I remember feeling such sadness then, watching as she tried to pull herself together: brushing her fingers through tangled hair, cupping a hand to her mouth as a hiccup escaped. Thinking that the person I was looking at then wasn't the Eliza everyone envied. That it wasn't the Eliza I looked up to, the one I spent my entire life wanting to be.

The person in front of me was someone else entirely.

It took her a few seconds to realize I was there, but then she turned around, somehow feeling the presence of another body behind her, and I registered the shock in her expression, the unmistakable shame.

"Margot," she said. "What are you doing here?"

"I came to make sure you were okay."

She was quiet, a subtle wetness in her eyes, and for a single, stupid second, I actually thought she might run over and hug me.

"You don't have to protect me," she said instead, crossing her arms tight across her chest. "I told you that."

"Obviously I do," I said, gesturing to the corner where she had just been. Dipping my voice an octave lower, trying to hide the judgment that was so clearly there. "Eliza, I don't even know who you are anymore."

"Yeah, well, neither do I."

"What is that supposed to mean?" I asked, taken aback.

She just scoffed, shook her head, and I took a few steps forward, the two of us suddenly close enough to touch. I could feel the wind whipping off the water in the distance, a welcome relief from the hot summer air, and I could tell she wanted to say something then. I could feel some big explanation for the way she'd been acting so close to barreling right out and I wanted to hug her, to slap her. To tell her I hated her and tell her I loved her—but at the same time, the wall we had built between us was too tall at that point. The stones too solid to tear back down.

I was exhausted, just so exhausted. I no longer felt that there was a point.

"Let's go home," I said at last. "You need to go home."

"I'm staying," she said, swaying some more.

"It's late, you're drunk. You need to go to bed."

"No," she said, her voice quivering a little. "I mean I'm *staying*."

I looked at her, still not understanding until I felt a stab of something sharp in my chest: rejection, pain, a terrible comprehension settling over me as I stared at her in the dark.

"What?" I asked, taking a step closer. "What do you mean you're *staying*?"

"I'm not going to Rutledge," she said. "I'm staying here with Levi. He'll graduate in a year and then maybe we'll go together. His dad was a Kappa Nu there—"

"Eliza, this is crazy," I interrupted. "You're being crazy. What *happened* to you?"

I felt the claw of tears then, their sharp nails scraping their way up my throat. I tried to swallow them down, push them away, but they sprang to the surface faster than I could contain them, gliding their way down my cheeks.

"We were supposed to go together," I said, my voice fragile and wet. "You can't just leave me—"

"I love him," she said with a finality that cut deeper than any lethal weapon, any sharpened blade. I could practically feel myself bleeding out then, the life leaking from my body as she watched it pool.

"I'm your best friend," I said at last, my voice barely above a whisper. "You're supposed to love me, too."

I noticed a little tremble in her lip, maybe a flash of regret like that day in my room, but before she could say anything, before she could respond, I spun around fast, ready to walk away and leave her there. So tired of caring about her more than she cared about me.

"Margot, wait—" she started, reaching out to grab my arm. I remember feeling the clasp of her fingers, her touch sending a surge of rage through my chest. In that single second, our entire life flipped through my mind like a movie as I thought about everything she had done to me, everything she had said. Every time she had left me, abandoned me, made me feel like I wasn't her equal, and before I could think twice, before I could relax, I whipped my arm away—violent, hard, way too fast—knocking her back with too much force. *"Margot!"*

I turned around just in time to see her stumble, eyes wet and wide as she reached out her hand like she was asking me to take it—but I didn't. I didn't take it. I don't even know if I could have reached her in time. I don't even know if it would have mattered, if I would have gone down with her, the two of us holding hands like we used to, fingers clasped together as we fell. But instead of trying, instead of helping, instead of swooping in to save her the way I always did, I simply stood right there, feet planted in place, watching in shock as her body tipped back.

The flutter of her dress and the wind in her hair making it seem, for a second, like she was flying.

CHAPTER 63

"I told you you had it in you."

I whip around at the sound of her voice, the silhouette of Lucy between the open shed doors making my stomach turn. I hadn't heard her follow me out here, hadn't registered the slap of the back door above the roar of the rain. The rumble of thunder masking her steps as she approached me slowly, a predator slithering up silently behind their prey.

Fresh tears burn my eyes as I remember the two of us on the beach again, me muttering about how I wanted to be bolder, braver, different than I've always been. Not the kind of person who let other people walk all over me, and Lucy's voice in my ear like a challenge, a dare—or maybe it was a reminder. Another little clue that she had been there, always, watching me in my lowest moments.

"I know you have it in you to be different. I've seen it."

"It was an accident," I say, shaking my head, the same thing I've been telling myself for the last two years. "I didn't mean to. I swear I didn't—"

"She never appreciated you," Lucy says, walking closer. "I saw the way she treated you before you even saw it yourself."

I imagine Lucy witnessing all those times Eliza rolled her eyes as I tried to help her, the way she and Levi hushed into a nasty silence as I approached them on the dock, and feel a shard of shame lodge in my chest at the thought of Lucy seeing me like that: so malleable, so weak. A rubber dummy that simply sprang back for more after taking a punch, ready and waiting to get hurt again.

My own words echo in my ears now, the four of us sitting on my bed on that very first night.

"The thing you need to understand about Eliza is that everyone loved her," I had said, thinking only I knew the real truth of it all. *"But just because you loved her, it didn't mean she loved you back."*

"You deserved to know," Lucy says, and I remember the sound that had alerted me to their presence: a kicked can followed by Eliza's low voice. The only reason I rounded that corner and even found them at all. I always assumed Eliza, Levi, and I were the only people up there, the only ones left, but I realize now: that noise had to have come from somewhere.

"It was you," I say, a sudden shudder cutting through me, quick and vicious, like swimming through a cold spot. The thought of Lucy pulling my puppet strings even then, even before I knew she existed. "You wanted me to see them like that."

"I wanted you to *do* something," she responds.

"Why?" I ask, imagining Lucy watching as I roamed. Knowing what Eliza was doing just around the corner and spotting that can, kicking it hard. Making a noise so I would find her.

"Because we're the same," Lucy says. "You and I are the same, Margot. Spending our lives wanting people who never wanted us back."

The sound of the rain turns to white noise in my ears as a flash from outside illuminates us both. The thought comes to me quick, before I can stop it, as fast and fleeting as the lightning itself: Lucy is right. We are the same. We were both rejected by the very people who should have loved us the most: her father, my best friend. All we wanted was acceptance and belonging. A chance at being a part of something bigger than ourselves.

"I know you know who I am," she says, taking a step closer. "I heard you and Sloane talking in your room. I know she looked me up at work, I saw you walk off with Danny at the party. I know you've been putting it together."

I think about how Lucy is always there, always listening, always hiding herself in plain sight. I guess she wasn't at Penny Lanes that day like we thought, instead creeping home early and listening to our whispers. Pushing her ear flush against the door. I guess she really did have one eye on me on that island after all and she had simply been biding her time with Levi, giving me space while she waited for me to figure it out.

"I saw what happened to Eliza that night and I took my chance," she continues. "I saw that I could actually step into the life I wanted after having to watch her live it from a distance."

I feel my body start to sway, that murky moral logic making my head nod gently along with her words. Strangely, in this moment, it feels like I understand Lucy more than I ever have before because I've felt that same way so many times: Maggie and me on the lawn outside Hines, the envy and awe as we watched Lucy from afar. Her comment on Halloween after we ran into each other, understanding how desperately I wanted to live another life. All those times I had looked at Eliza and felt that flame of resentment flare up in my chest when I saw the things she had that she always took for granted. Lucy had wanted them, too, and I can see it so clearly: her watching through the open window as we sat around the dining room table. The Jeffersons dancing in the kitchen and Eliza and me on the dock, staring up at the stars. Sharing our secrets like best friends do. Her curiosity growing, morphing, taking over everything and the impulse to keep getting closer, from the dock to the yard to inside the house. Flipping through Eliza's planner; realizing, once she fell, how easy it would be to simply show up where she should have been. Start her new life in the very spot Eliza's stopped.

Her best friend, her boyfriend, all of us ready and waiting for her.

"I've been trying to make you see it," she finishes. "I've been trying to get you to understand that you don't have to feel so guilty all the time. You don't have to keep punishing yourself. She deserved it."

I think back to that night at Penny Lanes, Lucy's soapbox about murder and death. The way she had looked at me and winked, spewing out justifications like she was trying to tell me it was okay.

"I would kill someone who deserves it."

I think back to all of us around the dinner table, that fragile stem twisting between her long, skinny fingers. Every little comment a chisel to my conscience, chipping away slowly, trying to make it disappear. I always thought it was Levi she was playing with, dangling the knowledge of what I told her like a cat clutching a mouse's tail. Pawing at him, making him squirm. Torturing him slowly just because she could. But it was never Levi—it was *me* she was trying to get to confess, all those little moments when she asked me questions about Eliza, her death, before sitting back and waiting patiently, quietly trying to pry it all out. She wanted me to put it together and I had tiptoed around it so many times, so eager to ease the crushing weight of it all. This burden to carry that was solely mine. So I had sprinkled in my own truths when I could, telling Lucy about an argument, an accident. The guilt I carried and all the different decisions I wished I could have made. I had been attempting to justify it, too: sitting on the porch with Mr. Jefferson, frantically searching for someone else to pin it on. For a way to channel my guilt into rage.

I chose Levi, of course, the only other person who could shoulder my blame. He had been there with her and everyone knew it. Other than me, who nobody saw, he was the last person to see her alive. And in a way, it was true: none of it would have happened if he hadn't come into our lives that day, Eliza's lips dipped below the water as she watched him curiously. His tan legs ambling down the dock, him handing her a cigarette. All his vices turning into hers, changing her into somebody she wasn't. Taking her from me even before she died.

I look at Lucy now, suddenly remembering the way she stood up and followed Levi into the trees, her eyes on mine like we were sharing a secret. Like she was granting my wish, that thing I had muttered to her in the kitchen. My hatred for Levi like a festering boil.

"Why did he have to die?" I ask, realizing now that it doesn't make sense. If Lucy was there the night Eliza fell, then she knew Levi had nothing to do with it. She knew of his innocence all along. "Why did you kill Levi?"

"I didn't," she says slowly, leaning forward like she's wondering when I'll finally fess up. "You did."

"No," I say, shaking my head, even though I can barely remember the end of that night. Even though Sloane said I had been looking for him, stumbling off on my own and waking up in the morning with mud on my pants. Even though I had that horrible feeling the next day, that sinking nausea, it wasn't the same as the way I felt waking up after that last night with Eliza: the horror of realizing it wasn't a dream. I'll never forget that feeling:

the terrible knowing that you're the reason someone else is gone. The blood on your hands that's always there, ever-present, no matter how hard you try to scrub it away. I understand better than anyone that something inside you changes after you've taken another life. Something cellular and permanent; an alteration of your very being, your very DNA. There is nothing muddy about it; in fact, it's crystal clear.

If I killed Levi that night, I would have known it in the morning.

"I didn't kill him," I say, even firmer now. "I had no reason to."

"Come on, Margot. You hated him," she says. "You told me yourself you wished it had been him instead of Eliza."

"Of course I wish it had been him," I say, remembering the way Lucy had ambled up to me that morning, her voice in my ear: *"It feels good, doesn't it? To finally get what you want."* "But that doesn't mean I killed him. You were the one who followed him out there."

"I was trying to calm him down," she says. "But he wouldn't listen to me. He was a lot drunker than I realized, yelling at me that he couldn't pretend anymore."

"Pretend what?" I ask.

"I don't know."

"So you just left him out there?"

"Yes," she says. "There was no reasoning with him like that. I tried for a while, but eventually I just left him alone to cool off."

We're both quiet, staring at each other, all our deceits tangling together in our minds until they're impossible to unravel.

"What about Parker?" I ask at last, my final card, shame at the accusation creeping into my cheeks mixed with a hint of pride that I know her secrets, too. "It's just a coincidence that your last boyfriend also died right after a big argument?"

Lucy looks at me like she's just been slapped, a mixture of shock and hurt as she processes the question. I think about us up on the roof, all those rumors Danny told me about her swirling around like a cloud of smoke. The gossip she absorbed from everyone back home and how she had tried to outrun it only to be met with the same thing here.

"I had nothing to do with that," she says, her voice suddenly so cold. "It's not my fault he got into a car after drinking too much."

"What were you arguing about?"

"If you must know, we were arguing about my dad," she says, those final two words sounding so strange in her mouth. Like she still doesn't think they belong to her. Like she's tried them on so many times only to find that they'll never truly fit. "My mom had just told me where to find him. I guess their agreement was that she would stay quiet as long as the money came—and then, one month, it stopped and she spilled."

I think about the envelope I found in Eliza's dresser and how it was made out to Lucy's address. All that cash inside, thousands of dollars. Eliza must have intercepted it, somehow, all those nights she snuck into her dad's office, poking around, stealing liquor from his private stash.

I close my eyes, wondering if she had any idea what she had stumbled across. The enormity of that single domino she inadvertently tipped over, removing it from wherever she found it and keeping it as her own.

"Parker told me not to go," Lucy says at last, the closest thing I've ever seen to tears in her eyes. "He said it was a bad idea, that my dad wouldn't want me, and that I shouldn't even be thinking of him as my dad, anyway. That real dads don't hide from their daughters with hush money. And maybe I should have listened to him"—she shrugs, wiping her nose—"but I was angry, okay? He was telling me hard truths that I didn't want to hear. After he died, there was nothing else keeping me in Fairfield. I had nothing left to lose."

I find myself nodding along, all these pieces that have been floating around for the last nine months now pushed together to reveal something whole. It makes sense, all of it, and despite the fact that Lucy has lied about so much, despite the fact that she's a master of manipulation, of misdirection and deceit, I find myself believing her now. I find myself wanting to somehow still make this work, wanting to simply give in to her web of secrets, so sticky and strong, because it's easier that way. It's easier not to fight them but to wrap myself up in them like a blanket, all silky and smooth as she crawls even closer, whispering her little lies in my ear. Because what the four of us had this year was good, real. I know it was, even if it wasn't entirely honest. There is no way those moments were manufactured: socked feet sliding around Penny Lanes and fits of laughter so intense, so pure, I thought my sides might split like a busted seam. My conscience healing slowly like scar tissue, something thick and hard growing over the spot in my heart that was once so raw. Secrets whispered in the night, bashful truths and audacious dares that wound us all together, so maddeningly tight that sometimes it hurt.

And that's the problem, I suppose, when so many lives become so intricately entwined: one snag, one single loose thread, and it all threatens to come undone.

"I didn't kill Levi," Lucy says now, drawing my attention back. "But that detective thinks I did."

I look at her, eyebrows bunched.

"He brought me in for more questioning," she continues. "People are saying they saw me follow him. That they saw us fighting. It's the same thing all over again."

"Maybe it really was an accident," I say, mostly to myself, but Lucy is already shaking her head.

"His neck," she says. "Those bruises."

"Trevor?" I ask, the next logical option. "Maybe they kept fighting and it went too far?"

"I don't know who it was, but I'm going to find out," Lucy says. "And I'm going to turn them in. I'm not going down for this."

"We'll figure it out," I say, but I see Lucy's eyes widen, some new understanding dawning on her as she starts to back up. The rain outside has slowed to a steady trickle now, a handful of stars peeking out from behind a blanket of clouds, and it makes me think of that night on the roof again, Lucy's hand in mine as she traced them for me. The constellations so close and clear it felt like I could reach out and grab them like a handful of sand.

"I don't want to keep running," she says, almost to herself. She backs up some more, closer to the doors, and I have the strange sensation that they're hiding from us now, all those stars. Aware of some impending disaster they don't want to witness. "I'm not going to take the fall."

"You won't have to," I say. "Lucy, we'll handle it."

"Margot, I think it was—"

But before she can finish, I watch her expression twist into something haunted, something strange, her mouth wordless and wide before her gaze travels down to her stomach, a bloom of red erupting through her shirt.

CHAPTER 64

AFTER

I trail Detective Frank into the station, whatever he wants to talk to me about apparently important enough to require bringing me in.

"I'll be fine," I said to Sloane and Nicole earlier as they watched me ease into the back of his cruiser, their lips set into two twin thin lines. I tried to smile then, tried to exude a sense of calm and control, although the metal partition cutting the car in half made the whole thing feel like a prisoner transport, the skin on my wrist where those handcuffs once hung tingling with the memory. "I'll meet you at the apartment when I'm finished."

Frank is unusually quiet now as he leads me down a long beige hallway, the entire building smelling like burnt coffee and body odor. I wipe one palm against the leg of my jeans, the other gripping a cup of coffee I had accepted just so I could hold onto something. There are so many scenarios running through my mind right now; so many reasons for why I could be here.

They haven't found Lucy, I know that for a fact, but there are the other things they must have found.

"I wanted to give you a heads-up before the news goes public,"

Frank says at last. He stops in front of a closed door, putting his hand on the knob before turning to face me. "Some bombshells are about to come out about your friend. I wanted you to be prepared."

"Bombshells," I repeat, my heart picking up in my throat. "What kind of bombshells?"

He searches my expression, eyes flicking back and forth for information. Like he still can't decide what I know and don't know; what I'm sharing with the police and what I'm keeping for myself.

He sighs when he doesn't find anything, turning back around and pushing the door open.

"I'd like for you to meet Lucy's father," he says. "Although I believe you two are already acquainted."

My eyes widen at the sight of him, feigning surprise, although it is still strange to see him here: Mr. Jefferson, ripped out of one reality and implanted into the next. I used to imagine him visiting Rutledge during parents' weekends; helping Eliza and me move into the dorm. Instead, I find him sitting on the far side of an interrogation table, his hands wringing nervously in his lap and his own cup of coffee sitting untouched in front of him.

"Margot," he says, looking even more ragged than he did in December. That wiry beard flecked with gray; those wrinkles like scars, deep and jagged, the physical proof of his emotional pain. "Margot, honey, I'm so sorry you got dragged into this."

I walk forward slowly, cautiously, slipping into the seat opposite him. It's ironic: the two of us sitting at a table like this, cups of coffee between us like Christmas morning, two months ago, right before everything changed.

"I had no idea she would go to this . . . extreme."

"Lucy?" I ask, finally finding my voice. I try to sound uncertain, confused, forever meticulous in the way I word my questions. Careful not to reveal something I shouldn't already know. "Lucy is your—?"

"Yes," he says, like he can't bear to hear the word that comes next. "Yes, honey, and it was a mistake. All of it was a terrible mistake."

I think of his words on the porch again; the torture in his voice as he rocked slowly in the dark. His own quiet admission, that secret he had been living with silently for the last twenty-three years.

"As a parent, you usually get it wrong more often than you get it right."

"I thought I was doing a good thing," he says to me now. "I was providing for them, at least. I bought them a house, paid their bills—"

He stops, pushes his hands hard into his eyes, and I realize, for the first time, that he isn't wearing his wedding ring.

"I barely even knew her mother," he continues, refusing to look at me. "It happened *one* time. She was practically a stranger."

I keep my mouth shut, knowing I'm supposed to be learning all this for the very first time. It's hard not to call him out on it, though. Not to point out that the house he bought them was practically a trailer; that the bills he paid were a sorry substitute for real responsibility. That he was doing a good thing only for himself.

"Then Lucy showed up at the house one day and I knew," he says, lowering his hands on the table, suddenly looking like a stranger himself instead of the man I always admired. The man who read my writing and danced with his wife in the kitchen; the man who sometimes felt like more of a father to me than my own. "I knew who she was immediately. She had her mother's eyes. That bright blue color."

"What did you do?" I ask, leaning forward, the curiosity in my voice authentic this time. Thinking of Lucy and me up on that roof; her fingers working at her necklace as she pulled me close like she was sharing a secret. She had danced around that moment so delicately before, with a ballerina's sweeping finesse, and the memory of her voice raises the skin on my arms now, so close to finally knowing what's real and what's not.

"I turned her away," Mr. Jefferson says, his voice devoid of any emotion. "I told her to leave. I had a family, Margot. A real family."

Had, the use of past tense, sends a fresh wave of tears to my eyes as I remember the two of us together on Christmas, Mrs. Jefferson notably absent. I wonder when she found out about Lucy, if it was before or after her own daughter's death. I wonder if she blames her husband for everything now. I wonder if that's why she left.

"Eliza and her mother were just upstairs," he continues, pulling my attention back. "I couldn't risk her ruining that."

I picture Lucy on the stoop, a bundle of nerves and his rejection knife-sharp as he slammed the door shut. I can still see her standing there, dazed and numb. Nowhere left to go so she just stayed and watched. Imagined what it might be like to be them.

"But apparently Eliza overheard us talking," Mr. Jefferson says next and I snap my neck up, surprise radiating through my chest like a tremor. "I didn't even know until the police told me. She never said anything."

"The police—?" I ask, turning to Detective Frank, suddenly remembering what he said to me after he searched our house, the two of us sitting together in the yard.

"I know about Eliza. Levi's old fling and your friend from before."

I think about the way Eliza sat in the kitchen with that faraway stare; the way she opened her mouth so many times like she wanted to tell me something only to snap it shut, swallow it down. The way she and Levi were always whispering, silencing themselves when I got too close. How she kept alluding to going through something I wouldn't understand.

"She knew," I say, the shock still settling in. "She knew about Lucy and she told Levi instead of me."

"Honey," Mr. Jefferson says, reaching out to grab my hand. "Sometimes it's just easier to talk to a stranger."

I swallow, watching Detective Frank as he walks closer to the table. No wonder Eliza and Levi got so close so fast. No wonder she thought she loved him, the only person in the world who knew her secret, this heavy thing she just had to unload. It's why she got so angry with me when I pushed her, challenged her, her bitter best friend who always assumed her life was perfect.

It's why she couldn't tell me, that ever-present fear of shattering the illusion.

"Levi went to his local PD over Christmas break and told them what he knew about Lucy," Frank says to me now, his voice from the yard still echoing around me: *It seems like a pretty big coincidence. Your next-door neighbor, your two best friends.* "Apparently Eliza only knew Lucy's first name, but Levi was starting to put it together. He remembered Eliza telling him once about someone breaking into her house."

I sit in silence, remembering how angry I had been at Eliza for confronting Levi about the break-in; how he had insisted it wasn't him. The way he looked at Lucy that first time in Penny Lanes like he somehow knew her, recognized her, jet-black hair like Mr. Jefferson's and tics like Eliza's that were too similar to ignore. The way he cocked his head on Christmas, eyeing us curiously from the door.

The two of them sitting on his bed, his body rigid as Lucy pulled him in for that kiss.

"Levi told the police in December that he thought Lucy might have been there the night Eliza fell," Detective Frank continues. I look at Mr. Jefferson, his palm cupped tight across his mouth like he's trying to keep a sob from escaping. "He was beginning to think Lucy might have pushed her."

I sit quietly, pulse throbbing in my neck, these next few seconds the most important of my life.

"He was told at the time that there was no evidence to support his claim, so it's possible he had been trying to get close to Lucy on his own to find some answers," he says, sighing, and I continue to nod, thinking back on what Lucy told me in the shed: Levi being drunk and angry, yelling at her in the woods about not wanting to pretend.

"We believe he may have confronted her about it on the island, which is what led to their argument."

Maybe he really was calling her out, flinging her arm off his leg like that. Sick of coddling up to a girl he suspected was a killer solely for justice, a quest for answers.

Maybe that's why his death barely even fazed her: another happy coincidence, another barrier eliminated in her brand-new life.

"Margot, we found some things in Lucy's bedroom that support all this," Frank finishes as a single tear slips silently down Mr. Jefferson's cheek. "Some things that will probably disturb you."

CHAPTER 65

BEFORE

"Lucy?" I ask, my voice trembling as I take a step closer.

I don't understand what's happening, even as her hands clutch at her belly. Even as the blood gushes from her stomach, suddenly everywhere, her eyes wide and afraid as it leaks through her fingers.

Her face suddenly a shade too pale, glowing white in the light of the moon.

"Lucy!" I yell, rushing closer. I can't figure out what happened, where it's all coming from, but before I can reach her, she slouches down, falls to her knees, and I register another body standing behind her, the knife from the living room red in her hand.

"I had to do it," Sloane says quietly, her voice shaking and a look of pure shock carved across her face. "I couldn't let her leave."

I run to Lucy's body, now crumpled on the ground, noticing the way her blood trickles dutifully into the floor grate beneath us, the very spot where that deer once hung.

The very spot where so many other things have bled out before her, dying slowly, their lives leaking out of them in one great pool of iron red.

"Lucy," I repeat, shaking her shoulders, clutching her stomach, though I can already tell that she's gone. Those ice-blue eyes are already dulling into a weak slate gray as the blood continues to seep from her wound and I push my fingers into the side of her neck, searching for a pulse I know isn't there.

"What did you *do?*" I scream at Sloane, looking up at her from the floor.

"She figured it out," she says, still standing at a distance, though her voice is already morphing back into that calm, controlled state. The way it always is. "It was the only way."

"Figured what out?" I ask, choking out a sob, suddenly thinking about the way Lucy's eyes had bulged just before she was stabbed; the way she had started to say something, that moment of knowing as she backed up toward the door.

"I'm not going down for this. I'm going to turn them in."

"It was you?" I ask, my mind hanging in some strange limbo between adrenaline and shock as I stare down at the body below me, my eyes following the single line of blood slowly leaking out of her mouth. Even in death, they're so much the same: Lucy, Eliza, their light extinguished as quick and violent as a shooting star. "You killed Levi?"

And then, like somebody simply snapped their fingers, flicked on the light, I see it all so clearly: the way Sloane's arm shot out to the side when Lucy appeared with the knife from the kitchen; the way she had begged me to talk to her that day in her room, folding that T-shirt again and again on the floor. The need in her eyes as she asked me about Halloween, what could have happened that night that made everything change.

"Margot," she had said. *"She's my best friend. Please."*

Sloane isn't protecting herself right now, that bloody knife still clutched in her hand. She's protecting the person she always protects.

"Nicole," I say, and I watch as she steps into view now, too. The two of them must have been just off to the side, behind the open shed doors, listening to Lucy and me talk in the dark. Absorbing our confessions, our secrets, all of them pouring out of us like water escaping two broken dams.

"I thought it was Trevor," Nicole says, her eyes wet with tears as her lower lip shakes. Her thin arms snaked around her waist like she's still trying to keep the pain inside. "It was so dark, and he was wearing Trevor's shirt."

"You thought Levi was Trevor," I repeat, the truth dawning on me now as the events from that night come roaring back. Remembering the way Trevor had tripped by the fire and struggled to stand; the way Nicole stood up and left, refused to watch it, never even seeing the fight that came after. Trevor spilling that rum, Levi laughing in the distance. The two of them switching clothes before Levi stalked off and into the trees. Those woods were so dark away from the fire and I can see how the two of them could look alike from the back: their hair color, their height. All those boys just a shade away from being exactly the same. "Trevor hurt you on Halloween."

I can picture it so easily now and I hate myself for not seeing it all sooner: Trevor hulking around that night with his shirt ripped off, that scary air to him like something bad had happened. Their fight the next morning and the way Nicole never wanted to go over anymore; him squeezing her leg on the boat, making her flinch.

I think of Nicole on the tile, so lifeless and limp. Vomit stuck to her hair and those finger-shaped bruises scattered across her arms as I tried to pick her up, bring her back to my room.

"Nicole, come on. Let's get in bed."

"I didn't want to," she says to me now, the humiliation in her voice still so deep. "I was so drunk and I didn't want to, but I couldn't get him off me. He made me do it, he held my wrists—"

"No," she had said, trying to push me away. *"No, stop."*

I had been so focused on Levi, remembering the way he gripped Eliza's wrists in the dark. The way he had been on our property; the way I had gotten so used to blaming him for everything.

"Levi walked in on us," Nicole continues, her gaze on the floor. On Lucy, staring straight back, the truth she had just worked out forever locked inside. "I remember him looking back and forth between Trevor and me, like he was trying to decide what to do."

I see Nicole and me on the island, that bottle in her hand. Me asking about Levi and her shaking her head, taking a swig.

"He didn't do a thing."

"He just left," she says at last, looking back at me. A plea in her eyes that cracks my heart open. "He just closed the door and left."

That's why Nicole and Levi avoided each other after that. That's why they would always dart their eyes, refuse to talk. Both of them so ashamed for reasons related, but also entirely apart. Levi knew what he was witnessing and he did nothing to stop it. He was a pledge, Trevor the president, the only person with the power to make his life a living hell. The person who reminded him of that again and again, just to prove a point.

"I tried to talk to Trevor about it the next morning and he got so mad," Nicole continues. "He started screaming at me for accusing him of something like that. He said it wasn't even possible, anyway, since we were dating."

"Nicole—" I start, but Sloane shakes her head, a silent cue for me to let her finish.

"I tried to just forget about it," she says, the tears streaming faster. "But I couldn't. Then that night, you were pushing me so hard, and I was getting so angry all over again. I couldn't stand the thought of us sleeping in that tent together, of him *touching* me—"

"It's okay," I say, walking toward her, finally, before pulling her into a hug. "Nicole, it's okay."

"I thought it was Trevor," she cries into my neck, little chokes erupting from her throat. "I went into the woods and I saw him stumbling around. He had tripped on a root or something and couldn't get up like that time by the fire and before I even knew what was happening, I was holding him down and he was too drunk to fight back."

I picture Nicole in the dark, her body pushed hard into Levi's neck. She's so small, so fragile, but her rage is big, all-consuming, growing inside her for the last few months. Adrenaline and anger and fear and hatred gnawing at her like an incessant itch. An open sore that could never truly heal.

"It felt good," she whispers, almost to herself, and I think of the thrashing, the choking, the mud lodging itself deep inside Levi's throat. The roles reversed; the power reclaimed. "That's the worst part. It felt good when I was doing it, until he stopped moving and I realized my mistake."

I look up at Sloane, staring at us from across the shed. The knife still hanging limp in her hand, blood dripping from the tip like that night on the boat as it leaked from Lucy's finger, little red circles dotting the floor.

"She would have told Frank," she says quietly. "She would have turned Nicole in."

"We don't know that," I argue, but Sloane interrupts me, shaking her head.

"Yes, we do," she says, pragmatic and even. Our voice of reason. "Lucy would have saved herself and you know it."

"But she didn't actually hurt anyone—"

"Are you kidding me?" Sloane snaps back. "She hurt all of us. Every single one of us."

We're all quiet, this familiar shed transporting us somewhere new now. Somewhere foreign and uncharted, though I've seen a glimpse of this place before: standing on the edge of that charred-black building, looking down, Eliza's body bent and broken beyond recognition or repair. Swaying slightly with the breeze and the realization that I could just turn around, walk back home, and nobody would be the wiser.

Lucy's voice in the wind like a whisper from the grave.

"If you knew you could get away with murder, would you do it?"

"All of this happened because of her," Sloane says. "She started it all when she walked into our lives."

I picture Lucy alone on the dock, her body the silhouette that kicked my fear into motion. My unease and my envy, all of it directed at the wrong person. If she hadn't been there, if she hadn't done that, maybe Eliza wouldn't have felt the need to hide it all from me. Maybe she would have talked to me, told me the truth about Levi and the envelope she found. Maybe we never would have gotten into that fight: the missing picture still on her wall, the things we had said never escaping our lips. The resentment that built up between us still flimsy enough to tear back down, not the concrete barrier Lucy erected from afar.

I turn to Nicole next, still nuzzled into my neck, the gentlest soul I've ever known. Lucy led her to Trevor like a cat chasing a mouse into the jaws of a fox. She used Nicole's kindness, her heart, her inability to let people down.

She maneuvered us all like chess pieces and people got hurt, people died.

"It was her or us," Sloane says at last. "She could get me

expelled. She could send Nicole to jail, Margot. This is the best for you, too."

I feel myself nodding, agreeing, because I know she's right. Lucy saw what happened between Eliza and me. She could have placed me at the party; she could have come clean about everything. None of our secrets would have been safe with her alive, dangling them over us the way she always did. Playing with us like another one of her games, her entire life an illusion she simply created and pretended to be true. The irony of it is that Lucy is the one who helped me see it, the necessity of her death: talking about murder with such indifference, one scale rising while the other one falls.

"Once you find the right person, the right reason."

It is possible to both love her and hate her; to trust and mistrust her. To feel so radically on both sides of the coin.

It is possible to want my friend back more than anything and to also want her to stay gone for good.

CHAPTER 66

We work quickly, quietly, wrapping Lucy's body in layers of game bags we found stored in the corner of the shed. We've seen the boys use them before, lugging fresh kill back to bleed out, the very thing created to keep a carcass fresh. Everything we need is right here, right in this very room, the perfect place to bring something to die: a hose to rinse the remaining blood from the floor, a brush to scrub all traces of her clean.

The smell of death already there, ever-present. Just another body to add to the count.

"I'm sorry," Nicole says for the hundredth time, practically shivering from shock as she stands off to the side. "I'm so sorry. This is all my fault—"

"No, it's not," Sloane says, crossing her arms, her anger toward Lucy hardened into a scab, crusted over, protecting her from feeling a single ounce of regret. "I already told you. It's hers."

"Where are we going to put her?" Nicole asks, the two of them staring down at Lucy in her makeshift coffin, long and lean and wrapped in twine. "How are we going to get her out of here?"

"We're not," I say, the plan that's started to formulate in my mind finally clear enough to communicate. "We're going to put her in the cave."

The cave, the basement. That little crawl space nobody knows is there. It's risky, I know, keeping her in the house like this, but it feels even riskier to move her somewhere new. We could be seen; she could be found. Plus, it's cool down there, so much cooler than the rest of the house, that draft that's always creeping into my bedroom and chilling the floor. It might become a problem once it gets hot, in the heat of the summer, but that's what the game bags are for and we'll be gone by then, anyway. Everyone will be gone. Kappa Nu is suspended; it's only a matter of time before they're disbanded for good. We won't be able to live here without them and they won't be hazing anyone anymore. They won't be using that space at all.

Once we leave, this place will sit empty, abandoned, the only people in the world aware of its existence never inclined to speak a word of it again.

"What do we do when the police start looking?" Nicole asks, panic creeping back into her voice. "People are going to notice she's gone. Her car is still here; she won't show up for work—"

"We're going to play dumb," Sloane says, a single bead of sweat trickling down her neck. "We're going to let them think she ran away."

"But why would they believe she just ran away?"

"Because they're going to find things," I say. "I'll show you when we get inside."

It's strange, the clarity of my thoughts as we walk back into the house. Like Halloween night, swallowing that pill, the edges of everything are as sharp as the knife that's been scrubbed three times and left to dry in the kitchen. It's two in the morning by the time we move Lucy, get the shed cleaned up and the gravel in the driveway rearranged to hide the pressure of her body being dragged across the yard.

The little door on the side of the house latched permanently shut, obscured by the azaleas, only visible if you know just where to look.

"Shouldn't she have that if she ran away?" Nicole asks as we walk into the living room, gesturing to Lucy's phone sitting abandoned on the floor.

"No," Sloane says, the remaining adrenaline making her fingers twitch. "They can track that. If it brings them here but they never find it, they'll know she's still on the property."

I walk toward the phone and pick it up slowly, the collection of stars on the lock screen sending a fresh wave of sadness through my chest. I swipe up, attempting to get inside and instead getting a grid of digits as I rack my brain for any combination that could have some type of meaning, but nothing comes to mind. Lucy never shared anything with us—no special birthday or anniversary; no unique mixture of numbers she held close. We knew so little about her, only her name, and I feel the sudden prickle of knowing on my neck as I punch at the digits and watch the screen open.

Her name, Lucy. 5829.

She didn't know much about herself, either.

"Here," I say at last, navigating to her pictures before flipping through them quickly, going back months, years, until I find what I already knew would be there. It's a picture of Eliza and me taken through her kitchen window, Mr. Jefferson sitting just by our side. We're all together, laughing, the image grainy enough to know that Lucy had tried to zoom in as she watched us from a distance.

Somehow, after thinking about the picture she stole from Eliza's bedroom, I had a feeling there would be more.

"Once the police realize she's missing, we'll let them find her phone and look through her pictures," I say, flipping some more, taking in the others: Eliza and me in her bedroom, stomachs-down on the mattress. Eliza and Levi on the dock, her head light on his shoulder as they huddled close on the wood.

"They'll figure out who she is," I finish. "We're just helping them put together a picture that already exists."

"You're going to let them think—"

"It explains them both," I say. "Eliza and Levi. It'll take care of everything."

"Why don't we just tell them ourselves?" Nicole asks, always so innocent. "Save them the trouble?"

"We can't give ourselves a motive," I say, shaking my head. "We don't want them looking into us or the house any more than necessary."

Nicole stays quiet, her expression unsure, but Sloane is starting to nod along now, too. I watch as she walks with purpose into Lucy's room, reemerging with her wallet as she pulls out Lucy's ID, a few credit cards. Things she would have taken if she decided to skip town.

"This is what Lucy does," she says. "She takes off without warning. In the beginning, we act completely unfazed. Totally unbothered to hear that she's gone."

"Like it's normal," I add. "But after a while, we start to get nervous, scared. Everything they learn about Lucy, we act like we're learning it for the first time, too."

"Then one of us has to crack, just for a second," Sloane says. We both look at Nicole, the weakest link. "Accidentally tell them something that will confirm their suspicions."

"Like what?" she whispers, her face draining into a ghostly shade of white.

"That night at Penny Lanes," I say. "The boys will remember it, too. They can corroborate it if they're asked."

Nicole nods, her cheeks hollow and pale before walking to the couch and collapsing onto the cushions, pushing her head deep into her hands.

"They'll just think we're naïve," I say, walking over to her now and rubbing her shoulders. "That our only crime is being too innocent to see her for who she really is."

"That we're just girls," Sloane adds, her eyes distant and detached. "Just a couple of harmless little girls."

CHAPTER 67

NOW

I enter the apartment to find Sloane and Nicole on the living room floor, boxes ripped open and all our belongings scattered across the room.

"How did it go?" Nicole asks, standing up fast, eyes hopeful and afraid at the exact same time. She's looking better, though, a certain buoyancy to her I haven't seen in months. The color blooming back into her skin and her cheeks filling out, all fleshy and pink like a ripening fruit.

"Good," I say, smiling weakly. "It's all good."

I watch her exhale and I take a seat in the middle of them, my head poking into the nearest box.

"Mr. Jefferson identified it all," I say, thinking about the things we planted in Lucy's bedroom; the evidence we snuck inside the locked drawers of her desk. Everything of Eliza's that I had kept: that tube of used lipstick, a scrunchie with her hair still tangled in the fabric. All of it painting a picture of a person obsessed—which Lucy was, in a way, although I suppose that means that I was, too.

"Kappa Nu is done," I continue. "None of them are facing charges except for Trevor."

I look at Nicole, surprise and relief flooding into her face.

"The other boys admitted that he was hazing Levi, singling him out. That Trevor's the reason he drank so much."

"It's going to be okay," Sloane says, fingers reaching out to grab Nicole's hand. All of us smiling at the thought of Trevor having to live with this forever; the consequences trailing him around for the first time in his life, for the rest of his life. "We're going to be okay."

We continue to unpack our things slowly, quietly, the magnitude of the last few months finally setting in. The fact that we actually got away with it, we got away with murder, not just once but three times over.

One was an accident, one a mistake, and one a necessity to save us all.

"I didn't know you had one of those, too," Sloane says suddenly, and I look up, tracing her gaze down to my neck.

To my hand, absentmindedly playing with the chain clasped tight around my throat: Lucy's necklace, that constellation of stars. The one I had plucked from her body when nobody was looking, a familiar urge I couldn't suppress.

"Lucy had one just like it," she says. "From that jewelry dispenser by the door at Penny Lanes."

"Oh, yeah," I lie, remembering what Lucy had whispered on the roof.

"I don't need him," she had said. *"But he gave me this."*

I picture her standing on the dock, listening to the music creeping out through the windows. Watching us dancing, singing, Eliza twisting the jewels around her neck as we looked up at the stars and found pictures in the sky.

Her body rigid by the door after Mr. Jefferson slammed it, banishing her to a life all on her own.

"He said it reminded him of me because I was named after that song. Lucy in the sky with diamonds."

Another lie, though whether that one was meant for me or herself, I'll never really know.

"I got it sometime over the summer," I add.

Sloane nods, looking back down, and I can't help but feel a pang of something new now, something fresh. Pity and understanding; the lengths that Lucy went to just to feel like her life was a little bit different, a little bit better, than what it really was. I dip my hand into my last box now, the one full of all my old books. The stories I used to get lost in, too; all the other lives I preferred to my own.

Dr. Jekyll and Mr. Hyde resting on top, that single person capable of both good and evil. Love and violence. Emotions strong enough to take another life.

I look around our little apartment, at us three friends now bonded by blood. I know better than either of them that this kind of violence never really washes away. No matter how hard they try to scrub it off, how desperately they attempt to keep themselves clean, it'll just keep seeping farther into their skin, their very foundation, all that blood running deep like a stain. What we did together is tattooed across all of us now, a permanent mark like a friendship bracelet tied tight around our wrists.

Like a broken heart drawn in sunscreen, only whole when we stick together.

In time, it may fade, but it'll never truly be gone—because if one goes down, we all go down, which might be the most steadfast act of friendship I've ever known.

ACKNOWLEDGMENTS

I'm going to start with a story. A story-within-a-story.

Some of what you just read is true.

During my junior and senior years at the University of Georgia, my roommates and I lived in a house off-campus owned by a fraternity. Our backyards were connected by a little old shed, so it was incredibly easy to move between the two properties. I once walked into that shed to find massive tobacco leaves hanging from the ceiling; another time, I walked into our kitchen to find a brother tenderizing deer meat with a mallet.

There really were specs of blood on the ceiling, and we really did eat it for dinner that night.

We decorated the living room with old vinyl records and it wasn't unusual to walk out of my bedroom to see random boys in the house at all hours: collecting our rent, which was ridiculously cheap. Attempting to fix all the things that needed to be fixed. The insulation was terrible, our toes always frigid against the hardwood floor; one winter, when the heater broke, my roommate slept in oven mitts to keep her fingers from freezing. Then one night, after several months of living there, we discovered the house had a basement—well, more of a crawl space. It was tiny and, to be honest, a little bit terrifying. We heard rumors of brothers being hazed down there in the past. The concrete walls were covered in graffiti and the only way you could access it was by a little side door hidden behind the bushes out back. And despite the fact that I truly don't think anyone ever went down there, learning of its existence after months of living in the room just above it was more than a little unsettling.

With that said, while the setting of this book was inspired by a very real place, everything else is entirely fictional, including and especially the characters themselves. The only character I stole from real life was the house itself, because trust me when I say: that house had *character*. It was weird and wonderful and I just had to memorialize it—but the rest of this thing, I completely made up. The brothers next door treated us with kindness and respect; the roommates I lived with are still, to this day, some of my very best friends.

Now that that's out of the way, I want to start by thanking the original girls of Hartford House for allowing me (no, *encouraging* me) to share this special place with the world. I look back and laugh at those years so often; the memories are too ridiculous to recount. That place left a mark on us, but we left our mark on it, too: our names are still written in chipped paint across the siding, our doodles still preserved in the concrete out front. Thank you so much for talking me into letting our time there live on in these pages. This book was so special to write.

To my agent, Dan Conaway, who wears a million hats and always wears them well: you've changed my life in countless ways and you have my endless gratitude. To Chaim Lipskar, Peggy Boulos-Smith, Maja Nikolic, Kate Boggs, Sofia Bolido, and everyone else at Writers House: thank you so much for all you do.

To my editor, Kelley Ragland: thank you for your continued trust and confidence. You have no idea how relieved I was when you first expressed your love for this book—a book that is so vastly different than ones I had given you previously. Your edits are spot-on, your opinions invaluable, and your support unwavering. Thank you, too, to everyone at Minotaur, St. Martin's Publishing Group, and Macmillan, especially Andy Martin, Jen Enderlin, Allison Ziegler (who titled this book!), Sarah Melnyk, Hector DeJean, Madeline Houpt, Paul Hochman, and David Rotstein. You guys just keep making my dreams come true.

To my UK editor, Julia Wisdom, and everyone at HarperCollins UK, including but not limited to Lizz Burrell, Susanna Peden, and Maddy Marshall: it's an honor to be working together again. I can't wait to bring more books overseas.

To my film agent, Sylvie Rabineau, at WME: thank you for everything you do to bring my stories to the screen.

To my husband, Britt, my favorite person on the planet: I'm so in love with our life together. Thank you so much for building it with me.

To my family: this past year has thrown us some curveballs, huh? Even so, there's nothing we can't tackle when we tackle it together and I'm so grateful for the little unit we have. I'm proud of us all—but especially you, Mom. I'm in awe of you daily and I love you so much.

To Brian, Laura, Alvin, Lindsey, Matt, and the rest of my extended family: thank you, as always, for your love and support.

To the librarians, bloggers, reviewers, TikTokers, bookstagrammers, book clubs, booksellers (especially Tammy Watkins at The Village Bookseller, my former high school English teacher who hand sells my books to anyone she can find), and readers around the world: you are the entire reason I get to do this for a living.

Thank you so much for reading my words and sharing my stories. Connecting with you all brings me so much joy.

To The Beatles, who wrote the lyrics that inspired both the character of Lucy and the first scene I wrote of this book (there are a few Easter eggs alluding to that, but I'll give you a hint: chapter 48).

Finally, a heartfelt thank-you goes out to my friends. Old and new, near and far, you know who you are and I'd kill for you guys.

ABOUT THE AUTHOR

Mary Hannah Harte

STACY WILLINGHAM is the *New York Times, USA Today,* and international bestselling author of *A Flicker in the Dark, All the Dangerous Things,* and *Only If You're Lucky.* Her debut, *A Flicker in the Dark,* was a 2022 finalist for the Book of the Month Book of the Year Award, Goodreads Choice Award Best Debut Novel, Goodreads Choice Award Best Mystery & Thriller, and ITW's Best First Novel Award. Her work has been translated into more than thirty languages. Before turning to fiction, she was a copywriter and brand strategist for various marketing agencies. She earned her B.A. in magazine journalism from the University of Georgia and M.F.A. in writing from the Savannah College of Art and Design. She currently lives in Charleston, South Carolina, with her husband, Britt, and Labradoodle, Mako.